PRAISE FOR BARRY EISLER

The Livia Lone Series

"An absolutely first-rate thriller . . . Emotionally true at each beat."
—*The New York Times Book Review*

"An explosive thriller that plunges into the sewer of human smuggling . . . Filled with raw power, [*Livia Lone*] may be the darkest thriller of the year."
—*Kirkus Reviews* (starred review)

"Readers may be reminded of Stieg Larsson's beloved Lisbeth Salander when they meet Livia Lone, and will be totally riveted by the story of this woman on a mission to right the wrongs in her past."
—Bookish

"You won't be able to tear yourself away as the story accelerates into a Tarantino-worthy climax, and when you're left gasping in the wake of its gut-wrenching vigilante justice, you'll belatedly realize you learned a lot about a social travesty that gets far too little attention . . . *Livia Lone* is a harrowing tale with a conscience."
—*Chicago Review of Books*

The Chaos Kind

"Another high-fatality, high-spirited revenge fantasy."
—*Kirkus Reviews*

"Eisler juggles the complicated plot and large cast, imbuing his diverse characters with robust backstory and emotional motivation."
—*Publishers Weekly*

"A spectacular revenge story. Eisler, who was briefly a covert operative for the CIA, has an energetic writing style: his dialogue gets right to the point, and his action scenes are clean and vividly rendered. The John Rain novels seem to fly under the radar of many genre fans, even though they deserve to sit alongside Lee Child's Jack Reacher novels and Vince Flynn and Kyle Mills's Mitch Rapp thrillers."

—*Booklist*

The Killer Collective

"Impossibly cool."

—*Entertainment Weekly*

"As usual with an Eisler novel, the plot is full of twists, the prose is muscular, and the action unfolds at a torrid pace. The result is another page turner from one of the better thriller writers since James Grady published *Six Days of the Condor* in 1974."

—Associated Press

"In this crackling-good thriller from bestseller Eisler, Seattle PD sex crimes detective Livia Lone, assassin John Rain, and former Marine sniper Dox form a testy alliance to combat a vile conspiracy involving corrupt and toxic government agencies . . . The feisty interplay among these killer elites is as irresistible as if one combined the Justice League with the Avengers, swapping out the superhero uniforms for cutting-edge weaponry and scintillating spycraft. By the satisfying conclusion, the world has been scrubbed a bit cleaner of perfidy. This is delightfully brutal fun."

—*Publishers Weekly* (starred review)

"Vicarious pleasure for anyone wanting to see the scum of the world get its due."

—*Kirkus Reviews*

"Eisler does a great job of creating individual personalities and tics with this group of uniquely trained professionals. A solid recommendation for fans of Robert Ludlum's Jason Bourne and Daniel Silva's Gabriel Allon."

—*Library Journal*

"Riveting . . . Barry Eisler pulls off an *Avengers*-like feat . . ."

—*The Mercury News*

"Eisler turns the heat up like never before to deliver a fun, fast-paced thriller that's tailor-made for fans of nonstop action."

—The Real Book Spy

"The fun of Eisler's super thriller is in the excitement, the chase, and the survival. *The Killer Collective* binds it together into a blazing adventure of espionage escape fiction, perfect to start the new year."

—*New York Journal of Books*

"Eisler's *The Killer Collective* packs a punch like a sniper's rifle. A solid grounding in up-to-the-minute technology and current affairs makes this a hot read for thriller lovers."

—Authorlink

"Heart-pounding! Eisler has created a more literary version of *The Expendables*—the movie series that brought together Stallone, Schwarzenegger, Jet Li, Chuck Norris, Jason Statham, Dolph Lundgren, Bruce Willis, and other action heroes . . ."

—*It's Either Sadness or Euphoria*

"Demonstrating the extraordinary expertise in the art of espionage and special operations—including surveillance detection, cover, elicitation, operational site selection, and more—that his fans and fellow practitioners have come to venerate, Eisler delivers another brilliant, fast-paced thriller, full of well-developed characters who remind me of the special operations and intelligence officers with whom I served and in some cases against whom I worked. For a retired senior CIA Clandestine Services officer still nostalgic for his espionage operations of bygone years, Eisler's thrillers full of intrigue, adventure, and suspense are a most welcome opportunity to get as close as is now possible to the real thing."

—Daniel N. Hoffman, retired Clandestine Services officer and
former CIA Chief of Station

AMOK

ALSO BY BARRY EISLER

Novels

A Clean Kill in Tokyo (previously published as *Rain Fall*)
A Lonely Resurrection (previously published as *Hard Rain*)
Winner Take All (previously published as *Rain Storm*)
Redemption Games (previously published as *Killing Rain*)
Extremis (previously published as *The Last Assassin*)
The Killer Ascendant (previously published as *Requiem for an Assassin*)
Fault Line
Inside Out
The Detachment
Graveyard of Memories
The God's Eye View
Livia Lone
Zero Sum
The Night Trade
The Killer Collective
All the Devils
The Chaos Kind

Short Works

"*The Lost Coast*"
"*Paris Is a Bitch*"
"*The Khmer Kill*"
"*London Twist*"

Essays

"*The Ass Is a Poor Receptacle for the Head: Why Democrats
Suck at Communication, and How They Could Improve*"

AMOK

BARRY EISLER

 THOMAS & MERCER

Text copyright © 2022 by Barry Eisler
All rights reserved.

Published by Thomas & Mercer, Seattle

www.apub.com

Amazon, the Amazon logo, and Thomas & Mercer are trademarks of Amazon.com, Inc., or its affiliates.

ISBN-13: 9781542005654 (hardcover)
ISBN-13: 9781542005647 (paperback)
ISBN-13: 9781542005661 (digital)

Cover design by Rex Bonomelli
Cover image: © heripic / Shutterstock

Printed in the United States of America

First edition

For Wim and Peggy, with love

The strong do what they wish and the weak suffer
what they must.

—Thucydides

Preface

Timor is one of the islands of the Indonesian Archipelago, across the Timor Sea north of Western Australia.

In the mid-nineteenth century, Holland and Portugal divided the island, making the western half Dutch Timor and the eastern half Portuguese Timor. After the Second World War and Indonesia's successful war for independence against the Dutch, Dutch Timor became part of Indonesia, while the eastern half of the island remained a Portuguese colony, with Portuguese and native Tetum both widely spoken. In 1974, the Portuguese began to withdraw, provoking a brief civil war among the East Timorese. In 1975, Indonesia invaded and annexed the eastern half of the island.

In 1991, when this story is set, Indonesia's occupation and a guerilla war waged by Falintil, the Armed Forces for the National Liberation of East Timor, had been grinding on for sixteen years.

1991

Chapter 1

Isobel crouched behind one of the thatched huts in the growing darkness, concealed among the giant nest ferns common to East Timor, straining over the din of cicadas for the sounds she dreaded: the thud of boots; the ugly, overconfident laughter; Bahasa Indonesian instead of Portuguese or Tetum. She heard none of it, but what if they were nearby, watching and waiting as she was, only more practiced at patience?

The strap of her medical bag was cutting into her shoulder, and for the hundredth time she adjusted it. Then she wiped a rivulet of sweat from her eyes and stole another glance past the edge of the hut. The girl was still there, standing by the well, an empty water jug on the ground beside her. A villager, obviously, her feet bare, her white shirt dirty, and her shorts not much more than rags. The girl's head was canted slightly, and her gaze seemed fixed on something in the distance, or perhaps on nothing at all. The incongruity of her presence made Isobel uneasy. Of course, under the circumstances, everything was making her uneasy. That was only natural. But knowing it was natural did nothing to calm her.

Maybe the girl was simply enjoying a slightly illicit rest—lingering longer than necessary before drawing up the water she'd been sent to fetch and then carrying it, perched on her head, back to her family.

Maybe.

The problem was, the American journalist had said she and Isobel should meet by the well, and they couldn't risk being seen. Kopassus had informants everywhere. Probably this young villager was as innocent as the girls Isobel treated at the clinic in Dili, and probably she hated the Indonesian soldiers as much. But hatred was often accompanied by fear. And more often still, eclipsed by it.

She's not an informant. Not a lookout. She's just a teenage girl. Sent to fetch water, and not in a hurry to finish the chore.

And then she surprised herself by almost hoping the girl *was* an informant. Because if soldiers saw her near Isobel and the journalist, and thought the girl was working with them, the things they would do to her . . . Isobel didn't want to imagine it.

Though neither did she need to imagine. She had heard more first-hand accounts than she would ever want to remember. And more than she would ever be able to forget. Some of the girls had been as young as twelve. Many of them had been made pregnant. Three had committed suicide, their shame and trauma more than they could bear.

Isobel glanced at her watch, a gift from her father in celebration of her graduation from UCLA Medical School on a scholarship five years earlier. And in gratitude for her return to East Timor, where she was needed far more but where she would always make far less. She had never regretted the decision to come back. Not even now, when at any moment she might be caught, tortured, raped by one soldier after another. And afterward, buried deep in some trackless part of the jungle, or worse, fed to the crocodiles of Timor's countless lagoons and mangrove swamps. For an instant, she was glad her parents were gone. And she was glad she had stopped in Aidabalaten on the way here, where she tried to visit once a year to swim in the sea that now held their ashes. If the worst happened, at least they would be spared the torment of knowing for the rest of their lives their daughter had been murdered, while lacking the proof their minds needed to ever fully accept it.

She looked at her watch again. The journalist was supposed to be here almost a half hour ago. The roads were treacherous around mountain towns like Maliana; could the woman have suffered an accident? Surely she wouldn't have been so foolish as to leave no buffer for the inevitable bus breakdowns, the washed-out roads, the random bad luck that made life in East Timor hard enough even before the Indonesians had come.

Unless . . . unless she had been taken. Not likely—the risks of holding an American woman, and a journalist at that, would be substantial. But the soldiers had murdered five Australian journalists in Balibo sixteen years earlier, on the eve of the invasion. No doubt those men, too, had felt protected by their nationality, their profession, their white skin.

She's fine. She's just late. She's coming.

The journalist's name was Beeler. Theresa Beeler. She had made a reputation for herself through her unrelenting coverage of the cruelty of the occupation, traveling to places other journalists feared to visit, almost daring the Indonesians to do something to stop her. There was a fine line between brave and reckless, and Isobel wasn't sure which side Beeler occupied.

Of course, the same could be said of herself.

Isobel had told Beeler about the medical clinic. About the girls she helped, and what had been done to them. *Proof,* Beeler had responded. *If you can get me proof, the world won't be able to ignore what's happening here any longer.* And the pain and fierce conviction Isobel had seen in Beeler's eyes made her believe it.

She adjusted the strap of the satchel again. Maybe she should have hidden it somewhere nearby. Then if the soldiers found her, at least they wouldn't find everything. But she had been afraid to leave it, to have it anywhere but on her body or in her hands.

Where are you, Beeler? Where are you?

She snuck another glance around the edge of the hut, expecting to see nothing but the dawdling girl. Instead, she was stunned to see Beeler walking toward the well, her short blond hair wet from sweat and clinging to her scalp as though she had just gone swimming in one of the streams that crisscrossed Maliana.

For a moment, Isobel was gripped by the urge to dash out, give Beeler the bag and everything in it, and be done. To rid herself of the weight of what she'd been carrying.

But she hesitated. Something about the way Beeler was walking. So cautiously, as though she had found herself in a minefield, or a trail thick with poisonous snakes.

And then she remembered—the woman had been adamant about something she had called bona fides. *They treat us like spies,* she had said. *So we have to act like spies. When I show myself, if I'm safe, I'll rub my chin. And you do the same if you're safe. Anything else means we're not safe. That we're under duress.*

Now Beeler was holding her arms stiffly at her sides. Nowhere near her chin.

Could the woman have forgotten her own admonition? It seemed unlikely. But maybe she didn't expect Isobel to have arrived yet? To be watching? And so was simply waiting to signal that all was well.

But in the last fading light, Isobel thought she could make out something in Beeler's expression. The woman was afraid. No, terrified. The lack of the bona fides had directed Isobel's attention to it. But only to confirm what she already sensed.

Something's wrong.

She felt her own fear then, a sudden, leaden weight in her bowels, a terrible tightness in her chest and throat. She tried to draw back but couldn't move. She struggled to rise from her crouch, but her legs were frozen, paralysis multiplying terror, terror deepening paralysis.

The girl watched Beeler's careful approach. She must have been wondering what this white woman was doing on the outskirts of occupied Maliana.

Isobel wished now she had insisted on meeting in town, which had modern buildings, a few paved roads, even some streetlights. But Maliana was only a few kilometers from the border, and the Indonesian soldiers occupying it preferred the comforts of town to the privations of the outlying villages. At the time, it had seemed a meeting on the outskirts would be safer. Now it felt like anything but.

Touch your chin, Isobel thought. *Please. Just touch your chin.*

But Beeler didn't touch her chin. She kept walking, her posture so rigid Isobel realized the woman was forcing herself to move forward, step by terrified step.

Beeler stopped several feet from the girl. For what seemed a long time, the two of them stood there, looking at each other.

Then Beeler turned to the trees behind her. "I told you," she called out, her voice higher than Isobel remembered. "There's nobody here. Just a girl I don't know. Probably from the village."

No one responded.

"There's no one here!" Beeler called out again. "All right? You made a mistake." She started to add something, hesitated, then said, "Please."

The moment stretched out, as frozen as Isobel's limbs. The buzzing of the cicadas was very loud.

The girl, perhaps sensing Beeler's terror, backed away. Instantly, six dark shapes emerged from the trees. The girl turned and started to run. There was a flash of light, and over the sound of the cicadas came a loud *crack!* The girl fell.

"Oh, God," Beeler cried out. "Oh, my God!"

Isobel felt a sudden warmth and wetness on the insides of her thighs. She realized her bladder had let go.

The shapes reached Beeler and surrounded her. Isobel could see them better now. They were soldiers in camouflage uniforms and floppy hats, all with rifles. One of the soldiers stepped forward and prodded the girl with his rifle muzzle, while another, farther back, kept his rifle trained on her. The girl lay still.

"I don't know her!" Beeler said. "I told you, there's no one here! I'm an American journalist and you have no right to detain me!"

The words were brave, but the pitch of her voice was even higher now, her throat constricted by terror.

One of the soldiers stepped away from the others, toward the hut Isobel was crouching behind, and turned his head leisurely back and forth. This one wasn't wearing a hat, and in the dim light, Isobel could make out something strange about his head. Then she realized—it was his haircut. A mohawk.

Her terror deepened. *Maybe it's someone else,* she thought. *Someone else with that haircut.*

Something about his bearing made Isobel sense he was the leader. The muzzle of his rifle was slung low, but he swept it slowly along, tracking his gaze, as though ready at an instant's notice to raise it and shoot. Isobel thought it was too dark, and the surrounding ferns too dense, for him to be able to see her head partially exposed from behind the hut. But she felt a dreadful certainty that he could sense her. Or smell her.

A long, frozen moment went by. One of the soldiers said something in Bahasa.

Another moment passed. The leader nodded at whatever the man had said and turned back to Beeler. In English, he said, "Come."

Beeler shook her head. "I'm not going anywhere. You have no right."

The man raised his rifle. "Come," he said. "Or we'll leave you here. In the dirt. Dead next to this girl you say you didn't know."

The man's English was very good. Did that mean he worked with the Americans? Isobel's terror grew worse.

Beeler didn't respond, but Isobel could hear her panicked breathing. *Help her,* she thought. *Help her.* But what could she do?

The leader raised his rifle higher and pointed the muzzle at Beeler's face. The man standing behind Beeler quickly stepped to the side.

"I'll count to three," the leader said. "One. Two. Th—"

"All right!" Beeler said, raising her hands. "All right. You win." Then she groaned, and Isobel realized the woman was crying, whatever bluff she had summoned exhausted now, evaporated.

A soldier took Beeler by the elbow, and they all walked off. A moment later they were gone, swallowed by the trees and the darkness, and the only sound was the cicadas again. It had happened so fast, and had been so surreal, it might have been a dream.

But for the girl lying in the dirt.

She might still be alive, she thought. *Help her.*

But she was still rooted to the spot. She understood physiology, of course; she knew that freezing was simply a biological mechanism, a survival reflex, the same in humans as in a rabbit that smells a jungle cat. But she had to move. The soldiers might come back.

A bead of sweat ran into one of her eyes. She felt herself blink to clear it. The sweat stung and she blinked again.

Do it again. Just blink. Blink your eyes. Keep blinking them.

She did. Her eyes weren't frozen. She managed a grimace. Then flexed her hands. And all at once, she could move again. She sucked in a huge breath and clamped a hand over her mouth to keep from screaming. She stood like that for a moment, clutching herself, rocking back and forth in mingled terror and relief.

She wanted to run. But the girl. She couldn't.

She tiptoed forward in a crouch, certain with every halting step that the soldiers would suddenly return. They would surround her, and take her away, and then, and then . . .

Stop. Stop it. Help this girl. You have to help her. That's all.

She reached the fallen girl, dropped to her knees, and eased the girl over until she was faceup, taking care to support the girl's back with her thighs, then edging away as she turned her. The girl coughed out frothy blood. Isobel checked the airway—the breathing was rapid and shallow, but she was alive.

But her shirt was soaked with blood. Immediately Isobel saw why—the bullet had exited the left side of the chest. Beneath the bloody material a hole fluttered, issuing the characteristic hissing sound. A sucking chest wound.

The shirt had buttons—faster to tear it open than to cut, and Isobel did so. She reached into the medical bag and pulled out some folded plastic wrap and a roll of duct tape. The clinic had long since run out of petroleum gauze, the aluminum-foil wrappers of which were perfect for sealing SCWs. But kitchen supplies could still be had.

She unfolded the plastic, placed it over the wound, and taped off three sides of it, using gauze to wipe away blood so the tape would adhere to the skin. She knew it was nearly hopeless. Without oxygen, a chest tube, a transfusion, surgery . . .

But she had to try. She couldn't just leave this girl to die.

For a moment, the girl seemed to rally. The plastic worked, sealing off the wound as the girl inhaled, releasing trapped air on the exhale. Isobel started to prepare an occlusive dressing for the downside wound.

The girl's lids fluttered open. She looked at Isobel and grimaced. Then she started to cry. *"Lae,"* she whispered in Tetum. *No.*

"It's okay," Isobel said, supporting the girl's head. "I'm here. I'm a doctor. It's okay."

The girl looked at her. Then her head eased to the side, and suddenly she was looking through Isobel, past her, again as though at something in the distance, or perhaps at nothing at all.

Isobel checked for a pulse. There was none.

She lowered the girl's head to the ground. Tried to collect herself. And all at once, couldn't.

She balled up the gauze she had used to wipe the blood and hurled it away. She pounded a fist in the dirt. Again. A third time. Then she knelt there for a moment, crying in rage and frustration, grieving for this girl she didn't even know.

At least they didn't take you, she thought. *At least they can't hurt you anymore.*

She felt a sudden wave of guilt that she had stayed hidden as the soldiers led Beeler away. She knew that even if she had been able to move, there was nothing she could have done. If the soldiers had seen her, they would have taken her, too. But still.

And maybe Beeler would be all right. Maybe they would be afraid to hurt an American journalist.

But Isobel didn't really believe it.

She retraced her path to the hut, again certain with every step that the soldiers would return.

But no one came. After a minute, she hurried back to the dirt road into town, her wet pants clinging to her, the smell of urine pungent in the night air. There was a stream at the edge of the village, low because of the season but deep enough to wade into and get clean. If anyone came, she would hide again. The satchel strap cut into her shoulder once more, but this time she welcomed the pain—proof that the bag's contents were still with her, that the soldiers hadn't won.

Now that she was away, her fear was intensifying, threatening to escalate to panic. She tried to push it aside, to force herself to think. *Think.*

What happened?

Someone must have told the soldiers. For the moment, Isobel couldn't imagine who. Maybe Beeler had said something to the wrong person. And the soldiers had caught her, and made her tell them where she was going, tried to make her tell them what she was doing in Maliana.

But she hadn't told them. If she had, the soldiers would have taken Isobel, too.

She felt a fresh wave of guilt. Despite the woman's tears and terror, Beeler had protected her. She had risked her life to save Isobel's.

Or given it.

Isobel forced herself to think again. The soldiers had known something was going to happen at the well. Or at least they'd suspected. And the girl they shot . . . Maybe they assumed she was part of it. That Beeler had been there to meet the girl. Which is why, once they had shot the girl, they had left without bothering to search the area.

Despite the fear and the guilt, Isobel felt a sudden surge of relief so strong it bordered on joy. Because whatever the soldiers knew or suspected about what Beeler was doing in Maliana, they couldn't have known what was in the satchel. If they had, they never would have stopped searching.

And then the fear gripped her again, worse even than before. Because they had Beeler now. If the man with the mohawk was who she was afraid he was, it would be very bad for the journalist. And if the woman so much as hinted at what was in the satchel, then not just Kopassus, but the entire Indonesian army would be searching for Isobel.

And if Beeler outright confessed, it would be even worse than the army. Much worse.

Chapter 2

C arl Williams sat on a steel bench bolted to a gray painted floor. The tables, also steel and also bolted to the floor, were all occupied, many by mothers with children, and the sounds of conversation echoed off the concrete walls. Carl wondered how often these folks came to the Huntsville Unit. Once a week? A month? There was a sense of routine in the air, and for a moment he marveled at what people could get used to. Maybe he should have visited more often himself. Maybe he could have gotten used to it, too.

Instead, he'd come only once, eight years earlier, just before leaving for Marine Corps Recruit Depot San Diego, to deliver the news that he'd joined up. That was 1983, when the old man was in Administrative Segregation, which among other things meant no visiting privileges, but Carl had written to the warden, himself a former Marine and veteran of the Frozen Chosin, and the warden had allowed the old man out so Roy Williams could see that his son was making a man of himself. In the end, none of it mattered. Roy had sat in his leg irons in this very room, barely saying a word, while Carl rattled on like a fool. At the end of the hour, two guards had stood Roy up and led him away. Roy hadn't even looked back as the barred door clanged shut behind him.

But Roy had been out of Administrative Segregation for years now, and in just over a month, would be eligible for parole. Carl's sister Ronnie was scared to death about it. So was their mother, Carl knew, though unlike Ronnie, Mary had always kept her fears to herself.

Carl snapped the front of his shirt back and forth a few times to get some air into it. It didn't do much to cool him down. If they had air-conditioning here, they sure weren't wasting a lot of money on it. Everyone was sweating—the visitors, the prisoners, the guards. In fact, the whole place smelled like sweat, even the check-in area where he'd been searched and had to show ID. And not good sweat, either, like in a gym or boxing club. This smell was more like . . . sadness. Resignation. Broken people and broken dreams.

He glanced up at the television set they had bolted to a ceiling corner. MTV was playing "Good Vibrations" by some guy named Marky Mark. The melody was hard to hear over all the people talking, but it sounded pretty upbeat. Earlier it had been Paula Abdul singing "The Promise of a New Day." Carl was grateful for the distraction, though he would have preferred a game—after all, the Houston Oilers were seven and one, and people were starting to talk about their playoff chances. But it seemed the prison administrators wanted to serve up some musical irony instead.

A sound cut through the conversation around him—the heavy steel clack of a prison door lock being thrown back. Carl looked over and saw him coming through. Roy.

His heart started pounding and he stood, as automatically as if he were coming to attention. Carl had seen a lot since the last time he'd been here—some in the Corps, and a whole lot more in Afghanistan. He realized he'd been expecting that being face-to-face with Roy again, he'd be facing him like a man, the man he now was. But he suddenly understood he'd been wrong about that. Because all he could see before him now was his father, who'd been taken away when Carl had been too small to really understand why. He'd missed his daddy back then, missed him badly, and had understood instinctively that he could never talk to Ronnie or their mom about it. He had to keep his doubts to himself, and his worries, and muffle the tears in his pillow at night. And so he had, until the tears came less often and less hard, and he understood better why Ronnie and their mom had been forced to do what they did, until he came to see that what they did, as hard as it was, was right.

He watched while Roy leisurely scanned the room. No leg irons this time, or handcuffs. And no guards. No smile, either, not even when he saw Carl. Just a nod, then another scan of the room. A prison habit, Carl supposed. But there was nothing furtive about it. More the air of a man surveying his realm.

When he had finished taking stock of the room, Roy strolled over. He looked as brawny as ever in his prison whites—more so, in fact. He'd always been heavy boned, but he'd put on weight, from the look of it all muscle. And though he was a tall man, standing close to six foot three, now he looked taller. His posture, Carl realized. It was so ramrod straight he could have been a Marine Corps drill instructor. He still had the goatee, and a full head of close-cropped, sandy-colored hair. The same color as Carl's, and everyone had always said the two looked a lot alike, the hair and the bones and build, too. As Roy got closer, though, Carl saw some gray was creeping in at the temples. Still, that was the only apparent sign that Huntsville had aged him.

He stopped a few feet from Carl and looked him up and down. Carl had filled out, too, since they'd last seen each other, but not like Roy.

"Another month wouldn't have made no difference," Roy said by way of greeting. "Could have met on the outside."

Carl was embarrassed that his heart was still pounding, and by all the confused emotions roiling inside him. Part of him thought he should hug his dad, or at least shake his hand. Maybe Roy wouldn't be closed to those possibilities. But he didn't exactly seem open to them, either.

"That a sure thing?" Carl said, just saying whatever to make a little time to get ahold of himself.

"It'll happen. Why, you hoping it won't?"

Ten seconds in and the old man was already trying to pick a fight. Weirdly, it calmed Carl down. At least now he understood what the tone was going to be.

"Why would you say something like that?"

Roy frowned. "You going to tell me your sister doesn't feel that way? Your mother?"

Carl didn't want to answer that. "I don't know. Have you given them a reason?"

"Sure, you don't know. You must think your old man's gotten soft in the head in here. They put you up to coming?"

"Why would they have to put me up to anything? You're my father."

Roy gave him another up and down. "You look like my son, I'll say that. Even wearing a goatee now."

Carl had grown a full beard in Afghanistan, which he'd since trimmed back to a goatee. He rubbed it as though to remind himself it was there. "Yeah, I guess I am."

"Bet your sister and mother don't care for it."

Roy was probably right about that. Mary hadn't said anything, but Ronnie had frowned when she first saw him. Carl had sensed why, but didn't want to think about it.

"They didn't say. They were just glad to see me."

Roy waved a hand as though the truth were too obvious to require confirmation. "Well, in just over a month, son of mine, the parole board is going to decide whether to keep me in here or let me out. Your mother and sister will be there, trying to make sure it's the first one. Telling everyone who'll listen what a bad man I am. The sort of thing they said that got me put in here in the first place. This time, they'll want you to join them."

Ronnie had already been testing the waters with Carl on this topic, though so far she hadn't come right out and said it. Roy, true to form, was less diplomatic.

"I don't know what they want," Carl said. "I'm back in town. I came to see you."

"Really? I see my boy twice in fifteen years. First time he's leaving town, second is when I'm coming up for parole. The world is just full of coincidences, isn't it?"

"This what you want?" Carl said. "You want to fight? Haven't seen you in eight years, and now we've got two hours, no, less because I've been waiting, and you want to spend the whole time fighting? Okay, fine, what do you want to fight about? Bet you got a whole list of things, I'll let you pick."

Roy didn't answer. After a moment, he offered a smile—not a particularly friendly one.

"I see my little man's all grown," he said.

Carl sighed and gestured to the bench. "You want to sit?"

Roy shrugged. "It's your visit."

Carl let the comment go. They sat a few feet apart.

For a minute, neither spoke. Then Roy looked at him. "Yeah, my little man. Standing up for himself at last. Wish you'd had the guts to stand up for me when I needed you."

Carl tried not to get exasperated. "I was ten years old. I barely even understood what was going on. The last time I saw you before you got yourself thrown in here, you hit me so hard I woke up in the hospital. Mom and Ronnie thought I was dead."

Roy laughed. "I knew you had a hard head."

Goddamn. He actually felt a swell of pride at Roy's confidence. It wasn't good. It wasn't right.

"Well, you sure did your best to bust it open. Mom's and Ronnie's, too. What were they supposed to do? It was like they were living with a rabid dog."

"That what they told you?"

"That's what I know."

"You don't know the half."

17

"Well, tell me, then. Tell me why the three people who lived with you were constantly having to explain to the doctors and teachers and police officers that they'd fallen down the stairs again, or walked into a tree branch, or gotten their leg caught in the door of the truck."

He knew it was all true, but it also felt like he was protesting too much.

"You weren't too young to know I was going through a hard time. There was a recession."

"It was a recession for everybody in Tuscola. But not everybody took it out on their family."

"I took it out on them? My own wife and daughter testified against me in a courtroom. Who the hell gave them the right?"

"Who gave them no choice?"

"To put their own husband and father in prison for fifteen years?"

"They didn't put you in for fifteen years. They put you in for three. You're the one who killed a man while you were here. That's on you."

Roy stared at him, and Carl immediately understood why his mom and Ronnie were so afraid. The stare was hateful, even murderous, but also so . . . cold.

"How does it work?" Roy said. "You're a jarhead now? You think you're tough?"

Carl didn't answer. What was the point?

"Come on," Roy said. "You see any action?"

The answer to that was complicated. Carl's timing in the Corps had been bad, the op tempo such that he saw more action in Slim's Tavern in Olongapo City than he did real fighting. It was part of the reason he got out. And then Desert Storm happened, just three years later. If he'd stayed, he likely would have been part of it. Yeah, his timing had been bad, all right.

On the other hand, if he'd gotten out any later, he would have missed the best of Afghanistan, where he'd spent nearly two years with the CIA as part of Operation Cyclone, fighting alongside the Mujahideen against the Russians, developing such a reputation for unconventional warfare that he'd been awarded the nom de guerre Dox, short for *unorthodox*. He'd seen a lifetime of action over there, up and down the northern countryside and even on raids into Uzbekistan, part of the Soviet Union itself, pissing off the Russians so badly they threatened to invade Pakistan if he didn't knock it off, which, after being repeatedly admonished by the CIA, he mostly did.

Not that he would be presented with any medals for his service in defeating the Soviet Union and ending the Cold War. He wasn't allowed to talk about it, or even to acknowledge that it had happened.

"I guess not, then," Roy said.

"I saw some."

"What kind?"

"What difference does it make?"

"Maybe I'm just curious, seeing as how you have a bullet hanging around your neck. What does that mean, you're some kind of badass?"

The bullet Roy was referring to was known as a Hog's Tooth—a 7.62 boat-tailed round with a hole drilled in it, which Carl had been wearing hung from his neck with paracord since receiving it upon graduation from Marine Scout Sniper School. That's when he became a HOG, aka a Hunter of Gunmen. A marksman not so trained was known as a PIG—a Professionally Instructed Gunman. There was no disgrace in being a PIG, and in fact, many if not most were fine marksmen. But to be a HOG was a different thing entirely. It meant you were the best of the best, a graduate of one of the most demanding and respected military schools in the world. Every HOG Carl had ever known wore his Tooth as one of his most prized possessions.

Which was exactly why he didn't want to explain to Roy. Roy would just belittle it.

"I told you," Carl said. "I saw some action."

"All right. Tell me, what passes for action for you? Were you all on your own, with a bunch of Negro and Mexican gangs trying to make you a woman?"

"What?"

"It's a simple question."

"You know the answer. It's why you're asking."

"Yeah, I know the answer. The answer is, whatever action you saw, or didn't see, you had weapons. Your buddies. Your unit. You had a radio, so if the shit hit the fan, you could call in an artillery strike. Hell, an air strike. *Come save me, cavalry, I need your help.* But see, your mother and sister got me locked in here without any of that. I was a twenty-nine-year-old white boy in a hellhole run by colored gangs. Gangs who had a slogan they lived by. You know what it was?"

"Look, I didn't come here—"

"You don't want to know what their slogan was?"

Carl didn't respond. Roy was going to tell him about the slogan. What Carl wanted had nothing to do with it.

"Their slogan was, 'Every white boy rides.' You know what that means?"

"I can imagine."

"Well, I don't have to imagine. 'Cause I lived it. I lived it every day and every night of being alone in a cage, surrounded by packs of animals who thought it was not just their right, but their sacred duty, to rip my ass apart until they were tired of it, then trade me around for cigarettes and to pay off gambling debts. I should have let them? That what you think of your father, that he should have let himself be ass-fucked by every Negro and Mexican convict in the Walls who wanted to take a turn?"

Roy's voice had been rising as his tirade went on, and a few visitors, and some inmates, too, looked over. Roy glanced their way, and suddenly they had more important things to look at.

"They had the numbers, and the organization, and the experience. I had one thing, and one thing only. How far would I go."

"So you killed someone."

Roy gave a short, harsh laugh. "Oh, not just someone. I killed the leader. Big buck called himself Juicy Fruit. Told me in the mess he was going to fuck me in my cell that very night, and there wasn't a damn thing I could do about it. *Gonna love you, white boy,* is what he said. *We're gonna beat you bloody and get them pants down. I'm going to go first, whispering in your ear the whole time while I make you my little girl. And when I'm done breaking you in, you're gonna give everybody else a turn, too. Yeah, everybody's gonna get a taste of you, white boy.* Then he turned back to his gang and they all started laughing. Except they weren't laughing for long."

Carl didn't like the way Roy was baiting him, but he asked anyway. "What'd you do?"

"Oh, old Juicy Fruit, he thought I was going to cower. Else he never would have turned away from me. You think I was a rabid dog at home? I jumped on his back and got my thumb in his eye. Brought my free hand around the back of my fist, and dug my thumb in 'til I was past his eyeball and had busted through the socket. Old Juicy Fruit was screaming and thrashing, his gang was hollering and beating on me, the guards started wailing away with their nightsticks. None of it mattered. I just kept on squeezing and digging 'til old Juicy Fruit stopped screaming and thrashing, and went nice and quiet and limp. Like I guess he wanted me. And I still kept digging, even then. You know what brains feel like when you get your thumb in them?"

Carl had seen his share of brains in Afghanistan, most of them in the form of the proverbial fine pink mist courtesy of a shot from his M40A1. But a bullet wasn't the same as a thumb.

"Can't say I do," he said.

"Well, why would you? You've never been sent to hell by your own wife and daughter. Much less lived there."

"I told you. You only got yourself to blame for this. Not them."

Roy said nothing. He just shook his head, as though too disgusted to even bother with a reply.

A moment went by. Then Roy said, "I realized later I was expecting old Juicy Fruit's brains to be rubbery. Maybe like . . . overcooked eggs. But I was wrong. Brains are softer than that. Like an overripe melon. Or maybe . . . custard."

Carl didn't know what the old man was trying to do. Threaten Ronnie and their mom? Intimidate Carl? Get him to understand? It seemed the safest course was to avoid responding, and that's just want Carl did. But after a moment, Roy started up again.

"One of the guards must have finally gotten in a good lick with his nightstick, 'cause I woke up in the hole with a lump on the back of my skull the size of a baseball and a clot of hair and dried blood felt like a bird's nest. Stayed there six months, too. Only time they took me out was to put me in front of the judge for my second sentencing. That was all right. I could have done them six months standing on my head, just enjoying the memory of old Juicy Fruit howling and thrashing while my thumb got all up inside his custard brain. You know the only part that was hard?"

Carl had a notion, but there was no point in volunteering.

"Only part that was hard was one of the guards giving me the news that your mother had divorced me. I thought he was just messing with my head. They like to do that sometimes, fill a man with fears when he's got no way to confirm the truth. Oh, your mother died. Or, oh your child was hit by a car and paralyzed. Heard your wife's sleeping with the neighbor. It don't take much creativity to torment a scared man locked alone in a cage."

Roy paused and scanned the room, then continued. "Guess you know, it wasn't no bullshit. I had no say in the matter, either, no sir. Something about me being an incarcerated felon. Not even anything for me to sign, that was between Mary and some state official. Now she thinks we're divorced."

"You are divorced."

Roy shot him a look. "We ain't divorced if I say we're not. And since we're not divorced, the marriage she thinks she's in with that jackass Henry Abbott is a sham, and those girls they had are bastards."

"Their names are Jane and Sue. They're not bastards. And like it or not, they're my and Ronnie's sisters."

"Not in my eyes, they're not. Why do you think my whore wife got me thrown in here? She went into her fake marriage with that jackass only a year later. What does that tell you?"

The comment, which took Carl straight back to all the taunts and fights in the aftermath, gave him a surge of angry adrenaline. "Don't talk about her like that."

"She's my wife, I'll talk about her as I please."

"She's my mother, and you will not."

"So you protect your mother, but not your father."

Carl hated how Roy could draw him in, then flip all his meanings around. Five years in the Corps, two in Afghanistan, and another just wandering the earth, only to come back to Tuscola and find himself a tongue-tied little kid again.

"It didn't matter," Roy said. "When they transferred me back to GenPop, old Juicy Fruit's gang was all, *We'll get you* this, and *We'll kill you* that. But you know what happened?"

"No, I don't."

"Turns out courage is contagious. There were plenty of other whites in here with heart. The problem was, they all felt alone as I did. All they needed was an example."

"You were their example."

"I was. We're outnumbered in here, you see, about six to one. The only way we win is by showing everyone else we'll go farther. We'll go harder. For us there's no limit. We don't care about the hole, or AdSeg, or consecutive sentences, or riding the lightning for killing a guard. There's no price we won't pay. There's only the price we'll make you pay."

"'We'?"

"That's right. Hell, I got a guy in here, had four months remaining on a twenty-year murder stretch, killed another convict for disrespecting him. Just like that. Now he's in 'til the end of days. But you think anyone will ever fuck with him again? Or anyone he's tight with? We're feared now, like it should be. And in this place, fear and respect, it's the very same."

It wouldn't have been productive to bring it up, but Roy had never drawn a distinction between those two things. When Carl had been small, he'd always been pleased at how much people seemed to respect his dad. It was only as he got older that he realized what it really was: people were afraid of Roy.

"Then what are you going to do?" Carl said after a moment. "Kill another inmate and die in here?"

"What I'll do is whatever needs to be done. You know what I call that?"

"No."

"I call it singularity of purpose. You care about a lot of things and I only care about one? You're going to lose. You can't stop a man who's not afraid of dying. You can't defend yourself against a man who doesn't care if he dies, too."

"And that's you?"

Roy gave another of his harsh laughs. "If Mary and Veronica don't like it, maybe they should have thought twice before putting me in here."

Veronica was Ronnie's given name. Mary had wanted to name her Ronnie, after the lead singer of the Ronettes, whose song "Be My Baby" was number two on the charts and playing nonstop on the radio while Mary was pregnant. But when Roy got wind that the singer's mother was half-black and half-Indian, he'd refused. They compromised on

Veronica—and Mary had immediately gotten her way by calling the new baby nothing but Ronnie from the moment she came into the world, with everyone else following suit. The only holdout was Roy, who for his whole life stubbornly refused to use anything but *Veronica*, and never stopped resenting Mary for making a fool of him with what he felt was a dirty trick.

"And you," Roy went on. "If you don't like it, maybe you could have spoke up for me at my sentencing instead of being their silent partner."

Carl sighed. "I already told you—"

"Oh, right. You was only ten, your balls hadn't dropped yet. Well, have they dropped now?"

Carl didn't answer.

"'Cause I'll give you a pass for last time. Fine, you were just a boy, barely knew what was going on, like you said. But you ain't no boy anymore, Mr. Marine who's seen some action and has a bullet hanging 'round his neck. You're a man now, son, whether you like it or not."

"I like it fine."

"Do you? Because being a man means making decisions. And sometimes those decisions mean taking sides. And you don't want to take sides against me again. One thing this place taught me is anyone who's not with you is against you. Well, which one is my son? Are you with me this time? Or against me?"

Carl shook his head. "What kind of question is that?"

"The only one that matters."

He didn't know what to do. There was one possibility he'd been clinging to. He'd told himself he wouldn't bring it up with Roy. But he was beginning to feel so desperate, he thought maybe he should take a chance.

"Listen," Carl said. "I might have a way to help. When you get out of here."

Roy's eyes narrowed. "What are you talking about?"

"I'm talking about money. Real money. To get you set up."

For a second, Carl thought he saw something in Roy's eyes. Concern? Alarm? Then it was gone.

"I don't need your help," Roy said. "And I don't need you being a damn fool and robbing a bank or whatever you're thinking and getting your ass thrown in here for your troubles."

"I'm not robbing a bank. It's government work."

"What the hell does that even mean?"

"I can't talk about it. Other than to say, it sounds lucrative."

"Oh, *lucrative*. There's a fancy word. You know what I think of fancy words? They're what people say to you when they're full of shit."

"Why would I be full of shit? You're my father, I want to help you. And don't tell me I didn't help you before. We've already been over that."

Roy looked away. After a moment he said, "The only help I want is for you to not get in my damn way."

They'd danced around long enough. And though he was afraid he already knew the answer, Carl said, "If they let you out of here, what are you going to do?"

Roy looked at him. "Do? I'll do whatever the hell I like."

"And what's that?"

Roy smiled, and even with all the blood and guts he'd seen in Afghanistan, Carl thought that smile was the most chilling thing he'd ever seen.

"I guess we're going to find out," Roy said.

Chapter 3

Ronnie was standing alongside the Pinto in the parking area when Carl came out. Most of the spaces were still occupied—the other visitors were getting their full two hours' worth. He squinted against the glare of the autumn sun and started walking over, not looking forward to the conversation he sensed they were going to have.

Ronnie waited until he was close. Then she said, "Went about how I expected?"

Carl shook his head. "I don't know."

"Then what are you doing out here so early?"

Ronnie had never been easy to fool. She was only a year older, but in many ways had been as much a mother to him as a sister.

He glanced at her belly. She wasn't showing yet, at least not that Carl could tell, but she'd told him he was going to be an uncle. The husband was a guy named Darryl they'd gone to high school with. Carl had missed the wedding—the CIA wasn't exactly generous about granting leave for contractors in Afghanistan—and it had created some discomfort that Carl couldn't even explain. But . . . Darryl was all right. Stable enough, and Ronnie and Carl's stepfather, Henry, had given him a job at Abbott Feed and Supply, the Abilene store that Henry owned and ran and that supplied half the ranches in Taylor and the surrounding counties. The problem was that Darryl wasn't half as smart as Ronnie, and Carl felt she was settling. It wasn't as though he could say as much, but even beyond his missing the wedding, he had a feeling she knew. She'd always known most of what he was thinking.

"Why didn't you wait in the car?" he said. "Could have been sitting this whole time with the air-conditioning on. Standing in the hot sun can't be good for that baby."

"I told you, I haven't been standing for long. I knew it would be a short visit."

"Well, you were right."

"I wasn't only right about that. He tried to get you to not speak at the parole board hearing, didn't he?"

Carl glanced back at the imposing red structure he'd just emerged from, its high brick walls stretching from one end of the street to the other, crowned with barbed wire, a white clock face somewhat incongruously perched at the top center. It was easy to see how the place had earned the nickname the Walls Unit.

He looked at Ronnie, thinking, *Here we go.* "He mentioned it."

"What did you tell him?"

"I didn't tell him anything."

"Why not?"

"Because I don't know, Ronnie."

Ronnie glared at him. "Mom and I are going to speak at that hearing. Roy knows we will. It's double or nothing now. His only concern is that you'll join us. If you don't, the parole board will wonder why. We're strongest with a united front."

Carl looked down at the cracked tarmac and didn't answer.

"Did he give you a sob story?" Ronnie said. "Try and make you feel sorry for him?"

"I wouldn't put it that way, no."

"Well, how would you put it?"

"He didn't have to tell a story for me to know he's suffered. What do you know about what it's like in there? What do I know?"

"You know what he told you, for starters. And it seems it's had the desired effect."

Carl threw up his arms. "He's our father, Ronnie. I mean . . . goddamn."

He looked away, not knowing how to tell her what he wanted to say. It was true Roy had always had a temper. And that he'd drunk too much. And that, at the end, it had gotten out of hand. But . . . Carl couldn't forget how they used to go hunting together, and how proud Roy was when Carl brought down his first buck, how he couldn't stop smiling afterward and telling everyone who'd listen, and some who wouldn't, how fine a shot his son was. Or when two bigger, older boys, the dumb and ugly Skove twins, Geeber and Guppy, had jumped Carl and given him a black eye, how Roy had smashed their father's head into the hood of Roy's pickup so hard it left a dent like someone had taken a sledgehammer to it, and for years after, Carl would see that dent and remember Roy telling the twins' father, *If your chickenshit boys so much as look at my son the wrong way ever again, I promise when I'm done with you, you won't have a tooth left in your head.* He couldn't forget the way Roy used to hold his hand when they'd go down to the lake to fish, or how he would tousle his hair when he was dozing in the passenger seat after, or how he'd carry him inside from the car and lay him down in bed and kiss him softly on the head when they were back. Or how Roy taught him engines, and showed him how to use various tools at the construction sites where Roy worked as a carpenter, and how Roy would look up from leveling a floor joist or framing a window or cutting a roof rafter and smile at the sight of his small son watching. Or the time Carl hit a grand slam in Little League and he was running the bases and all he could hear over the hollering from the stands was Roy, shouting, *That's my son, that's my boy!* Or the smell of his Old Spice cologne, or of the unfiltered Old Golds he liked to smoke on the porch in the evening because Mary wouldn't have it in the house, or a dozen other things he never thought about anymore, but that had all come flooding back the moment he'd seen his dad again.

"Carl," she said. "Look at me."

He didn't want to, but he did as she asked.

"Mom and I need you to speak at that hearing."

"And say what?"

"That you believe he's a danger. To our family."

"I don't know that's true."

"Did you look him in the eye in there?"

"Of course I did."

"Then you know it's true."

"He's been in there fifteen years! A third of his damn life. And I'm supposed to convince the state to hold him even longer?"

"That's exactly what you're supposed to do. We got lucky before. We're not going to get so lucky again."

"He didn't even try to convince me. Not really."

"What do you mean?"

"I mean . . . if he were that worried about my testifying, I think he would have tried harder to . . . I don't know. Make a case for himself. Pretend to have learned his lesson, and that it was all water under the bridge or something. But he didn't."

"Maybe he just couldn't, you ever think about that? Maybe he's got so much anger, he can't hide it, even when he knows he should."

Carl gave her a glum nod. He didn't disagree exactly. But there was something about the way Roy had eyeballed that room. The confidence of it. Like he knew all the angles and had it all figured out. With Carl, or without him.

"Anyway," he said after a moment, "it might not even work. He's smart. He's got nothing but time to think and plan. I don't know anything about parole boards and prisons. He does."

He hated the way she just kept looking at him. Like she was expecting something he didn't know how to give.

He thought about what he'd said to Roy before—the lucrative opportunity. The same guy who'd set him up with the contract work in Afghanistan—Magnus Magnusson, a Marine major at the time, now a light colonel—had told him about it over the phone just a few days earlier. "Southeast Asia," Magnus had said, and he wouldn't be more specific than that. "They need a sniper, and they mentioned you specifically."

"How'd they even hear of me?" Carl had said.

"It seems your exploits in Uzbekistan have become Agency lore."

"Hell, I thought they didn't like my invading Soviet territory. They were always telling me not to."

"Well, you have a fan somewhere that counts. Anyway, if you're interested, it would be short-term, high-risk, and a lot of money. That's all I can say."

It had to be a CIA op. But where? There were some contentious talks going on about the status of the US bases in the Philippines, so maybe there? Some kind of joint exercises in Thailand? Or maybe Indonesia. Kopassus, the Indonesian special forces, were part of the Pentagon's International Military Education and Training Program— IMET. It was hard to say. Southeast Asia was a big place, and Uncle Sam always had a lot going on there.

"Okay, who do I talk to?" Carl had said.

"I can put you in touch."

"I don't know when I'm going to be in DC. I'm home now in Tuscola."

"I'm sure the guy who's interested will send someone to talk to you."

He still didn't know who was interested, or where, or what for. But Magnus's contact was coming to Tuscola tomorrow. Carl wanted to tell Ronnie. But it was all so uncertain. And even if he knew the details, he wouldn't be able to tell her any more than he'd told Roy. He doubted she'd be any more impressed.

Part of what was paining him was how Roy had looked worried when Carl told him he had a way of making big money. It was like the mask slipped, and for a second his tough-guy father couldn't hide that he actually cared that his son was going to do something stupid that could get him in trouble. He wanted to tell Ronnie about that, too. But he knew she'd just explain it away. And the truth was, that would have hurt too much for him to give her the chance.

After a moment she said, "We protected you, Carl. When you were small. Now you need to protect us."

"What the hell do want me to do?" he said, his voice rising. "Kill him?"

"You want him to kill us?"

"You don't know he's going to do that."

"No, we won't know 'til it's done."

He had no answer to that, though he badly wished he did.

She sighed. "Think about it. We're standing here, trying to figure out whether our father is going to kill us all if he gets out of prison. Mom. And Darryl. And the girls. And Henry, who's been a better father to us than Roy ever was. And me. And your baby nephew. And the best you can come up with is, 'Maybe he won't.'"

He almost told her to have Darryl do something about it. But Darryl would wet himself if Roy so much as looked at him.

But it was more than that, too. Married or no, this wasn't Darryl's business. It wasn't even Henry's.

It was family business. Blood family.

The problem was, Roy was as much his family as Ronnie. And Mom.

He hoped the Southeast Asia thing might offer a solution. He didn't know what he would do if not. He only knew that whatever he did, if he got it wrong, he'd regret it for the rest of his life.

And maybe even if he got it right.

Chapter 4

Isobel trudged southeast along a nameless, unpaved road, her boots squishing in the mud, crickets chirping in the trees around her. She didn't know where she was going. But it was the opposite direction from the one the soldiers had taken, and for now that was all that mattered.

Her lower half was soaked from washing in a stream, and she felt blisters developing on her feet. She was hungry. And she was getting cold. She badly wanted to return to the guesthouse she had stayed in the night before. But she was afraid to retrace her steps. Somehow the soldiers had known about Beeler. About the meeting. They might have known more.

She wished they had met in Dili. But Beeler hadn't wanted to take possession of the package there. The airport was too tightly controlled. Better to hand it off near the border, which Beeler had snuck across many times. She could smuggle the package out that way, then fly to Bali from El Tari in West Timor, just another anonymous American tourist visiting the Indonesian paradise.

But on this side of the border, Beeler wasn't anonymous. Was that what had happened? Had the soldiers been watching the woman? Following her?

Beeler's reporting was well known. It was what had brought her to Isobel's attention; it was why Isobel trusted her. But that same reporting would have been infuriating to the Indonesian government. And if Beeler was that worried about flying out of Dili, and worried enough to insist on the bona fides, didn't it mean that she was also worried she might be . . . watched? Isobel had thought the reason for the chin-touching signal was Beeler's concern that Isobel, the amateur, might have been followed. But Isobel realized now that didn't make sense. Beeler would have been at least as concerned about people following her.

But how could they have learned about the meeting?

Maybe . . . Beeler saw them. Maybe saw them too late, too close to the well where the meeting was set. So she tried to run. And they grabbed her. The leader of those soldiers . . . There was something cunning about him. Maybe he saw the area around the well and thought it looked good for a secret meeting. Maybe he wondered what Beeler could have been doing so close by. And then he saw the girl. And made Beeler march forward, believing the girl was Beeler's contact.

If all that was true, they wouldn't have known much before the meeting. But now they had Beeler. Soon they might know everything.

She shivered in the cool, moist air and focused on walking, just walking. It was full night now, but the sky was clear, and a crescent moon offered just enough light so that she could find her footing.

She came to a small village, not much more than a collection of thatched-roof dwellings and a concrete mercantile. One of the dwellings, larger than the others, had a porch and a rusty Bintang Beer sign hanging in front. It might have been a guesthouse, at least once upon a time, when towns like Maliana had catered to adventurous Western tourists eager to see nearby Marobo Hot Springs.

She walked up a pair of creaky wooden steps. There was a bare incandescent bulb set into the porch ceiling, around which moths and other insects swooped and whirled.

"Hello?" she called out in Tetum through the screen door.

She heard footsteps on a squeaky floor. A moment later, a thin, midthirties man in torn jeans and a faded tee-shirt appeared. "Yes?"

"Hello," Isobel said again. "I'm sorry to bother you. I missed the last bus to Dili, and I've been walking. I saw your sign and wondered . . . If you're a guesthouse, I'd like a night's lodging."

The man scratched a stubbly chin. He looked tired. Well, everyone was tired. The war.

"We haven't had a guest in a long time," he said slowly. "We're not really doing it anymore. But of course you can stay."

A woman of about the same age, similarly clothed and also tired-looking, appeared just behind the man. Probably his wife. "We used to charge three thousand rupiahs," the woman said, glancing in apparent irritation at her husband. "Or if you have US, two dollars."

She must have been afraid Isobel would take her husband's words as an invitation to stay for free. Judging from the appearance of their dwelling and of the village, they must have needed the money. Isobel couldn't blame the woman for wanting to be sure they'd be paid.

"Of course," Isobel said. "I can pay you in rupiahs. And for a meal. I'm . . . I haven't eaten."

The woman's expression shifted from irritation with her husband to suspicion about Isobel. "What are you doing here?" she said. "Where are you from?"

"I'm a doctor," Isobel said. "From Clínica Médica Internacional de Dili. Here to help with a typhoid outbreak. But I got lost, and fell in a stream, and . . ."

She should have thought of all this sooner. How to account for herself and her circumstances. Instead, she was practically babbling.

But it didn't matter. The moment she'd said the word *doctor*, the woman's eyes had widened. "Doctor?" the woman said. "You're a doctor?"

Isobel nodded. "Yes."

The woman pulled open the door so quickly her husband had to jump out of the way. "Please," she said. "Please. Come."

Isobel followed her wordlessly through the kitchen and living area to the common sleeping quarters in back. On a pallet on the floor, dimly illuminated by a small table lamp, was a girl of about eight, clothed only in a pair of track shorts, lying on her left side and facing away from them. She was trembling slightly and moaning. The room was cool, but the girl's back glistened with sweat.

"Please," the woman said again. "Please."

At a glance, it could have been anything. Malaria, tuberculosis, dengue fever, typhoid fever . . . All were endemic to the island, and all had gotten worse since the Indonesians came. Of those possibilities, dengue fever offered the best chance for recovery, as long as it didn't progress to one of its more severe forms. Malaria was generally worse. If the malaria-causing parasite was *Plasmodium falciparum*, it would be much worse.

Isobel went to the pallet and knelt alongside it. But there were too many shadows.

"I need to examine her," she said. "Do you have a better light?"

Instantly, the husband was gone, returning a moment later with an extension cord. He plugged it into a wall socket, then unplugged the table lamp. The room was dark for a moment as he inserted the lamp plug into the extension cord. Then it was light again, and the husband picked up the lamp and carried it over, holding it above the girl.

"Your daughter?" Isobel said.

The woman nodded. "Yes."

"What's her name?"

"Alonsa."

Isobel turned to the girl. "Alonsa. My name is Isobel. I'm a doctor, from Dili. I'm going to examine you. Okay?"

But the girl, listless and still moaning, seemed barely aware of her

Isobel placed the back of a hand on the girl's forehead. It was burning hot.

"Bring the light around," Isobel said to the father. "I still can't see."

She reached into the satchel for her stethoscope. If, despite the fever, the pulse was slow, it could be typhoid. Which Isobel could treat—she was carrying Cipro in her bag.

And then she saw it—swelling out of the girl's right trapezius. A large boil, almost four centimeters. It was classic: erythematous, edematous, weeping small amounts of pus through the skin. Here and there was some crust in areas where skin cells were dying.

Isobel pointed at the boil. "How long has she had this?"

"Weeks," the mother said. "They gave us antibiotics in Maliana."

Isobel shook her head. "Antibiotics won't work for this. The infection is sealed off. The medicine can't reach."

She pulled a pair of nitrile gloves from the satchel. "Alonsa. You have a boil on your shoulder. I know it must be sore. But I have to touch it. All right?"

In response, Alonsa only moaned.

Isobel reached out and palpated the boil. Instantly, Alonsa cried out and jerked away.

That would have to do. The size was bad enough. But in addition, it was notably soft. Just the one touch told Isobel there was a great deal of pus beneath the surface. Warm compresses might have worked a week earlier. Not anymore.

Isobel looked at the man and the woman. "It needs to be cut open. Do you understand?"

The mother glanced worriedly at the father. He nodded to her, and then at Isobel.

"What are your names?" Isobel said.

"I'm Mateus," the man said.

"Joana," the woman said. She started to cry. "Please help her. We've been so worried."

Isobel nodded. "I need you to boil water. To make sure it's sterile. Two liters. Do you have a plastic bottle? A water bottle, that kind of thing?"

Joana swiped away the tears with the back of her fist. "Of course."

"Good. I don't have a proper syringe to irrigate the boil—to wash it out—once I open it. We can use the bottle for that. We'll drive a heated nail through the cap to make a hole, then fill the bottle with the sterilized water. Okay?"

Joana nodded. "What else do you need?"

"A tarp to cover the pallet. And rags. Do you have anything for disinfecting? Hydrogen peroxide? Rubbing alcohol?"

Joana nodded again. "Rubbing alcohol."

"Bring that, too. We'll use it to sterilize the rags. The wet rags, plus the pus in that boil, plus the water I'll be using to clean it out . . . We'll need the tarp for all that. The pus is infected, and it can infect other people. Everything it touches needs to be burned, or buried, or washed in hot soapy water. Okay?"

An hour later, they were ready. Alonsa shrieked and jerked away when Isobel tried to inject lidocaine in the skin around the boil. That was good. She still had strength. Mateus held her so Isobel could finish numbing the area.

Before she made the incision, Isobel had Joana hold a rag above the scalpel. And sure enough, the moment the blade parted skin, a pressurized bolus of pus shot into the rag. The accompanying smell was pungent and awful, and only years of acclimatization kept Isobel from gagging. Joana, she noted, never so much as turned away.

Alonsa moaned, but the moan was more of relief than of pain. Isobel began wiping away the pus away with a rag and gently pressing the area to express more. She noticed Mateus looking inside the satchel—either because he was curious about the contents of a doctor's bag, or because he didn't want to watch the procedure being performed on his daughter, or both. It was all right. The medical supplies were on top, concealing what she had planned to give to Beeler.

In five minutes, it was over. Isobel had broken up all the loculations, drained the pus, and thoroughly irrigated the wound with pressurized sterilized water shot through the nail hole in the cap of the water bottle. After that, it was simply a matter of packing with iodoform gauze and dressing the wound. She explained to Joana and Mateus that they would need to remove the packing in a day or so, clean the wound, repack, and change the dressing daily for a while after, but beyond that the wound should take care of itself. She would show them how and tell them more in the morning. No, she saw no need for systemic antibiotics at this point, which was good because she was carrying only limited supplies. The antiseptic and anesthetic iodoform, and the dab of bacitracin she'd placed on the dressing, would likely be more than enough. Alonsa should begin drinking water and other fluids as soon as she was able, along with paracetamol every four hours for the fever.

She left out her uncertainty about whether the boil was the sole cause of Alonsa's distress. She would examine her again in the morning. But for now, she felt optimistic.

Joana and Mateus thanked her copiously, Joana wiping tears again as she did so. Isobel had seen the reaction many times before. For people who lacked access to a hospital or even a clinic, a doctor's intervention could seem like magic, a miracle. From her own perspective, an incision and drainage, or I&D, couldn't be more routine. Of course, she would have preferred a sterile saline solution and a 60 cc syringe, but the fundamentals were the same. As they'd taught her at UCLA: *The solution to pollution is dilution.*

She told them Alonsa should begin to improve soon now, and that she was happy she had been able to help. It was true, she was happy, and not just for Alonsa and her parents. For a moment, she'd been able to feel like herself again. To forget the helpless terror and shame of watching the soldiers lead Beeler away. And the horror of holding the girl the soldiers had shot, unable to do anything to save her.

They gave her dry clothes to change into. Mateus killed and cleaned a chicken, and Joana basted it with a mix of oil, shallots, ginger, garlic, soy sauce, lime juice, palm sugar, and chili paste, then cooked it skewered over coals. These people had little food, and they were using so much of it for her. She felt guilty. Of course, they would have been insulted had she tried to decline. And they would have insisted anyway.

And maybe she was rationalizing. All she knew for sure was the dinner seemed the most delicious she'd ever had.

At one point, Joana remarked that it was lucky Isobel's medical bag hadn't gotten wet when she'd fallen into the stream. The woman was obviously smart and noticed incongruities. Isobel sensed she had made the remark in all innocence. But it frightened her anyway. She'd had no backup plan for what to do if things went badly with Beeler, as indeed they had. She'd had no story prepared when she came to Mateus and Joana's door. And what story she improvised was strange and filled with inconsistencies. She was a doctor, not a spy, and it seemed the one had done little to prepare her for the other.

Isobel helped Joana clear the dishes while Mateus prepared what years before had been their guest room, more recently used for storage. Her belly full, Isobel was suddenly as exhausted as though she'd taken a drug. She used the privy and washed up with some well water. When she came back in, Joana was emerging from the sleeping quarters, wiping her cheeks again.

"She's okay," she said, her eyes welling up. "She's sleeping. I think . . ."

She paused, collected herself, and said, "We had two others. Both gone. Alonsa is our baby. I think God sent you to us. To save our little girl."

Isobel shook her head. But it wasn't modesty. It was the knowledge of what had really sent her to this house. The death of another innocent girl. And an unknown fate for Beeler.

Afterward, lying on her pallet in the dark of the guest room, Isobel couldn't shut off the film spinning through her head. The crack of the rifle shot. The girl falling. Beeler's high voice. The soldiers leading her away. The girl, staring at Isobel with doomed and terrified eyes.

She was a doctor in a war-racked country plagued by endemic illnesses, operating in substandard conditions and with grossly inadequate supplies and facilities. She had seen more death and suffering than she would ever be able to keep track of. Some of it she barely remembered. Some she would never forget. But she had never witnessed someone murdered in cold blood right in front of her. In its clarity, its wrongness, its evil, it was unlike anything else she had experienced.

The clinic treated anyone, for anything, with no questions asked. The Indonesians knew that Isobel treated Falintil, the guerillas. But they overlooked it because the soldiers needed doctors, too. And likewise, Falintil tolerated her treating the soldiers, something that in any other context they would have punished as treason.

Sometimes, in the privacy of the examination room, men Isobel knew were with the resistance would hint that perhaps Isobel could do more. Pass messages. Report on things she had seen. On what she might overhear from the soldiers.

She had always declined. Partly it was fear for herself. Partly it was fear of doing anything that could jeopardize the clinic and the girls she helped there. And partly it was knowing she already was doing more, with Beeler.

But if Beeler could no longer help, and if Isobel couldn't get the package out as she had hoped . . . she would have to find another way to combat these monsters. For her parents. For these kind people. For Beeler. And for that poor, murdered girl Isobel had been unable to do anything at all to help.

She didn't know what it would be. But given the chance, she would do it.

Even if she died trying.

Chapter 5

It was a five-hour drive from Huntsville to Tuscola, but Mary held dinner until they were back, and now there were seven of them around the table. Mary and Henry, of course, and Ronnie and Darryl, who had an upstairs room in the house. And Janey and Sue, Carl and Ronnie's little sisters. Janey was thirteen and still a skinny little freckled thing. Sue, two years older, had turned into a beautiful young woman with a dazzling smile. It made Carl realize how long he'd been away. When he'd left for boot camp in San Diego, they were barely five and seven. He wished he could have seen more of them as they'd been growing up, but he'd been climbing the walls to get out of Tuscola, and not just because of what had happened with Roy. There was plenty to love about the town, but it was tiny and no one ever seemed to leave. He needed something bigger, he just did. And yet here he was, and with the same problems he'd had before. It was like he'd never left.

No one had asked about the visit with Roy, though Carl knew Ronnie would be talking about it with their mom later, after everyone else had gone to bed. Only Henry had mentioned it. Before they sat down for supper, he patted Carl on the back and said, "I'm glad you went to visit your father." Carl didn't know what he was really thinking, but he never doubted Henry's intentions. He'd earned Carl's trust under hard circumstances, mostly by being patient with Carl's ambivalence, and by always being open yet never pushing. It didn't hurt that he was a good provider, building up the feed store from nothing, turning it into a thriving family operation, and buying them all a nice house with some land on Alamo Drive, instead of the shack they'd lived in with Roy over on Callahan by the railroad tracks. Henry was a gentle, doting dad to the girls, and was just as good to Ronnie and Carl. Carl knew he loved them all, and Carl loved him, too. But he couldn't help feeling guilty about it, as though loving Henry was a betrayal of Roy.

Mary made chicken-fried steak with gravy and cornbread, Carl's favorite. He wondered whether she was subtly showing her appreciation for the discomfort he must have felt visiting his father. Or was it more that she was trying to keep him onside? Either way, the smell of that fried meat, breaded in flour and buttermilk with onion and garlic and pepper, made him feel like a kid again, before anything bad had happened and he'd been able to take whatever blessings life offered entirely for granted.

They sat in the dining room because with Carl back and all of them eating together, the kitchen was too small. The girls sat on either side of Carl and carried most of the dinner conversation, with little Janey asking loads of questions about Carl's adventures far from Tuscola. She already had the bug, Carl realized, the recognition that even Abilene, the closest metropolis, wasn't at all a big town, and the need to see what lay beyond.

"But why didn't you come back sooner?" Janey said. "Mom says you left the Marines four years ago."

"That's true," Carl said, swallowing a mouthful of cornbread smeared with honey. "But I still had some out-of-town contract work to do."

Janey cocked her head. "What does that mean?"

Carl smiled at her. "It's like . . . you know how Mom and Ronnie and Darryl are full-time employees at the store?"

"Uh-huh."

"But how even so, when it's hay-baling season, Henry hires some extra help, but just temporarily?"

"Uh-huh."

"Well, that was me. Just giving old Uncle Sam a little extra temporary help."

Janey nodded as though contemplating. She was at the age where she was caught between recognizing that her older brother was being deliberately vague, on the one hand, and being dissatisfied enough with his answers to keep pushing, on the other.

After a moment, she resolved her dilemma by saying, "Did you have to kill anyone?"

Henry, sitting at the head of the table, said, "Honey, that's not a polite question to ask a man."

Not for the first time, Carl admired his stepfather's deft touch. He'd told Janey exactly what she needed to understand, but the rebuke was delivered with so much love that Janey wouldn't be stung by it. If Carl had been forced to say the same, his sister might have been embarrassed.

Janey turned to Henry. "Why not?"

"For one thing," Henry said in his patient, gentle way, "it's personal. For another, for the answer to be worth anything, it requires context. And the context itself could be personal. It's the kind of thing a man will talk about if he wants to. And if he doesn't talk about it, it means he doesn't want to."

"Also," Mary said from opposite Henry, "it's not proper dinner conversation."

"But Mom—" Janey began.

Mary shook her head. "That's enough, young lady."

Janey slouched in her chair and crossed her arms with a grunt. Carl couldn't help but laugh. She'd always had a will, and it was only going to get stronger as she got older.

Sue, older and so a bit less direct conversationally, said, "Anyway, you're done with your temporary work?"

He couldn't imagine a worse venue to bring up the opportunity he might have with Magnus's contact. He didn't even know what the opportunity was, or whether, under the circumstances, he could realistically take it.

He flicked the tip of Sue's nose, the way he used to do when she was smaller, and she laughed. "Done with that temporary work," he said, not wanting to lie but also wanting to avoid the truth. "But you know Uncle Sam, he's always hiring."

"So you're going to stay?" Janey said.

Damn, you might be even smarter than Ronnie.

He could feel everyone looking at him. He laughed uncomfortably. "Well, I'm here now, ain't I?"

"Aren't I," Ronnie said with a slight frown.

Carl winked at Janey. "Oops."

Janey laughed, and Ronnie's frown shifted from irritation to exasperation. Carl scrunched up his nose at Ronnie like he used to when they were small, and she rolled her eyes, which had always been her standard response. It was funny how fast being back could make it feel like they were kids again.

"I saw your picture on the wall of Jim Ned," Sue said. "With the football team."

Jim Ned was the local high school, where almost ten years earlier, Carl had played linebacker and tight end. "What are you doing, looking at those old pictures?" he said.

"I wasn't looking," Sue said. "I just saw them."

He laughed. "They must be all faded and cracked by now."

Sue laughed, too. "It wasn't that long ago! I still remember watching you play."

Carl bit into a forkful of the steak and gave Mary an appreciative smile. "I suppose you might be right. Being back here, it doesn't feel long ago at all."

Chapter 6

Joko Sutrisno squatted in the moist dirt where the evening before the girl had fallen, the grass around him dewy, birds calling from the trees.

In the faint morning light, he could see the depression where the body had lain, dark with blood, along with footprints left by someone who had come and carried the body away. Those footprints were of bare feet, large and wide and therefore probably male, and led to the village. But another set, leading from the depression to the back of a nearby hut, were of boots. Judging from the small size and narrow width of the prints, he guessed a small woman. That the prints were made by boots suggested an outsider. And the lack of wear on the soles meant either that the boots were new, or were worn only infrequently.

He examined the area around the depression. Small, semicircular indentations alongside the shape of the girl's body, hitting the dirt close to where the girl had lain and then sliding away. Knee marks, obviously. For their size, though, they were deep in the dirt at the point of impact. That suggested they were made by a small, light person, dropping to the ground and hitting hard. Someone heedless of hurting her knees.

He ran a hand absently along the line of close-cropped hair running down his otherwise shaved scalp, considering.

Heedless why?

Because she was intent.

Intent on what?

On helping the fallen girl.

And who would help a fallen girl?

AMOK

Whoever it was, the knee marks, along with the shape of the depression itself, suggested she had known how to safely and efficiently turn a casualty from prone to supine. Long ago, Joko himself had been trained by American advisors in what they had called the logroll technique.

And there were several other deep indentations alongside the depression. Not from a foot. Or a knee. But maybe . . . a fist.

Other possibilities began to materialize, but he pushed them to the side. He sensed he would find more, and after twenty years in Kopassus, he had learned that sometimes it was better to wait.

Tracking was a strange art, and he'd never known anyone better at it than he. There was a deliberate, conscious element, which, had he been so inclined, he could have articulated. There were obvious things, like the size of footprints, and whether the print had been left by a bare foot or by a boot. But Joko's skills went far beyond that. Treads, for example. There was heel wear—lateral, medial, rear, depending on the person's gait. Sole wear. Obliteration of elevation and grooves in high-pressure areas. Nicks and cuts. And then there was stride, from which he could determine height, fatigue, caution, speed, whether the person was bearing a load, and more. To a tracker like Joko, elements like these could be combined into a profile as conclusive as a fingerprint.

But there was also a kind of   magic to it. Where he could, if not see, then somehow *feel* the things that had happened earlier in a place, things that had happened before he had been there. In the village he had grown up in, near Bandar on the island of Sumatra, there had been elders who claimed to be able to commune with the spirits of the dead. To do so, they would enter a kind of trance. They could talk, but you could see that part of them had gone somewhere else. Joko didn't believe in spirits. Certainly he had never been troubled by one, despite the many lives he had taken. But he understood that feeling of . . . connecting with people who had departed. This more mysterious aspect of what Joko did was best invoked by quiet and solitude. His men understood this. Or at least they understood that when he was tracking, their commander preferred not to be disturbed. He would brief them afterward, once he had found whatever could be found and felt whatever could be felt.

He put down a hand, lowered his head until his face was inches from the ground, and sniffed. The overall smell was of blood, along with the natural smells of the earth. But there was also, faint but just perceptible, urine. Maybe the girl had a full bladder, which would have emptied itself when she had been shot.

Maybe.

His men were nervous. Word of the girl's death might have gotten to Falintil. The guerillas might be nearby, hoping to track and ambush the girl's killers. And Joko had brought a team of only five. For one thing, he needed to move fast. But he also needed a force to remain with the American journalist—both to guard her, and to fight off any rescue attempts. Taking her was causing problems. Apparently, she had failed to check in with her news bureau. The American authorities were already complaining to counterparts in Jakarta. The shit was rolling downhill, as shit always did.

It was a stalemate. He couldn't let her go. But he couldn't get rid of her, either.

But Felix would know what to do. And would be able to intercede, if necessary.

Joko had wanted to bring Beeler to Felix right away. He'd almost done so. But then he realized, while he and his men bivouacked the night before, that something had been wrong by the well. His instincts had told him as much at the time, but he had ignored them. Something he had learned not to do, and yet he had done it anyway. The mistake infuriated him and had to be corrected.

He had tracked Beeler to the well and was sure she had come to meet a source. But when Beeler realized his squad was following her, she tried to run. So his men had taken her. Joko saw the girl, and knew he had been right about the place. They forced Beeler to walk out to the well. But when the girl tried to run, one of his men had overreacted and shot her. Nothing to be done at that point but leave before there were problems.

But even before they made camp, Joko had that nagging feeling he knew to trust. The feeling that he was overlooking something, ignoring it, misinterpreting it.

And then he realized what it was. Beeler. The way she had called out to him that nobody was there. *Just a girl I don't know. Probably from the village.*

It was louder than it needed to be. It was said to Joko, but it was intended for someone else.

And the girl . . . she had just stood there. Confused, not frightened. It was only when she saw Joko and his men that she ran.

She was nobody, Joko now knew. But there had been somebody.

He looked more closely at the dirt around the depression. The balls and toes of the bare feet had left deep impressions, suggesting the man had merely squatted here. And his footprints were deeper on the return to the village. Because the man was carrying the girl on the way back, and so was heavier overall.

Joko tilted his head. He didn't close his eyes, but he was seeing something that was no longer there. A man coming. Seeing the girl was dead. The man squatting, lifting her, and carrying her away.

But the kneeling person was different. The boots. The intentness. The turning the girl over. The hiding behind the hut.

Joko stood and began walking in slow, concentric circles, looking closely at the ground. It took him only a moment to see it: a white button, about a meter and a half from where the girl had fallen.

The girl had been wearing a white shirt. And . . .

Someone had torn it open, hard enough to pop a button and send it flying a full meter and a half.

Why?

To render aid.

None of his men had checked the girl carefully. Based on where she had been shot, she was either dead or soon would be. But someone else had looked more closely. Someone more concerned.

If the kneeling person had immediately recognized that the girl was dead, there would be no point in tearing open the shirt. But if the girl was still alive . . .

He continued circling. Five meters from the depression, he saw something else: a ball of bloody gauze. He had been so intent on the depression itself that he had initially overlooked it. The villager. The man. He had gauze with him? Tried to attend to the girl's wounds, and, seeing it was futile, dropped the gauze?

Joko didn't think so. But the woman, the one who had tried to render aid . . . the ball of gauze lay at a distance that suggested the woman had thrown it. Yes, she was frustrated. Frustrated that she couldn't save the girl. Those marks . . . She had been pounding her fist into the dirt.

He walked slowly, following the barefoot tracks in the direction of the village, examining the ground closely along the way. Thirty meters along, he saw patches of matted grass, some of the blades pushed back into the moist dirt. Blood again. The barefoot tracks were all around those patches.

The man had set the girl down here. Then circled the body, probably to find a different way of carrying it. Even small bodies were heavy, and, before rigor, awkward. In the initial shock of discovery, the man had picked up the girl ineffectively. He had needed to adjust . . .

He looked around and saw a sheet of clear plastic.

He picked it up. There was duct tape around three sides. And it was crusted with dried blood. A field-expedient seal for a sucking chest wound. Maybe it had come loose. Maybe whoever had picked up and then carried the body had pulled it off, whether out of confusion, or curiosity, or to see if anything more might be done.

He walked back to the first depression, then followed the boot prints to the back of the hut, noting the short length of the stride.

Along the hut were numerous giant ferns. A good place to hide and from which to watch.

He looked at the back of the hut. It was coated with dust. Smudged in one place by a hand. Too large to be a child's. Too small to be a man's.

He knelt and put his face close to the ground. Sniffed. Considered. Sniffed again.

Yes. It was urine. Faint, but no doubt.

Someone had been very frightened back here. Her bladder had let go. Her pants had absorbed most of it, but not all. Some had dripped. More had dripped when she had gone to her knees to help the girl.

He looked at the boot prints leading away from the village. The stride was shorter leaving the village than it was on the way to the girl. On the way to the girl, the woman had run. Leaving, though still in a hurry, she was beginning what she thought might be a long march. And the gait was slightly uneven. Not enough to be explained by an injury. But . . . something was making her favor her right side. A backpack, worn over a single shoulder? Not impossible. But it would make no sense to carry a pack that way. More likely a satchel. Perhaps one the woman had been carrying for a long time. Something heavy that had begun cutting into her neck.

He smiled, knowing he would find her.

He called his men over. "We're looking for a woman," he said. "About fifty kilos. Maybe one hundred sixty centimeters."

Not for the first time, his men stared at him with mouths agape and awestruck eyes. Some of them, he knew, suspected he was a sorcerer, sensing his dark magic was what kept them all alive. Joko never disabused them. Their belief in his power gave him power. Besides, he didn't know that they were wrong. There were shamans on Sumatra who practiced magic—who believed that if you ate the heart of your enemy, you would gain his strength. Joko shared that belief, consuming the hearts of fallen Falintil fighters, and sometimes of civilians, too, if Joko judged the civilian brave enough. None of his men had once joined him—their terror and revulsion were too great. And that was fine. They were strong men. But it was important that he be stronger.

He pointed to the boot prints.

"She tried to help the girl," he said. "But the girl was beyond help. And then she went this way. Because she was afraid of us, and because it was the opposite direction from ours."

"If she was afraid," one of his men asked, "why would she try to help the girl?"

Joko looked at the man. "Because she's a doctor. And she was the one Beeler was here to meet."

Chapter 7

After dinner, Henry invited Carl to join him outside. Henry liked to sit on the porch for a bit after supper, especially when the days were longer, with Jim Beam being his custom rather than the Old Golds Roy had favored. Carl, who preferred his hard liquor to be clear, skipped the whiskey in favor of a couple of Lone Star beers. Out of politeness, Carl had invited Darryl along, but Darryl declined, leading Carl to wonder if the women hadn't put Henry up to some kind of interrogation.

They sat for a while on the cushioned chairs, backs against the house, in comfortable silence. Carl realized he'd missed how quiet Tuscola was in the evening. Abilene and the interstate were twenty miles away, and the only sounds on the porch were the breeze and the plaintive whistle of a Santa Fe Railway locomotive passing in the distance. The latter reminded him of growing up in the shack on Callahan, chasing trains despite all Mary's oaths that she would beat him senseless if she ever caught him playing on those tracks again, trying to scare him with true stories of other idiot boys who'd horse-played on those tracks and got splattered to death by a train for their troubles. But Carl had never stopped. And despite everything, remembering made him nostalgic.

He'd missed it all while he was gone, but now that he was back, he felt restless again. Too many memories, he supposed, and of course plenty of them weren't even memories; they were still the here and now.

Mary was still pretty, but he could see she was getting older. Roy's and hers had been a shotgun wedding, when she was only a senior in high school and Roy, who'd dropped out, just a year older. Her parents had been dead set against the marriage. They'd already forbidden her from seeing Roy, who they thought was trash even though their economic circumstances weren't a whole lot better than his, and learning—from her pregnancy, no less—that she'd defied them, put them over the edge. Devout Catholics, they were caught in a paradox—against an abortion, and against marrying. They solved their dilemma by disowning their daughter, something they came to regret after Ronnie and then Carl came along. They tried to make amends, but the damage was done, and Ronnie and Carl had never felt much for either of them. It was a little different with Sue and Janey, where there was more water under the bridge, plus a more respectable father. But part of what had made things so hard with Roy was that Mary had no one she could go to with her troubles. For her to finally resort to the police and the courts was a sign of just how desperate Roy had made her.

Not that Carl had appreciated any of that right away. In fact, it had taken years. The turning point came when he was in high school and reading the Jack London book *White Fang*, where a starving she-wolf, White Fang's mother, stole the kittens from a lynx's lair to feed her own starving young. The mother paid a terrible price for that, one she'd sensed coming. After reading the story, Carl had looked at Mary in a new light. Though he never said anything about it to her or Ronnie, either. He felt too bad about how long it had taken him to understand.

But even before all that, seeing the way Henry was with Ronnie and him, and then with Sue and Janey, had been a revelation. That Henry would raise a hand, or even his voice, to anyone in his family, was unthinkable. Before Henry, Carl grew up thinking that being afraid of your own father's temper, of his fists and his belt, was normal. Now he knew there wasn't a more abnormal thing in the world. Family was the place where violence was impossible. Out in the rest of the world, there was plenty of it, and Carl himself had meted out his fair share.

But that was it. If violence was possible, it wasn't family. And if it was family, then violence wasn't possible.

He sipped his beer, enjoying the evening air and Henry's quiet company. Not much more than a stone's throw to his left was the high school. To his right, the football field where, for four brief years, he and his teammates had been like gods with the Jim Ned Indians. And behind them, across the railroad tracks, Tuscola Cemetery, where, just before the summer of his sophomore year, a graduating senior, Marla Phillips, had taken him on his first trip to heaven in the middle of a burial plot owned by the Cox family. The two of them had laughed afterward about the name, the breeze cool on their sweaty skin, and joked about whether the ghosts might have enjoyed the show. He never understood why people called it losing your virginity. Lying in the grass half-naked and catching his breath alongside Marla that night, Carl hadn't felt he'd lost anything. On the contrary, he felt he'd gained something even more wonderful than he'd imagined, and the world had never seemed more exciting, more promising, more filled with joyous possibility.

"Good to be back?" Henry asked.

Carl wondered whether the reminiscing had shown on his face. "Yeah," he said after a moment. "I mean . . . it's complicated, but yeah."

They chitchatted for a bit about the store. It sounded like it was really thriving now. There had been a rough couple of years at the beginning, when there was a lot of gossip about Mary marrying Henry after getting Roy put in prison. People were divided on what had happened. Everyone knew Roy was trouble. But there was also a sense that you handled your troubles yourself, not by airing your dirty laundry in public. And like Roy, there were plenty of people who suspected Mary had set Roy up so she could have Henry. Didn't Henry own his own store, after all? He wasn't rich, but for Tuscola, he was successful, and certainly a better prospect than Roy. Late one night, Carl had overheard Mary and Henry talking about whether they should move, maybe to Fort Worth or San Antonio. Mary was all for it. But despite the loss of some people who were newly avoiding him, Henry had built up a loyal customer base in Abilene. He was afraid to start over. And he was concerned that if they ran from their troubles, it would look like they were ashamed, and that in their absence the gossip would set like cement. Better to stay and ride it out, let the gossip die down and fresh news become stale. Probably Henry had been right. But in the meantime, there had been a lot of schoolyard taunts about what had happened, and an equal number of fights.

He glanced over at Henry. He knew his stepdad must have been thinking about it—the visit with Roy, the upcoming hearing. "Ronnie and Mom ask you to invite me to sit out here with you?" he said.

Henry laughed. "Of course they did."

Carl laughed, too. "I feel like they're not getting their money's worth."

Henry shrugged. "All they asked was that I get you out here to sit. And I've duly complied. You know how hard it is for me to say no to them. To any of my girls."

Carl laughed again. He didn't know much about business, but he was surprised Henry had figured out how to do so well. The man was just so kind, seeming always to think the best of people, always knowing the right thing to say—not in a slick way, but in a way that made you know he respected you and really cared. His habit of extending credit to deadbeat customers gave Mary fits, but on the other hand, his goodness and generosity had probably gone a long way toward shifting opinions about the whole Roy scandal.

Henry took a sip of his Jim Beam. "You really back for a while?"

If it had been Ronnie asking, Carl would have known it was a gambit. With Henry, it was a safe bet the question was innocent.

"I might be. I . . . got a few things I'm looking into."

There was an opening there, but Henry, true to form, didn't exploit it. "You know you always have a job in the store. We could use you."

Carl laughed. "You don't want that. Ronnie and I would fight all the time. No one would ever get anything done."

"Will you at least be here long enough for deer season?"

Carl had spent more time stalking deer with Henry than he had with Roy. The truth was, Henry was the better hunter, and certainly the better teacher, giving young Carl an education in everything: aging, sexing, and sizing track; knowing which trees were going to drop their acorns and when; ways to slip up on a bedded buck; how to move silently in any terrain. He'd taught Carl that ninety percent of the game was knowing the quarry, and predicting it. Roy, on the other hand, preferred a tree stand to still hunting, making up in brute patience what he might have lacked in knowledge and skill.

Carl upended his Lone Star and finished it. "I don't know," he said. "I'm . . . not sure how to handle what's going on with Roy."

Henry nodded. "I don't envy your position. I feel I've been able to give you some useful advice over the years, but on this one I'm afraid I'm not the right person."

The man was being modest. Carl had never known anyone with sounder insights. Maybe Ronnie, but with Ronnie you always had to wonder what was in it for her. Henry never felt like he had an interest, other than your interest.

Though on this topic, Carl could see how, even for Henry, disinterested advice would be a struggle.

He cracked another Lone Star and took a swig. "If you want to give it a try, I'm willing to listen. Probably could use some good advice."

There was a long pause before Henry said, "I can't tell a son to go against his father."

Carl chuckled. "I guess you can say no to your girls, after all."

"They didn't ask me. Not exactly."

"I think you must not have been listening."

"Maybe."

Carl looked at him. "You going to testify?"

There was another long pause. Then Henry said, "It would be a bad idea. Beyond not having much to add due to my not having been there when Roy was abusing y'all, it could easily backfire because of . . . appearances."

Carl didn't like to think of what Roy had been doing as abuse. Wife beating. Child abuse. It sounded like things that happened to other people, not to him and his sister and mother at the hands of their own father and husband. He realized he'd have to guard against the temptation to look back and minimize how bad it had really been. Rationalizing might help him forgive Roy, and also provide an excuse for avoiding a hard decision.

"Yeah," Carl said, after a moment. "I suppose."

"Ronnie and your mom don't want me to anyway. But if they change their minds, I will. We've been a family for almost fifteen years now. If they want to trot me out to demonstrate that and provide some context for what came before it, I'll take that risk."

"You think he's dangerous?"

Henry looked into his glass and sighed. "If you want to know more about what to expect from him, maybe I can help with that. As to what to do about it, that's going to have to be up to you."

"What have you got in mind?"

"There's a fellow I extended a hand to when not many others would have. Still temps for the store when we need the help. Mostly, though, he works at the Purple Sage."

"The honky-tonk?"

"That's the one. On 277, south of the base."

The base was Dyess Air Force Base, which abutted the western limit of Abilene. "I used to sneak in there," Carl said. "In high school."

Henry nodded. "I know."

"You never said anything."

"Would you have listened?"

Carl nodded in appreciation of the man's unimpeachable good sense. "All right. And this friend of yours . . . he knows Roy?"

"They did time together at the Walls."

"How well do they know each other?"

"Why don't you ask him? His name is George Whitaker."

"Will he be there tonight?"

"I think George is there every night. He buses and cleans and straightens out whatever needs to be straightened out, including the occasional unruly customer."

"How will I know him?"

"You shouldn't have a hard time picking him out. I expect he'll be the only black man there."

Chapter 8

Isobel was paralyzed again. The girl by the well was alive, but the soldiers were dragging her off. The soldiers were laughing and the girl was screaming, "Don't let them! Don't let them!" Isobel kept pulling equipment from her bag and throwing it at the soldiers, but everything she threw turned into gauze that unfurled in the air and floated harmlessly to the ground. Birds were calling from the trees, loudly and insistently, as though to accuse the soldiers. But the birds had no more effect than the items Isobel was trying to throw. They called more loudly—

She woke and could still hear the birdsong, and for a moment was confused. Then she realized. It had been a dream. A bad dream. But the birdsong was real.

She threw off the sheet, sat up on the pallet, and rubbed her eyes. The curtains on the room's one window were sheer, and she could see it was light out. She hadn't expected to sleep at all, but somehow she'd managed.

She peeked through the curtain and saw what she had been expecting: a line of about twenty villagers, all ages, from infants to the elderly, standing in front of the porch. The news had already gone out a doctor was here. And these were only the locals. As word spread, people would come from farther afield.

She had never begrudged it before, and didn't now. She had no idea what she should do anyway. Go back to Dili? She supposed so, and eventually, she would have to. But it felt like the wrong direction. The border was only a few kilometers away. This was where Beeler had wanted to meet.

Her one hope was something Beeler had said: that if anything happened to her, she had contingencies in place so that her news bureau would know and could intervene. She hadn't said more than that. At the time, Isobel wondered whether she ought to do something similar with the clinic. But in the end, she had been afraid of arousing suspicion. She had told them only that she needed a few days off, that it had been too long since she'd visited the spot where her parents' ashes were scattered. Her colleagues were surprised because she hadn't taken more than a day off in years. But for the same reason, no one begrudged her.

She needed to pee. She pulled on the shorts Joana had lent her, then slipped into her boots. She picked up the satchel, then realized how strange it would look to take her medical kit to the privy. Mateus had already seemed curious about it. It wouldn't do to walk around with it everywhere she went, clutching it as though it contained the most precious thing in the world.

Though of course it did.

In one corner of the room was an old freezer, the kind used to display ice cream in shops. Maybe Mateus and Joana had stocked it in happier times, when there were tourists in the area. But for now, it was plainly unused—unplugged and covered with dust.

Isobel slid open the glass top. Stacked within were photo albums. Isobel picked up the one on top. Inside were pictures of children— Alonsa, when she was younger, and two others, a boy and girl, older than the Alonsa in the photos, but close to the same age she was now.

No wonder the freezer was dusty. Mateus and Joana must have been unable to bear looking at the albums they had placed inside it. But they couldn't throw them away, either.

Isobel put the satchel on the pallet and started carefully removing the contents. Stethoscope. Blood-pressure gauge. Bandages. Splints. Betadine and other antiseptics. Precious antibiotics.

Concealed beneath it all were two videotapes, each containing two hours of footage. She placed them under the photo albums in the freezer, then slid closed the top.

Immediately she felt better. She didn't know how long she would be here. But now, if she were caught, they wouldn't find the videos. At least not on her.

A sudden fear gripped her: *What if someone finds the videos and thinks they belong to Joana and Mateus?*

But no, there was no chance of that. Anyone who saw the videos would assume they were home movies, kept alongside a collection of family photo albums.

She realized that wasn't the real concern. The real concern was that if the soldiers caught her, they would make her tell them where she had hidden the videos. She had tended to enough of their victims to know exactly what their interrogations entailed. Strangling. Electric shocks. And rape, of course. Always rape.

They don't know about the videos. If they did, they wouldn't have just left with Beeler. They would have kept searching.

But what if Beeler tells them?

It didn't matter. With or without the videos, they would do to her what they wanted to do. The interrogations were always just an excuse.

She repacked her bag and left it on the pallet. She spent a moment collecting herself, then walked out into the kitchen area.

Joana was standing in front of the small stove. Isobel smelled coffee and something else—something delicious.

"How's Alonsa?" Isobel said.

Joana's face lit up in a smile perfectly poised between joyous relief, and fear that the relief would prove fragile. Isobel knew the expression well. But if Alonsa continued to improve, the balance would shift to relief.

"Much better," Joana said. "She's sleeping again. Her fever is down. She was able to drink some juice, and I gave her the medicine."

Isobel nodded, pleased. "I don't want to wake her. I'll check on her later. I need the privy. And . . . it looks like there might be some people who need attention."

Joana glanced toward the porch, then back at Isobel. "I'm sorry. The neighbors' boy is sick. We told them—"

"Don't worry. It's fine." And then, unable to help herself, she added, "What's that you're making? It smells delicious."

Joana smiled again. "Pisang goreng. And sasoru. For you."

Pisang goreng were banana fritters. Sasoru was a rice porridge made with ginger, carrot, and mustard greens. Both were traditional Timorese breakfast treats, and both were some of Isobel's favorites. She hadn't eaten either in a long time. In Dili, she had gotten in the habit of more Western fare. When it was available. For everyone, food was scarce. Which made what Joana was doing all the more remarkable.

"You'll need it," Joana added. "There are . . . a lot of people."

Isobel didn't mind. She had labored long hours before with much less than pisang goreng and sasoru for sustenance. Besides, it all felt like a good omen. Finding these people. Helping their daughter. And now helping others in the village on top of it.

Maybe Beeler would be all right. Maybe her contingency would work. She'd be freed, Isobel would give her the videos, and everything would work out. In the bright light of morning, amid the birdsong and the delicious smells of Joana's cooking, she felt sure they would find a way.

Chapter 9

After coming in from the porch, Carl pulled on an old pair of jeans, his favorite Tony Lamas, a black tee-shirt, and a straw cattleman. He would have liked to take out his bike, a 1977 Harley-Davidson Sportster he'd bought used in high school with the money he'd saved doing summer construction work, but even though he'd changed the oil, added fuel stabilizer, and pulled the battery the last time he'd been home, that was too long ago to trust the gaskets, and he hadn't had a chance to replace them all since being back. So he borrowed Henry's pickup instead, and headed out to the Purple Sage.

He found himself taking a meandering route, maybe because he wasn't necessarily eager to hear what George Whitaker might tell him. The shack on Callahan was still there, and in no ways improved. And the Allsup's, where he'd hung out after school arguing about sports and playing videogames. And Lantrip's, of course, always a popular destination when skipping classes. Oh, and there was Mr. Bludgus's house, the math teacher nobody liked, where Carl and his friends Montie and Clint had once left a paper bag filled with dogshit on the porch, setting it on fire, and ringing the bell, then howling with laughter while the doofus stomped it out, all of it hilarious until by bad luck a patrol car happened by, and they all got to spend the night in jail and the next day scraping burnt dogshit off old Bludgus's porch.

He drove on, chuckling at the memory. There had been a few tough stretches, sure, but some good times, too, weren't there? He thought so, but maybe he was bullshitting himself. Maybe it was just a human instinct to put a nice, comforting gauze over the lens you used to view the past.

He pulled over by the football stadium and got out, then stood for a while listening to the crickets in the fields around him, smelling the cut grass, looking out at the big Texas sky. It was a clear night, indigo overhead and still a line of pink in the west, with a sharp crescent moon rising. He picked out the Summer Triangle, still visible: Vega, Altair, Deneb. It was strange—Roy had been the one to teach him the names of the stars and constellations, but he realized now he'd never asked Roy who'd taught him. Roy had no book learning to speak of, and his own father, Duke Williams, had died before Roy was even born. Duke had been awarded the Navy Cross for heroism with the 2nd Marines during the Battle of Okinawa, then came home from the war to Abilene, married his high school sweetheart, and promptly died in a freak road accident, with Roy born not long after. Duke's war record and tragically early death forever elevated him to icon status—not just among the family, but throughout the town as well. Roy, who grew up wild, wasn't looked on quite as favorably, though it was true, too, that people were generally sympathetic to his circumstances. At least Duke, who Carl knew only through a handful of fading photos and stories from his grandmother, provided a posthumous example for Carl to try to live up to, a dead role model in this case being preferable to the live one.

Of course, he wasn't sure he'd really lived up to anything. He'd served, but he had no medals to show for it. He supposed that being part of the secret effort that broke the back of Communism in the Cold War might be considered equivalent to breaking the back of the Imperial Japanese Army in World War II, but Duke got a tickertape parade, and Carl . . . He wasn't sure what he got.

He walked along the track that ran around the gridiron. There were a few people jogging, but the light was too dim for anyone to make out faces. That was fine. He didn't much care to see anyone he knew. The whole town must have been buzzing about how Roy was coming up for parole. Carl didn't want to have to answer any questions about it, or imagine what people were thinking behind the chitchat, either.

All right. Enough procrastinating. Time to talk to this man George. Though he wondered if even the talk might be just another form of delay. At Infantry Training School, he'd learned about the dangers of hesitating to engage, and of rationalizing that what was needed was always a little more intel. Maybe he was just afraid to make a decision. Well, shit, who wouldn't be?

The Purple Sage occupied the basement of an old stone warehouse just past the Abilene city limits. He approached it along 277, watching as fast-food joints gave way to widely spaced single-family houses, and drove on until the houses were gone, too, until he was surrounded by nothing but cow pasture, with only the road, the telephone lines, and some barbed-wire fences a reminder that there might be a few people around among all this empty terrain.

He saw the neon sign ahead, glowing purple and green in the darkness. A moment later, he was pulling into the parking lot, the tires crunching on the gravel and raising a trail of dust behind him. It was still on the early side, but judging from the number of trucks, he had a feeling there would be a crowd.

For a moment, he just sat there, taking it in. There was some scaffolding along one of the side walls where it looked like the stonework was being repaired, but other than that, it might have been a postcard from his boyhood. Well, one thing was different: back in the day, he and his friends had been able to get in only on certain nights, when Billy Ray Johnson, who'd played offensive and defensive tackle at Jim Ned before graduating a few years ahead of them, had worked the door. Now he could go anywhere. So why did he feel so damn hemmed in?

He got out, put on his hat, and headed over. From inside he heard a band playing Steve Earle's "Copperhead Road," the music punctuated with the periodic stomp of a line dance. And there, still hung on the red metal door, a sign they'd always laughed at in high school: *Cowboys—No shirt, no service. Cowgirls—No shirt, free beer.*

A guy with biceps on the verge of busting through the sleeves of his tee-shirt was sitting on a stool beside the door. He was as big as Billy Ray, but it was someone else.

"ID?" the guy said.

Carl pulled out his wallet. "You bet."

The guy took his ID, looked at it, went to hand it back, looked at it again, then stared at Carl.

"You're Carl Williams."

"I am unless I'm using someone else's ID." It was a bit of a curt thing to say, but he wasn't thrilled to be recognized.

The guy gave a small, embarrassed laugh. "Right, sorry. I'm Pete Wenzel. I went to Clyde. We played against you."

Clyde was another 3A Division 1 high school team. "The Bulldogs," Carl said. "Of course."

Wenzel went to shake Carl's hand, realized he was still holding the ID, and gave it back. They shook. Carl put the ID back in his wallet, thinking this was exactly the kind of thing he'd hoped to avoid. Maybe he should have borrowed Darryl's ID, though it would take a blind doorman to confuse Darryl's soft features for Carl's.

"You here to see your friends?" Wenzel asked.

"What do you mean?"

"A bunch of your teammates are here. I thought maybe you were having a reunion."

"No, I'm afraid I've lost touch with the gang. Who are we talking about?"

"Dollar Jackson, for one. He played a whole semester with Alabama. And Rabbit Abernathy, he got recruited by the Aggies, but he never played. And the Skove twins. They were away for a while, but now they're back. Did a little time, I heard, down in Ramsey for robbing a liquor store."

Oh yeah, the Skove twins. It was funny, they'd left Carl alone after Roy had straightened out their father, but every time they'd ever looked at Carl, they felt like a couple of mean dogs whose owner had barely gotten them to behave.

"That right?" Carl said. "Well, I hope they've learned the error of their ways. But no, I just thought I'd have a beer and listen to some music."

"What are you doing in town?" Wenzel asked. "I heard you joined the Marines."

Carl smiled at Wenzel's chattiness. He supposed checking IDs all night could get dull. Well, what the hell. He wasn't in a hurry.

"That was a while ago. I'm out now."

"How was it?"

"I suppose I could fairly say it was an adventure."

"You see any action?"

The question was an uncomfortable echo of what Roy had asked him earlier that very day, though doubtless driven more by curiosity and maybe vicarious longing than by the desire to score a point.

"Well, I once had to kidnap a guy in the Philippines who'd shacked up with his mamacita and drag him back to the ship before they declared him AWOL. But that was about the worst of it. I got out before Iraq, so my timing wasn't good. How are you doing?"

"Oh, same old. Got married. Have a baby girl. You know how it is."

Carl didn't know, though the notion frightened him anyway. He started to hold out his hand to indicate the chitchat was over, but Wenzel was too fast.

"But you must have done a lot," Wenzel said. "I mean, the Philippines, and . . . what else? What was the best part?"

Carl laughed. Because how could he even begin to convey some of the things he'd seen? Growing up in Tuscola, he wouldn't have believed it himself. Not until he'd been there. But okay. If Wenzel wanted to hear, there were a few tales to tell.

"I guess my favorite was getting liberty in Olongapo—that's a city on Subic Bay in the Philippines. To get to it, you cross a river so filthy and odiferous everyone calls it Shit River. On the other side of which is a long strip of girlie bars with all kinds of depravity. Beggars pulling at your sleeve, hawkers trying to sell you everything from monkey meat to their own sisters, jeepneys honking their horns to chase the crowds out of the way. Live music pouring out of every bar you pass—and you'd think you were listening to Johnny Cash and Aretha Franklin and Led Zeppelin themselves, the singers were so good. San Miguel beer for fifty cents a bottle. And the smells—everything from grilled meat to all kinds of spices to diesel smoke to sewage and back again. And beautiful women, and I mean beautiful."

"I heard about that," Wenzel said, a little rapture creeping into his voice. "I heard they were friendly, too."

"Oh, they were. But there were limits. If you bounced from girl to girl, they'd call you a 'butterfly boy,' and they didn't like that. Once you settled on one, they liked to keep you dedicated for as long as your ship was in port. And they'd know when it was leaving, too. 'No, *Tripoli* not leaving until next Friday. You butterfly boy.' Damn, they were good. If the military had intel networks like the girls ran in Olongapo, the Cold War would have been over before it even started."

"How about the food?"

"Oh, yeah. Though some of it was weird—not just the monkey meat, but baluts, which are two-week-old fertilized eggs pickled in brine. I mean, we're not just talking about an egg, there's a little duck or chicken inside there, partially formed feathers, eyes, feet, you name it. Peel the shell and down it all goes."

"Oh, man, you ate those?"

"Yeah, they're not bad. You'd be surprised what you can eat after a dozen San McGoos—what we called San Miguels—and not much time to hustle back to the dock and beat the curfew. And I think there was even weirder fare, too. The woman I used to buy the baluts from, I'd ask her about some other things she had on the shelves behind that little window of hers, and she'd shake her head and say, 'Those not for you.' And I'd say, 'Okay, but what are they?' And she'd say, 'You not worry, not for you.' Eventually I stopped asking, but I still wonder."

Wenzel laughed. "I can't imagine what could be worse than one of those eggs."

"Truth is, I can't, either. Maybe she was just messing with me, I don't know. But I miss the place, I'll say that. I know Ernest Hemingway said it was Paris was the movable feast, but if you ask me, that boy had never been to Olongapo."

"I wish I could visit."

"Well, it would be hard now. The base is closing, and the town depended on it. Plus just a couple months ago, old Mount Pinatubo erupted and dumped about a foot of ash on everything. I don't know what's in store for the place, but I doubt it'll be the same."

Wenzel nodded, his expression wistful. "Least you got to see it."

Carl nodded. "Like they say, *Don't cry because it's over. Smile because it happened.* Anyway, I'm going to go have a beer and relax. If you're not too busy on my way out, maybe we could catch up a bit more then."

Wenzel brightened. "That'd be fine. Go enjoy yourself."

Carl gave him a nod. He pulled open the door, the hinges squealing and the Steve Earle suddenly louder, and headed down the rickety wooden staircase.

The familiar smell hit him a moment later: tobacco smoke and beer and salted popcorn. His eyes took a moment adjusting to the dim light, but he recognized the gal standing at the bottom of the stairs—the owner, Arlene Juenke, who somewhere north of sixty seemed to have ceased aging. She took his five-dollar cover but showed no sign of recognizing him. That was a relief, and also understandable—he hadn't made a habit of conversing with the management back when he was sneaking in here.

He turned the corner and couldn't help but smile at how unchanged it all was. The ceiling was low, made of red tin, and gave the space an intimate feeling. The walls were still decorated with hunting trophies, confederate flags, beer memorabilia, and posters of country greats like Patsy Cline, Loretta Lynn, and Hank Williams. Between the restroom doors stood an old-fashioned scale, which, for five cents, would give you your weight and your horoscope. There was a small stage to the right, occupied by a couple of cowboys with guitars and a microphone and a third guy playing the drums, the all-important tip jar set out in front of them. Behind the stage, a pair of jukeboxes for nights when they didn't have live music. At the far end, the bar. Along the wall, a pair of well-worn pool tables, each illuminated by an overhead Lone Star beer light and surrounded by bar patrons intent on their games. In the middle of it all, the sawdust-covered dance floor, a couple of dozen people line-dancing to the music, whooping and clapping and giving the whole place a shake every time they stomped their boots in unison.

He strolled over to the bar, which was barricaded three deep, and managed to ease his way through the boisterous crowd. A television was playing in one corner—a Wildcats game, unsurprisingly. And there was none other than Marla Phillips, the gal who'd been his first that long-ago night in the cemetery, tending bar. It was like the cherry on top of the sundae of feeling like he'd been shot back in time, and he smiled at the pun he'd made with the *cherry* reference. And just that moment, Marla looked over, caught his eye, and lit up in a surprised smile of her own.

"Carl Williams!" she called out. "Of all the gin joints in all the world. Get on over here and give me a hug."

He was more than happy to oblige, though leaning across the bar was a little awkward. Marla solved the difficulty by snaking an arm around the back of his neck and planting a serious kiss on his mouth.

Nessie, short for *the Loch Ness Monster*, who'd been slumbering quietly until then, took the opportunity to stand bolt upright.

She broke the kiss but didn't release his neck. "I've been hoping to see you."

"I didn't know that. Although I'm starting to figure it out."

She laughed. "People have been saying you might be back. On account of your dad."

He looked around, suddenly feeling he was in a fishbowl. "Is that right?"

"Tuscola. Everybody knows everybody's business."

"I guess that's another thing that hasn't changed around here."

"Yeah? What else hasn't changed?"

The band struck up Merle Haggard's "I Think I'll Just Stay Here and Drink," and the crowd cheered. Carl shook off the discomfort of knowing people were talking about him. The music helped. The sight of Marla helped more.

"You," he said, taking the opportunity to look her up and down. "No, forget that, you look better than ever."

It was true, too. She'd been a slim cheerleader in high school, but she'd filled out nicely, and the cleavage he could see at the opening of her V-neck tee-shirt made him want to look again, and then some.

She raised her arms and gathered her hair back in a way that offered a delicious view of her body, then gave him a big, slow smile. "Carl Williams, are you flirting with me?"

"Just telling the truth."

"Uh-huh. You always were a sweet-talker."

Lord, it was like being sixteen again, and damn if it didn't feel good. "I don't know about that," he said, smiling. "Now, what's a fellow gotta do to get a beer around here?"

Someone from over to the left yelled, "Marla, I been waiting!"

"And you can wait a little longer," she shot back. Then she leaned close and said quietly, "Fella's got to tell me he'll stick around 'til I'm off tonight."

Well, if Nessie had been at attention before, now it was more a matter of high alert. He nodded, feeling his heart pounding at the prospect. "I'll stick around."

She gave him about the sexiest smile he'd ever seen and popped the cap off a Lone Star longneck. "In that case," she said, holding his eyes and waggling her head a little, "this one is on the house."

Someone shoulder-checked him hard from the left. He looked, and there was Geeber Skove, big as ever and twice as ugly, standing too close and smelling like too much beer. "Carl Williams," he said, more loudly than was needed given their proximity. "So you're the reason I've been waiting so long."

Marla took the Lone Star she'd just cracked and set it in front of Geeber. "Oh, Geeber, you ain't been waiting that long. Here."

Geeber slid the beer over to Carl. "I don't want his beer. I want my own."

Carl was glad Geeber had sent the bottle his way. Because if there was one skill acquired by any Marine who'd been deployed on a WestPac float, with port calls in Olongapo and Pattaya and endless carousing at the local nightclubs and bars, it was how to measure the distance from the base of the bottle of beer you were drinking to the head of the person who was annoying you while you drank it.

"Where's your brother?" Carl said, his tone artificially cheerful. "It takes two of you as I recall."

Geeber gave him a menacing smile. "Two's more fun. But one'll do the job."

Carl lifted the bottle in a mock toast. "I don't know, Geeber, the way you say it, it sounds like you've been jerking off a lot." He took a sip and set the bottle down. "But I suppose that's between you and yourself."

Marla stifled a laugh. Geeber's face darkened.

Carl noted an old electric fan on the bar, from back when such things were made of steel rather than plastic. "Listen," he said, holding the neck of the bottle loosely. "Don't trouble yourself trying to think of something clever to say. I don't want to wait that long. I'll buy you a beer if you think you can be friendly. Otherwise, I'd rather be left alone."

Geeber frowned while his pea brain tried to figure out what was going on. Carl realized he wasn't afraid of Geeber anymore, or of his brother, Guppy, for that matter. It seemed at least one thing had changed, and he was glad for it.

"I heard your murderer daddy might get out of prison," Geeber said. "That why you're back here?"

Carl took a deep breath and let it out. It couldn't be more obvious that Geeber was baiting him. But that didn't mean it wasn't working.

"Way I heard it," Carl said, his fingers still light around the neck of the bottle, "doing some time might not be something you want to offer an opinion about. Glass houses and all that."

Geeber's mouth moved, apparently in the hope that his brain would kick in and give it something to do. If he so much as raised a finger, Carl was going to backhand the base of the bottle straight into his face. That would bring up the dimwit's hands and stagger him back. At which point, Carl would snatch up that fan and brain him with it.

"Geeber," Carl heard Marla say. "Why are you always trying to start trouble?"

Geeber didn't answer. He just kept looking at Carl.

But Carl didn't return the stare. Because another thing he had learned in all those WestPac bars and nightclubs was to resist tunnel vision. The guy right in front of you might be the main problem, but you couldn't assume he was the only one. So while Geeber's brain struggled to find a way to justify its own existence, Carl looked past him. And sure enough, there was the other brother, Guppy, moving in behind Geeber.

"Good news," Carl said to Geeber, while still watching Guppy. "It looks like your partner's here. So you won't have to do it all by your lonely self tonight."

Guppy frowned, then broke into a smirk as he recognized Carl. He threw an arm around his brother's neck and cackled. "Carl Williams. Look what the trash people forgot to take out."

It seemed whatever restraint their frightened father had exercised over them had evaporated in the intervening years. Carl wasn't sorry. They'd had it coming since they were kids, and he was going to enjoy giving it to them. In his peripheral vision, he saw Marla signal someone. Bouncers, probably. Too bad.

"Can I ask you two a serious question?" he said, looking from one to the other.

Each of them frowned in concentration, but neither answered. Damn, they were like a couple of outfielders letting the ball drop because they didn't know who was supposed to catch it.

Carl raised his left index finger as though emphasizing a point, which had the useful effect of obscuring that his right fingers had curled thumb-down around the neck of the bottle. "How is it possible," he said, squinting as though trying to solve a difficult puzzle, "that the two of you have gotten even uglier since high school? And dumber, too."

They both reddened, each probably hoping the other would know how to respond.

"Inbreeding," Carl said. "That would be my guess. Am I right?"

Guppy said, "Say that outside, asshole."

Carl smiled. "I'd be happy to repeat it anywhere you like. But would outside really give you the time you need to figure out an answer? Maybe we'd be better off making an appointment, say, a week from now?"

Geeber, maybe feeling left out, said, "You're dead."

Carl smiled. "I don't think I am. If I were dead, I wouldn't be able to stand here and keep telling y'all how dumb and ugly you are."

"You coming outside?" Guppy said. "Or are you yellow?"

Carl was so ready to go at it he'd forgotten all about Marla. All that mattered to him was that they go first so they couldn't jump him from behind. He'd keep enough distance as they went up the stairs to make sure they couldn't turn and get in a kick, but not so much that they'd be able to make it to their vehicle and access a weapon, which in Texas meant a baseball bat if you were lucky, and a shotgun if you weren't.

But before he could say, *After you,* two very large men appeared alongside the twins, each placing a hand on their shoulders, and not at all gently. They were bigger than the twins, which was big indeed, and looked a whole lot tougher besides. One of them was white, probably in his forties. The other was younger and black—from what Henry had said, George Whitaker.

"Gentlemen," the white one said in an exceptionally no-nonsense tone. "The management of the Purple Sage would like to ask the two of you to take the rest of the evening off. Thank you for your patronage tonight, and if you need any help getting out to the parking lot, we would be happy to assist. Or you're welcome to get there by yourselves. Which would be your preference?"

The Skoves blinked, and Carl knew right away they'd comply. He'd seen it many times before. There was just something so sobering about a man that big being that polite. You knew instantly he wasn't being polite because he had to be, but because it didn't matter. Mean or nice—he could split your head either way. The combination of intimidating size and courteous demeanor produced a kind of reflexive gratitude in the person on the other end of it, who recognized he was being given a marvelous gift—the chance to avoid the beating of a lifetime. Along with a bonus, that if he moved quickly, he even had an opportunity for a face-saving exit. All he had to do was say—

"We were leaving anyway," Guppy said. "Let's go, Geeber." Then he gave Carl a *We ain't done with you* look.

"Goodnight, fellas," Carl said. "You really are even uglier. And dumber, too."

Guppy tensed as though to launch himself. The white guy stopped him by shifting a little more weight into the hand on Guppy's shoulder, then gave Carl the kind of look he'd seen from many a teacher and drill instructor back in the day.

Carl held up his hands in an exaggerated gesture of innocence. "I'm only saying it because it's true."

"Carl," Marla said, "that is enough. Geeber, Guppy, it was nice seeing y'all. Now goodnight."

The Skoves slunk off, the two bouncers watching them.

"I'm sorry," Marla said to Carl. "Those two are always hitting on me. Geeber must have gotten jealous seeing me with you."

"Can't really blame him," Carl said. "And it's not their fault they're dumb and ugly, either."

"Enough," the white guy said. "The only reason we didn't toss you, too, was because we don't need a fight in the parking lot. Speaking of which, you might want to take a good look around out there when you leave tonight."

Carl, who was well acquainted with how a sore loser could back up on a guy outside a bar, didn't need a bouncer to explain it to him. "I'll be sure to do that, sir. Thank you for the advice."

The guy looked on the verge of tossing Carl out on his ass, fracas in the parking lot or no. Carl knew he was being a jerk. The guy was just doing his job, and doing it well. He realized the Skoves might not be the only ones looking for a fight.

"I'm sorry," Carl said. "It was a long day. I really do appreciate your help. I didn't need it, but I appreciate it."

"Mike," Marla said, "I apologize for my friend. He has a speech impediment. It impedes him from shutting the hell up, even when he knows better."

"I can see that," Mike said.

He and the black guy started to shove off. "Hang on," Carl said to the black guy. "Pardon me, but are you George Whitaker?"

Mike kept going. The black guy turned and looked at Carl warily. "Who are you?"

"Carl Williams. I'm Henry Abbott's son. Stepson. He told me maybe you and I could talk."

The guy looked at him for a long, silent moment. There was something a little off about his face—an asymmetry or something. And then Carl realized—the left cheekbone was sunken, as though it had been caved in.

Feeling uncomfortable, he said, "I mean, you are George Whitaker, is that right?"

The man glanced around the room, then back at Carl. "Yeah."

Carl held out a hand. "Well, it's nice to meet you, sir. I apologize for being any trouble, but I sure would be grateful if you have a few minutes to talk."

Whitaker glanced around the room again, then looked at Carl as though weighing a heavy decision. Ignoring Carl's hand, he said, "I'll be on break in twenty minutes. There's a storeroom across from the stairs. We can talk in there."

Chapter 10

Twenty minutes later, Carl stood before a wooden door opposite the bottom of the stairs. A sign was hung from a nail: *Employees Only*. He glanced at Arlene, whose back was to him, then knocked. The band was playing "Ramblin' Fever," and he wondered if anyone inside could even hear over the music. But right after the knock, the door opened inward, and there was Whitaker, hanging back as though he preferred not to be seen. Carl stepped inside. Whitaker swung the door shut, and the music was instantly muted—the wood must have been heavier than it looked. Well, it figured, the whole building was made of stone.

"Thank you again for taking the time," Carl said, looking around. It was a long space with a low ceiling. At the far end, a stairway led up into the darkness. There were several big sacks in one corner, each with sawdust leaking out—surplus for the dance floor. On a shelf were some cleaning products. Some safety gear attached to a wall, including a fire extinguisher and one of those four-cell Maglite police flashlights. One night in Pattaya he'd been on the wrong end of one of those, the aftermath of which had involved twenty-two stitches over his left ear.

He was surprised at how nervous he felt. It was the topic of conversation, of course, along with the discomfort of talking to a stranger about family business. On top of which, he was afraid of what he might learn from this man, and how the information might bear on the decision he had to make.

Whitaker didn't respond, and Carl's nervousness edged into irritation. "You mind telling me why you won't shake my hand?" he said.

Whitaker looked at him with an expression somewhere between annoyance and pity. "You want me to shake your hand in the middle of a roomful of a hundred white folks?"

That did nothing to alleviate Carl's confusion. Racial relations in Texas could be tense, it was true, but as far as Carl knew whites and blacks could shake each other's hands without worrying.

Whitaker shook his head, apparently at how slow Carl was. "Your father is Roy Williams," he said.

"That's right. That's what I was hoping to talk to you about."

"I know that. And so does anybody else that sees us talking."

Finally, Carl started to understand. "You mean—"

"Your father is up for parole in a month. You planning to testify at that hearing?"

"I . . . haven't decided."

Whitaker shrugged. "If you do, and your testimony hurts Roy's chances, Roy won't take kindly to anyone he thinks was whispering in your ear. Especially a black ex-con he knows personally."

"You know him, then."

"Yeah. I know him."

From the tone of it, it didn't sound like Whitaker and Roy had been close friends. Not exactly a surprise, given Roy's views on black prisoners at the Walls. Carl felt terrible that his stupidity might have put the man in a bad position.

"I'm sorry. I didn't realize . . . I mean, I could have met you anywhere. Why now, in here? People could know we're talking."

"My break started ten minutes earlier than I told you. And you'll stay in here for five or ten minutes after I leave. But it doesn't really matter. If there's damage, the damage was done the moment you held out your hand."

"I'm sorry for that, but no one—"

"Folks will think what they want to think. They always do. It's more on your stepfather than it is on you. Henry Abbott is one of the smartest men I've ever met. But he doesn't always appreciate the way things are. Now, what is it you want?"

What did he want? Suddenly faced with the question, he didn't know how to answer.

"It's just . . . I've been away for a while. Roy . . . he got sent to prison when I was young."

"I know the story."

"You do?"

"Cons don't have much to do to pass the time. They talk. People talked about Roy a lot."

"Is it true he killed a guy named Juicy Fruit?"

Whitaker looked at him for a long moment. "Where'd you hear about that?"

"Roy told me. I saw him earlier today."

Whitaker shook his head as though resigned to something awful. Whatever favor Henry had done the man, it must have been substantial.

"I'm not going to tell Roy we talked," Carl said. "I hadn't seen him for years before today. I won't tell anyone. Not even Henry, if you don't want me to."

Whitaker shook his head again. "Like I said, the damage is likely done."

"Why do you keep saying that? Roy's in prison. He's not here."

"You don't understand who your father is, do you?"

Carl tried to puzzle through how to respond to that. After a moment he said, "That's what I'm hoping you can help with."

There was a desk in the corner, an old office chair in front of it with stuffing coming out of the seat. Whitaker eased himself into the chair, took a pouch of tobacco from a pocket, and set it on the desk. He gestured to a folding chair against the wall, then started rolling a cigarette. Carl pulled out the chair and sat. A minute later, Whitaker struck a match and brought it close. He took a deep drag, shook out the match, blew out a cloud of blue smoke, and extended the cigarette to Carl.

Carl shook his head. "No, thank you."

Whitaker nodded, and Carl sensed the man was pleased his polite gesture hadn't been accepted. For a moment he just sat there smoking, his expression somber and faraway, as though he was remembering things he would have preferred not to discuss.

"Yeah, your father killed Juicy Fruit. That was a few years before my time. But people still talked about it. It turned Roy into a kind of . . . hero among the white cons. Before Roy, it was black and Mexican gangs that ran the yard. Roy . . . he changed all that. Got a reputation. Formed his own gang. The guards realized they could use him, so they made him a tender. A tender's a con with privileges. A kind of . . . convict guard. The tenders run the prison. Enforce the rules. Do things the guards want done but aren't allowed to do themselves."

He took a drag on his cigarette, then went on.

"Roy and his gang were so effective, the guards gave them more and more leeway. Armed them with blackjacks and billy clubs. Looked the other way when it came to protection and gambling and smuggling. Roy got the prison running nice and smooth, and made sure the guards were cut in on all the different rackets. It's like organized crime moving into a neighborhood. Some crime—the kind the police like because they profit from it—is allowed. Other kinds are put down."

Another pause, another drag on the cigarette.

"The guards thought they could control Roy. What they didn't see was that when Roy's men left prison, they didn't leave his gang. Pretty soon, Roy had reach inside the Walls and out. It got to the point where even the guards were afraid to cross him. Then about ten years ago, some judge struck down the whole prison tender system. Well, inside the Walls, that decision was nothing but a piece of paper. There's judges, and court orders, and announcements from on high. And then there's the way things are. You understand what I'm saying to you?"

Carl, who was familiar with the difference between the Marine Corps Manual and life in the field, and the way CIA personnel were instructed to overlook Mujahideen proclivities they were legally bound to report, understood perfectly.

"This is why you're concerned about us being seen together," he said. "Roy can get to people outside the prison."

Whitaker raised his eyebrows and nodded slowly, as though Carl was a plodding but apparently educable student.

"The reason I wanted to talk to you," Carl said. "It's . . . my mother and sister. They're scared of Roy. They want me to testify with them at the parole hearing. Remind the board of what he used to do to us. Tell them we all feel he's still a danger to our family."

"Is he?"

"Listening to the way he talked today, he might be. He blames us for his being in prison."

"If you or your family becomes part of what keeps him there, ain't gonna be no *might.*"

"We already are part of it, remember?"

"Well, that's not good."

Carl thought for a moment. Something was off, but he couldn't put his finger on it. And then he realized.

"You say he's got reach outside the prison."

Whitaker nodded. "That's right."

"Doesn't that mean that if he wanted to, he could have . . . hurt my mother and my sister anytime? And Henry, too. I haven't even been around to protect them."

Whitaker took a drag on his cigarette and looked Carl up and down, as though doubtful he'd be worth much against Roy. Carl wasn't insulted. He was doubtful himself.

"Maybe he's been waiting for you to be back here," Whitaker said, blowing out another cloud of blue smoke. "So he could have some people hurt you all at once. Or maybe he doesn't want to have other people hurt you. Maybe he wants to do the hurting himself. And that's what he's been waiting for." He turned his head to the right and pointed to the crushed-in cheekbone.

"Roy did that?"

Whitaker nodded. "I was a young, scared convict. All I knew was that I'd better stand up for myself, show people I had heart. Well, I picked the wrong guy to stand up to."

"I'm sorry."

"Not your fault. I don't believe in the sins of the father."

They were quiet for a bit. Then Carl said, "I've barely seen him since I was ten years old. It sounds like you know him better than I do. I got a way I might be able to make some money. Can he be . . . bought off?"

Whitaker took a last drag from what was left of his cigarette, then dropped the butt in an ashtray, where it continued to smolder. "Who can say? Depends on how wedded he is to his grievances. And how much money you're talking about. But here's the thing about a convict: a convict takes what he can take. There's no honor among thieves. You make a deal with a convict, you better have the power to enforce it. You don't have that power, a convict will take what you offer, and then demand more. So what's to stop your father from taking all your money and then doing what he wants to do anyway?"

He thought of his conversation with Ronnie outside the prison. How he had told her that Roy could have made a case for himself, could have pretended to have learned his lesson, but hadn't. He knew Whitaker wouldn't believe it, but Carl didn't think Roy was the type to fool people. Roy wanted you to know exactly what he was about, even if what he was about was hurting you, or worse.

Whitaker pocketed his tobacco pouch and stood. "I need to get back. Wait a few minutes at least. Probably it's closing the barn doors after the horses have run off, but it can't hurt."

Carl stood, too. "I'm sorry again for—"

"Forget it. You want to make it up to me? See those stairs behind you? Use them when you leave. They lead to a back door. It's locked from the outside but you can open it from inside. Five'll get you ten those two troublemakers are waiting for you in the parking lot."

"Ah, they're not so tough."

"I didn't say they were tough. But there are two of them. And they're mean."

"Yeah, and ugly, too."

Whitaker surprised him by breaking into a laugh. "You just don't know when to stop, do you?"

Carl smiled. "So I've been told. Anyway, thank you, sir. I'm sorry again for any trouble I might have caused, and I really appreciate your time. And everything you told me."

He held out his hand. This time, Whitaker shook it.

Chapter 11

Carl waited a few minutes after Whitaker had left, thinking about what to do. If the Skove boys were intent on an ambush, and patient enough to stick around until closing, it wouldn't do to leave with Marla. A fight could ruin the rest of the evening, and Marla's presence could impede his tactics. He wanted the dumbasses to understand where the nom de guerre *Dox* came from, and the best way to do that was to have only them to worry about.

So maybe he and Marla could pick another place and meet there later. Yeah, that would work. And he had a thought about where.

He went back to the bar to tell her, and wound up getting stuck talking to Dollar Jackson and Rabbit Abernathy, and a couple others besides. They were all married, most with kids, and one already divorced. They had jobs in retail and construction, and a few were ranch hands, and they all still went to the games on Friday nights in the fall, and when it came to conversation over beers at the Purple Sage, it was a little politics and a lot of glory days. Everybody asked why he was in town, even though of course they already knew, but at least they were polite and didn't press when his answers were vaguer than they might have liked. In some ways, it was nice to see them all. But even so, it all made him acutely aware of the undertow of small-town Texas. You could swim far out, so far you thought you'd crossed the horizon, but then the tide would roll in and drag you right back onto the beach.

At some point, he managed to disengage sufficiently to lean across the bar and say to Marla, "Listen, I'd still like to get together later if you would. But I can't stay right now. Maybe we could meet somewhere?"

She leaned closer and gave him that sexy smile again. "And where did you have in mind?"

"Well, it's a beautiful night with a crescent moon. I was thinking about lying on my back over at Tuscola Cemetery and looking up at the stars."

She waggled her head again. He didn't remember her doing that from high school, but he liked it now. "Why does that sound familiar?" she said.

Damn, if this went on any longer, Nessie was going to bust loose and cause a panic. "I don't know," he said. "Maybe we should find out."

She gave his hand a quick squeeze and said in a low voice, "I'll be there just after two."

He nodded, holding her eyes for a moment, then said goodnight to the boys and made his way through the crowd to the head by the horoscope scale. He didn't know if the Skoves would be waiting, but he'd nursed his beer anyway, preferring to fight sober to drunk when presented with a choice. But still he needed to take a leak, and it was better not to fight with a full bladder, if fight there would be.

He headed back into the storeroom where he'd talked with Whitaker, once again without Arlene noticing. It seemed that being stealthy at the Purple Sage in his younger days had been good practice. There was something in the storeroom he wanted, and it wasn't just access to the back staircase. And there it was, hanging from the wall—the Maglite flashlight. He pulled it from its holder and nodded in satisfaction at its heft. "I promise to return it," he said aloud, "or to replace it if it breaks against Geeber's or Guppy's head."

He went up the stairs, the band breaking into "Folsom Prison Blues" behind him and the crowd roaring and stomping its approval. He stopped at the top landing and put his ear to the door, but there was no hope of picking up anything with the music playing and the crowd hollering.

He realized that when he opened the door, anyone nearby would know it from the sound. Well, he'd have to take the risk. If he saw the Skoves, he'd pull the door shut and try again another way. But he didn't think they'd be back here. If they were smart, they'd understand that he was smart, and because going out the back was the smart thing to do, that's what they'd expect. But they were dumb, and the essential quality of being dumb was lacking the capacity to understand that you're dumb. They went out the front; it would likely be beyond them to imagine that someone else might do it any differently.

After a minute, his eyes had adjusted to the dark. He pushed the bar on the door, opened it a crack, did a quick sneak-and-peek, and pulled it closed again. He hadn't seen anything out there, just a cow field and a few trees in the faint moonlight.

He opened the door again, wider this time, grimacing at the way its hinges squeaked, and did a longer scan. Still nothing.

He eased through sideways, then looked and listened again, holding on to the push bar so he could duck back in if necessary. Again he saw nothing. There was a doorstop on the stoop outside, maybe for when employees came out here for some air and didn't want to get locked out. He crouched, got the doorstop in place, and eased the door back onto it slowly, to minimize the squealing. Other than the music from below, still all quiet.

He crept around the corner, moving low in the shadows of the scaffolding attached to the side of the building. He reached the front and saw them right away, illuminated by the glow of the Purple Sage road sign: Geeber and Guppy, uglier than ever and even dumber than that, leaning against the side of their pickup, about a dozen empty beer cans at their feet. Also propped against the pickup were a couple of aluminum baseball bats. The police flashlight suddenly felt a lot smaller than it had inside.

But he had a better idea. Under the scaffolding were several piles of stones in a variety of shapes and sizes. He knelt and set down the flashlight, then took off the cattleman, wishing he'd worn felt rather than straw. He picked up a rock and was about to put it in the hat when he noticed a metal bucket that looked like it was used for mixing cement. That would hold more rocks than anything made of straw, and more securely. Not to mention, it would save the cattleman. He set the hat back on his head and filled the bucket with a dozen good-sized stones—likely more than he'd need, but you never want to run out of ammo. Then he stood and walked out into the parking lot.

Geeber saw him first, and instantly grabbed the nearest bat. Well, *instantly* might have been a strong word—it seemed all that beer might have slowed Geeber down a touch, but he sure didn't pick up that bat to wave hello with it. Guppy, who had his head back and was in the process of draining a beer, must have realized from Geeber's move that something was afoot. He jerked his head forward, coughed, sputtered, and wiped the back of an arm across his mouth. Then he tossed the can and grabbed his bat, and the two of them came striding forward.

"Okay, asshole," Geeber said, swinging his bat like he was auditioning for the Baseball Furies in that movie *The Warriors*. "Who's the dumb one now?"

Carl was already holding a rock about the size of a fist. "Still you," he said, and launched it.

Back when he was playing high school baseball, Carl's position was shortstop. Jasper Felds was the pitcher, partly because no one could hit his world-famous slider. But Carl could put the ball over the plate just fine, and his fastball was good enough to make him the preferred sub for Jasper when the occasion required. So even though the rock he'd just hurled as though it was a fastball floated a touch high to be considered within the strike zone, it was close enough for government work, and blasted right into Geeber's noggin.

Geeber's legs must not have gotten the message that his head had been hit, as they kept right on churning. But because his head went the other way, something had to give, the something in this case being his body, which was caught in the brain/legs crossfire. He cried out, dropped the bat, and landed on his back in a cloud of dust with a thud big enough for Carl to feel.

Guppy paused to glance at his fallen brother, then looked at Carl. "You yellow fuck!" he cried, and sprinted forward like a lone soldier charging a machine-gun nest, intent on glory. Carl snatched another fist-sized rock from the bucket, took a moment to aim, and launched it downfield, right over the proverbial plate. Or in this case, into the plate, the plate being Guppy's ugly nose. There was a beautiful *smack!* and a spray of blood. Guppy's hands flew to his face while his feet kept going, and he wound up doing an even better pratfall than his brother, though landing similarly, on his back with a giant thud.

He doubted there was any need, but still Carl took another rock from the bucket before strolling over. His heart was beating hard, and he realized he'd been more scared than he'd let himself notice. Only when the fight was done could he afford to acknowledge the fear. He'd noticed the same reaction many times on ops in Afghanistan. It interested him that although this wasn't remotely as dangerous, his body seemed not to know the difference.

The two of them were lying in the dust and gravel, holding their faces and moaning and rolling back and forth. No doubt about it, it was a pleasing sight, and he smiled.

"You know the saying," he said. "Sticks and stones will break my bones, but stones will get there first."

It seemed Geeber tried to respond. It might have been *Fuck you* or something equally clever, but it was mixed with a lot of groaning, and Carl couldn't be sure.

"Something you boys ought to know about Marine snipers. We prefer to fight at a distance. In fact, we prefer not to fight at all. We'd rather just kill you and get back to drinking and fornicating and other such pursuits. Well, I reckon it was a hard lesson, but now you know better."

AMOK

In his peripheral vision, he sensed movement from the front entrance. He looked and saw Pete Wenzel running his way.

"What the hell was that?" Wenzel called out.

"Oh, nothing. These dumbshits were causing trouble inside. Check with your bouncers, Mike and George—they threw 'em out, and even warned me to be careful when I left."

Wenzel looked at the fallen brothers. "That's the Skove twins."

"Yeah," Carl said, staring down at them. "Much as they might wish otherwise, I suppose they're stuck with it."

He set down the bucket of unused stones and picked up the baseball bats, then looked at the twins again. "Consider yourselves lucky," he said, still thinking of *The Warriors*. "Next time, I'll shove these bats up your asses and turn you into Popsicles."

There was a fair amount of moaning in response, and another unintelligible something that might have been the previously attempted *Fuck you.*

"Whatever you say. But if I see you two again anywhere near me, I will assume the worst and respond accordingly. At which point, you'll think catching a couple rocks in your ugly heads was nothing but foreplay. You understand me? Just moan for yes."

They moaned.

Carl nodded, satisfied. There was more he might have done to emphasize the point, but not in front of Wenzel. He didn't expect the law to get involved, but if it did, he'd be a former Marine with the accounts of the bouncers, and of Marla, too, to back up his side of the story. On their side, the Skoves would have their sterling robbery and prison record. About as much of a slam dunk as you could ask for in these things, and the only way he could screw it up now would be to start kicking them when they were already down right in front of a witness.

He looked at Wenzel. "Can I ask you a favor?"

"Uh, yeah."

"I borrowed a flashlight from the storeroom before coming out here. It's around the side of the building, on the ground alongside a bunch of stones. I'd be grateful if you could return it for me."

"Sure. No problem."

"Thank you. And now I think I ought to leave. I'm sorry we didn't get a chance to catch up a little more."

Wenzel laughed. "It would have been fun. But . . . looks like you had some fun anyway."

Carl smiled and glanced at the twins. "More than they did, I'll say that."

He went back to the pickup and drove away fast. He wasn't expecting any more trouble from the Skoves—when they got to their feet, all they'd be looking for would be the nearest emergency room—but still, once you put out the fire, no sense standing around and watching the smoke.

Shortly after turning onto Buffalo Gap Road, he started laughing, harder and harder. He pulled over to the shoulder, cut the engine, and just sat there, cracking up. He replayed the whole thing in his head, what he'd said about the Popsicles especially—it was a good line, from a good movie.

The truth was, he'd been lucky. They were big sons of bitches, and if his aim had been off or their heads had been harder, the two of them might have done a lot of damage with those bats. Well, his bats now. The Muj liked to take trophies, and he'd picked up the habit while he was over there. One of his favorites was a Kizlyar Korshun, a knife he'd liberated from a dead Spetsnaz following a raid. The baseball bats didn't quite compare to that, but still they were proof of life and an emblem of victory.

The laughter got harder, and he realized he was shaking. He waited, laughing and shaking, letting it roll through him. And then he started crying. Because the Skoves were so easy and obvious. Even if he'd lost the fight, it was still about nothing. Just testosterone, really. But Roy . . .

He didn't know what to do about that. How to fight it, or whether he should fight it, or whose side he was on or even why there were sides.

Maybe that's why he was so eager to talk to Magnus's contact about this Southeast Asia opportunity. Combat was stark and simple. Just kill someone, someone who's trying his hardest to do the same to you.

But family . . . that was a different story. Family was like navigating a minefield in a pit filled with quicksand in the dark of night during a thunderstorm.

The tears tapered off, the shakes along with them. He wiped his face with the back of a hand. Yeah, he would talk to this guy tomorrow. Another secret war might do him good. Clear his head and fill his pockets. Help him figure out a way through the real war. The one he was trapped in right here in Tuscola.

Chapter 12

Joko and his men lay proned out inside the tree line east of the village, the sun slanting through the leaves and branches behind them. It was frustrating to not simply march in and take the woman. But she was surrounded by scores of villagers, and she was helping them. Doctors in such remote areas were virtually nonexistent. If Joko tried to remove this one, there could be a fight. And while there was no doubt about how such a contest would end, it would likely involve the kind of brutality Felix had been trying to reduce because it was counterproductive.

He raised his binoculars and watched as the woman stuck a tongue depressor into a small boy's mouth, the boy's long and somewhat theatrical *Ahhh* just audible from Joko's position. The woman followed up with a flashlight, looked, withdrew the implements, and said something that made the boy laugh. The woman smiled in return, a smile sunny enough to give succor all on its own.

Joko wanted so much to go in without waiting. She'd be shocked. They'd all be shocked. Their moment of hope shattered, and nothing for the villagers to do but watch as Joko and his soldiers led the woman away, hoping they themselves would be spared.

But he knew it would be better to come back, in force, when the woman was asleep, or more likely gone. Then, under cover of darkness, Joko's men could enter individual huts and interrogate people separately, and quietly, about who this doctor was. It was important in such matters to let each villager know that others were cooperating. To make them understand that information corroborating accurate information was the key to freedom and other rewards. And that information contradicted by separate intelligence was the key to suffering. And death.

Many times, this means of persuasion was so effective that no physical action was even necessary. This pleased Felix, who was strict about interrogations that left marks. Felix had taught them how to do what needed to be done without leaving marks, but he had also advised that fear was better than force. Once you used force, the fear of force was over. The only fear would be of more force. Such a cycle could be problematic. Fear, by contrast, left no marks. Or at least none that could be discerned.

Of course, Felix didn't have to concern himself with the morale of Joko's men. Beeler was a prize the men had expected to enjoy, but with Jakarta breathing down his neck, Joko had made them wait. He would try to find them some consolation.

Joko knew that units untethered in the countryside, far from Jakarta, would inevitably suffer breakdowns in discipline. Eventually, unit integrity would come to depend on only two things: how much your men needed you, and how much they feared you. You could buy cooperation by allowing, even encouraging, the men to slake whatever appetites they might have, whether by stealing, raping, or wantonly killing. But cooperation lasted only as long as the currency used to purchase it. Loyalty was different. Loyalty wasn't bought. It was earned. By need. And fear. And Joko always made sure to instill both. In abundance.

Now the woman was checking the temperature of another boy, this one smaller than the one before. The woman gave the mother a packet of pills. Probably Cipro or other antibiotics, perhaps for typhoid fever. There had been floods here not so long ago. Floods were always followed by typhoid.

Joko didn't care about the boy. What mattered was, if the woman had antibiotics, she worked for a clinic that had Red Cross contacts. Probably that meant Dili. And a skilled doctor in Dili, with access to antibiotics, would inevitably be in frequent contact with Falintil.

He had seen enough. He turned to the men alongside him and signaled that they should fall back. Their expressions registered some surprise, but of course they did as he commanded.

When they were deeper in the jungle, they circled up. "We need to go back for Beeler," Joko said. "We'll return here when the timing is right."

His sergeant, Bambang, glanced toward the village, but it was too far to see. "What if the doctor is gone later?" he said. "We came here for her."

Joko shrugged. "We know a lot already. Probably enough to find her in Dili or wherever else she came from. And when the journalist realizes how much we know, she may tell us more."

Bambang glanced back again. "And if she doesn't?"

Joko looked at him. "This doctor must have treated twenty villagers already. If she's gone when we return, we'll interrogate the people she helped. They'll know a lot. Where she came from. Maybe her name. And other details. Besides. I have a feeling this doctor is . . . special. Felix will want us to give her room for a while. Let her think she's eluded us. Let her continue whatever it is she's been doing."

"We can only roll her up once," Bambang said, knowing Joko's preferences in such matters.

Joko smiled. "Yes. Better to watch and wait before we do."

His men all nodded, but he sensed their disappointment. He understood. The woman was young and attractive, which gave them the urge. And part of Falintil, which gave them the right.

Of course, in the end, all Timorese were part of Falintil. When clearing out a rat's nest, you didn't discriminate among the vermin. It was only a question of how you got rid of them.

He glanced back toward the village, still frustrated. He almost admired the woman. She had overcome her fear and helped the girl by the well. Her attempts had been futile, but that was no fault of hers.

AMOK

And she was passionate. The ball of gauze she had hurled. And those fist marks in the dirt. Her will would be strong, as strong as her heart.

He would make that strength his. When the time came. And he sensed that time would be soon.

Chapter 13

Carl crawled into bed at a little past six. He was drained, and not just figuratively. That was two rides on the merry-go-round with Marla, and they weren't short rides, either.

He pulled up the covers and smiled. Years earlier, that first time . . . Well, there was never going to be anything quite like that. The astonishment of it. The revelation. The wonder. But there was something to be said for familiarity, too, a little more comfort and context.

The day before had been a long one, no doubt. And while staying out with Marla had made the night even longer, that was different. One way or another, everything else that day felt like it had been forced on him. Marla, though . . . that had been nothing but a sweet surprise.

She'd been married but was divorced now, with no kids, so it wasn't complicated, and she wasn't bitter, just relieved. They'd laughed a lot. She'd heard from Wenzel about what happened with the Skove twins, and when she got out of her car and slipped into his arms, she told him jokingly he was her conquering hero. Then they walked over to the Cox plot, as tradition seemed to require, kissing and pulling at each other's clothes on the way, and it was beautiful, all of it so natural and unexpected. And then after, they'd lain there on the grass, crickets chirping softly around them, just looking at each other in the waning moonlight, talking and reminiscing. He'd even told her a little about Roy and the overall conundrum.

"Everybody knew at the time," she'd said. "I mean, about what he was doing. People talked about it. I don't remember it being called child abuse or spousal abuse or anything like that. Maybe back then we didn't have those words. But people knew."

"Yeah, I guess they did. Hard not to, with all the marks he was leaving."

"But you know how it is around here. People get involved when they ought to mind their own business, and mind their own business when they ought to get involved."

He laughed. "Probably that's people everywhere."

"Maybe. But I remember hearing my parents talk when your mom and sister pressed charges. They thought it was the wrong thing to do, airing the family's dirty laundry in public like that."

"A lot of people felt that way."

"Did you?"

He thought about that for a minute. "It was confusing. I loved my dad, but we'd all gotten afraid of him. Still, I think once the law became part of it, I was more embarrassed that people were talking about us than I was afraid of Roy."

"I can understand that. You were just a kid. I remember you were pretty wild, though."

"Yeah. People used to taunt me, especially after my mom married Henry. I spent a fair amount of time defending her honor."

"That why you were such a hellion on the gridiron?"

It was true he'd had a reputation for being rough. He hadn't been the biggest, or the strongest, or the fastest, but everybody knew that when Carl Williams put a lick on you, you'd be remembering it all through the weekend, and probably longer.

"Yeah, I guess it's safe to surmise I had some unresolved issues. Of course, my detractors would likely say, 'Oh, *had?*'"

She laughed. "Being a Marine didn't straighten that out? Judging from seeing you with the Skove twins earlier, I'm guessing the answer is no."

"The Skove twins? They were provoking me."

"I'd say you might have done a little provoking yourself."

"That was counter-provoking. It's different."

"Oh, you mean they started it?"

"Well, they did, didn't they?"

"Uh-huh." But her tone was more skepticism than agreement.

He laughed. "All right, I see your point. I don't know. I just took so much grief back in the day over Roy and my mom and Henry. I guess I got in the habit of never letting it go. It was like that with football, too. The other players would talk shit to me. Call me white trash. And my reaction was, *I'll show you who's the trash.*"

He could have added, but didn't, why those *white trash* taunts had been so particularly hurtful. Beyond the insult itself, the people who hurled it were telling him that he was just like his father. And it wasn't right that *You're just like your father* should be a slur. The worst part was, Carl had been afraid there could be truth to it. Maybe he still was. And that was why anyone who used those words was going to get hurt, never mind how much Carl might have gotten hurt in the process.

And then he thought of Roy, talking about *singularity of purpose.* But surely that was different?

Marla said, "Was it like that in the Marines, too?"

"You mean people provoking me?"

She laughed. "And you counter-provoking."

He remembered a certain asshole instructor he'd busted up. "Sometimes."

"But they didn't know about Roy."

"I don't think so."

"Then maybe the way you are . . . is just the way you are."

He wasn't sure. He'd never had these kinds of problems in Afghanistan. He did things his way there. No one complained that he was boisterous and liked to whoop it up, or told him a sniper couldn't have a loud personality. Even that guy Rain, the half-Japanese one with the stick up his ass, respected Carl's ability and his results and treated him accordingly, even if he never did once laugh at any of Carl's jokes. Nobody cared that he was unorthodox—hell, they celebrated it by naming him Dox.

On the other hand, it was true that he had always enjoyed tweaking the higher-ups. Up to and including launching those incursions into the USSR to do it. So maybe Marla had a point.

He smiled at her. "You know, you're pretty smart for a country girl."

"You trying to rile me, mister? You'll have to do better than that."

His smile broadened. She really was smart.

"What?" she said, looking at him.

He shook his head. "I just keep feeling nothing has changed in Tuscola. And maybe it hasn't. I sure never expected to be back with the first girl I was with, but here we are."

"Wait a minute. I was your first?"

"Unless I'm forgetting another night with another girl that was about the most memorable of my life."

"Sweet-talker. But I can't believe this. Are you sure? You were so confident. I thought you had loads of experience."

"Some. But not that."

"Damn. You were a natural." She gave him that sexy smile. "And you've gotten even better, you know that?"

He smiled back. "Had a few opportunities to practice."

She laughed and punched him in the shoulder. "Scamp. But fine, then. Practice on me."

And so he had, all the way until the sun came up and the birds started chirping. At which point, a maintenance crew arrived, and he and Marla had to pull on their clothes and slink out of the cemetery like criminals.

She'd given him her number and told him he'd better call. He wanted to. He liked her. She was smart and funny and easy to be with. But it all made him feel . . . troubled, too. Like this whole place had a kind of gravity, and a girl like Marla could easily become part of it.

He glanced around the room. Being back in the bed he'd slept in as a kid, surrounded by the various football and baseball trophies he'd won in high school, was so familiar it was simultaneously surreal—just another part of Tuscola that hadn't changed at all, and that seemed to be waiting for him to slide right back into it.

He closed his eyes and thought about Marla again. He wondered whether he could be happy with a girl like her, and why he seemed instinctively to resist the notion. And then he thought about Roy, and what the hell was the right thing to do.

He couldn't answer any of it. After a long while, he slept.

Chapter 14

It was almost dark when Joko arrived at Felix's encampment near Betano.

This was the southern edge of the island, across the Timor Sea from Australia. Felix moved his forces frequently, but preferred to be close to the coast for resupply and, if necessary, rescue by American vessels. Indeed, Australian guerillas fighting the Japanese in these very jungles had been supported at the port in Betano by Allied naval forces. Then, the West had fought with the Timorese against the Japanese; now the West was against the Timorese and aiding Indonesia. Joko understood that some would find the constant changing of sides to be ironic. He wasn't interested in such things. Alliances weren't determined by friends. They were determined by enemies. And as enemies changed, so did alliances.

Joko and his men had to be careful to show themselves as they approached. More than once, Falintil had probed Felix's positions, and Joko wasn't going to risk one of Felix's men mistaking Joko's unit for a hostile force. Nor would he take a chance on entering the encampment without a guide. The perimeter was booby-trapped—surrounded by trip-wired claymores.

So as he and his men came to a clearing at the bottom of the ridge they had climbed, Joko whistled loudly. For a moment there was nothing, just the buzz of insects in the trees around them. Then he heard an answering whistle from inside the trees ahead.

Joko stepped forward. *"Olá,"* he called out.

A moment later, a hard-eyed white man in jungle fatigues and a buzz cut emerged from the tree line, his folding-stock Franchi SPAS-12 shotgun held at low-ready. Joko had seen him before—he had a scar that suggested something had missed his left eye by a miracle, and went by Waster. Joko's own weapon, a US-made CAR-15, was slung over his shoulder in patrol carry. Not only did Americans get the best toys; it was also understood that they had the right to deploy them more aggressively. Joko didn't appreciate having to approach like a dog with its tail tucked. But Felix was the bigger dog.

Joko waved. "Good to go?"

Good to go was lingo he had picked up from Felix twenty years earlier, in Vietnam. He liked it. He was proud of his English, which he'd honed in Ranger School at Fort Benning. It made him feel like an American. An American soldier.

Waster didn't move the Franchi from low-ready. "How many in those trees?"

"Twelve."

"Let's start with just you. Stay close to the ridge. The center of the path is mined."

Joko turned. Most of his men were only two meters back, but he was pleased to note he couldn't see them. "Bambang," he said.

There was movement inside the trees as Bambang stood and crept forward.

"Boss."

"Wait here. Keep Reeler well to the rear."

Bambang nodded and faded back into the trees. Joko turned and walked toward Waster, who was saying something into a radio. Joko kept close to the ridge as Waster had instructed. As he moved, his boots dislodged some small rocks. A few seconds elapsed before he heard the echo of their impact far below. Anyone approaching Felix's position would instinctively keep to the center. Which of course was why Felix had placed his mines there.

Joko followed Waster about fifty meters deeper into the trees, pass-ing other sentries along the way, mostly white, two black, one Asian. Doubtless all Americans. And all with small arms like HK MP5s, Uzis, and more Franchis. Anything they wanted, it seemed, as long as it wasn't US-made.

They came to another clearing. At its center, surrounded by sand-bags, was a collection of large, heavy-duty tents. From one of them emerged a bald white man in wire-rimmed glasses, tall and thin to the point of emaciation, stooped even though the tent was high enough not to require stooping. Felix. Joko wondered whether his friend was leaving the tent to greet him, or to keep him from seeing what was inside. It didn't matter. The main thing was, Felix would know what to do about Beeler.

"Joko," Felix said, smiling and walking over. "You have something for me?"

From time to time, Joko would bring Felix a promising prisoner for interrogation. When Felix was satisfied he had learned all that could be learned, he would decide what to do next. If the prisoner could be turned, he would be released. If a show of justice was called for, he would be imprisoned at Lembaga in Dili. If neither of those two courses was feasible, he would be shot. Any of these outcomes was satisfac-tory—what mattered in the end was that the prisoner was neutralized.

They embraced. Joko noticed something had changed from the last time they had seen each other, about a month earlier. Felix wasn't old—not yet sixty—but now his smell had more . . . age to it. And he had lost weight. Not that there was much to lose to begin with.

"You haven't heard," Joko said. "Maybe that's good."

Felix stared at him. Sometimes the wire-rimmed glasses gave Felix the appearance of a harmless, aging academic. Other times, com-bined with his gaunt frame, the glasses could make him look like an ascetic. But when Felix was disturbed or angry, the intensity of his gaze magnified in those lenses gave him the feel of a scientist, with the person subjected to his stare a small creature fixed for vivisection.

"What haven't I heard?"

Joko pressed a thumb against a mosquito that had alighted on his forearm, squashing it. "My men took an American journalist. Theresa Beeler."

Felix's stare continued. "'Took' her?"

"We were following her. You know that. Her stories about Falintil . . . She has access."

"Yes, but your mission parameters were observe-only."

"We thought she was about to go operational. One of my men overreacted."

"You didn't kill her?"

"No, she's unharmed. We're holding her."

Felix's stare showed a touch of concern. "Where?"

Joko inclined his head in the direction he had come from. "In the trees on the other side of the mined clearing. She's blindfolded. She doesn't know where she is. We came from Maliana."

Felix glanced in the direction Joko had indicated. "Why would you bring her here?"

"I don't know what to do with her."

"Do? Keep the blindfold on her, take her far away by a different route, and let her go."

"It's not that simple."

Felix sighed. "Of course it's not. What happened?"

"She was in Maliana to meet a source. One of my men shot a village girl. Beeler saw it."

Felix shrugged. "All right. She saw too much. If no one knows you took her, get rid of her. Make sure the body can never be found. In fact, make sure there *is* no body to be found." After a moment with no response from Joko, Felix said, "Apparently, that's not so simple, either."

"No," Joko said. He briefed Felix on what he'd heard from Jakarta—that the US State Department had contacted Indonesian counterparts, expressing "grave concern" that an American journalist had gone missing in Timor.

When Joko was done, Felix shook his head as though in despair. "Did you acknowledge that you have her?"

"Of course not. And they knew better than to ask directly. But they made their point clear. 'If you find her, make sure she's escorted out of the country unharmed. The Pentagon doesn't care, but the State Department does, and we can't do anything that could jeopardize the flow of American arms and other aid.'"

Felix pushed back his thinning hair. "All right. If everyone has preserved some degree of deniability, at least you have options."

Joko wasn't much heartened by Felix's use of *you*. *We* would have been better.

"Your men," Felix went on, shaking his head again. "I thought they were better disciplined. The whole point—"

"I know. The whole point is to move from a hatchet to a scalpel."

Felix nodded, apparently not realizing Joko was trying to forestall the lecture, not encourage it. "Jakarta could have done nothing when Falintil took over," Felix said. "Or you could have cleansed this half of the island, before the world started watching."

Felix was in professor mode. The most efficient way to deal with it was to just let him get it out. So Joko nodded, but otherwise didn't respond.

"But you didn't," Felix went on. "You settled on the most popular but counterproductive position between doing nothing, on the one hand, and genocide, on the other."

"Brutality," Joko said, beating Felix to it.

"And why doesn't in-between brutality work?"

"Because brutality fosters rage. And rage is the fuel insurgencies run on."

"Yes. Brutality is like strong medicine. It has to be administered in calibrated doses. Otherwise, it creates undesirable side effects."

Joko and his men had traveled fast and hard. He was tired, and worried about the pressure from Jakarta. He needed Felix's help, not a lecture he had heard a dozen times before.

"Old habits," Joko said, quoting another aphorism of Felix's. "They die hard."

Felix nodded. "Which is why I'm here. To help Indonesia professionalize its efforts. To administer the necessary brutality, but in a calibrated fashion."

"You know I agree with you, Felix. You trained me, remember? But you also taught me about the fog of war. Murphy's Law. *Shit Happens.*"

Felix chuckled, perhaps amused to realize that Joko had learned his lessons so well he was now deploying the teachings against the teacher.

"The situation isn't good," Joko continued, "but for now, I can't let her go. And I can't get rid of her. All I can do with Jakarta is play for time. But there might be a way out. You know in every crisis, there's an opportunity."

Felix raised an eyebrow at the obvious quote of another Felixism. "Yes?"

Joko told him about the doctor. "She came a long way," Joko said. "Almost certainly from Dili. Alone. For a meeting close to the border. Why?"

"Why indeed?" Felix said.

"Whatever it was, it was important. We've talked before about how Falintil communicates, both internally and with the outside world. They're afraid of radio intercepts. Some of it is couriers. But some of it—"

"Conduits," Felix said.

"Yes. And what better conduit than a doctor? She can treat anyone—Timorese, Javanese, foreign—in total privacy. And pass one guerilla's message on to the next. Or broadcast a message to multiple guerillas. Or hand over stories, film, whatever, to foreign journalists."

Felix looked away as though considering. Then he said, "How confident are you of your theory?"

"How well can I read sign? How well do I read humans?"

Felix smiled. "That's a good answer. You can find her?"

"Of course."

"You have someone you can get close to her?"

"That's more difficult. An Indonesian won't work, obviously. And there are enough Jakarta sympathizers among the Timorese that the move would be obvious. The woman is smart. With keen instincts."

Felix didn't ask how Joko could know such a thing after only a brief observation from a distance. His confidence made Joko proud.

Felix was silent, his expression contemplative. Joko knew he had an idea. He waited for Felix to formulate it.

After a moment, Felix said, "There's a man I've requested. A sniper. Former US Marine. Black-ops experience. Deniable, like all my men. I want him for perimeter security because Falintil has been increasing its probes. But I'm thinking . . . maybe that could wait."

"A sniper? To spy on this doctor?"

"From everything I've heard and read, he's an unusual man. Not a sniper's personality. Not a spy's, either. Boisterous. Unpredictable. Some discipline problems. An apparent affinity for UNODIR, which is not necessarily a vice. In Afghanistan he was called Dox, short for *unorthodox.*"

Joko was well familiar with the American military acronym UNODIR—Unless Otherwise Directed. It was a way of alerting command to an action you were about to take without leaving anyone time to tell you not to. Related to another special ops concept he had learned from Felix: *It is better to seek forgiveness than ask permission.*

"Too much of a wild card for her to suspect?" Joko said.

"That's what I'm thinking."

Joko didn't like the admiration with which Felix seemed to regard this Dox. It made the man feel like a rival. And of course, in more practical terms, the more support the man had from Felix, the more independently he might think he could operate from Joko.

But those were concerns for later. What mattered now was that Felix was warming to his idea. So Joko smiled and said, "If this sniper learns something valuable about the doctor's role with Falintil, what she was doing with Beeler . . ."

Felix nodded. "It could help Jakarta overlook Beeler's . . . disappearance. Even the handwringers at State might find themselves in a more forgiving mood. Right now, everyone sees the journalist's disappearance as pure cost. But if we could show that the cost was actually a payment, made in exchange for something of great value . . ."

Ah, the *we* Joko had been hoping for.

"And if he learns nothing?" Joko said.

Felix shrugged. "We'd be no worse off than we are now. With the same range of options."

Joko liked the sound of that. "Brutality?"

"Calibrated brutality. But yes."

"Beeler?"

Felix nodded. "And the doctor, too, I'm afraid."

It was almost enough to make Joko hope the sniper would fail.

Chapter 15

Carl sat alone at a booth in the back of Huddle House, a diner in Tye just north of the air force base, drinking black coffee and digging into a Big House Platter. Willie Nelson was singing "Nothing I Can Do About It Now" through some ceiling speakers, which felt appropriate. The place was about half-full, mostly old folks enjoying a breakfast out, but also, judging from the number of eighteen-wheelers in the parking lot and the profusion of Caterpillar Diesel and other such caps inside, a lot of truckers, too.

The waitress, a plump middle-aged woman with a swish and a nameplate on her uniform reading *Evonne,* came by and gave him a bright Texas smile. "More coffee, honey?"

He slid his mug over to make the reach easier for her. "Ma'am, I'll take all you've got."

She laughed and filled the mug. "Sugar, if you took all I've got, it would ruin you for sure."

He was so surprised, all he could do was laugh. He wondered if she was entirely joking. But he'd seen Marla twice in the three days since that night in the cemetery, and while it wasn't like they were formally committed to each other or anything, he didn't much care to be with more than one woman at a time. Well, there had been those twins in the bathtub at the Sukhothai in Bangkok, but that was different.

Still, as much as he enjoyed her, even Marla felt like just . . . marking time. He had to decide what the hell he was going to do about Roy. And for that, he needed to hear the details of the mysterious Southeast Asia opportunity Magnus had told him about. Which is why it was good that the night before, Ronnie had taken a phone message—a friend of Magnus's who wanted to meet at Huddle House the following morning.

At eight o'clock sharp, a fiftysomething guy, trim, with an Errol Flynn mustache, walked in. Carl, who'd been checking each time the door chimes rang, made him for out-of-town. He was wearing a flannel shirt, but the weather was too warm for flannel, unless you had the sleeves cut off, which this guy didn't. Plus it looked new, like something an out-of-towner, maybe someone accustomed to wearing a suit, might choose because he thought it would help him blend in with the locals.

The guy looked around, his gaze settling quickly on Carl. He nodded once and headed over. When he got close, Carl stood.

The guy held out his hand. "You must be Dox," he said in a slightly fussy Yankee accent.

They shook. "People around here don't know me as that," Carl said. "That was more an overseas thing."

The guy nodded. "Short for *unorthodox*."

"Apparently so." He didn't much care for the man's way of not so subtly demonstrating that he knew a good amount about Carl, while Carl knew nothing about him. He gestured to the cushioned seat across from him. "You want to order something?"

They sat. The guy picked up one of the laminated menus, took a quick peek, and said, "What's good?"

The guy looked like the type who played racket ball three times a week at the club and fancied low-sodium egg white omelets and decaffeinated beverages. "Try the cheesy bacon grits," Carl said. "They're my favorite. Or the biscuits with the sausage gravy. Can't go wrong there."

The guy looked like he was struggling not to wrinkle his nose. Evonne came over, holding a carafe. "Coffee?"

"Decaf," the guy said. "Thank you."

Carl thought, *I knew it.*

Evonne looked like she was struggling against a nose-wrinkle herself. "Whatever you like, honey. I'll be right back."

"How about the biscuits?" Carl said, enjoying himself despite feeling tired from the hours he'd been keeping.

The guy shook his head. "No, thank you." He turned to Evonne. "Do you have a fruit plate?"

She stared for a moment as though he'd grown a pair of antennae. "We could make one."

The guy nodded. "That would be perfect. Thank you."

Evonne departed. Carl said, "You look fresher than I feel. Where'd you come in from?"

"The East Coast."

The irritation Carl had felt a moment ago, when the guy had been a little too pleased about his information advantage, edged up a notch. "Are we being intentionally vague here?"

"Sorry. Occupational hazard. I'm in from Andrews Air Force Base."

"By way of Langley?"

"Correct."

Maybe it was just that he was tired, but Carl felt himself beginning to develop an antipathy. He was obviously just trying to break the ice a little. Why did the guy need to respond as though Carl was a schoolchild who'd just offered the right answer and deserved a pat on the head?

But he pushed the feeling away. He wanted the job. Or at least to know what it was. "What do I call you?"

"Mossberg."

For whatever reason, that irritated him, too. "Purveyors of fine guns. Is that Mr. Mossberg? Or Moss? Or Mossie?"

"Just Mossberg."

"Okay, Just Mossberg, how about if you tell me a little about who put us in touch. Just to establish your bona fides."

Evonne swung by, put a plate of cut melon on the table, and filled Mossberg's mug from an orange-lidded carafe. "You fellas let me know if you need anything else," she said and moved off.

Mossberg waited until she was out of earshot, then said, "Your former Marine commander, Magnus Magnusson, speaks highly of you. So does a former Peshawar station chief named Rob Kee."

"Kee? He was the one who was always telling me to stop invading Russia."

"No, it was the seventh floor that was upset about that. Kee was a fan of your Uzbekistan antics and would have been happy to have you do more. He was just following the higher-ups' orders. Apparently, he was secretly glad you wouldn't follow his."

The seventh floor was the executive suite at CIA Headquarters in Langley. "Huh. How do you like that? Wish I'd known. Me and my Muj could have taken Samarkand."

Mossberg eyed him as though trying to decide if he was serious. He mostly wasn't. The truth was, he and the boys had never gotten farther than Termez, just over the border, and even those were just hit-and-run raids to taunt Ivan and improve morale. They didn't have nearly the numbers or supply lines to hold territory. Not that it wouldn't have been fun to try. Thinking about it made him miss those days. He never was sure who he liked taunting more—Moscow, or Langley.

Carl said, "So Kee's the one who wants me for this Southeast Asia op?"

Mossberg started in on his fruit. "Kee's a died-in-the-wool cold warrior," he said, swallowing a forkful of melon. "He was promoted after Peshawar—he *is* the seventh floor now. And apparently, you're his kind of guy."

"Well, it's good to have low friends in high places. But what about you? What do you do?"

"Think of me as the personnel department. I keep track of certain types of men with various skills and experience and needs, and stay abreast of operational requirements. Then I help fill positions with the right people."

"A kind of matchmaker, it sounds like."

"I suppose that's one way to put it."

"And you think I'm the right match."

"I'm sure of it."

Carl had no problem with confidence. But smug was irritating. "Why?"

Mossberg took another sip of his decaf. "You're a former Marine and outstanding sniper. There was an incident of insubordination involving an instructor at one point, but that's easily overlooked. The CIA is more tolerant of youthful indiscretions than the regular military."

Yeah, the dreaded "youthful indiscretion." The instructor in question had set Carl up, and then, after Carl punched his lights out, wrote a fitness report describing him as "temperamentally unsuited" to be a sniper. Carl could have been court-martialed for what he'd done, but Magnus had pulled strings and saved him from that. Still, the incident tarnished his record. It was part of why he wound up in Afghanistan, something else Magnus had helped with.

"I'd say I proved myself in Afghanistan," Carl said. "And then some. You know how many personal kills I racked up there?"

"Eleven."

"Eleven confirmed. Three of them at over a thousand yards."

Mossberg didn't respond, and Carl realized the man had been baiting him. Maybe he should have tried to reschedule this meeting for when he was feeling a little less tired and cranky. Well, too late now.

He took a sip of coffee to give himself a moment to get a grip on his irritation. "All right. You're looking for a sniper."

"We were. What we have in mind now is a little less . . . orthodox."

Carl looked at him, making no attempt to hide how unimpressed he was. "I get it. Now's when I'm supposed to say, 'Oh, unorthodox—that's me.'"

Mossberg offered a *Fair enough* dip of the head. "However you want to characterize it. The sniper work is important, but not urgent. What's urgent is, we believe we've identified one of the key players in the Communist underground that's currently bedeviling Indonesia's East Timor pacification efforts."

"East Timor? I thought that was some kind of civil war."

"The geopolitics are complicated. But the *Reader's Digest* version is, Jakarta has been trying for sixteen years to subdue a Communist insurgency called Falintil on the eastern half of the island of Timor. Their efforts have been as bloody as they've been subpar. Not long ago, we sent a specialist to refine those efforts. His name is Felix, and he was remarkably effective against the Vietcong before Congress cut the balls off our war effort there."

Carl didn't consider himself a historian, but he had some notions about human nature, one of which was that the loser in any conflict was always motivated to shift the blame. Not that this was the right time for a debate on the topic.

"What did your man Felix do in Vietnam?"

"Have you heard of the Phoenix Program?"

"Sure, the assassination campaign."

"It was much more about intelligence than it was about neutralization. But yes. Felix designed it. And ran it. He's doing something similar in East Timor. We call the operation Surgical Hatchet."

Dox couldn't help laughing. "You really call it that?"

Mossberg looked a little peevish, which Dox didn't mind at all. "It's a perfect description. The hatchet is heavy and sharp. But it's being used with surgical precision."

"I'm just saying, anyone who wants to perform a surgical procedure using a hatchet can count me out."

"You're being too literal. And at the risk of compounding that problem, what the Indonesians were doing against Falintil was the terror equivalent of fighting fire with fire. Now, of course, fire is an exceptionally useful tool—arguably the most important ever. But it has to be used properly. Otherwise it burns the wrong things."

"Like in this case, what?"

"In this case Indonesian President Suharto's prestige. His grip on power. A Communist insurgency in the Indonesian Archipelago could spread. Suharto could be toppled. A civil war could break out. China could move in. In fact, just last year China and Indonesia resumed diplomatic relations. In short, America could get burned here by losing to China its closest Southeast Asian ally and military partner."

"I don't know. I mean, who am I going to invade? Lot of ocean between Indonesia and China. I guess I'll need some ships."

Mossberg grimaced. "No invasions this time, please. How soon will you be ready?"

Carl looked at him. "You know what Texans don't like, Mossberg? Besides a carpetbagger, that is."

Mossberg raised his eyebrows.

"A hard sell," Carl continued. "You haven't even told me what the job is. All you've told me is what it isn't—sniper's work."

"As I—"

"No, don't tell me again what the job is *for*. Tell me what it *is*. What I'd be doing, not why. You understand the difference?"

Mossberg leaned back and took a sip of his decaf. It was probably getting cold. Carl was glad Evonne hadn't bothered to refill it.

"There's a doctor," Mossberg said after a moment. "Her medical work is a cover for her role in the insurgency. We want you to get close. Report on her movements, her meetings, her state of mind. We believe we can use all that to draw a more accurate wire diagram of who's who in Falintil. Close down their communication channels. That will enable a more surgical approach to Jakarta's pacification efforts."

"Sounds like you need a spy. I'm a sniper."

"You don't have a sniper's personality, but that didn't stop you from racking up eleven confirmed kills in Afghanistan, three of them from over a thousand yards. Why would it matter that you don't have a spy's personality, either?"

"I'll take that as a compliment."

"Take it any way you like. It's coming straight from Kee. And from Magnusson. They think you're right for the job."

"What makes you think I want it?"

Mossberg looked at him. "Do you want to know what I have about you in your file?"

Carl said nothing. Of course he wanted to know. But damn if he would give the man the satisfaction.

"You had a difficult childhood," Mossberg went on. "You longed to escape your suffocating small-town upbringing. You wanted the discipline and structure of the military. And glory, too. Well, you got the discipline and structure. The glory, not so much."

Carl wasn't impressed. "We got a lady in town, Mrs. Jarvath. She does palm readings out of her house by the funeral home. You sound just like her."

"You said you proved yourself in Afghanistan. Fine. I know you liked it there. You certainly stayed long enough. Almost like you didn't want to come home. I mean, did you repeatedly invade Uzbekistan just so you could come back to Tuscola? You can't even tell war stories here. All your stories are classified."

That hit closer to home. Carl said nothing, and after a moment Mossberg went on. "And yet here you are. Where the same thing that made you run away has now brought you back to Tuscola."

Carl drummed his fingers on the table. Mossberg was walking his observations in like mortar rounds, and Carl was beginning to take fire. He badly wanted to tell the man to go fuck himself. It would have felt good to show the know-it-all little carpetbagger that in fact he didn't know shit. But he was too off balance. He needed to hear the rest.

"Your mother and sister can testify all they want," Mossberg said. "So can you. It won't matter. Roy is going to be released."

Carl looked at him, stunned and trying not to show it. "How could you know that?"

Mossberg shrugged. "I would have hoped that by now, you'd understand I make it my business to know things. Your father has bullied, bribed, or blackmailed everyone he needs to."

Carl didn't buy it. "You're wrong. He's worried. He told me I better not testify."

"He doesn't fully understand how effective his campaign has been. And even if he does understand, he's not going to take chances. Beyond which, have you ever considered that perhaps your father doesn't want the indignity of having his only son, joined by his ex-wife and only daughter, publicly trying to convince the state of Texas to keep him in prison forever?"

Carl didn't want to believe it. But Mossberg seemed so certain.

"You're sure he's getting out."

"Bet on it. Unless."

"Unless what?"

Mossberg shrugged. "Unless the CIA wants him to stay."

Carl shook his head, trying to get his mind around it. "What the hell are you going to do, write the parole board?"

"We would be more subtle than that."

"Subtle how?"

"We could eliminate the unhelpful pressure. And replace it with a more helpful variety."

"I see we're being intentionally vague again."

"This time it's not a habit. This time it's sources and methods. Ones that would be illegal for the Agency to employ in a domestic environment. But think about it. None of you would have to do anything. Testify for, testify against, don't testify at all. Roy would remain in prison no matter what. And he would never know why."

Carl didn't know what was the right thing to do about Roy. He couldn't see trying to keep him in that hellhole. But if he got out and did something to Ronnie and their mom and the girls and Henry . . .

But if he took this job, it would at least give him money. Money meant options. And maybe he would be able to see the Roy situation more clearly if he was looking at it from far away. That might have been a rationalization, he knew. There was FEAR, meaning False Evidence Appearing Real. And there was the other definition—Fuck Everything and Run. He wasn't sure which was in play in his mind just now.

It didn't matter. He didn't want to say yes. Didn't want to give this prick the satisfaction. But he didn't see an alternative. He put his hands behind his neck and stretched to crack his back, hoping the nonchalant move would conceal his ambivalence.

"Ah," Mossberg said. "The Hog's Tooth."

Carl felt for the round—it had pulled out of his shirt when he was cracking his back. He leaned forward and slipped it under his collar.

"A Hunter of Gunmen," Mossberg went on. "No mere Professionally Instructed Gunman."

Carl looked him up and down. "You're no Marine. I don't need Mrs. Jarvath to tell me that."

"No."

"Then how do you know about the Hog's Tooth?"

"I told you. I make it my business to know things."

"Yeah? Do you know why I don't like you?"

"Because I'm supercilious and condescending."

"That's redundant. And no, that's why *no one* likes you. *I* don't like you because you use the truth the way other people use lies. And that's even worse."

For a long moment, neither of them spoke. Then Mossberg said, "May I take that as a yes?"

"You haven't even told me about the pay."

"The pay is five thousand a week. Plus a fifty-thousand-dollar bonus. May I take that as a yes?"

Carl leaned back and looked at him. "You may."

That seemed to settle it. Mossberg didn't offer his hand. Carl wouldn't have shaken it if he had.

Chapter 16

T he moon was high overhead, and even without night vision, Joko could see the hut they wanted. The one Joko had seen the doctor going in and out of when she had been here treating the villagers.

Joko, Bambang, and three other men crept forward, their boots silent on the dewy grass, the moving parts of their weapons taped for noise suppression. Early on during the occupation, night raids had been more difficult. There were dogs in the countryside, and dogs were quick to bark. But as the occupation had ground on, people had gotten hungrier, and dogs had become less plentiful. Without the dogs, surprise was easier.

Not that Joko expected resistance. But he never took docility for granted, either, especially when he invaded someone's home. Surprise was disorienting, and disoriented people had a harder time rallying an effective defense. That was why tonight he was using a five-man team when two would have been enough. The appearance of overwhelming force made the actual use of force less likely—one glimpse of the power in Joko's command, and thoughts of fighting back would vanish even before they had cohered. Joko had been a long-distance runner in high school, and he knew it was better to blow past someone you were overtaking rather than to approach gradually. The gradual approach was a signal to the man ahead that he had a chance to outpace you. But fly by him fast enough, and he wouldn't even bother to try.

They crept forward, insects buzzing in the trees behind them, the moon casting long shadows among the huts they passed. Joko was nearly certain the doctor wouldn't be here. He doubted she had intended to stay as long as she did, and sensed that she had lingered only because she was confronted by so many villagers begging for her ministrations. It was possible he was wrong, of course; though that happened only rarely. But if he was, he and his men would interrogate the doctor and everyone else in the house, let them all think he was satisfied with their answers, and then let them go. Either way, he would learn who the woman was and where she had come from, and Felix's sniper-spy could then get close to the woman and probe her involvement with Falintil.

Joko's favorite approach in these matters was extreme stealth—the goal being to reach and surround a pallet before the man and woman sleeping on it had even stirred. The couple would wake to weapon lights and rifle muzzles in their faces and be instantly paralyzed by absolute terror. Sometimes Joko's men would rape the woman then and there, while the husband was forced to watch. That game they called Viddy Well, after a scene they liked from the movie *A Clockwork Orange*. Since Felix had arrived, though, such games had to be curtailed. These days, when the men needed companionship or just some fun, they tended not to let the girl go afterward. It wasn't exactly what Felix wanted, but it spread fewer tales of Kopassus brutality, which was ultimately the point of Felix's "professionalization" efforts.

What galled him, though, wasn't the rules. It was the hypocritical application. Because Joko knew that some of Felix's men liked to play games of their own, and if Joko knew, Felix must have known as well. It was all part of the arrogance of wealth and whiteness—*games for me but not for thee*. Joko resented that Felix's men got the best weapons and the most latitude and at the same time looked at Joko, who accomplished so much more with so much less, as somehow inferior. Not Felix himself; Felix had always been good to Joko. But his men. Joko could see it in the way they looked at him, hear it in their voices when they talked to him. He could almost smell it on them. And he hated them for it.

Yes, they all thought they were so professional, here to manage Joko's pacification efforts. To teach him all their high-minded, scientific, American management techniques. But what had happened? Within a matter of months, they were reaving and raping as they pleased. Could anything have been more predictable? Having guns when no one else did made men feel like gods. Gods could do as they liked. And men who *could* do as they liked *would* do as they liked. It was only a matter of time, and exposure to the trappings of godhood. Americans who thought they were immune didn't know the truth of their own history, from Sherman's March to Vietnam.

He and his men crept closer. The problem with extreme stealth was simply how difficult it was. One creaky floorboard could be enough to wake the inhabitants of a house and give them time to prepare. A blitzkrieg approach was the surer thing: rather than worry about noise, you simply obviated it with speed. But with the blitz, there was never that delicious moment of silently surrounding the pallet, savoring the seconds before people woke in shock to find you standing over them.

There was a compromise, though, and they would use it tonight. Extreme stealth, yes, but at any compromising noise, an instant switch to speed. They'd used the compromise before, in most situations finding it to be the best of both worlds.

There were three wooden stairs in front of the hut, leading to a small porch and the entrance door. Joko avoided them. Stairs squeaked, and besides, his men were all in the habit of staying clear of trails and other obvious routes of ingress and egress because Falintil was adept at laying booby traps. Instead, one by one they went to the end of the porch, turned and put their butts on the edge, swung up their legs, and approached the door that way.

Bambang tried the knob, then turned to Joko and shook his head, indicating the door was locked. This was unusual in the countryside, where many huts didn't have locks, and even for those that did, the people inside didn't bother. Why would they? These hill people had nothing worth stealing. And everyone knew that against Kopassus, a lock was little more than a joke.

So what was different about the couple living in this hut? Obviously, guilty knowledge. Which made perfect sense—after all, they had just harbored a person who was working with Falintil and passing information to foreign reporters. Maybe they didn't know that, but they would have sensed something was amiss about the woman, about whatever story she had told them to account for her presence in Maliana, and their attendant anxiety was already manifesting in new behavior, such as locking their door at night.

But guilty knowledge was good. It was always close to the surface, and people who had it were easy to interrogate. In fact, it was the basis for polygraphs, which contrary to popular understanding didn't detect lies as such, but rather the anxiety produced by guilty knowledge.

Under other circumstances, Joko and his men might have drawn out the approach. Perhaps by trying to pick the lock; perhaps by entering through a window. But tonight wasn't about games. It was about intel.

Joko nodded to Bambang. Bambang looked around to confirm everyone was ready. The other men nodded.

Bambang pulled a pry bar from his pack and worked it carefully into the doorframe. Of course, they could have easily kicked the door open, but the reverberation from that kind of action could be loud enough to wake others in the village.

There was no need for a three count; they'd all worked together on enough ops to know the overall tempo. Bambang tensed, then shoved the pry bar hard. There was a crack of wood and a pop as the hardware gave. Bambang rushed inside, pushing the door ahead of him, making sure it didn't crash open, closely followed by Joko and the other three men. Joko heard a woman's voice yelling in Tetum—"Someone's here!"—and saw the pallet at the end of the room. Joko and two of his men switched on their weapon lights and raced forward. Bambang and the remaining man peeled off to the hut's other room.

The man on the pallet was fast—he was already on his feet by the time Joko's men reached him. The woman was only sitting up, but she had grabbed a big kitchen knife. She must have been keeping the knife right next to her—more behavior caused by guilty knowledge.

"Put it down," Joko said to her calmly but firmly in Portuguese. Then he turned to the husband. "And you, back on the pallet. Or we'll kill everyone in this hut."

The man looked past Joko with terrified eyes, toward the hut's other room. Beyond looking, though, he did nothing. He raised his hands and slowly sank back onto the pallet. But the woman held on to the knife. For a moment, Joko thought she might not comply, so extreme was the desperation in her expression.

He heard a muffled scream from behind him and for an instant wondered if it was possible he was wrong about the doctor not being there. But no, a moment later, Bambang and the other man brought out a squirming girl. She was wearing an old tee-shirt that had ridden up as she struggled, exposing faded underwear. The couple's daughter, presumably. She must have been inside the hut the whole time Joko and his men had been watching from the trees earlier. That's why they hadn't seen her.

"Put her on the pallet," Joko said in Bahasa, and his men dumped the girl alongside her parents. The mother pushed the girl behind her as best she could and held on to the knife.

"Put it down," Joko said again, switching back to Portuguese. "We're here for information. About the doctor who stayed with you. Cooperate and nothing will happen. Refuse to cooperate and you'll die right where you are."

The woman's lips were peeled back in a feral expression of hate. Joko didn't mind. He had provoked every kind of hate, sometimes incidentally, other times because he wanted to. Tonight, he had planned only on collecting the information he needed and then leaving. But the woman's fierceness was beginning to excite him.

Joko raised his rifle so that the muzzle was pointing at the woman's face. Still she held on to the knife. He smiled—and swiveled so that the rifle was pointing at the daughter. The girl cried out and her father scrambled to shield her.

"Put it down!" the man said to his wife in Portuguese. "Are you crazy?"

Joko noted that the husband addressed her in Portuguese rather than Tetum. He wouldn't know that Joko spoke Tetum; the Portuguese meant he wanted Joko to be able to understand him. To know that he was trying to cooperate.

But the woman didn't put down the knife. She continued to stare at Joko with her feral eyes. So impressive was her hate that he wondered whether she would succumb to the urge to leap at him.

"You won't make it," he said. "You'll only die before your daughter's eyes. And her a moment after. Is that what you want?"

Her hand shaking, the woman lowered the knife to the floor.

"Push it over to me," Joko said. "Slowly and carefully."

The woman, her eyes never once leaving Joko's face, complied. Of course, it wasn't inconceivable she had another weapon concealed under the pallet. But even if she did, if she moved for it, she would be dead before it mattered.

"Good," Joko said. "We're going to ask you some questions. Which of you wants to stay with your daughter? I'm sure you're concerned about her, but as I said, if you cooperate, none of you has anything to fear."

If. So much power in that word. So much promise.

"I'll stay with her," the mother said immediately, still shielding the girl with her body.

Joko noted the intensity of her protective instinct. If he needed additional coercion, the proper tool couldn't have been more obvious.

"Fine," Joko said, looking at the woman. "We only have a few things to ask. If your answers and your husband's answers match, this will be easy for you, and we'll leave quickly. If your answers don't match, this won't be easy for you. And we could be here for a long time. Do you understand?"

The woman nodded, her eyes burning.

Joko looked at the husband. "Do you understand?"

"I understand," the husband said.

For whatever reason—fear or hatred or both—the woman wanted to give as little as possible. Hence the mere nod. The husband understood their situation better. He was doing all he could to signal his cooperation. Hence the verbal reply.

Joko could tell from the woman's eyes and demeanor that she was intelligent. She would know as well as Joko, if not better, that her husband was going to cooperate. That would make her afraid not to, lest their answers not match.

"And you?" Joko said, looking at the girl. "Do you understand?"

The girl nodded. "Yes."

More like her father than her mother, it seemed. Not that it mattered. Joko had addressed her only to let the parents know their daughter was at risk, too—at least as much as they were.

Bambang knew what to do without being told. He and one of the other men led the father to the girl's room. The woman didn't even glance at them as they walked away. She was watching Joko too intently. The way a cobra watches a mongoose.

It didn't matter. The mongoose was faster. And this cobra had already been defanged.

"What's your name?" Joko said, looking at the mother.

"Joana."

He looked at the girl. "And you?"

"Alonsa."

Joko smiled. "That's a pretty name. For a pretty girl."

Joana, her voice shaking, said, "Ask us your questions. And then leave."

Joko looked at her. "I am asking my questions. Whether we leave depends on your answers. What was the doctor's name? Lie to me and I'll know it."

"Isobel," Joana said immediately.

"Her last name?"

"We didn't ask and she didn't say."

"Where is she from?"

"Dili. She works at a clinic there. Clínica Médica Internacional de Dili."

"What was she doing in Maliana?"

"She said she was here to help with an outbreak of typhoid. But that she got lost."

"Did that make sense to you?"

"No. It didn't make sense, but we didn't ask beyond that. All we cared about was that she was a doctor. Because a lot of people here are suffering." Tears sprang to the woman's eyes. "Suffering because of men like you."

Joko understood the outburst. The woman was obviously telling the truth, and therefore giving up someone she was grateful to. It didn't matter that she had no choice. Her guilt over the admissions demanded that she lash out.

But understanding the outburst didn't mean that Joko had to tolerate it. Another American expression he liked was *Give them an inch and they'll take a mile.* He had found it to be particularly true of the Timorese.

"Careful," Joko said, with a glance at Alonsa. "You're not suffering now. But you could be."

The woman was immediately silent. But the hatred never left her eyes.

A moment later, Joko was conferring with Bambang. The husband's answers matched perfectly those of his wife. They were lying about nothing, and they were holding nothing back.

They let the husband rejoin the women on the pallet. "Thank you," Joko said. "You were very helpful. We apologize for the intrusion. I'm afraid we did some damage to your front door upon entry—"

"We'll take care of it," Joana said.

Joko understood—there was nothing this woman would accept from him, no matter how badly she needed it. And why should she?

Still, he didn't like it. The defiance had never left her eyes. Not even when she had been struck silent by his reminder that she wasn't suffering, but could be.

The husband was a different matter. There was no defiance there, only gratitude, as strange as that might seem to someone who didn't know better. Even though Joko had invaded the man's house. Held him and his family at rifle point. Forced them apart and interrogated them separately, two of them on their own sleeping pallet. But the man understood there were other things Joko could have done, much worse things—and yet hadn't. It was amazing, how grateful people could be for the things you didn't do even in the face of what you did.

But the woman. Her insolence frustrated Joko. Because as long as the Timorese could stare with such hate even down the barrel of a gun, this half of the island would never be subdued.

Bambang looked at Joko. Joko knew what he was thinking. The same thing Joko was. *Let's see how insolent she is while we make her watch us fuck her daughter.*

He could feel himself getting excited at the prospect.

The woman must have sensed it, too, sensed that she had provoked him, that the "easy" interaction Joko had held out to them was about to become anything but. She dropped her head. "I only meant . . . ," she stammered. "I only meant . . . I know how busy you and your men must be, sir. I wouldn't want to have you waste your time on something as trivial as a door."

The father and daughter must have picked up on the same danger the woman had sensed, because they dropped their heads, as well.

Joko watched them all for a long moment, enjoying his power over them, their complete helplessness and submission. He couldn't reasonably require more.

Still, it would be so satisfying. To have gotten the information he wanted in exchange for a promise of restraint . . . to have them submit so utterly . . . and then to do everything to them anyway. All while letting them understand the reason for their ruin was the woman's stupid pride, her refusal to know her place and to accept Joko's dominion, and by extension, that of Kopassus.

He wanted to. But Felix knew Joko had come here to interrogate this family. Felix would learn what had happened, one way or the other. It was galling, given what Felix's own men were permitted, but for Felix to learn that Joko had gone outside parameters on a mission as sensitive as this one, especially after Joko's men had killed the girl by the well, especially after they had abducted the American journalist . . . Well, it wouldn't be good.

"That's considerate of you," he said. "Do I need to mention what would happen if I learned you tried to get word of this visit to the doctor?"

"No," the husband said immediately. "We understand completely."

Joko waited so they could stew a bit longer in their fear. But he'd already decided. He'd have to leave these three unharmed.

After a moment, he cocked his head toward the door, indicating to Bambang and the others that it was time to go. It was a shame, though. His men were hungry, and there was enticing food right in front of them.

Well, they could always find the food they craved somewhere else.

Besides, it didn't mean they were done with these three. When they didn't matter anymore, when Felix would have forgotten about them . . . that's when it would be time.

Time for another visit.

Chapter 17

Carl's flight landed in Dili at a little before noon. It had been a long trip—Abilene to Dallas, Dallas to Los Angeles, Los Angeles to Tokyo, Tokyo to Singapore, Singapore to Jakarta, and finally Jakarta to Dili. Over forty-eight hours door to door. And to think that despite the five-thousand-a-week paycheck and the bonus, that pencil neck Mossberg had initially tried to nickel-and-dime him by insisting the whole thing be done in coach.

"How do you fly?" Carl had asked him, and Mossberg had answered with a cagey, "It depends."

"Does it ever depend on your cover?" Carl said.

"Among other things," Mossberg said.

"Well, my cover, if I understand correctly, is that I'm an advance man for Western corporate interests, scouting locations for the airfields those interests will need for when the war is over, and it's time to start exploiting East Timor's minerals and timber and oil for the good of the local populace. Is that right?"

Mossberg grimaced. "I think you might want to focus more on how proper airfields will enable more efficient transportation of NGO personnel like doctors and aid workers to the people and places that most need help. And how this will benefit the local population directly, and also indirectly via employment opportunities for laborers and support staff."

"Yeah, yeah, we're bringing jobs to East Timor. However you want to put it. The companies in question have a lot of money, though, don't they? Maybe not quite as much as Uncle Sam, but plenty."

Mossberg, probably sensing where this was going, grimaced again. "Yes."

"So might it seem incongruous for said companies to send a valued contractor—a man with geological and engineering expertise and military experience doing site surveys and battle-area preparation—halfway around the world in cattle class?"

Mossberg was silent. After a long moment, he said, "I'll see what I can do."

But now, as the plane touched down, Carl found himself wondering whether what had initially felt like a victory had in fact been a setup. Because of course someone living his cover would fly first class. Mossberg would have expected Carl to push back against anything else. And, expecting some form of pushback, would have looked for a way to channel it in an acceptable direction, and thereby neutralize it. It made him wonder what else he might have bargained for if he'd been a little shrewder. Well, too late now. Besides, he'd gotten what he needed. He thought.

The plane hit the tarmac with a hard thump, then rattled over a series of what felt like giant gopher holes as it slowed. Carl smiled to himself as it shuddered to a stop, thinking, *Don't worry, I'm here to build some better airfields.*

There wasn't any kind of a wait to get off the plane—there were only three other passengers, one of whom wore a priest's collar, and the other two Carl made as Red Cross or such. He headed down the steps onto the tarmac, pack slung over his shoulders, and was instantly struck by the wet heat. But not in a bad way. It felt like the other places he'd visited in Southeast Asia—Thailand, Cambodia, Bali, various islands in the Philippines—all of which he'd loved. It smelled familiar, too, some fruit or spice he couldn't place but that he associated with nowhere outside the region. And those colors—reddish soil he could see at the edges of the landing strip, gray-blue sky, pale fog clinging to the green hills. It all might have felt idyllic, but for the camouflage netting strung up around some of the surrounding buildings and over a few parked planes, reminding whoever disembarked that although things might be quiet just this moment, Dili was still a war zone.

He passed through customs easily enough. The terminal was as hot and wet as the tarmac—which made sense, since the structure was open-air. It wasn't much, just the one gate, a lone kiosk, and the space itself even smaller than the airport in Abilene he'd left from. But despite the size, it was so empty that he could hear his footfalls echoing. Here and there he saw bored-looking Indonesian soldiers with M16s slung over their shoulders. They eyed him with curiosity, but no one gave him a hard time.

In front of the exit to the street, he spied a young man holding a hand-lettered sign: *Bill Dox.* The name on the passport Mossberg had arranged for him, and the backstopped legend. It felt right. Not so much the use of his last name, *Williams*, for *Bill*. But *Dox* instead of *Carl. Carl* was for the world of Tuscola—his family. Marla. Even Roy. People who'd known him before Afghanistan. *Dox* was for this world.

The young man waved, apparently recognizing the only white guy in the vicinity of the airport. "Mr. Dox?"

Dox nodded. "Howdy."

The young man gave him a sunny smile. "I'm your driver. Here from the hotel."

Dox looked him up and down. "The driver, huh? Pardon me for asking, but are you old enough to drive?"

The young man nodded just a touch too vigorously. "I'm seventeen."

Dox was aware that this didn't necessarily answer the question, but he decided to let it go. Of all the things that might kill him in Timor, it seemed a teen driver was unlikely to be at the top of the list.

"What's your name?"

"Fernando, Mr. Dox."

"Why don't you just call me Dox? Mr. Dox makes me sound like my father."

Fernando cocked his head. "You are American?"

"I am."

"And you prefer to be called by your last name?"

"As long as it's a term of endearment."

Fernando laughed, and Dox couldn't help smiling at the young man's joie de vivre.

"Then call me Fred," Fernando said. "That's an American name, yes?"

"It is indeed," Dox said. "And while I could be wrong, Fred, I'm getting the feeling you got hired for this job more for your language skills than for the presence of a valid driver's license. Wait, don't answer. Better if I don't know."

"Thank you, Mr. Dox. Dox. I learned my English from Australian television. G'day, yes? But I really am a very fine driver."

Dox nodded, noticing for the second time the mismatch between the inquiry and the response.

"We'll take the beach road," Fernando continued. "Slightly slower, but worth the views. You might want to sit in front. You are a large man, even for an American, if I may say."

Whatever the status of his driver's license, Fernando did drive competently, albeit slowly, navigating potholes and bomb holes and apologizing for each bump along the way. Dox had to admit, the cover legend Mossberg and the Agency had come up with made a fair amount of sense. Whoever won or lost, eventually the war here was going to wind down, and someone would have to clean up the mess.

Which would be good. It was a beautiful country—swaying palm trees lining the road, blue water and white beaches, a lush-looking island in the distance that Fernando told him was called Atauro. He'd decided while traveling in the region after Afghanistan that Southeast Asia was his kind of place. But it was strange to be back operationally in an environment that before had been an idyll.

The drive was only about eight kilometers, but between the condition of the road and two military checkpoints, it was almost an hour before they arrived at the Hotel Turismo. It was a strangely sleepy place—two stories, whitewashed concrete trimmed with brown wood, rows of verandas overlooking the road and the ocean beyond it. The parking lot in front, shaded by flowering trees, was nearly empty, an ancient BMW sedan, a rusting Volkswagen microbus, and a pair of mud-splattered olive-drab military jeeps the only evidence the establishment harbored any guests other than ghosts.

Dox had no luggage other than his rucksack, which Fernando insisted on carrying while accompanying him up a short flight of stairs to the entrance. The door was open, which Dox knew from experience meant no air-conditioning and plenty of mosquitos. It was quiet inside, even hushed, and their footfalls echoed off the tiled floors and plaster walls. The corridor was surprisingly cool, and unexpectedly dim in contrast to the bright day they'd come in from. From somewhere unseen came the rhythmic sound of slowly dripping water.

They came to the front desk. It wasn't much more than a table with a red plastic chair behind it, on which perched an ancient woman, a breeze from a desk fan fluttering the edges of the newspaper she was reading. She watched as Dox and Fernando approached, her expression impassive.

"Bill Dox," Fernando announced, before Dox could say anything himself. And then, in Portuguese Dox was able to make out because it was close enough to Spanish, "The American. Ocean view. Second floor."

Dox wasn't sure why all the particulars were necessary, given that he was probably about the only American within fifty miles, and possibly the only guest of the hotel as well. The woman presented him with a piece of paper. He signed it, and she handed him a key on a plastic fob.

"*Obrigadu barak,*" he said, Fernando having briefed him on the Tetum version of the Portuguese for *Thank you.*

The woman laughed, revealing a mouth stained so red it was almost black. *Betel chewing*, Dox realized. He'd heard about the stimulant and knew it was popular in the region, but he'd never come across it before. He'd tried qat in Afghanistan, and while it was all right, he didn't expect it to put chewing tobacco out of business, or coffee for that matter. He'd be sure to give betel leaves a go, though for the sake of his smile, he doubted he'd make it a lifelong habit.

"Lalika temi," the woman responded. From the crash course Fernando had offered on the way over, Dox knew this was *You're welcome*.

Fernando, who seemed to have cornered the market not just on hotel driving but on bell captain duties as well, insisted on carrying the ruck to the room. They took the stairs to the second floor, passing no one, and again Dox was struck by the solemn stillness of the place. Either they were having a very quiet war here, or this was some kind of calm before the storm.

The room was small, neat, and functional, with the promised ocean view and, most importantly, mosquito netting over the bed. He was tired, but he'd slept enough during several of the flights. He thought he could hold off until nightfall so as to get acclimated more quickly to the new time zone.

He turned to Fernando. "All right, Fred, I think I'll unpack and do a little exploring. But if your duties allow, tomorrow and thereafter I could use a driver. I need to start scouting for the kind of terrain that'll be suitable for aircraft takeoffs and landings."

"Of course, Mr. Dox. You can count on me for anything you need."

"I thought you were going to call me Dox."

"If you insist."

"You prefer Mr. Dox?"

Fernando tilted his head back toward where they had come from. "I think my employer would prefer it."

"Does anyone else here even speak English?"

"You make a fair point."

"Well, call me whatever you like."

Fernando gave him the sunny smile. "As long as it's a term of endearment."

"Exactly," Dox said with a laugh. He handed Fernando a hefty tip. "Grateful to you for the ride and the language lessons, and for carrying my bag."

Fernando held out his hand. "It's very nice to meet you, Mr. Dox."

"And you as well, Fred." They shook, and Fernando was gone.

Dox locked the door. In five minutes, he had finished unpacking and was enjoying a shower. The water was anemic and lukewarm, but still it felt like heaven after two days of travel.

He didn't bother to dry off—he knew he'd be sweating soon enough anyway. He just combed his hair; pulled on a pair of cargo shorts, a cotton safari shirt, and sneakers; and went out to explore.

Chapter 18

T he first thing he did was take a stroll around the hotel, both to acquaint himself with points of ingress and egress and also to locate somewhere to conceal a bug-out bag. War zones could be tricky, quiet one minute and crazy the next. It was never a good idea to assume you'd be able to retrieve things from your primary location if things went sideways. Hence the bug-out bag. The contents varied depending on circumstances, but in this case included currency, extra passport, knife, flashlight, waterproof matches, mylar blanket, duct tape, paracord, water filter, energy bars, fishing gear, and medical kit, all compressed into a large fanny pack. Plus several nonlubricated condoms, of course—not so much for close encounters, which tended to be not a priority when you were running for your life, but for their versatility as water carriers, water-proofers, and so on. There was always the temptation to add one more item, but you had to account for concealability, accessibility, and portability. This bag was his smallest, and he'd supplement it as he became more familiar with the environment. But in the meantime, if the shit hit the fan around here, a little bag would be a whole lot better than nothing.

He found a spot in an alley lined with trash cans at the south end of the hotel—a cinder-block wall pockmarked by what looked like artillery fire. He found a suitable hole, hid the bag inside it, and strolled on, checking his surroundings to be sure no one had seen him.

He headed out onto the main drag, such as it was. It was all low-slung buildings in various states of disrepair, punctuated here and there by vacant lots. A lot of rusted corrugated metal and cinder block, a lot of sagging awnings, a lot of unfinished construction that looked like it had been started a while before and wouldn't be finished for a long time to come.

There were uniformed Indonesian soldiers about, all of them brandishing M16s and looking on edge, and Dox wondered whether there had been a recent incident to account for the tension in the air. It couldn't be like this all the time—the occupation was in its sixteenth year. After that long, no matter how much underlying hostility, things would likely settle into a routine. At least that's how it had been in Afghanistan, where the war was eight years old when he'd arrived. But the soldiers he saw patrolling didn't feel like part of a routine. They felt like they were expecting a problem.

The people were tired, he could see it, and thin. A few glanced at him suspiciously, but most kept their eyes averted. He was a little surprised by that. As a white man, he expected he'd be more of a curiosity. Well, probably everyone here had experienced some kind of trouble with the Indonesians, or knew someone who had, and didn't want to do anything but keep their heads down and survive to the next day. He noticed there were no dogs about. Everywhere else he'd been in Southeast Asia he'd always seen dogs, resting in the shade, or trotting along in packs, or foraging by a dumpster. And then he realized with a start—the dogs must have been eaten.

Good lord.

He didn't know much about things like complicated geopolitics, as Mossberg had termed it, but anything that reduced people to eating dogs . . . Well, something was rotten in Denmark. You didn't have to be a grand strategist to know that, and in fact you could probably see it more clearly if you weren't.

But he was here to do a job, which if all went well would help him find a way to resolve the Roy situation. He had to try to focus on that.

He kept walking. But while being in a new place usually felt nothing but good to him, this time was different.

Chapter 19

T hree days after arriving, Dox was sitting at a round plastic table in the hotel's courtyard, sheltered from the overhead sun by a faded umbrella. Mossberg had told him this would be the time and place to meet his handler. Dox didn't understand why they would do it right out in the open, but the hotel was empty, and he supposed they knew what they were doing.

The courtyard was a grassy enclave enclosed on three sides by the hotel and with a wooden fence on the fourth. A pond sat at its center, crossed by a short wooden bridge and shaded by a skinny palm tree. The air was so still and sultry that even the insects in the bushes and trees seemed too tired to do anything but offer a weak background buzz. There was a floral scent Dox didn't recognize, along with the smell of the damp earth, and mold, and a whiff of diesel. He loved it instantly.

He'd spent his time so far living his cover—having Fernando drive him to various places that would be suitable for landing strips, asking lots of questions, giving himself a crash course on the country, the culture, and most of all the terrain. He felt he'd gotten a lot done, but of course it was really all just background. This meeting would be the start of the operation itself.

Within a minute of his arrival, a waiter emerged from a doorway. Dox watched as the man approached. Unlike Fernando, this was no teenager. He seemed somehow ageless instead, and Dox had the feeling this was someone who had been with the hotel for a long time, and who had probably seen a lot—maybe even more than he'd wanted to.

"Good afternoon," the man said in English. "Would you like to order something?"

"Thank you," Dox said. He glanced at a sign over the doorway the man had come through—*Victoria Bitter*. "I believe I'll try a Victoria Bitter. Ice cold if possible."

A minute later the man returned with a dewy bottle and glass balanced on a tray. He set them on the table and started to pour.

"May I ask you a question?" Dox said.

"Yes," the man said, his tone uncertain.

Dox had spent enough time with the spooks in Afghanistan to have picked up a few tricks. One was that whatever you asked risked revealing the intel you were missing. Two was that it was therefore sensible to conceal your real interest within a thicket of harmless questions. And three was that it was easier to keep people talking than it was to get them talking, so it was best to start with something harmless.

"Those plants over there," Dox said, pointing to some nearby vegetation. "With the beautiful hanging red flowers. I don't think I've ever seen something like that on my travels. What are they called?"

"I believe you would know it as hanging lobster claw, sir."

"Huh. Now that you mention it, I can see where it gets its name. Is that what's giving off that lovely smell?"

"I'm not sure, sir. It could be the hibiscus, but most people can't smell hibiscus. So perhaps jasmine."

"Jasmine. I thought I recognized it. Maybe it's a little different here than where I'm from."

"Where are you from, sir?"

Mossberg had told him to hide in plain sight. Which was fine. The truth was, he didn't know any other way to play it.

"I'm American," Dox said. "From the great state of Texas. Guessing you don't see so many Texans out this way? Or Americans generally, for that matter."

"That's true, sir. More Australians and New Zealanders."

Dox looked around. "I don't see any at the moment."

"Yes sir, it's been quiet."

That was noncommittal enough to suggest a degree of caution. Even fear. Maybe there were unseen people watching. Which again made him want to know—why this garden for a meeting?

Dox glanced at the man's name tag—*João Pereira.*

"João," he said. "Would it be all right if I call you that?"

The man frowned, perhaps in confusion. "Uh, yes."

"Thank you. I like to know a man's name. I'm Dox. I don't know how long I'm going to be here, João. A few weeks at least, maybe longer. I'm getting to know the lay of the land and I could use some pointers. Am I right in thinking you've been with the hotel for a while?"

João straightened a touch. "Almost a quarter century, sir."

"Well then, you're just the man I need. I—"

He stopped. Because suddenly João was looking past him, his expression that of someone confronted by a growling dog, and trying not to give it a reason to bite.

Dox glanced back. And saw three Indonesian soldiers advancing on him, all in tiger stripes and boonie caps. Two were on the flanks, M16s held at patrol carry. The third, a small but hard-looking man, was in the center and slightly ahead. He was carrying a CAR-15, the carbine version of the M16, preferred by special-ops types. The leader.

The three of them stopped a few feet away. The leader looked at João and gave a single sideways tilt of his head.

João glanced at Dox and managed, "If there's nothing else you need, sir." He was walking briskly away before Dox could even respond.

Dox instantly disliked the soldiers. Because of João's obvious fear and his dignified attempt to hide it, for starters. Along with the interruption of their conversation. On top of which, the arrogance with which the leader had signaled that João should scram.

But nothing to be done about it. It was their war. Dox was just here to do a job. Besides which, they had all the guns.

"Your papers," the leader said.

Dox's mind flashed on that night with Marla: *I'd say you might have done a little provoking yourself.*

But before he could stop himself, he said, "Don't you think that kind of thing sounds better in the original German?"

The leader stared at him, and Dox had the sense that the man didn't quite get the joke. But also the sense that the man didn't like that he didn't get it.

"You're a foreigner," the man said. "All foreigners in East Timor are required to carry their passports at all times and to present them upon demand. Ignorance is no excuse. If you're breaking the law, you'll be punished."

"Well, where's your passport? You're Indonesian, right? Ain't you a foreigner here, too?"

The man's stare hardened. Then, without so much as a glance at his men, he said something in Bahasa. Instantly Dox was looking at the muzzles of two M16s, both pointed at his chest.

"Your papers," the man said, his eyes flat. "I hope for your sake you're carrying them."

Dox slowly raised his hands, fingers splayed. He'd met a few killers in his time. Not the kind who did it as part of a job. There were plenty of those, and he himself was one such. No, there was another kind, the kind that did it because it was what they liked. Because they were good at it. Because killing made them feel alive.

This guy was that type.

So while he wanted to say, *I'd prefer a simple "please,"* he understood that some people you could fuck with. And some it was better not to.

"It's in my back pocket. Okay if I stand and reach for it slowly?"

The man smiled, and something about the smile confirmed the *some it was better not to* diagnosis. "You can reach as fast as you like."

"It's kind of you to offer, but I'll keep it slow."

He stood and handed over the passport. The man opened and examined it. The two soldiers to his flanks, still as statues, continued to point their rifles.

"William Dox," the man said. "American." He looked up from the passport. "What are you doing in East Timor?"

"Site surveys. I gather your government is planning on some post-war rebuilding, which will require airfields and such. I'm here to do the advance work."

"You're military?" the man said. He hadn't given back the passport, which wasn't necessarily a bad sign, but it wasn't a good one, either.

"I used to be. Engineer. I built bridges and buildings and watch-towers, cleared runways, even dammed a river or two. Who else do you think the suits could get to come to a war zone and do this shit, some pencil neck with a yard stick and a degree from MIT? Good luck with that. But these days, no, I'm strictly private sector."

Usually when Dox talked this much, he could feel the person on the other end start to soften, or at least get confused. But this guy didn't so much as blink. Literally—he just kept staring.

"Airfields," the man said after a moment.

"That's right."

"You must know a lot about the subject."

"I hope so. Otherwise, my employer is wasting its money."

"And your employer is . . . ?"

"REESE Incorporated. That's Rare Earth Engineering and Surveying Enterprises. Would you like a card?"

The man said nothing. Just the stare. His nostrils twitched, and Dox had the weird sense the man was smelling him.

He decided to take the silence as a yes and handed over a card. The legend was backstopped, the address and phone and fax numbers real. There were even people who would answer calls and respond to letters. Say what you would about Christians in Action, they counted on lies being probed, and made sure to be ready.

The man glanced at the card, then back to Dox. "You must be a topography expert."

There were a lot of advantages to being from a small town near Abilene, among them the way some people assumed it meant you were dumb. Thereby proving who the dumb ones really were. And while this guy wouldn't know Abilene from abalone, Dox had the sense that he was making the same kind of mistake. Because his use of the word *topography* felt like an attempt to show off his English skills. And if he was focused on showing off, it meant he wasn't focused on what mattered. Which was if he thought Dox would get tripped up by even the most cursory questions, he was about to be disappointed. After all, Christians in Action weren't the only ones who knew a thing or two about getting their lies straight.

"Topography," Dox said. "Well, sure, there's drainage, grading, slope, and obstacles and dimensions and such, especially when you're looking to clear ground for an airstrip. But that's not the half of it. You've also got your soil type and composition, and those'll kill you, especially in the rainy season. We had crushed volcanic rock runways in Sudan—such as in Rumbek where I sojourned for several years—that were usable in any season. But then we also had cotton soil runways, which were a problem for fixed-wing aircraft in both extremes of dry and wet. A lot of people don't know it until it's too late, but in the rainy season cotton soil can turn into a gooey mess. I've had to run at a dead heat to get on a plane and off a runway just because I saw clouds moving in—yeah, the rain can come that fast in Sudan, let me tell you. And once that cotton soil is wet, you need at least two days, and more like three, under Sudan's sunny skies to dry it enough to get out—and even that's pushing it. Conversely, in extreme heat, cotton soil cracks. Furrows so big it's dangerous to run a bush plane tire over them. Hell, there was this one time—"

"Shut the fuck up," the man said.

Dox glanced at the M16s, which were still pointed at his chest. That, plus the man's tone, made it seem compliance was the right way to go.

The man stared at him. "You think I'm an idiot?"

Dox held up his hands in a gesture of innocence. "On the contrary. I'm impressed by your English. Where'd you learn it? It's pretty good."

The man kept staring. "Pretty good? It's better than yours."

Dox offered what he hoped would be perceived as a friendly smile. "Like I said, pretty good."

The man said nothing, and Dox had an unpleasant feeling that a decision was about to be made.

"You're lying to me," the man said.

And . . . it didn't look like the decision was apt to be the one Dox was hoping for. "Why would I lie?"

"Because you're a spy."

"A spy? Do I look like a spy?"

"You look like a dead man."

Dox felt a chill behind his ears and down his spine. This was going badly and getting worse, and he couldn't figure out how to turn it around.

"Look," he said. "At your request, I gave you my passport and my card. I'm an American, here at the invitation of your government. How else would I have even gotten into the country? If you'll check my credentials, you'll see I'm telling the truth."

"You lie to my face, stupid American?" The man added something in Bahasa. Instantly his men took a crisp step back and to the side and raised their rifles so the muzzles were pointing right at Dox's eyes.

"I'm not lying," Dox said, his hands still raised. He had a weird and detached sense that every word coming out of his mouth might be the last. "I'm not trying to be disrespectful. I'm just respectfully asking if you would please be kind enough to check my credentials. You can always shoot me afterwards if you still want to, isn't that right? I'd be more than happy to wait."

The man stared at him, his eyes cold and unreadable, and Dox could tell none of it had worked; he hadn't managed to distract the man, or reason with him, or do anything else that was going to change what was about to happen, which was that two 5.56 millimeter rounds were going to punch through his face and blow out the back of his skull, and no one would even know what had happened to him, his mom, Ronnie, he'd let them all down—

The man started laughing. Dox thought, *What the fuck?* and felt his legs wobble.

The man glanced at Dox's shaking knees and laughed harder. Dox felt a sudden murderous rage, but there was nothing he could do, neither to stop his knees from knocking nor to stop this guy from laughing at him. He supposed it could have been worse—at least he hadn't pissed himself.

The man laughed for what seemed a long time. His men didn't so much as crack a smile. They kept the muzzles of their rifles trained on Dox's face. It was clear that if the man's mood changed and he uttered a single command, they would fire.

Finally the man's laughter died down. He said, "What brings you to the island of Grandfather Crocodile?"

Dox blinked, so surprised that for a moment he couldn't respond. The man had just given him the bona fides for the contact Dox was here to meet. Which meant . . . this man *was* the contact. It all suddenly made sense. The meeting, right here, out in the open . . . Well, why not? The way the man had played it, to anyone watching it would look anything but clandestine.

"I, uh," Dox stammered, thoroughly flummoxed. Then he managed to mentally locate the response bona fides: "I came for the waters."

The man laughed again. "You were so scared, I thought you were going to make water."

Dox slowly lowered his arms and put a hand on the table to steady himself. He wanted to say, *Let's see how you do when I'm the one pointing the rifle at you.* But mad as he was, he wasn't mad enough to be that stupid.

The man held out Dox's passport. Dox took it with a shaking hand and returned it to his back pocket. The man said something to his soldiers. They lowered their rifles.

"All right," Dox said. "You've had your fun. I was told you'd have a file?"

"While we were talking, I had it placed in your room. Under the mattress. It contains photographs and all particulars for the subject. Memorize and then burn it."

"Never would have thought to do that. Thanks for the tip."

The man said nothing. For a moment, Dox thought he was going to order his soldiers to raise their rifles again, or worse. Killing a CIA contractor would be a bold move for someone under orders to make contact, and Dox felt more confident now that he knew this guy was his handler. But he'd have to watch himself anyway. The guy didn't seem like the most stable specimen ever, on top of which, Dox's urge to counter-provoke was definitely making its presence known.

The man removed his boonie hat. Dox had seen the shaved sides of his scalp and assumed a high and tight, maybe a recon, but now he saw it was a straight-up mohawk, nothing but a short, thin strip front to back.

"I see you're a Travis Bickle fan," Dox said. "You sure you need the haircut, though? People would probably get the feeling you're a psycho even without it."

The man looked at him. "Bickle wasn't a psycho. He was the movie's hero. He rescued Jody Foster's character, Iris; he was celebrated by her parents and the city; and he earned the desire of Cybill Shepherd, too."

"I think you're being too literal there. Everything that happened after the shootout was in De Niro's head as he lay dying."

The man frowned, which gave Dox tremendous satisfaction.

"You made a mistake," Dox went on. "It happens. But don't worry, it'll grow out."

"Her name is Isobel Amaral," the man said, managing a better-than-most effort to ignore Dox's taunts. "She's a doctor. Her English is good. She's young and very pretty. Maybe you'll get to have fun with her."

Dox didn't answer. His taunts had been restorative, it was true, but still he felt a strong desire to put a hurt on this man and knew he had to manage it.

"Her clinic is just a few blocks from here," the man went on. "She's there today."

"Yeah? What am I supposed to do, just go in for a checkup?"

"East Timor has all sorts of tropical maladies. Malaria. Typhoid. Dengue fever. Tuberculosis. Ask for a briefing."

Dox felt his animosity boiling over again. "You know, amigo, your English is tops, but maybe you're not quite as bright as you think. My company would have made sure to brief me, and to inoculate me, before sending me out here. In fact, my company—the Company—did. It'd make no sense at all for me to go to a local clinic asking for the same."

The man's cold stare returned. Dox realized he was the type who would be dangerous when he thought you were scared—and even more dangerous if it seemed you weren't.

But before he could finish processing the thought and what it might mean, the man's right hand blurred forward. Dox saw a flash of metal and jerked back. For a second, he thought the man had missed. Then he felt a flash of hot pain. He glanced at his left shoulder—blood was flowing out of a long cut through the material of his shirt and the skin and muscle beneath. He slapped a hand over the wound and grimaced.

"You're right," the man said, smoothly returning a karambit to a sheath on the right side of his belt. "It would make more sense for you to go to the clinic to have that cut sewn up. You can even say you provoked an Indonesian soldier, who taught you a lesson about who you are and what your life is worth here. Maybe that will help establish your bona fides. Maybe you and Amaral will even bond over it."

Dox looked from the man to the two soldiers flanking him and back again.

"Nothing?" the man said. "Not even a thank-you?"

Dox tried to suppress his rage. It wasn't going to help him. Maybe just get him cut more. Or killed.

After a moment, he felt a little more in control of himself. "So you're my handler."

"Yes. Although I don't know what I did to deserve it."

"A comedian, too, I see."

"I never joke. Along with the file under your mattress, you'll find an encrypted radio. Use it to contact me for anything you need."

"What do I call you?"

"My name is Joko Sutrisno. You can call me Joko."

Dox stared into the man's eyes. "Joko. All right. I won't forget this, Joko."

Joko smiled. It wasn't a warm smile. Not at all. More like something you'd see on the face of a boy looking forward to boiling a frog alive, or to pulling the wings off some flies.

"I don't want you to," Joko said. "Dox." He said something to his men. The three of them turned and walked away.

Dox watched. All at once, his legs were shaking again, this time worse. He wanted to steady himself by grabbing the table, but the one arm was hurt and the other was busy stanching the wound.

He sank into the chair and waited. The shakes passed surprisingly quickly. He wondered at that, then realized why.

It was the sudden certainty that somehow, at some point, he was going to kill this Joko.

The only shame of it was that probably the man wouldn't see it coming. But Dox would try to make sure he did.

Chapter 20

Dox walked through town, pressing a handful of cloth napkins tight against his shoulder.

João had seen what happened. As soon as the soldiers were gone, he had rushed out with some napkins to stanch the blood. Then he ran and got Fernando, who was still at the hotel and wanted to drive Dox to the clinic. Dox wouldn't let him.

"It was just some asshole," Dox had reassured them. "Drunk on power. But right now he's my problem. I don't want him to become yours or anyone else's. Just tell me how to get to the clinic. I understand it's close by, and if so, I'm happy to walk." They'd been reluctant, but they were scared, too, and they didn't insist.

He pressed the napkins more tightly to his shoulder and kept moving, trying to focus on what he was here for. He hadn't even had time to read the damn file before that *pendejo* had cut him. But there was some truth to the notion that the wound would be a solid reason to visit the clinic, and might even help establish some degree of trust.

Not that it would make any difference later, of course. When it was time for payback.

He found the clinic easily enough—it was a long, white building with a green cross painted over the entrance. Just as Fernando had described. There were dozens of people lined up on the sidewalk outside. Dox wasn't sure about decorum or how they performed triage in these parts, but at this point, despite the napkins, his entire arm was covered with blood, and it was dripping from his hand, too. He hated to be rude in a new place, but he thought he'd better not wait.

He went through a pair of swinging doors into a rectangular, fluorescent-lit waiting area with faded gray linoleum flooring and walls painted powder blue. On either side was a corridor, each presumably leading to treatment rooms. The windows were open, and a big fan, loud enough to be a jet engine, was creating a welcome breeze. The air blowing past him smelled of antiseptic, which under the circumstances was reassuring. There were a good thirty people, leaning against the walls and seated in plastic chairs, but none seemed to be bleeding out or otherwise in immediate distress.

An older woman in a white nurse's dress and cap the likes of which Dox hadn't seen since he was a child, at least not outside a fetish video, noticed that he was bleeding onto the linoleum and rushed over. *"O que aconteceu?"* she said in Portuguese. It wasn't close enough to Spanish for Dox to recognize, but *What happened?* seemed a good enough guess for government work.

"Somebody cut me," he said.

"Sem inglês," the nurse said, looking at his shoulder. For some reason, he thought she looked suspicious of him. But maybe he was being paranoid.

She motioned with her hand. *"Venha. Venha comigo."*

Dox followed, looking around. There were other women in nursing attire, tending to some of the waiting people and bustling to and fro, but he didn't see anyone who looked like a doctor. Of course he wanted to get patched up. But how was he going to make contact with this Isobel Amaral?

A petite woman in a white smock with a stethoscope around her neck emerged from one of the treatment rooms alongside a young mother carrying a crying little boy. The woman was stroking the boy's hair and speaking to him reassuringly in Tetum. On instinct, Dox called out, "Does anyone here speak English?"

The woman looked over. Dox caught her eye and felt weirdly certain this was her.

"Hello," he said. "I'm bleeding bad, can you help me?"

The woman said something to the young mother, who nodded eagerly. Then she patted the little boy's back and walked briskly over to Dox. Like the nurse, her expression seemed suspicious—even a little afraid.

"What happened?" she said, leaning in and looking at his arm.

Dox had intended to check her name tag, but he was suddenly so taken that for a moment he forgot. Her eyes were soft brown, and kind but at the same time no-nonsense. A row of freckles was splashed across her nose and cheeks, which made her look younger than she probably was, and her hair was back, exposing the smooth brown skin of a long neck. A delicate pair of clavicles showed inside the collar of the smock.

"Pardon me," he said, looking back to her face and trying to collect himself. "Are you a doctor?"

"Yes," the woman said, frowning with evident irritation. "What happened?"

He glanced, but couldn't see the name tag. "Somebody cut me. Some asshole soldier. Pardon my language. It was a little upsetting."

The woman straightened and looked at him. Now her expression seemed confused. Because he had called a soldier an asshole? He wondered—had she seen some of Felix's people? Maybe that's why she seemed suspicious. She thought Dox was working with the Indonesians. Or maybe she was just wondering what an American was doing in Dili, let alone in her clinic.

The woman said, "All right. Rosa is a nurse. She'll have a look. If you need stitches, she'll take care of it." She turned to leave.

"Hang on," Dox said, trying to think of a way to improvise. "I mean, you said you're a doctor."

The woman turned back to him, but damn it, he still couldn't see the name tag. "I assure you," she said. "Rosa is—"

"My name's Dox. And you are?"

The woman glanced at wherever she had been heading when Dox had first called her over. "Dr. Amaral. As I was saying, Rosa has stitched up more cuts than anyone else here. More than I have. You'll be in very capable hands." She started to turn away again.

"Wait," Dox said. "I'm sorry, it's just, I'm new to these parts, and I'm a little, uh, germophobic. I'd really be more comfortable being attended to by an actual medical doctor rather than just a nurse." He glanced at Rosa. "No disrespect, of course."

The woman looked at him, and he could tell she was getting irritated. "We have over fifty people waiting, and every one of them would like to see a doctor. We don't have enough to go around."

"I could help with that," Dox said before he had a chance to even think. "I mean, my employer could make a contribution to your clinic. If you treat me."

The woman stared at him for a moment as though she couldn't believe his presumption. "Your employer?"

"Yes."

"And who is your employer?"

"Rare Earth Engineering and Surveying Enterprises. They sent me out here to do site surveys. Airfields and such."

The woman kept staring. He had the sense that as irritated as he'd made her, she was trying to decide whether his offer was real.

"How much?" she said.

Dox had no idea how much. He glanced around and said, "Five hundred dollars."

"Five thousand."

"What? Six hundred."

"Six thousand."

"Hey, it doesn't work like that. You're going in the wrong direction."

"Seven thousand."

"A second ago you said five!"

"Then make it five. Or again, you can have the exceptionally competent Rosa take care of you."

"I don't know if I can—"

"You work for a rich Western corporation?"

"Well, I'm outsourced, but—"

"They don't need the five thousand dollars. Look around you. We do."

Dox glanced around, then back to her. "I see your point. All right, it's a deal."

"You have the money with you?"

"No. I mean, not all of it. But I'll get the rest."

"When?"

"Don't you care that I'm standing here bleeding?"

"Yes, that's why I offered to have Rosa take care of your injury."

"It's not an injury, it's a wound. Look, I have a few hundred US with me. I'll get the rest."

The woman said a few words in Tetum to the nurse, then looked at Dox. "Give what you have to Rosa."

"You mind giving it to her yourself? My wallet's in my left front pants pocket. I'd get it, but if I let go of my shoulder, I'm concerned I might bleed out right in front of you and thereby cause you to violate your Hippocratic oath."

The corner of the woman's mouth twitched. Was she trying to keep a straight face? He had a feeling she would have a beautiful smile. He realized he wanted to see it.

She took out his wallet, extracted all the bills, gave them to Rosa, and said a few more words in Tetum. Rosa nodded and walked away. The woman returned the wallet to Dox's pocket. He was very aware of how close she was standing, and that she was touching him, albeit briefly.

"My name's Dox," he said.

"Yes, you said. It's a strange name."

"Well, it's my last name."

She took a step back. "It's still strange."

"I suppose so. What's your name?"

"I told you. Dr. Amaral."

"Come on. I mean your first name."

There was a pause, and maybe the woman was thinking she shouldn't tell him. Then she said, "Isobel."

He smiled without even meaning to. "Isobel. That's a pretty name."

She shook her head as though he'd served up a line, even though he really hadn't meant it that way. "All right, Mr. Dox, come with me and we'll have a look at your wound."

"Thank you for appreciating its wound status. It makes me feel more important. But would you mind calling me just Dox? My first name's Bill, but my friends call me Dox."

She looked at him. "That's your friends. I'm your doctor."

"Well, what if we were friends?"

She shook her head as though incredulous. *"Oh, meu Deus."*

"Hey," he said. "Are you trying not to smile?"

"No."

"Because you can if you like. I wouldn't object."

She sighed. "Do you want me to stitch up your shoulder? Or would you rather just stand there bleeding?"

"I actually forgot I was bleeding. Maybe that's why I feel light-headed. What's your medical opinion?"

"My medical opinion is that you should stop talking—if you can—and follow me to a treatment room so I can examine your shoulder."

She turned and walked briskly away. He hustled after her, and a moment later he was sitting in a small room while she cut away what was left of his bloody shirtsleeve. The room, already cramped, was divided by curtains into three sections. Under the curtains, he could see the feet of people waiting to be looked at. Wound or no wound, it made Dox feel guilty for what he'd done to jump the line.

"This is a deep cut," Isobel said. "And clean. It must have been a very sharp blade."

"I have no doubt of it," Dox said.

She swabbed the site with alcohol, then pulled a syringe from a plastic package. "Lidocaine," she said. "It'll sting for a second."

"That's fine. I've been stung worse." He looked away, though. He never did like to watch a needle go in.

"What happened?" she said, and he felt the promised sting.

He told her about the encounter at the hotel, of course leaving out the parts about the guy actually being his Agency contact.

"It happens sometimes," she said. "If they weren't bastards before they came here, they become bastards after. How did you get into Timor, anyway? The Indonesians allow very few Westerners."

"You ever get any here at your clinic?"

She glanced at him suspiciously. "Not often. Why?"

Yeah, he'd been right. These folks had dealt with Felix's people. And didn't like them.

"Just wondering if I'm the first Westerner you've treated."

She held his eyes for a moment, then went back to his shoulder. "You're not."

He could feel a little pressure from the sutures she was putting in, but that was all. "Anyway," he said. "As to how I got in, REESE is a big corporation. And I don't have to tell you, money talks."

"It didn't talk you out of getting cut."

"No, I don't think the fellow who did it was much interested in money. He struck me as the type who's in his line of work more out of love."

A moment later, she affixed a big bandage to his shoulder. "Thirty stitches. You'll have a scar, but it'll be straight at least. Change the bandage if it gets wet. You can buy some extras at the window by the exit. And some antibiotic cream."

He flexed his arm. "You've got a nice touch. I didn't feel a thing."

She gave him a long-suffering look. "Yes, lidocaine can do that."

"Oh, now you're making fun of me, I can tell."

She pulled off the nitrile gloves she was wearing and tossed them in a metal basket. "I have to go. You've put me behind schedule."

"Well, maybe we could get together on another occasion? When you're not as busy, I mean."

This time, she didn't look like she was trying to suppress a smile. She looked pissed.

"Do you think you're entitled?" she said. "Because you're American and I'm Timorese? Because you're white and I'm brown? You think because your money can buy medical services, you can buy anything?"

It all caught him totally off guard. "No," he said. "I don't think any of that. At least . . . I don't think I do."

He felt suddenly confused. He'd set aside the knowledge of what he was really doing here, and why he was supposed to get close to her. It hadn't been hard—he was drawn to her, more than drawn, and he'd just been going with that. He didn't think he'd been doing anything different with her than he'd done with anyone, anywhere else he'd ever been.

On the other hand, some of those other places, like Olongapo . . . it was true American dollars could buy almost anything there. He remembered seeing Marines throwing coins into Shit River and laughing as desperate kids dove in to retrieve them. Dox had never even been tempted to do something like that, but did he feel entitled there in other ways? It would be hard to argue that he didn't.

"I didn't mean it the way it sounded," he said. "But . . . what you said about the Indonesian soldiers. That if they weren't bastards before they came here, they become bastards after. I can see where that would apply to a lot of things. But . . . anyway, I don't even know what I'm trying to say. I'm sorry."

Her expression softened. "I didn't mean to compare you to them. I don't think you're like that."

He was supposed to be a spy, so her confidence should have pleased him. Instead, it made him feel guilty.

"I really didn't mean to be rude. I appreciate what you did for me here. I was bleeding a lot, but I shouldn't have jumped the line. How do I get the clinic the rest of what I owe you?"

She shook her head. "You seem like a nice guy, Dox. But we both know the minute you walk out of here, you'll forget all about the rest of what you promised."

"That's not—"

"It's all right. The money I took from your wallet is a lot for a clinic like this one. It was a good bargain."

They were quiet for a moment. Then he said, "We don't know each other, Isobel, but when I make a bargain, I hold up my end. So though it pains me to say it, now you're the one insulting me."

She looked at him as though trying to gauge whether he was serious. "You're really going to give us the rest of that money?"

"Of course I am."

"Why?"

"Because I told you I would. Now, I expect I'll get it from my company. But if I can't, it'll come out of my own pocket."

She looked at him, the anger he'd sensed a moment ago gone. "I feel like I should say no. That was a deep cut. Maybe it's true I had you under a little duress. But . . ."

She looked down for a moment, then back to him. When she spoke, her voice was low, almost as though she was sharing a secret, or admitting something shameful. "We really need it."

"It's okay. I'm glad you're letting me help."

She nodded.

"Even though it was of course wrong of you as a physician and healer to take advantage of my circumstances."

Her mouth dropped open and her eyes widened in indignation. He smiled to let her know he was just giving her a hard time.

She smiled back. "Very funny."

He might have made another crack, but he couldn't think of one. And had no desire to, either. Her smile, even in exasperation, was even more lovely than he'd imagined. For a moment, all he wanted was just to look at her.

He realized his mission here was going to be more complicated than he'd been expecting.

"I'll be back with what I promised," he said. "It might take me a day or two, but you can count on it."

She nodded, then smiled again. Smaller than the last time, but there was no exasperation in it.

"We'll see," she said.

Chapter 21

It was evening, and Isobel was sitting in the nurses' lounge, enjoying an egg sandwich and a short break. It was a small room, devoid of creature comforts save for a plastic table and chairs and a worn upholstered couch. But its single window faced west, and Isobel always enjoyed the way the room felt late in the day, the fluorescent overheads turned off, the setting sun spotlighting one corner, the diffused illumination giving the room a comforting, golden glow.

Mostly it had been a straightforward day. A variety of childhood fevers. Some bad cases of diarrhea. A lot of advice to give on sanitation and hygiene, because being a doctor in Timor was as much about teaching self-care as it was about administering medical care. So much of what was killing the country's children wasn't even disease. It was the vulnerability to disease—the poor nutrition and resulting reduced resistance, compounded by poor hygiene and lack of cleanliness, leading to more disease and more disease vectors. The magnitude of it all . . . Sometimes it overwhelmed her.

The trick was not to look at the big picture, but instead to focus on the individual cases—each person, each child, she was able to help. She knew other doctors who were able to maintain that focus. They did no less good than she did, and they seemed happy, too. Or at least happy enough. And what was wrong with that? Nothing.

But no matter how hard she tried, sometimes she couldn't help feeling like all she was doing was bailing out a sinking boat with a tiny tin cup. A cup with holes in it. It was exhausting her, and the boat was sinking anyway.

She ate the sandwich slowly to make it last, chewing carefully, washing down each small bite with a big swallow of water. She knew from her studies that food rituals were associated with disorders like anorexia and bulimia, and with ordinary chronic hunger, as well. And while here at the clinic they weren't going hungry, it was also true that no one ever had enough to quite get full.

The little victories were what kept her going. The young mothers who listened when she told them that by far the best food for their babies was breast milk, not anything imported from the West in a can. Or that lots of water could be better than cough medicine for even a nasty cough. That for the most part, their money was better spent on food than on medicine.

But so often, people didn't listen. They believed that if something came from the West, if it was expensive, if it was scarce . . . it was what they needed. That if only they could obtain such treasures, it would make their children healthy and happy and strong, like the Australian children they had seen on television.

The sandwich was disappearing too fast. She nibbled around the crust and chewed more slowly.

It was always hard. But as overwhelmed as Isobel felt in the face of all the ordinary health problems that had grown rampant everywhere after the Indonesians had invaded, it was the rapes, and the terrible aftereffects of the rapes, that haunted her most. Those sobbing girls, some so ashamed they couldn't even tell their families, and the trauma they recounted . . . It was almost unbearable. She would tell them it wasn't their fault, that they had nothing to be ashamed of, that the shame belonged only to the men who did such things . . . but the words were barely a balm.

At first, when some of the girls reported that their attackers had been Americans, Isobel thought they must have been mistaken. The Indonesians were restricting foreign access, the better to conceal the brutality of their occupation. How could these girls have been attacked by Americans? Where would they even have come from?

AMOK

And then Isobel started to see them herself. Sometimes, not often, they would ride through town in their jeeps, stopping only to buy food or medicine or other supplies. They were dressed like civilians. But their hair was short. They were young and looked fit. And they wore the same kinds of watches and sunglasses the Indonesian soldiers wore. Probably the Indonesian soldiers were imitating them.

Isobel had collaborated with many aid workers. These men were nothing like them. They didn't engage with the people. Instead, they kept apart from them, saying little, buying what they needed, disappearing back to wherever they had come from.

Once, two of them had come to the clinic carrying a third between them, the middle one with his arms around the necks of the other two and their arms around his back. The middle one had suffered a crush injury across his legs, which were covered in blood and dragging behind him. *An accident,* one of the men had curtly explained. He was scary-looking, big and with a nasty scar running vertically above and below his left eye. Even in response to her questions, he would offer no further details. Only, *Fix him. And you better do it right.*

Isobel tried. But the man had developed rhabdomyolysis—crush syndrome—from his injuries, and resultant hypovolemic shock. It didn't help that his comrades had mistreated his case, tying off his legs with tourniquets and opening one of them with a prophylactic fasciotomy. Isobel had staff hydrate the man, but they got no further than that. Within minutes, he had an arrythmia. They attempted defibrillation, but the clinic's unit was ten years out of date, and anyway it was too late. The man proceeded to cardiac arrest, and died on the table.

The men who brought him had been furious, accusing Isobel and her staff of inadequate treatment. Isobel had gotten angry in turn, pointing out the refusal of the men to share potentially important diagnostic information and their contraindicated field treatment. The man with the scar had become so angry that he reached for something under his shirt, and Isobel had caught a glimpse of a gun. But the other man had stopped him. They said nothing more, simply loading their dead comrade into a jeep and vanishing like ghosts.

But they weren't ghosts. Sometimes people saw them at the edges of the forest, and what they were doing there no one could say. Sometimes they would drive by a farm, watching the workers like owls staring at mice. And sometimes they would catch a girl, when she was alone in a field or at her chores, and drag her off, like monsters from a fairy tale.

Isobel felt as helpless about their presence as everyone else. But one day, she realized there was something she could do. Or at least, try to do.

Some of the girls could barely speak of what had been done to them. But others refused to let the soldiers silence them with shame. They wanted to fight, and their voices were their weapons. All they needed was someone to hear them.

Isobel had bought an old VHS video camera and some cassette tapes from a store selling scavenged electronic equipment. She started to tape the girls who were willing.

The stories were horrifyingly similar. The earlier rapes had been carried out by Indonesian soldiers. There were whole villages where the women had been separated from the men and then systematically raped, sometimes for days on end. These were not isolated incidents or the actions of rogue soldiers. The methodology was always the same, the soldiers clearly implementing a central policy.

Which wasn't to say there was no variation. Even in the midst of such atrocities, again and again in the victims' recounting there was one unit that stood out. A squad of Kopassus soldiers, commanded by a Sumatran named Joko, identifiable by his signature haircut—a mohawk. Joko's men were particularly sadistic. And Joko himself inspired exceptional terror, apparently by actually eating the hearts of any Falintil fighters who dared resist him.

More recently, the mass rapes seemed to have abated. Isobel didn't know why. But the less systematic variety was still widespread. And the perpetrators were no longer primarily Indonesian, with less frequent atrocities being committed by pro-Indonesia Timorese militias. Now there were non-Indonesian foreigners involved as well. And while the victims couldn't name their attackers, they described them. Girl after girl gave similar accounts. Mostly whites, along with two blacks and one Asian. American accents. And one, who the others called Waster, who had a scar on the left side of his face from something that had narrowly missed his eye.

The same man, Isobel realized from the girls' descriptions, who had wanted to shoot her for being unable to save his comrade.

After three months, she had enough material, more than enough. She was stalling, she realized, afraid to take the next step.

But eventually, she had contacted Beeler. She told Beeler who she was and what she had. Beeler told her what to do—the meeting in Maliana, the instructions, the bona fides.

Isobel went to meet her. And then everything had gone wrong.

At the time, she thought it would be better to leave the tapes close to the border, where Beeler had wanted to do the exchange. She had been terrified that she might be caught with them—both for what it would mean for her, and because if she were caught, the stories those girls had suffered—re-suffered—to tell would all be lost.

But now she wondered. Unless Beeler reappeared, there would be no way to know what had happened to her. At some point, Isobel would have to assume the worst. She would have to find, and find a way to trust, another Western reporter.

There were men she was certain were with Falintil. Sometimes they would come to the clinic with wounds that could only have been sustained in combat. Should she give the videos to one of them? Could she trust them? She had been tempted. But the risk seemed too great. Not just the risk that she would entrust the videos to an incompetent, or worse, a turncoat, or to someone who might be tempted to do anything with the girls' testimony but find a way to have it heard. She had also been afraid to involve herself too directly with the guerillas. Kopassus had burned clinics to the ground in revenge for disobedience, more than once with the staff and patients still inside. She couldn't put her clinic and her people at such risk. Not when there was a better way.

But who else was there? The Indonesians allowed in almost no reporters. The ones with permission were useless or co-opted. Beeler was different—she had learned how to sneak in across the border. Very few were willing to take a risk like that.

Not that Isobel could blame them. For all she knew, Beeler was dead now. Or soon would be.

The American who had come to the clinic earlier that day—Dox. At first, Isobel had thought he was one of the Americans—the monsters, the rapists. But then she realized she'd been wrong. He looked like them, it was true. But he said he was staying at the Turismo, while those other Americans . . . Well, no one knew where they came from or where they went.

Beyond which, Dox talked far more. Not just more than the Americans—more than anyone she'd ever met. And there was a . . . kindness to him. An awkwardness she couldn't deny was endearing.

She felt bad that he had thought she was comparing him to the soldiers. She could think of no worse insult than that. She was glad she had been able to explain herself. But would he really come back to the clinic with the money he had promised?

For some reason, she thought he would.

Of course, she was foolish to believe it. But they needed the money so much. There was a black market in Timor—the same, Isobel supposed, as in any other war zone. Sometimes, the clinic was able to buy imported medicines from the Indonesian soldiers. But the prices were exorbitant, and they accepted only Indonesian rupiahs. And US dollars, of course.

For a second, she wondered whether this man Dox might smuggle the videos out of the country for her. But she immediately rejected the idea as absurd. She didn't know him. She couldn't trust him. Besides which, how could she ask something like that of a stranger? It could easily mean his death.

Her sandwich was done. She folded the plastic bag she had brought it in and peeled an orange, separating the segments, removing and eating the translucent skin from each one before enjoying the sweet fruit inside it, all to make the treat last. The sunlight was creeping down the wall, suffusing the small room with its glow. A last golden burst before the day faded to dark.

She wondered if she liked him. She hadn't been involved with someone for longer than she cared to remember. Since medical school, really. Sometimes she asked herself why. It wasn't for lack of interest on the part of some of her colleagues. But she was never interested in return. Some of it was the horror of the war, she knew that. And while they had taught her in medical school how important it was to maintain a professional distance, lest the pain of countless patients become your pain, their trauma your trauma, the clinic was different. Her patients were her people. And the disease they suffered from was the occupation itself. It was a disease that afflicted every Timorese. How could she distance herself from that?

There were times, though, when she wished she could. She was doing everything in her power to help. What good would her own misery add to it?

Dox had been right, though. About her trying not to smile. Maybe that's why she dressed him down the way she had? Was she protesting too much?

But she was being foolish. He wasn't coming back. And even if he did . . . so what? He was from another world. She knew that world—she had spent four years in it, in Los Angeles, the city of angels. Everything had been clean, and neat, and efficient. And most of all, safe. And in retrospect, all of it felt like a dream. She had awakened, and now she was here, where she was needed. For Dox, Timor would be the opposite. It would be like diving off Atauro Island. He would enjoy himself swimming among the exotic fish along the coral reef. Take photos. Maybe even form a few interesting memories. And then he would return to the boat that brought him, and leave. He didn't belong in these waters. And she didn't belong in his boat.

She finished the last segment of the orange, chewing it slowly, savoring it. She thought again about Beeler and again was hit by a wave of anxiety and guilt. She told herself for the hundredth time there was nothing she could have done. Beeler, the girls, the whole occupation itself . . . Why did bad things, things she had no control over, make her unable to enjoy good things? Life was so short and so perilous, it seemed a waste not to appreciate what she could.

She sighed. Whatever she was going to do about the videos, she would figure it out another time. For now, she had to get back to work. The clinic didn't close for another hour.

She stood and was on her way to the door when it opened. A large man with bushy hair and a shaggy beard was on the other side of it. Santiago, the man who handled the clinic's garbage and contaminated materials. Ordinarily she saw him only in the very early hours, and the sudden sight of him now, blocking the doorway, startled her. She took a step back.

"I'm sorry," Santiago said in Tetum, glancing down the corridor and then back at her, "I didn't mean to surprise you."

She had always suspected he was with Falintil, or at least that he helped them in some way. She realized that was part of what had startled her. It was as though Falintil had been reading her mind.

"It's okay," she managed. "You're here late. Or early."

"Yes. I need to talk to you."

If she had been startled before, now she was actually frightened. "Is everything all right?" she said.

He glanced back again, then stepped inside and closed the door behind him. "There was a man here today. He goes by the name *Dox*. He isn't who you think he is."

Chapter 22

Dox found the file and the radio under his mattress as Joko had promised. He pulled out both, sat on the bed, and started reading.

Isobel Amaral. Born right here in Dili in 1961. Making her thirty—four years Dox's senior. He smiled, thinking, *Older woman.*

Parents deceased. No siblings. A scholarship to UCLA medical school in 1982, which explained her fluency in English. She must have been a good student, because after her residency they made her an offer to stay on. Instead, she came back to Timor—to a war zone. Why would a person do such a thing? Give up money and comfort and security, in exchange for privation, discomfort, and danger? Since the file said she had no family, the obligation must have been to something else. After all, if Mom and Ronnie and Henry and the girls had relocated or were otherwise gone, Dox doubted he'd return to Tuscola, even for a visit. Maybe when he was an old man, if he made it that far, for reasons of nostalgia. But he wouldn't settle there. The world was too big, and he wanted to see too much of it.

Hell, even with his family there, even with the Roy situation coming to a head, the first chance he'd seen he'd taken off. He'd told himself it was for the money and how the money could help defuse Roy, but looking back he realized that was a rationalization. Like old George Whitaker had said, you couldn't buy a man like Roy. Roy would just take what you offered and then do what he wanted anyway.

And then that *pendejo* Mossberg had made him a different kind of offer—play ball, and we'll keep Roy in prison, no questions asked. And

Dox had jumped at it as the solution to all his problems. But maybe that was a rationalization, too. Maybe all he really wanted was to run away, rather than stay at home and face things squarely, whatever that entailed.

Because how did he know Mossberg would even hold up his end? Well, he'd seen the Hog's Tooth. With that, and if he knew anything about Dox, the man would realize the collateral for his promise was his own life. But you never knew with these CIA types. They lied and manipulated for a living. That kind of thing could become a habit, even an end to itself. The truth was, the only benefit Dox could really count on from being out here was that being here meant he didn't have to be there. Maybe that's all he had really wanted.

And maybe Mossberg knew, too. Didn't the man say it was his job to know things? Maybe he knew Dox better than Dox knew himself.

Maybe, asshole. But I'm learning.

He realized he should probably call home just to let them all know he was fine. But Ronnie had given him a hard time about leaving, and she wasn't one to change the subject just because someone asked her to. Marla had taken the news of his departure better than his family had. "Don't stay away too long," she'd said, and if the smile she gave him was forced, he couldn't tell. "I can't promise I'll be waiting."

He sighed. Reading about the woman wasn't making him feel better about his reasons for coming. The opposite, in fact. Because everything in the dossier suggested a person of unusual conscience, courage, and conviction. If he'd gotten a look at the dossier Mossberg had put together on him, would it read anything like that?

He doubted it. Courage under fire, sure, but *moral* courage? He wanted to think so, but he didn't see a lot of evidence for the proposition. Conscience? In some matters, like ones having to do with personal debts or debts of honor, hell yes. But how far did his conscience extend beyond that?

And conviction? What did he really believe in?

Well, his people, of course, meaning primarily his family. And also some comrades-in-arms, a few friends, and standup types like Magnus who he knew had his back. And there was Texas—*Don't Mess with Texas*. But nobody had messed with Texas since the Civil War and Reconstruction. Saying *Don't Mess with Texas* was just that—a saying. He didn't have to actually do anything about it.

It wasn't that being a Marine didn't entail sacrifice and risk. It certainly did, and the country had a long honor line of Marines who'd been called upon to sacrifice everything, and had. But it was also true what Roy said—as a Marine and then in Afghanistan, Dox had always had weapons. His buddies. His unit. Cavalry he could call if the shit hit the fan, even though in fact the cavalry wasn't always available or, if it was, it might not get there in time to make a difference.

But Isobel came home to a war zone to fight her battles . . . with what? Nothing but the knowledge she'd earned at medical school and her own beliefs, it seemed to him. And if she was mixed up with the guerillas, too . . . Well, who could blame her? Which side would he himself be fighting for if he were Timorese?

The truth was, he admired her. And wanted to protect her. Which under the circumstances was not going to be helpful or appropriate. Not least because it was all combining with what he'd felt the moment he'd laid eyes on her at the clinic.

He was attracted to her.

She was pretty enough, but he didn't think anyone would argue she was beautiful. Her ears stuck out a bit. And her forehead was maybe a little long. And not everyone liked freckles. But even as he ticked off these ostensible imperfections, it felt like an attempt to talk himself out of something words had nothing to do with. Worse, every time he considered one of the supposed imperfections, he realized he was feeling the opposite—that he liked her ears, and thought her forehead gave her a lovely, dignified look, and her freckles were adorable.

Listen to yourself, amigo. You really are in trouble.

Yeah, he was. He'd been in trouble from the start, and when she'd finally smiled at him, it had made the rest impossible to deny. Hell, her body was nice, too, he could tell even with that smock she'd been wearing. He realized that was another reason he'd been trying to focus on her ears and forehead and freckles. He didn't want to think about those delicate clavicles, or the way the fabric of her uniform clung and fell away in all the right places. Or, under the circumstances, in all the wrong ones.

Oh, man. What the hell was he going to do?

He didn't know. He'd left his insuperable complications in Tuscola for the glorious simplicity of combat. And walked straight into more complications for his trouble.

Well, one thing he could do. He'd promised her the money. And he was damn well going to make sure her clinic got it.

He wondered for a moment whether there was a pattern here. He'd told himself getting money was the way to solve the situation with Roy. And now he was telling himself the same thing about admiring and being attracted to this woman he was supposed to be exploiting.

He didn't know. Maybe he was rationalizing yet again. But it didn't matter. He wasn't going back on his word.

He powered up the radio and pressed the *Talk* button. "It's Dox. You there?"

He released the *Talk* button. There was a squawk of static, then Joko's voice. "Yes."

He pressed the *Talk* button again. "Still within range, I see."

"I'm always within range. The system has repeaters. How's the arm?"

Dox wanted to show the asshole how good the arm was by punching his face with the fist on the end of it. It would be worth a few popped stitches. But that kind of thing could wait. A dish best served cold and all that.

"I need five thousand US," Dox said. "I have a Western Union account, and I know they have a branch right here in Dili. Wire it to me."

"For what?"

"It's what it cost today to get my arm stitched up after you cut it."

"It should have cost you five dollars, not five thousand."

"It cost what it cost. And I had to spend it because of you."

"I'm not delivering money to that clinic. I might as well send it directly to Falintil."

"You told me to use this radio to ask you to provide whatever I need. That's what I'm doing. If your offer was bullshit and you're now going back on your word, that's fine. I'll explain to Mossberg I'm unable to proceed with this op and why. The two of you can sort it out from there with Felix. *Comprendez?*"

There was a pause. Dox sensed he had irritated the asshole. *Good.*

"You know," Joko said, "you talk a lot different on the radio than you do in person."

"Yeah, it's a funny thing about people, how they talk differently when they have a couple of M16s pointed at their faces. You're a genuine student of human nature to take in something as subtle as that, Joko. I doubt anyone else has ever noticed it before. And by the way, as *talk* is a verb, it gets modified by *differently*, which is an adverb, not by the adjective *different* you mistakenly used instead. I know you're proud of your English, but sloppiness like that is the sort of nonsense up with which I will not put."

He released the *Talk* button and waited. Joko said nothing.

Dox smiled and pressed the button again. "Nothing? Not even a thank-you?"

After a moment, Joko said, "I'll have the money wired to your account."

Dox should have been satisfied, but instead felt a wave of unease. This wasn't the Skove twins he was counter-provoking. This was a dangerous and capable man. And the suddenness with which this man had gone from trading insults to ignoring them, as though he'd thrown a mental switch, spoke of discipline, and intent. And not the kind of intent Dox was apt to welcome when it expressed itself down the road.

He needed to be smarter. He realized he was trying to recover some face after the way Joko had laughed at his quivering legs in the court-yard earlier. But that was no excuse for being dumb. He knew the two of them were on a collision course. Letting the man know he knew was the same as warning him. And what kind of sniper warned his targets they were being targeted?

"I appreciate the support," Dox said. "And look, maybe we got off on the wrong foot here."

Joko offered a small, cold laugh. "Don't worry. It's how things end that matters."

Chapter 23

Isobel stared at Santiago. The man with the cut shoulder. Who she'd been thinking about, daydreaming about. He wasn't who she thought he was? Who was he?

One of those Americans. Your first thought was the right thought.

And she had helped him. That might have made Falintil angry. But she was a doctor. She had no choice.

"What do you mean?" she said, afraid to say more.

"He's a spy. Helping Kopassus."

Instantly Isobel felt sick to her stomach. She took a step back and sank heavily into the chair she had just gotten up from.

"Don't be afraid," Santiago said. "Falintil knows you didn't know."

She wondered how anyone could be so confident of what she did or didn't know, and sensed Santiago was saying it to lull her. Which only made her more afraid.

"I don't . . . How do you know he's a spy?"

"We have people at the hotel where he's staying. They saw his interaction with the Indonesian soldiers and thought it was strange. Perhaps . . . an excuse for him to come to the clinic, hmm?"

Though she had suspected Santiago was with Falintil, and knew that he knew she suspected, still neither of them had ever acknowledged anything. And yet now Santiago was speaking on Falintil's behalf. He was even describing Falintil as *we*. Some frightening, invisible line had been crossed.

For a moment she couldn't speak. Then she said, "I'm sorry, I . . . I don't understand."

Santiago looked at her and said nothing, and suddenly she was sure Falintil knew about the videos, and Beeler, and everything. But would they be angry? Getting the videos to the Western media would help all of Timor. She had only kept her plans from Falintil out of fear of . . . fear of . . .

Of getting involved.

Yes, of getting involved. With Falintil or any other group. How could she know who to trust? The videos were too important, the girls' stories too precious to let anyone else handle. She wouldn't let anyone else direct her. Or veto her. Or try to make her do anything she didn't know was right for those girls.

"My question is why," Santiago said. "Why would he be interested in the clinic, hmm?"

Santiago had a habit of ending many of his sentences with *hmm?,* even ones that weren't technically questions. She had always found the habit strange, but never intimidating. She felt different now.

"What do you mean, 'interested'? This interaction with the soldiers . . . He came here with a bad cut. I sewed it up. Thirty stitches. I think that was his interest."

She realized Santiago seemed . . . different. Ordinarily he was quiet and deferential to the point of meekness. She was seeing a hidden side of him. The Falintil side.

Not a hidden side. The real side. What he shows you at the clinic is an act.

"You sewed it yourself?" Santiago said.

Isobel was suddenly worried. "Yes. I . . . He didn't want a nurse to do it."

Did he know more? For some reason, Isobel was afraid to say anything about the money Dox had offered, or the money she had taken.

Santiago said, "Did he ask for you by name?"

"No, just for a doctor."

"And then? Did he want to know your name?"

Isobel wanted to lie, but was too afraid to. "Yes. But so what?"

"Think about it. Everything that happened from when this man Dox came into the clinic. You thought it was a coincidence. But would anything have been different if he had been intent on meeting you? You, specifically."

The notion struck Isobel as almost clinically paranoid. But she thought about it, and . . .

He *had* wanted to know her name. Not just her last name. Her full name. And had he been trying to read her name tag? She'd seen him glancing, and had assumed it was her breasts he was trying to get a look at. His glances had been discreet, and she realized now that on some level she had been . . . pleased. That he would react to her that way.

"I don't know," she said.

"How did he get treated by a doctor for something as trivial as a cut, rather than by a nurse?"

Isobel realized her reluctance was going to get her in trouble, or, if she was already in trouble, then in worse trouble. Either Santiago knew the answers to these questions, or he had very good instincts. Or both. Regardless, Isobel would look better if she volunteered information rather than having it dragged out of her.

Some detached part of her mind wondered whether that was the idea, that an interrogator wants his subject to believe the interrogator knows more than he really does. Maybe to make the subject afraid to hold back. If so, it was working.

"He offered to have his company donate to the clinic," Isobel said. "We took some cash from his wallet. He promised to come back with the rest."

"How much?"

"Five thousand US."

Santiago laughed. "How do you rate the chances of his coming back?"

For an instant, Isobel felt weirdly protective of Dox's honor. "I think he will," she said.

Santiago gazed at her as though in wonder at her foolishness. "A rich white employee of some American corporation makes a promise to the poor benighted Timorese peasants to come back later and pay the five thousand dollars he owes . . . and he keeps his word? In the absence of any reward or punishment or connection to our country at all? In what possible universe could such a thing happen, hmm?"

Isobel was suddenly crestfallen, certain he was right. How could she have been so stupid? None of it had made sense, except as Santiago was explaining. She'd misinterpreted everything.

Why, though? How could she have missed something so obvious?

She thought of Dox's face, and the way he seemed unable to stop talking, and the way he had looked at her, and realized she had missed it all because of some ridiculous, girlish attraction. It made her furious to think she could be so immature. So naive.

"I thought he would," she said. "But . . ."

Santiago shook his head. "It's all right. We hope he does come back. We want you to get to know him."

Isobel had been frightened as she prepared the videos. But that had been on her own initiative. The girls didn't know the details; they only knew, and only wanted, that their stories would be heard, and they trusted Isobel to find a way. And Isobel's only contact had been Beeler, a woman Isobel herself had selected for the role.

This was different. It was being thrust on her. By people she didn't know and didn't trust, for reasons she couldn't understand. No one had asked her before; only her conscience had impelled her. She realized she was being more than just asked. She was being commanded. Because what would happen if she were to say no?

"I'm a doctor," she said, knowing how weak it sounded. "Not a spy."

"The one doesn't preclude the other," Santiago said. "But there is something we don't understand."

She tried not to let her fear show. "What?"

"Why is he interested in you? You, specifically, hmm?"

The videos, her mind tried to say, but she pushed the thought away before it could appear on her face.

"I don't even know that he *is* interested in me. At least not beyond my treating his injury."

"No, he's interested. There's no other way to explain the sequence of events. What do you make of the timing of his arrival?"

He doesn't know why. Doesn't know about the videos. "The timing?"

He looked at her doubtfully. Even suspiciously. "This man arrives right after those scum killed Sebastião Gomes? And only a few days before the procession from the church to honor him? You think this is a coincidence?"

Gomes was a resistance member. Accounts were confused, but it seemed he had gotten into a fight with pro-integration Timorese militias at the Motael Church. One of the pro-integration people was stabbed to death; Gomes was taken outside by Indonesian soldiers and shot. In a few days, there would be a procession from the church to the Santa Cruz cemetery, where Gomes was buried. The potential for violence between the resistance and the militias, and from the Indonesian soldiers, too, was high. Everyone at the clinic was nervous about it. But they all felt they had to be there—to honor Gomes, and to show the Indonesians they were unbowed.

Still, Isobel didn't understand the connection. "What would this Dox have to do with any of that?"

"He could be a provocateur. He could be working with Aitarak or one of the other militias fronting for Indonesia. Every time the Indonesians slaughter innocent people, they claim they were attacked. You know this."

"Okay," she said, afraid to say anything else.

Santiago sighed. "No one cares about us. Don't you see? America wants to sell arms to Suharto. It wants Indonesia as a military bulwark against China. Their president and secretary of state were in Jakarta the day before the Indonesians invaded. They knew. They gave the green light."

She understood all this. Everyone did. But she didn't understand why he was saying it.

"We're poor," Santiago went on. "We're not white. What oil there is off our coasts, Jakarta has already promised to Western interests. And remember, that oil—the Sunrise and Troubadour fields in the Timor Sea—was discovered only a year before Indonesia invaded. Another amazing coincidence, hmm? So the sooner Indonesia crushes us, the sooner the oil they've stolen can be exploited, the sooner what Indonesia has been doing here can be swept under the rug, and the sooner the people who rule America can stop pretending to want Indonesia to leave while at the same time arming them to the teeth."

She still didn't know why he was telling her all this. All she knew was that it was frightening her that he was.

"I don't know what you want from me," she said.

"The CIA has soldiers operating in Timor. We all know this. You know this. Several of them have been to the clinic. This man must be connected with that."

Isobel felt a jolt of fear. How much more did Falintil know about her, about what she hadn't told them? How closely was she being watched?

"We've tried to capture one," Santiago went on. "But they're much better armed than we are. We have bolt-action rifles and count every bullet. They have claymores. Grenade launchers. M60 machine guns and endless ammunition. The closest we came was the man you treated here, the one with the crushed legs. That was a roadside bomb. And we lost twelve men in the fight afterward. We can't do it that way."

"Do what?"

"Tell the world that America isn't just ignoring what's happening here. America is *supporting* what's happening here. The rapes, the massacres, the torture, the burnings . . . They're not happening because America is ignoring them. They're happening because *America is doing them*."

His intensity was frightening her more.

"I still don't understand," she said, and heard the unsteadiness in her own voice.

"The only way we'll ever get the Indonesians to leave," he said. "The only way we'll survive. Is to get Americans to care about what's happening here. We have to show them this isn't a foreign war. It's *their* war. *Their* atrocities. Just like in Vietnam. And then, just like in Vietnam, public opinion will change, and Congress will cut off its arms sales and other support to Jakarta and pressure the Indonesians to leave because Indonesia's war here will have become an embarrassment to the rulers of America. And the rulers of America don't like to be embarrassed. It's bad for business."

She shook her head. "What am I supposed to do?"

He shrugged. "Even well-trained men, disciplined men, forget themselves on the pillow."

She was stunned, sure she was mishearing. "What?"

He laughed without warmth. "Have I offended your virtue?"

"I . . . can't believe what you're asking of me."

He stared at her. "Just a minute ago I told you the price we paid trying to capture one of them. Twelve men dead. Which itself is only a drop in the bucket of Falintil's losses over the last sixteen years. And what of the country at large? They're starving us. Destroying us. Raping and torturing and killing us, and you're going to faint at the prospect of using whatever weapons God has given you in this fight to drive them out and save our people?"

She remembered the vow she had made at Joana and Mateus's house. That she would find a way to combat the Indonesians and their evil. But . . . her way. Not by subordinating herself to the whims of this man and his movement.

"I am saving our people," she said. "Or trying to. One person at a time, the best way I know how."

"You're ministering to people trapped in a burning house," he said, his voice rising. "We have a chance to put out the fire. Every one of us has a call to answer. Every one of us has a role to play. For every one of us, if there is something we *can* do for our freedom, then we *must* do that thing for our freedom. Are you different? My men have given their lives, and in the face of that, you're concerned about a stain on your virtue?"

She glanced at the door, worried he might have been overheard.

He chuckled. "You see? It's as I told you. When they're swept along by passion, men forget to be careful."

She glanced away, confused and afraid.

"Isobel," he said. "Look at me."

She did. She had always been Dr. Amaral to him. She understood that he was addressing her now from a new position. Not an equal position. A commanding one.

"I'm not telling you that you have to sleep with this man," he said. "I'm telling you that if you *can* sleep with him—if that's what it takes, if that's what brings him to trust you, if that's what induces him to share with you things he's sworn never to divulge—then, yes, you *will* sleep with him."

Her fear was now shot through with disgust. She wondered how different he was, really, from the Indonesian soldiers he hated.

"Don't look at me that way," he said. "My men are killing for our freedom. And dying for it. By comparison, any sacrifice you make is nothing."

She was suddenly enraged by his gall. "Why don't you let him have his way with you?" she said.

He stared at her. "You think this is funny?"

"No. What if he wanted to? Would you? To get him to open up to you?"

He glowered at her so furiously that she thought he was going to step in and strike her. She forced herself not to flinch.

"No more jokes," he said after a moment. "We all fight with the weapons we have. You have a body. You should be grateful God has given you an opportunity to use it for our people."

He paused as though expecting a response. She wouldn't give him the satisfaction.

After a moment, he continued. "So you're going to spend time with this spy Dox, hmm? Cultivate him. Make him trust you, and fall in love with you, and tell you all about what he's really doing here and who he works for and why they sent him."

She knew she had lost. That if she said no, she would be their enemy. And that they would treat her as such.

Still, she couldn't stop herself from saying, "What's stopping you from asking him yourself? You said you tried to capture one of the others."

Santiago's expression softened, apparently at the recognition that he had won, that he had secured her acquiescence, that now she was only trying to save a little face.

"That was before," he said. "Before, we didn't have you."

The words felt like a door closing on the cell he had trapped her in.

"It's hard to make a man tell you what he doesn't want to," he went on. "Even under torture, people will invent anything if they think it will end the pain. Better a voluntary confession to start with. You see? Your role isn't just to make him tell you. It's to make him *want* to tell you."

"And then?"

Santiago smiled. "Then, of course, you'll betray him. To us."

Chapter 24

Two evenings after Isobel had patched him up, Dox was waiting for her in the bar of the Hotel Turismo, feeling not like a local, but at least like a respectable foreigner, dressed as he was in a pair of faded jeans, a blue linen shirt, and his don't-leave-home-without-them Tony Lamas. The establishment wasn't much—just a small room overlooking the garden where Joko had done his Benihana routine, with half a dozen bar stools and four tables. Not the kind of place that was likely to ever present much of a threat to Rick's Café Americain, but still comfortable and convivial enough.

The light was soft and low, and the music was nice, Frank Sinatra of all things, singing a song called "Summer Wind," which wasn't Dox's usual speed but for which he decided it was time to make an exception. The place was well kept, too—a polished wood bar, with a big mirror, glass shelves, and a nice array of libations behind it. João, in a white shirt and black vest and bow tie, was doing the pouring. There were about a dozen other people enjoying the oasis, some he thought must be aid workers, and one fellow in a priest's collar sipping a Victoria Bitter. *A priest walked into a bar,* he thought, and chuckled. He knew a few jokes like that, but none that involved aid workers. And there were a few Indonesian soldiers with local girls. He wondered how those girls would fare if the Indonesians wound up losing and getting kicked out. Not well, he supposed.

He'd gone back to the clinic that morning with the money, which Joko had wired to his Western Union account as promised. He'd given it to the nurse, Rosa, because Isobel was with a patient. But Rosa signaled to him that he should wait, and ten minutes later, Isobel came out. She seemed stressed, he supposed from the medical problems she was dealing with. Or maybe some problem with the guerillas? That was hard to imagine. But Mossberg and this Felix must have had some kind of intel they were relying on, and anyway his job was just to get close to her and see what he could learn about what she was doing when she wasn't at her official duties.

"Well," she had said when she saw him. "You came back."

Something in her expression or her tone struck him as wary. "What, were you hoping I wouldn't?" he had said, trying to make her smile again. But she hadn't.

"My arm's doing fine," he said, flexing it a bit to show her. "I suppose the work was expensive, but I feel like it was worth it."

She nodded, but that was all.

Shit, he'd felt a connection when he'd been here last, he was sure of it. But now she seemed tense. Something must have happened. He realized he preferred that to the alternative, which was that she had just spent a little time thinking about him and decided she wasn't interested.

"I can see you're busy," he said. "But . . . if you ever have some spare time, would you maybe want to get together?"

"For what?" she said, and the way she said it, so flatly it was almost a challenge, made him certain he was striking out, both personally and professionally.

"Well, I don't know the town," he said. "Or what people do here in their leisure hours. I've been all over the place doing preliminary site surveys, but . . . I was thinking maybe just a walk along the beach. Or there's a nice bar in the hotel. We could have a drink there. If you'd like, I mean. If it would be okay."

The way she was looking at him, he decided he was making a damn fool of himself. "That said," he added, "I confess I'm getting the feeling you wouldn't want to."

She shook her head. "No. I want to."

He didn't think he'd ever heard a woman say those words with less conviction. If it was just personal and he didn't have ulterior motives, he would have found a way to let them both off the hook, or at least tried to.

He felt all mixed up. It wasn't in him to pressure a woman—it wasn't fair to the woman, and wasn't good for his pride, either. But he was supposed to cultivate her.

"Are you sure?" he said, not knowing what was the right thing to do. "I mean, it's nice of you, but I know you're busy, and I don't want you to feel pressured."

"I want to," she said again, and it was horrible, it was like she was choking on the words.

He had an idea. "I'll tell you what," he said. "I'll be in the hotel bar tonight from nine o'clock. If you get off work before then and you'd like to join me for a drink, I'd be very pleased. But if anything comes up, or you're busy or whatever, it's really okay. Okay?"

She nodded. "I need to get back to work," she had said, and turned and walked away.

And now he was on his second Bombay Sapphire martini, which was doing an exemplary job of steadying his nerves, and which also was a credit to the skills of the man who made it, the redoubtable João, who had shaken it hard with lots of ice and only a few drops of vermouth, the way God intended.

While he'd been waiting, three white people he made as American had come in—a tall man who looked half like Henry Silva—the bad guy from *Sharky's Machine*—and half like Warren Beatty; a smaller, pretty woman with shoulder-length brown hair, serious eyes, and a strong chin; and another man, this one with a disarming smile and brown hair so wavy he might have been caught in a windstorm. Dox watched as they paused at the bar to order Victoria Bitters, which seemed to be the official beer of the hotel, after which they took a table and started talking intensely in low voices. They didn't look like spooks, and they didn't look like aid workers. And no priest collars, either. He wondered what they were all doing in Dili. After a little while with no sign of Isobel and halfway through the second martini, he decided to find out.

He strolled over. As soon as they saw him coming, they stopped talking and looked up, apparently not wanting him to overhear.

"Howdy," he said, stopping short of their table. "Pardon me for interrupting, but you're the first foreigners I've seen here. Well, the Indonesians of course, but you know what I mean. What brings you to town?"

"We're reporters," the woman said. "What are you doing here?"

"Site studies," Dox said. "I work for a company called REESE Incorporated. They're planning on building air strips and such when the war is over, and it's up to me to figure out where."

The woman looked at him with those serious eyes, and he had the sense she didn't believe a word of it. No one said anything else, and for a moment it was awkward.

"Reporters," Dox said. "I thought Indonesia wasn't letting any in."

"There was supposed to be a delegation," Henry Silva/Warren Beatty said. "From Portugal. Accompanying the UN Special Rapporteur for Human Rights on Torture. Jakarta got pressured into allowing in a few journalists to cover the event. The event was canceled, but not our visas. So here we are."

"I was just here to film a documentary on diving," the wavy-haired guy said in a British accent. "But there's a memorial procession tomorrow, for Sebastião Gomes, the young activist who was killed. I'll be filming that instead."

Dox nodded, irritated at himself for guessing the man's nationality wrong. "That explains it," he said. "I thought things felt pretty tense out on the street."

The woman raised her eyebrows. "You don't know about Sebastião Gomes?"

"I arrived just a few days ago. I know a fair amount about soil composition, gradation, and other such matters, but no, I'm playing catch-up on the local political scene."

"What's your name?" the woman said.

"William Dox. But call me Dox. Everybody does."

There was a quick round of handshakes, and they all introduced themselves. Henry Silva/Warren Beatty was Allan Nairn; the woman was Amy Goodman; and the wavy-haired fellow was Max Stahl.

When the intros were done, Goodman gestured to the empty chair. "Would you like to join us?"

And have my story probed by you? Dox thought. *I'd rather go another round with old Joko.*

"That's kind of you," he said, "but I'm waiting on a friend. Besides, I get the feeling y'all have a lot to talk about. I'm staying here at the hotel, though. Maybe we'll run into each other again."

They all lifted their glasses to that, and Dox went back to his table. He checked his watch—nine thirty, and still no sign of her.

He sat and sipped. He was uncomfortable with the whole situation, and the alcohol was helping him think through why. Or at least it seemed to be. He wasn't much accustomed to cloak and dagger or to deceit in general, and he realized he was more in his element among people who were just honestly trying to kill each other as hard as they could. Not that deception wasn't a critical element of combat, but it was honest deception, everybody knew it was there. It couldn't really be said to be cheating, after all, if all the players know everyone else is cheating and everyone knows that everyone knows.

But this kind of stuff . . . What was he supposed to do, play with her feelings? Not that there would be much chance of that, judging from the reception she'd given him at the clinic earlier that day. Regardless, though, wasn't that what he was trying to do? Fool her? Manipulate her? And who could say, maybe put her at risk at the same time?

Well, maybe she wouldn't show up. That was one way to solve the problem. He'd just have to tell old Mossberg the subject didn't like the stink of him, and that was that. If they needed a sniper here, he'd be happy to shoot some people. But this skulking-around-and-manipulating-women shit, it wasn't for him.

He sipped the martini. The worst part was, he still wanted her to come. He wanted to see her. And talk to her. And look at her.

But hell. No good could come from any of that. Better if she just didn't—

A woman walked in. She was wearing dark blue jeans and a matching V-neck blouse, and had long, beautiful black hair. It took him a second to realize—it was Isobel.

He gave her a little wave and stood. She nodded and walked over. She seemed taller than he remembered from the clinic, and he saw she was wearing heels.

She stopped a few feet away. "Hi."

He looked at her. She was wearing a little makeup, and even with her hair down he could make out a flash of gold earrings. Without thinking, he said, "Wow." And then, recovering himself, added, "I mean, you look different when you're off duty. In a good way, I mean. I mean, you look good at the clinic, too, just more like a doctor. Not that being a doctor means you don't look good. It's just more of a doctor look. If you know what I mean."

Damn it, he was babbling. Probably he should have held off on that second martini. And then he realized she hadn't said anything at all, and her face . . . She looked worried. No, worse than worried. Stricken.

"Is everything all right?" he said.

She shook her head and her eyes welled up. "Rosa. The nurse you met. She was killed."

He felt like he'd been hit. "What?"

She didn't answer. After a moment he added, "Killed . . . What do you mean? What happened?"

She gave a quick wipe of her eyes with a wrist. "The money you brought. She went to deposit it at the bank. Someone robbed her."

Joko, he thought. *You son of a bitch.*

"People saw what happened," she said. "A man tried to grab her bag. Rosa fought him. And he . . . he punched her in the face. She fell down."

She started crying again. "And still she held on to the bag. She knew what that money meant to the clinic. And the man . . . He kicked her. Stomped on her throat. Then she let go of the bag. But she died. People carried her to the clinic, but her trachea was crushed. We tried to save her. But she had already asphyxiated."

She paused and tried to collect herself. Dox snatched a napkin from the table and handed it to her. She wiped her face.

"Her family is in Ossu, in the mountains. We can't reach them. We haven't informed them yet. They don't even know, their mother, their daughter . . ." She stifled a sob.

"Isobel," he said. "I am so sorry." It wasn't untrue, God knew. But it wasn't the half of it, either.

She nodded but didn't respond.

"I don't know that you should be here," he said. "I mean, is there anything I can help with? Do you need to go anywhere? Can I do anything?"

She held up a hand. "I just need a minute. I'm sorry."

"Why did you even come out tonight? I feel terrible. Do you want to sit for a minute? What can I do?"

"I'm okay. Thank you. Yes. Let's sit."

He pulled her chair out from the table, not that she needed it, but he wanted so badly to do something for her. She sat and put her elbows on the table, her fingertips against her forehead.

He took the chair next to her. "Would you like something to drink? Water or anything?"

She glanced at his martini. "What's that?"

"Bombay Sapphire martini."

She shook her head. "Ugh. I hate gin."

"That's all right, we can still be friends."

She laughed a tiny bit at that, and it made him glad that he was able to do anything, even just make her chuckle for a second, if it made her feel better.

"I'll have a vodka," she said. "In a glass like yours."

"A vodka martini? With vermouth?"

"No, no vermouth."

"Any vodka you like?"

"I don't care."

He liked that, that she wasn't pretentious about her preferences. "Okay, hang on, I'll be right back."

He walked over to the bar. His mind was swirling from a combination of the gin and too many thoughts and feelings to make sense of. He knew he'd gotten Rosa killed. That fucking Joko . . . No wonder he'd decided to hand over the money. He knew he was going to steal it right back. And steal it from people who really needed it, too.

This poor woman was in pain, and he wanted badly to help. But he barely knew her. He didn't know the place, he didn't know the culture, he just didn't know what to do.

He told João to fix an ice-cold vodka, up, then headed straight back to the table. It struck him then, really struck him, how beautiful she was. Sitting alone at the table like that, a petite woman with her makeup a little smudged, and but with so much dignity and determination and strength.

The makeup, though. That was odd, wasn't it? And she was dressed nicely, too, heels even, and earrings. Under the circumstances, why would she have gone to the trouble? At most he would have expected her to show up just to tell him she was sorry, something terrible had happened and tonight wasn't going to work. Hell, she could have just phoned the hotel and had the call put through to the bar. It wasn't like she had seemed head over heels for him at the clinic earlier in the day. The opposite, in fact. And he wasn't an old friend she could go to for comfort in the face of tragedy.

Something was off, but he was too buzzed and preoccupied to figure out what. He'd have to ponder it later.

"João's bringing you a drink," he said. "But if you change your mind, please just tell me."

She nodded. "I'll be all right. Still just . . . shocked."

"Of course. How could you not be?"

João came with the drink, set it on the table, and headed back to the bar. Isobel seemed not even to notice.

Dox waited a moment, then raised his glass. "Here's to Rosa," he said. "She seemed like a nice lady, and I imagine she helped a lot of people here. And I'm sure she felt lucky to have you as a colleague, like you were lucky to have her."

Isobel nodded and her eyes filled again. They touched glasses. Isobel drained about a third of hers, blowing out a long breath and shuddering for a moment after it went down.

"I don't drink much," she said, apparently to explain the reaction.

"Well, it's never too late to start."

She gave him another small laugh and then teared up again. He realized that in the state she was in, she might be vulnerable. That if she needed a shoulder to cry on, it might be a way to get her to trust him.

And as soon as the thought formed, it made him feel ill. He realized he couldn't do it. It wasn't for him. Not that spying wasn't an old and noble profession, and God knew the scooters and shooters needed solid intel to figure out who to blame and where to aim, but he just wasn't built for it. He'd stick to killing people who were trying their hardest to kill him first, at least up until one of them beat him to the punch fair and square.

Yeah, he'd find a way to explain to Magnus, who might catch a little heat for suggesting someone who quit practically before he got started, but probably nothing worse than that. After all, it was Kee who'd really pushed for Dox in the role, and if the CIA decided they didn't like him anymore after this, so be it. As for Mossberg, he was always welcome to just go fuck himself. There had to be another way to deal with the Roy situation.

The second he decided, it was like a big weight came off him. Some of it was the decision, no doubt, though maybe the Bombay Sapphire was lending a hand.

She was still crying. "It's all right," he said. "I like to have a good cry myself from time to time."

She laughed again and wiped her eyes with the napkin. "When do you cry?"

Before he could even consider what was about to come out of his mouth, he said, "Well, I cried when they put my daddy in prison."

She looked at him. "When was that?"

"When I was ten."

"That doesn't count."

"Why not?"

"You were a little boy. I'm a grown woman."

"I don't know. I think we're all a little younger inside than we like to admit."

She looked at him. He couldn't tell what she was thinking.

"What?" he said.

She shook her head. "Why did your father go to prison?"

"Oh, the usual story. He used to get drunk and hit my mom and my sister and me. Eventually it got so bad that away he went."

She gave him that look again.

He smiled at her because he couldn't help it. "Why do you keep looking at me like that?"

There was a pause, then she said, "You seem so nice."

"Just seem?"

She took another swallow of vodka and shuddered again. "Did your father really go to prison?"

He was taken aback. "Why would I make up a story like that?"

She shook her head. "I don't know."

Did she suspect him? Did someone . . . warn her?

"I wish I were making it up," he said. "But alas. What about you? Are you close with your family?"

"My mother died when I was small. I still remember her, though, teaching me to bodysurf in the ocean at Aidabalaten."

"Aidabalaten?"

"A beach town about two hours west. It's where my parents met, and they used to take me there for a family vacation every year when I was small. It was only later I realized the trips were also for their wedding anniversary. The ocean there, with them . . . Those are some of my earliest memories. My best."

"From what I've seen, the beaches here look beautiful. I'd be in the water all the time."

She smiled, but her eyes were sad. "Being in the ocean, floating on the waves . . . It's one of my favorite things. But . . . it's hard to find time. These days it's mostly just once a year."

"A special occasion?"

"When my mother died, my father and I scattered her ashes in the sea at Aidabalaten. And when he died, I scattered his there, too. I try to visit once a year. It feels good to be in the water where they rest. I turn on my back, and look up at the sun and sky, and let the waves carry me along. I can feel the two of them there. And for a few minutes, it's as though we're together again."

"I'm sorry you lost them. But I like your custom. And I'm glad you were all close. You must have made them happy."

"I tried. It was my father's dream to see me graduate from medical school. He drove a cab here in Dili and would never let me help with anything. It was always *Study, study, study. If you want to be a doctor, Isobel, you have to study.*"

"Did he get to see his dream come true?"

She nodded, smiling as though remembering. "I graduated from UCLA on a full scholarship, and you should have seen him that day. Talk about crying . . . He was wearing the only shirt and tie he ever owned, and I think he soaked them. I was embarrassed at the time, but now . . ."

She shook her head and blinked away tears.

"Sounds like you made him proud," Dox said. "I mean, how many dads get a day like the one you gave him?"

"You never gave yours one?"

Dox laughed. "If I did, he never mentioned it. I mean, I was a US Marine, and so was my grandfather, he was decorated for heroism at the Battle of Okinawa in World War Two. But that was a lot for my father to try to live up to, and I reckon he never did. So my joining up . . . I guess it made him feel like less than his father, and less than his son, I think you could put it that way. So the rest of my family was proud of me, but it was more complicated for him. In fairness, though, being in prison, I suppose he had other things on his mind."

He realized he was talking too much. "I'm sorry, I didn't mean to offer my entire memoirs. I've been here in the bar for a while—not your fault, I didn't know when you might come, or even for sure if you were going to—and this is my second go-round with one of Joao's expert martinis."

She smiled. "You do talk a lot."

He laughed. "I know, I've been told. But I listen, too. Hopefully, that's a saving grace."

She looked at him as though trying to figure something out. "Why do you talk so much?"

He laughed again, embarrassed. "What? I don't know, I never gave it any thought. It feels like the right general amount to me, but I guess it always does for the one who's doing the talking."

"I just . . . It's not what I expected."

"Well, what would you expect? You don't even know me."

She shook her head. Then she lifted her drink, drained it, closed her eyes, and shuddered again. She set the glass back on the table and blinked a few times.

"You know," he said, looking at her empty glass, "for someone unaccustomed to alcohol, you sure made short work of that vodka. Maybe you like it more than you realized? João told me it was Smirnoff, in case you want to know what to ask for next time."

She didn't answer. The way she shuddered as she drank suggested she hadn't been going so fast because she enjoyed the taste. More like someone looking for liquid courage.

She blew out a long breath, then looked at him. "I feel better," she said slowly.

"Well, that means you're doing it right. Are you sure, though?"

She nodded. "I can see why people drown their sorrows. I want another."

"I'm sorry you have sorrows to drown. But maybe you shouldn't try to drown them all at once. Maybe just take them for a little swim, instead. I find that works better."

She laughed at that, harder than the chuckles she'd offered earlier. Which on the one hand gratified him, because it made him happy to make her laugh, and also because she looked so beautiful doing it. But on the other hand, it concerned him. Because even beyond what had happened to Rosa, something was off here. Someone had told her something, or she was worried about something. She seemed to like him, and at the same time to be almost . . . confrontational, even hostile. He couldn't quite place it, maybe because he was pretty buzzed himself.

She shook her head and looked away. "I don't know what I'm doing."

"I'm not sure what you mean by that. And I don't know you well, but from what I can see, what you're doing is being a good doctor to people who need one."

Her eyes filled up again. "I'm a good doctor? I left her there tonight. Rosa. She's all alone in the basement, in the morgue cooler. No one to watch over her."

Dox tended not to be sentimental about these things, believing as he did that you couldn't really be left alone when you were dead because you were just, well, dead. But he understood that not everyone was like that.

"Would you like it if we went back there?" he said.

She looked at him. "Are you serious?"

"If it would make you feel better, of course. Rosa doesn't have to be by herself. I'll stay with you until your coworkers are back, or her family comes, or whatever happens next. I don't mean to intrude, just if you don't want to be alone. But I'd be honored to keep a vigil with you."

Her tears spilled over. "I want to trust you."

He wanted so badly to touch her, but he was afraid it would come across the wrong way. And he didn't know what to say, either. What came out was, "You can."

Chapter 25

Twenty minutes later, they were in a windowless, rectangular room, about thirty feet long and fifteen feet wide. It didn't look like a morgue, at least not Dox's conception of one. It was more like an unfinished basement, a metal table and a horizontal refrigerator at one end being the only giveaways regarding its true function. Well, that and the smell of bleach. But it was peaceful, and cool, and it had a nice hush to it. Along one of the long sides was an old, upholstered couch covered in a blanket. There was nowhere else to sit, so they sat alongside each other on that.

"I really appreciate your doing this," she said. "It's not quite as nice as the hotel bar."

Dox looked around. "I guess we're a little overdressed for it, but that's all right. The truth is, I'm not in the habit of hanging out in morgues. I don't think I've ever been in one. But I'm more about the company than I am about the place."

She smiled. "Thanks."

"So do you come here often?"

She laughed. "Actually, yes. Well, not often. But it's the only place in the clinic that stays reasonably cool even on hot days. That's why we put this couch here. People use it as a break room. Do you think that's strange?"

He thought of his nights with Marla in Tuscola Cemetery. "Some would," he said. "But . . . I don't think there's anything more natural in life than death. Sometimes I wonder at all the euphemisms. I guess no one wants to dwell on how short a ride it is, but still there's probably something between dwelling on it, on the one hand, and being in denial, on the other." He paused, then added, "Sorry, I'm talking too much again, aren't I? I think that's partly from the martinis. I'm going to give it some more thought when I'm sober."

"I don't think you talk too much."

"Really? I thought that's what you meant before."

She shook her head. "No."

He looked at her. "You know, you make me feel a little off balance."

She chuckled. "I can't imagine anything that would make you feel off balance. You'd just talk your way through it."

He laughed. "That's a nice compliment. I wish it were true."

"It is true. You know, you always say the right thing."

It was a nice echo of something he admired about Henry, and he smiled. "You mean I say so many things that some are bound to be right?"

She shook her head. "Like when you said, how many dads get a day like the one I gave mine. Thank you for that."

"You're welcome."

"And what you said about Rosa. That we were lucky to have each other as colleagues. And you didn't even know her."

"Well, she must have been special for you to have such high regard for her."

She gave him a sad smile, then looked down. "That's what I mean."

They were quiet for a moment. "Hey," he said. "I have a really strong urge to put my arm around you. But I don't want it to come across the wrong way."

She didn't look up. "What would be the wrong way?"

"Any way you didn't like, I think."

She nodded but didn't otherwise respond.

He didn't know what she wanted. Was he being selfish in the way he wanted to hold her? He hoped not.

He reached out and put his arm around her. She didn't stiffen or move away, but she didn't curl into him or anything like that, either.

He wanted to see her face, but she was still looking down. "Like I told you," he said. "You make me feel a little off balance."

She turned her head to look at him, and he saw she was crying again.

"I'm sorry," he said. As gently as he could, he touched his fingertips to her face and wiped away the tears. One cheek, then the other. Her mouth was slightly open, and without thinking, he brushed his thumb across her lips.

"I think you're lovely," he said. "Not just when you're dressed up, either. When you were in your doctor's outfit, too. I thought it the first time I saw you."

She didn't say anything. But she kept looking at him.

He wanted to kiss her. Not a big kiss. He just wanted to feel her lips against his.

He leaned slowly forward. He thought she might have frowned slightly—he wasn't sure. But she had plenty of time to see him coming, and she didn't draw back.

For a moment, their lips just brushed together. It felt good to have her so close. He caught a whiff of something floral—soap or shampoo—and instantly liked it.

He wasn't sure what she was feeling, and he supposed it would be strange to start making out not ten feet from the body of her murdered colleague. He was about to draw back when she lurched forward and jammed her tongue into his mouth.

Instinctively he drew back and broke the kiss. She was breathing hard, but not in excitement, he thought. The sudden way she'd done it, it was like she'd been psyching herself up to eat something distasteful, and had tried to swallow it all at once to get it over with faster.

"I'm sorry," he said, still more than half-drunk and reeling with surprise. "I didn't . . . I mean, that escalated a little faster than I was expecting."

She looked at him, then shocked him by trying to kiss him again. And again it was way too aggressive, at least for him. It didn't feel like she was excited—more like she was trying to rip off a Band-Aid as fast as she could so it stung less.

He tried kissing her back, but he realized he was on autopilot. It wasn't what he wanted, and anyway it felt all wrong.

He pushed her gently but firmly away. "Hang on," he said. "Hang on. What's going on here?"

She didn't answer. She just looked at him, breathing hard. But somehow it wasn't excited breathing. It was . . . agitated, or angry or something.

"I don't know what you're trying to do," he said. "I like you, Isobel. And I feel like you like me. But what you just did . . . That doesn't feel like you liking me."

She looked at him. "I like you."

He thought he'd never heard something more rote. "Well, thank you for that, but what you were just doing . . . It felt like something else."

She kept looking at him, her expression somehow an accusation.

"Did someone tell you something about me?" he said.

She frowned. "What difference does it make?"

"I don't know. But it doesn't feel good to think that someone might be casting aspersions, and I don't even know who they are or what they're saying. I mean, how would you feel if you thought someone was telling me tales about you?"

"Was someone?"

In his drunkenness or just in his general dumbassedness, he hadn't seen that coming. "Not exactly."

"What does that mean?"

How could he answer that? "Look, the company I work for . . . It's bigger than the company I mentioned. And that's the only lie I've told you. Everything else has been true. And anyway, I quit. I decided earlier tonight, and maybe even before tonight, and I'm going to tell them, too."

"Tell who? Quit what?"

"Hang on, it's your turn. Who told you about me?"

"You don't understand what things are like here. With the resistance, it's *Either you're with us, or you're against us.*"

"Which are you?"

"I was neither until you got here!"

"What does that mean?"

"Are you a spy?"

"Is that what someone told you?"

"Are you? Don't lie to me. And if you won't answer, that's the answer."

He tried to think of a way to respond that would compromise neither his position nor his integrity. He couldn't find one.

"I was supposed to be a spy, all right? Except I turned out to be the worst spy in the history of spying. I quit before I even got started."

"Are you with those other Americans?"

"What other Americans?"

"We see them from time to time. I treated one of them here at the clinic but he died. You don't know the one with the scar on his face? The one called Waster?"

"I try not to associate with people with nicknames like that."

"Answer the question."

"No, I don't know any Waster, scar or no scar."

"People think they were sent by the CIA."

"I don't know the specifics of what they do here, and I don't know any of them individually. I think the original plan was for me to join up with them, mostly for glorified guard duty. But then someone got the idea that I should cultivate you instead."

"So you were supposed to meet me?"

"Yes, I was. And that's exactly when I quit."

"Why? Why were you supposed to meet me?"

He blew out a long breath. "Apparently, the Indonesians think you're somehow wired into Falintil."

"That's a lie! I told you, I had nothing to do with Falintil until you got here!"

"You keep saying that—I don't know what you mean!"

"Falintil is who told me you're a spy! I never had anything to do with them before that! They told me I had to get to know you, and to . . . to . . ."

She shook her head and looked away.

He stared at her, putting together some of the pieces that had been hanging askew.

"Goddamn," he said after a moment. "That's why . . . Oh, goddamn. Isobel, I'm sorry."

She nodded. "Yeah."

"That's why you kissed me like that. You didn't want to, but you thought you had to."

"I do have to."

"No, you do not."

"Easy for you to say."

"Easy? I've never said anything harder."

For a second she looked enraged—and then she started laughing. So did he. The laughter built and built until they were both convulsed with it.

They sat there for a long time, just cracking up. It would start to die down, and then get going again.

Finally it abated. "All right," Dox said, catching his breath. "We need to figure out what we're going to do."

Instantly the dregs of her laughter were gone. "If Falintil finds out we talked like this—"

"They're not going to find out."

"How can you be so sure? They're everywhere. The man who told me I had to . . . be with you. Santiago. He knew so much about me. About the clinic."

"Well, I'm sure not going to tell anyone we talked like this. Are you?"

"Of course not."

"Then it's our secret, and no one else is going to know."

"They were watching you at the hotel. They saw the soldier cut you. They thought it was staged."

Dox thought for a moment about who at the hotel might have gone to Falintil about his interaction with Joko. Fernando? João? Someone else?

It didn't matter. He couldn't fairly blame them.

"Well," he said, "it was half staged, I suppose. I sure didn't know it was coming. But the guy who did it, asshole calls himself Joko, the idea was that it would explain my trip to the clinic."

At the mention of the name, she almost flinched. "That's the one who cut you?"

"You know him?" Dox said.

She shook her head quickly. "No. But . . . I've heard of him."

"What have you heard?"

"Did he tell you . . . why he thinks I'm working with Falintil?"

"No, no one ever gave me specifics."

Twice she started to speak and then stopped. It was obvious she knew something, something she didn't want to tell him.

Finally, she said, "Kopassus . . . They use rape as a weapon of war. I've . . ."

She trailed off, shaking her head.

"I'm sorry," Dox said, wanting to say more, and wishing he knew how to say it.

She blew out a breath. "I've treated their victims at the clinic. Joko's name has been mentioned again and again. Even with the terrible things the soldiers do to my people, Joko and his men have made a reputation for cruelty."

The topic seemed to make her even more nervous than she'd been earlier. Well, that wasn't such a hard thing to understand.

"That tracks," Dox said. "I told you, I was a Marine. A sniper. And you know, all Marines are killers. It's right there in the job description—*Every Marine a rifleman,* as the saying goes, and that doesn't mean you just carry a rifle or clean one. Your job is to kill people with it. And Marines are good at their job, the best. But that's just it—it's a job. Something that sometimes has gotta get done. But this hombre Joko . . . Everything about him tells me he's the type who likes his job just a little too much. Like I said, he struck me as someone who's in his line of work for love, not money."

"Some of the girls I've treated," she said. "They told me . . . he eats the hearts of his enemies. Do you think that's true?"

Dox had seen his fair share of barbarity in Afghanistan. Whole villages razed by indiscriminate Soviet shelling, with helicopter pilots using fleeing survivors for target practice. And when the Mujahideen captured a Russian soldier . . . Well, the payback they inflicted could border on medieval. Burnings. Dismemberments. Which the Soviets would repay by razing more villages, and on and on. On top of which, the Soviets had a predilection for raping Afghan girls, which the Muj liked to pay back by gang-raping captured Russian soldiers, usually before tying them to a pole or tree or whatever else was handy and stoning them to death. But he'd never heard of anyone making a meal of a dead Ruskie, and certainly not of a live one. The Muj hated the *dushman*, their name for the Russians, about as much as humans could hate anyone, but still they didn't go so far as to dine on them. And saying *Even the Muj wouldn't do it* was saying a lot.

"I wouldn't have thought so," he said. "If I hadn't had the pleasure of meeting him myself."

She grimaced. *"Meu Deus."*

They were quiet for a moment, and then she said, "That money you gave us . . . It was from him?"

"Yeah. Or through him, anyway. And then he stole it back. He's the one who killed Rosa. Or had her killed."

She looked gut-punched.

"I'm sorry," he said. "I didn't . . . When I offered, I just didn't have any idea . . ."

She shook her head quickly. "It's not your fault."

"Either way, before this is done, I'm going to make him dead."

She looked at him. "You really mean that?"

He nodded. "I wouldn't say it except in the literal sense. *I love you* and *I'm going to kill you.* If you hear me say either, you better believe it's true."

He paused for a moment, realizing that maybe he was giving her the wrong impression. "I feel I should clarify," he added. "The first one I've never actually said, except to my mom and my sisters, but that's not what I'm talking about. Anyway, when I say it, I'll mean it. If you know what I mean."

He forced himself to stop before the hole he felt he was digging got even deeper.

"But what do we do?" Isobel said. "About . . . this situation."

He was relieved they seemed to be past the part of the conversation he'd stumbled into, about all the sincere loves he'd never declared. "Well, on your end, I suppose you tell this Santiago fella that you seduced me like the vixen you are, and I was putty in your hands, but I stuck to my story about being here solely to carry out site surveys, despite obviously having fallen hopelessly in love with you."

She chuckled, but seemed unconvinced.

"You could add that you found me a marvelous and generous lover, and that one night with me ruined you for all other men forever. We want to stay as close to the truth as possible."

She laughed again, a little more this time but still not much. Then she shook her head. "I don't think . . . What if he doesn't believe me?"

"About my being a marvelous lover?"

This time she didn't laugh. "The whole time he was talking to me, I felt he would know if I was lying."

"If this is your way of telling me we have to actually go to bed together, I want you to know I'm willing to make that sacrifice."

"I'm being serious. Just . . . the overall falsity. I don't know if I can lie that well. Well enough to pretend that . . . that even if we went to bed, I've kept my distance from you. That I don't trust you."

He looked at her. "Then you do trust me."

There was a pause. She said, "Yes."

He took her hand and kissed the backs of her fingers. "Thank you, Isobel."

"And you trust me?"

He nodded. "I do."

There was a slightly awkward moment where he was still holding her hand and wasn't sure if he should let it go. "I think you should kiss my hand now," he said. "Just to keep things symmetrical."

She laughed and softly kissed his hand. And held on to it.

"Careful," he said. "I could get used to that."

She gave his hand a quick squeeze, but then let it go. Oh well, it was an imperfect world.

"What should I tell Santiago?" she said. "If he thinks I'm lying to him, Falintil . . . I'm afraid of what they'll do to me."

He thought about that. If this Santiago had instincts like the ones Isobel thought he had, they needed to be careful. Being the "good guys" in a conflict was a relative term, and had nothing to do with ruthlessness. Hell, the Muj were the good guys in Afghanistan, and look what they'd been capable of. In some ways, the good guys could be even worse than the bad guys because they were more motivated. Most of the Russians sent to Afghanistan were conscripts; they knew the war was pointless and all they wanted was to get home. But for the Muj, the war was a holy calling, a cause. And the parameters for what it meant to betray a cause could get pretty broad, including even failing to be adequately passionate about it, or not properly appreciating the all-powerful righteous authority of the cause's leaders.

"I'm going to think out loud here for a minute," he said. "Cloak and dagger's new to me. But maybe . . . On second thought, the simplest thing would be the wrong thing."

"The simplest thing . . ."

"Would be for you to tell Santiago you didn't find anything suspicious about me. We went out, we came back here, you asked me a bunch of probing questions, I passed every test. See, the problem is, he already thinks I'm a spy. He's already convinced of it. The fact that he's not wrong isn't even relevant. What matters is, if you tell him you found no evidence in favor of his belief, at a minimum he'll get frustrated. Sooner or later, and maybe even right away, he'll decide you're lying to him. Which we don't want."

The way she was looking at him, he could tell she trusted him. Which made what he had to say next hurt.

"So what you tell him is, he's right: I admitted to you I'm a spy."

"What?"

The more he thought about it, the surer he felt. "Yeah. You want to stick as close to the truth as you can. Tell him we had a drink at the hotel, which he probably already knows if his network is as good as you think. And that we came back here exactly the way we did. And I kissed you. And you tried to get me to do more, but I was a perfect gentleman. I said I wanted to take things slow. Which generally I do, by the way. Anyway, you tell him . . . you pressed me on what I'm really doing here, and I told you there's more to it than just site surveys but that I couldn't say more."

"I can't tell him that. If they realize you're a spy . . . who knows what they might do to you?"

"Well, they already think it and they haven't done anything yet other than tell you to take me to bed. Which if that were the penalty for spying generally, I think there might be a big jump in the growth of the global espionage business."

She gave him a small, worried laugh. "I don't know . . . I don't think it makes sense. I mean, why would you admit something like that?"

He thought of what he'd said to Mossberg: *You use the truth the way other people use lies.*

"To fool you. To trick you."

She flinched as though he'd raised a hand to her.

"I'm sorry, Isobel, but it's true. And it worked, didn't it? My being honest with you, it's made you trust me, hasn't it?"

It stung how hurt she looked, and confused. But he had to finish what he was saying.

"Well, what if I weren't being totally truthful with you? That's the way a con works. You feed someone some truth, and then they think you're honest. That's when their defenses go down, and you can tell them the lies that count. And listen . . . I'm sorry, but you should always be aware of that with me. I want you to trust me, I really do, but you can't trust me and also lie to Santiago. You said it yourself: he'll know. So hold on to some doubt about me. Worry about it. And feel all that when you talk to him. That's how you'll fool him—but you won't even be fooling him. Not really. You'll tell him I admitted I'm a spy, and that I told you I have feelings for you, feelings that made me want to be honest with you."

"I hate what you're saying."

"I do, too."

"Are you being truthful with me?"

"If I am, it could be because I'm trying to manipulate you."

She shook her head and looked away. He watched her, feeling suddenly bleak. But he knew it was the right thing to do. It had made him so happy to be honest with her, and to feel her trust. Now he was being honest to get her to distrust him.

Without turning back to him, she said, "I think maybe you're better at this spying stuff than you think."

"I don't care. Let someone else do it."

They were quiet for a moment. Then she turned to him.

"What about you? What are you going to tell Joko?"

"The same. We want our stories to match. And the closer we stick to the facts of what happened, the easier that'll be."

"You're going to tell him you admitted to me that you're a spy?"

"That's the plan."

"But he might . . . I don't know what he'll do to you. Or to me."

"I know. But remember, they haven't done anything yet. Joko thinks you're mixed up with Falintil, and rather than move directly, he told me to cultivate you. And likewise, Santiago thinks I'm a spy, and rather than having Falintil move directly, he told you to cultivate me. I don't know why any of that would have changed. In fact, both of them are likely to interpret what we tell them as progress. They could always change their minds at some point, but I doubt that would happen right away."

"But they could."

"Yeah, they could. I'm not saying there's no danger here. We're just trying to manage it, but . . ."

He let the words trail off while he tried to reason his way through.

"Here's the thing," he said. "It sounds like Santiago suspects me because someone saw me with Joko. And thought the way it went down was suspicious, like an excuse to come to the clinic and meet you. Okay, fine, he was right about all that. But why is Joko interested in you? I mean, where's he getting this notion that you're mixed up with Falintil? You said you haven't been, so why is he suspicious?"

Her mouth moved as though to form words, but none came out. Yeah, he could tell she had a good idea of where Joko's suspicion was coming from, and that it was frightening her. When she'd stumbled like that earlier in the conversation, it was when she'd started talking about rape, and how the Indonesians used it as a weapon of war. Was it something about that? Isobel had witnessed something, or knew something, or even had endured something herself, and was passing information on to Falintil? But she said she wasn't mixed up with Falintil. He couldn't figure it out.

But it was better if he didn't know, at least for now. "Wait," he said. "Don't tell me. You don't trust me that much yet. And you shouldn't."

"When you say things like that, it makes me trust you more."

"Maybe that's my game. I mean, I was sent to figure out what you've been up to. If you're on the verge of telling me, it means my mission is going well. You don't want that. You want to think I'm trying to play you. And that's what you'll tell Santiago."

"He asked me, too. Why whoever you're with would be so interested in me."

"What did you tell him?"

"That I didn't know."

But she did know. He could feel it. Joko thought she was working with Falintil, but she wasn't, and even Falintil didn't know why the Indonesians suspected her. Whatever had drawn Joko's attention, it didn't involve Falintil. She was doing it on her own.

If he knew what it was, maybe he could help her. But she wasn't a good liar. So when she reported back to Santiago, she had to be able to tell him something that was at least adjacent to the truth.

"Okay," he said. "That's good. It doesn't matter if he doesn't believe you. He'll want you to spend more time with me, so you'll have to keep reporting to him, thereby giving him lots of additional opportunities to probe your story."

"That sounds horrible."

"Well, it's no picnic, but it should buy us time."

"To do what?"

"I haven't gotten that far yet. But . . . what do you think about this Sebastião Gomes procession tomorrow?"

"How do you know about that?"

"I met some reporters at the hotel bar. They seem to think it's going to be a big deal."

"Western reporters?"

He nodded, wondering why she seemed so interested in that. "Two Americans and a Brit."

"What are their names?"

"You think you might know them?"

She shook her head. "Just asking."

It didn't feel like just asking, but he didn't press. He said, "Goodman, Nairn, and Stahl. Does that mean anything to you?"

She shook her head again. "Just that it's good the procession will be covered. Everyone I know is going to be there."

Well, maybe he'd been reading too much into her interest. "Are you going?" he said.

"Of course."

"I'd honestly rather you didn't. The streets feel tense to me. I have a feeling things could get ugly."

"It doesn't matter. We can't let them cow us. And anyway . . . it wouldn't look good to Santiago if I didn't go."

"Tell you what: as far as I'm concerned, he and Joko can have each other."

She didn't answer. He could tell he wasn't going to be able to talk her out of going to the procession. He wished she would have listened, but at the same time admired her stubbornness.

"I'll stick close," he said. "People have seen us together, it won't look strange. In fact, to Santiago and Joko, it'll look like progress."

"Why? Even if things get ugly, what could you do?"

"Oh, just keep my eyes and ears open. Tell some jokes if it turns out to be boring."

She gave him an uncertain laugh. "How do you know all this . . . spy stuff? You say you're not good at it, but . . ."

"That's fine, you're being suspicious of me. As you should be. Look, I told you I was a Marine. Well, afterward, I was embedded for a few years with the spooks in Afghanistan. And like they say, *Lie down with dogs, wake up with fleas.* Or in this case, spend enough time with professional liars, and you start to get a feel for what makes them tick."

"Which is what?"

"Well, they like lying, for one thing. They're good at it, and people naturally enjoy doing what they're good at. I mean, why do people run three-card monte games? They get satisfaction from fooling people, and there's a buck in it. For spooks, you get paid to fool people, and you're licensed by Uncle Sam himself."

There was a long, quiet moment while she seemed to ponder all that. Then she said, "There's something I want you to know."

"I told you, you shouldn't—"

"If you're lying to me, I'll hate you."

He thought, *You might, by the time this is over.*

What came out was, "I guess I'd deserve it."

Chapter 26

Once they stopped talking, Isobel realized how exhausted she was. The combination of unaccustomed alcohol, and fear tapering off, and grief settling in. She briefly considered asking Dox more about the journalists he mentioned—but then she would have to tell him why she was interested, and that would have meant telling him about the videotapes. And even if she could trust him that much, could she trust any of these reporters she'd never heard of? She didn't think so, but regardless, for a moment she castigated herself for leaving the tapes in Maliana. Now she wished she'd kept them. But she'd been so afraid of being stopped, searched . . .

She had stretched out on the couch, not meaning to fall asleep, but waking sometime later to find herself covered with the blanket, Dox sitting alongside her.

"You should sleep," she said, looking at him through half-closed eyes.

He shook his head. "Then I wouldn't get to look at you while you sleep. Besides, I told you, I'm keeping a vigil."

She felt a pang of guilt at that. "Then I should get up."

"No, you shouldn't. You'll have patients to see in the morning, and Rosa would have wanted you to be fresh."

It brought tears to her eyes. "I told you. You always say the right thing."

"Just telling the truth."

After all they'd discussed earlier, she didn't know how to respond. So she said nothing, simply taking his hand instead, and falling asleep again holding it.

Sometime later, she woke to the sound of the doors upstairs. Dox was still there, still awake. She sat up, rubbed her eyes, and checked her watch—six o'clock.

"Shit," she said in a low voice. "That's probably Santiago. He usually gets here before the clinic opens to collect the medical waste. You should go."

"You going to be all right?"

"Yes."

"Remember what I told you: stick to the truth. The truth can be a hell of a way to lie."

"Don't worry, I won't forget that."

Dox went up the stairs. Isobel used the bathroom, taking a few minutes to collect herself and think through what she would say to Santiago. She'd look for him upstairs so he wouldn't think she was trying to avoid him.

But when she came out, she pulled up short. He was sitting on the couch.

"It's still warm," he said.

She didn't know what he meant. But she didn't like the lack of any standard greeting. "What is?"

He gestured to the cushion beneath him as though it was the most obvious thing in the world. "The couch. From end to end. But"—he leaned closer to the upholstery and sniffed like a dog—"I think you must only have been sleeping."

She suppressed a surge of anger and disgust. "We were."

"You slept together but didn't sleep together?"

"We kissed. I tried to get him to do more. He wouldn't."

Santiago looked doubtful at that. "Is he . . ."

"I don't know. As I said, maybe you should try to get him to sleep with you."

His face darkened. "If you don't know how to seduce him, maybe it's because you need to practice, hmm? You think that's it?"

She glared at him but said nothing.

He patted the couch. "Come. Practice on me. We'll practice everything, hmm?"

You're just like them, she thought. *You make me sick.*

"Do you want to know what happened?" she said. "Or is this all just a pretext?"

He waited so long to respond that she thought he was going to tell her it *was* just a pretext. And she wouldn't have been surprised.

Instead, he said, "What happened?"

She told him. The hotel bar. Coming back to the clinic. The kiss. The admission.

He frowned at the last part. "He told you he was a spy?"

"Not in those words, but yes, it was obvious that's what he was implying."

"Why would he tell you something like that?"

She shrugged. "He seems . . . taken with me."

Santiago laughed. "Taken with you? You couldn't even get him to go to bed with you."

"He said he wanted to take it slowly."

"How can women raise strong sons and also be so naive, hmm? He wants you to trust him. He told you a little truth to conceal all the big lies."

It was exactly what Dox had predicted. She wondered fleetingly if men like Santiago were incapable of believing someone else could be telling the truth because they themselves were incapable of it. She pushed the thought away, along with the satisfaction she felt. She was too afraid it would show on her face.

"What lies?" she said.

"What he's really doing here. Did he tell you anything of that?"

"No."

"Did he tell you why he's interested in you specifically?"

"No."

"Did he say anything about Falintil?"

"No."

Santiago rubbed his chin as though pondering. "It's strange, I admit. You've never had anything to do with Falintil. And yet this man seems to believe otherwise. Meaning that whoever sent him believes otherwise. Kopassus, the CIA . . . Someone thinks you've been misbehaving. You're sure you have no idea why?"

"I'm sure."

He sighed. "All right. I suppose nothing to be done. Other than to keep seeing him. The little truths he's shared seem not to have had their desired effect. Let's see if he shares some bigger truths, hmm? Maybe eventually he'll share enough that we'll see all the lies behind them."

It seemed Dox's predictions about how Santiago would react were accurate. But again, she allowed herself to feel nothing about it. She could do so later, when Santiago was gone. When he wasn't looking at her.

"You'll be at the procession?" he said.

She nodded. "Of course."

He returned the nod, then stood and walked to the stairs. He started up—then turned back to her.

"Oh, one thing I almost forgot. How was your vacation last week?"

She looked at him, suddenly afraid and trying not to show it. "My vacation?"

"Yes, your vacation. You went away for a few days, for the first time in years. Maybe the first time forever. Have you forgotten?"

Her heart started pounding. *He knows,* she thought. *He knows, he knows . . .*

She felt it showing in her face. Her distress. Her fear. Her weakness.

And then inspiration struck. "It wasn't a vacation," she said, letting some of the roiling emotion express itself in her tone as indignation.

"No?"

"I was visiting the spot where I scattered my father's ashes. And where he and I scattered my mother's."

He frowned. "I thought your parents were buried here, in Dili."

No, you did not, you liar.

He had no idea what had been done with her parents when they died. Or where. He was inventing it, to try to trip her up.

I was right before, she thought. *You don't know as much as you want me to think you do.*

"I don't know what could have given you that idea. My parents were cremated. Their ashes are in the sea at Aidabalaten. I try to visit at least once a year, but as you say, it's been too long. I'm sorry, though. Should I have asked for your permission?"

He stared at her for a long moment. "There's something you're not telling me, Isobel."

"There are all sorts of things I'm not telling you," she said, trying and failing to control her growing anger. "Because *they're none of your business.*"

He came down the stairs and stalked toward her. She wanted to back up but wouldn't let herself.

He stopped just inches away. "Let me tell you what is my business. My business is *the nation.* Are you part of that nation, hmm?"

She could feel her anger getting the better of her. She didn't care.

"If you think you and the nation are the same," she said, "you're in the wrong clinic. Because you don't need a medical doctor. You need a psychiatrist."

He stared at her, his jaw clenched, air whistling in and out of his nose. She was sure he was going to hit her. But still she wouldn't flinch.

"I'm cooperating with you," she said, her voice rising. "Even with your disgusting instructions. And I'm reporting to you afterward. If that's not enough, then you need to ask yourself what this is really about, Mr. Defender of the Nation!"

He drew back his hand but she didn't care. She wouldn't give him the satisfaction of seeing her shrink away. He could hurt her, but she wouldn't let him know she was afraid.

A long moment went by. Then he lowered his hand.

"You say you're cooperating," he said. "I hope for your sake that's true. Because if I learn it's not true—if I learn you're doing anything behind my back, if there's something you're not telling me, if you're doing anything at all that frustrates my ability to save our nation from the Javanese, let me tell you, Isobel: what Kopassus does to innocents is as nothing compared to what Falintil does to traitors."

He turned and walked up the stairs, then closed the door behind him. As soon as she was sure he was gone, her legs started to shake. She collapsed facedown on the couch and sobbed into the cushions, as quietly as she could, to be sure no one could hear.

Chapter 27

T he swaying tops of the palm trees were lit by the rising sun when Dox arrived at the hotel. He took the stairs to the second floor, relishing the thought of a quick shower before hitting the rack for a few hours. But as soon as he turned onto the corridor, he saw Joko's soldiers flanking his door. They kept the muzzles of their M16s lowered, which was good, but which also seemed a minor detail compared to the fact of their presence.

But no way was he going to let them know that the sight of them made him nervous. "How y'all doing?" he said cheerfully. "You're up early."

They looked at him impassively. It occurred to him that they might not speak a lick of English. Their boss's was so good, he assumed theirs would be, too.

"You boys speak any English?" he said. "My Bahasa is sadly lacking. And without a common tongue, I fear our friendship will be stillborn."

He might as well have been talking to a pair of staring statues. He shrugged. "Well, it's been good chatting. I guess now's the part where I get to enjoy your boss's company at least as much as I've enjoyed yours."

He knew the door wouldn't be locked. He turned the knob and walked in.

Joko was sitting on one of the two twin beds, a pistol in his right hand. At the sight of Dox, he broke into his sociopath's smile. "Good morning, Dox."

Dox plonked down on the opposite bed, facing him, as though it was the most natural thing in the world to find Joko sitting there. "How you doing, Joker?"

"It's Joko."

"Oh, right, Joko. My bad."

Joko shook his head. "You think you're the first American idiot who's made that crack?"

Dox laughed. "Hell, no. I'll bet there've been hundreds. You know with you, Joko, I'm guessing all sorts of jokes write themselves."

"That's good. I want you to laugh. I like it."

"Finally, something we can agree on."

"You're laughing now, but when the time is right, you'll be begging. The contrast will make the begging so much more satisfying. So by all means, indulge yourself while you can. I'll thank you for it later."

"We'll see who thanks who. Or technically *who thanks whom*—I know you're a stickler for proper English. Anyway, to what do I owe the pleasure? Other than your desire for a theatrical display of your prowess in getting into my hotel room. Which by the way has a lock a one-armed, nearsighted, feebleminded child could pick, so if you want to intimidate me, you're going to have to get more creative."

"Maybe I'll have my men point their rifles at you again. It was fun watching your legs shake."

"Whatever blows your hair back, Joko. What little of it there is. Now, what do you want?"

Joko smiled. "Do you ever think about how easy it would be for me to kill you?"

"I think if it were easy, amigo, you would have done it already."

"Maybe I'm savoring the prospect."

There was an echo in that of what George Whitaker had said about Roy, but he pushed the thought away.

"Honestly, Joko? That wouldn't surprise me. I mean, on a scale of one to ten, you seem pretty twisted. But no, I think the real reason is you need permission from your master."

Joko's eyes narrowed slightly, and Dox sensed his guess was probably right. Thank God.

"I don't have a master."

"Whatever you want to call Felix. I was brought here to carry out a mission. And until that mission has been completed or overtaken by events, the people who sent me on it will be pissed if you fuck it all up just because you were unable to manage your obvious proclivities."

Joko laughed. "You think I need Felix's permission to kill someone?"

"Not someone. Me."

The truth was, Dox wasn't sure of any of this. It made sense, of course, but lots of things made sense on paper and then didn't hold up so well when they bumped into the real world. But he'd played enough poker on floats and in Afghanistan to know that once you bluffed, either you saw it through, or the other players were going to see your cards.

So he said nothing, instead affecting a slightly bored look.

After a moment, Joko said, "You know, on my island, Sumatra, we believe things you Westerners could never understand."

"I'm sure there's a whole boatload of things we Westerners could never understand. So forgive me if I seem less impressed than you were hoping."

"For example, we believe that if you eat the heart of your enemy, you gain his strength. And that if you kill enough of your enemies, and eat enough of their hearts, you yourself can never be killed."

Dox knew there would be no upside in acknowledging that he'd already heard about Joko's culinary habits. "Well, if it was a big fella's heart you were eating, I could see where you'd gain a little weight, sure. I don't know about his strength. And I've yet to meet anyone who couldn't be killed, though it's true some can be harder than others. But like you said, there's a lot we Westerners don't understand."

"Do you want to hear how I know it's true?"

"Not particularly, but I can't imagine you allowing a little thing like that to get in the way of telling me."

Joko smiled. "It's because when I kill a man, I make sure to eat his heart."

"Do you have a family recipe for this kind of thing? Or is it something you improvise, over a cookfire?"

"I never cook my enemies' hearts. To gain their power, you have to eat them raw."

"Of course you do. How could I not have realized? But I'll tell you what, Joko. Your heart is safe from my dining table. For a lot of reasons, including that your heart strikes me as the most putrid organ in your entire body, which is saying a lot, and even the thought of any part of you in my stomach? Makes me want to puke it up in advance."

Joko stared at him. The man did have an intimidating stare. It made sense that he'd resort to it upon realizing that in their battle of wits, he kept coming up short.

After a moment he said, "How did it go last night?"

Once again, Dox was struck by the man's discipline—by the way he could instantly turn off his ego and get back to substance, a quality Dox had to admit he himself sorely lacked. He had a feeling that what enabled Joko to do it was the man's expectation that soon enough his ego would have all the satisfaction it craved, plus interest.

"You're watching me," Dox said. "You're a subtle man, I know, and it wouldn't be like you to come right out and say it. But I want you to know that I got the message, same as I did finding you sitting here on one of the beds in my hotel room."

Joko stared at him again, and for a moment Dox wondered if he was overestimating the man's self-discipline. And the degree to which

Felix could control him. Even a well-trained dog could be provoked. And a rabid one was apt to do anything at all.

"How did it go last night?" he said again.

"It went fine. I think she likes me. I doubt you could blame her. I'm sure you feel the same yourself. Although it's true that the five thousand I donated to the clinic might have helped. Did you know, though, that someone stole that money right after I delivered it?"

Joko offered a slight, satisfied smile. "Really?"

"Yeah, really. Murdered a nurse named Rosa, too, who was bringing it to the bank. A nice lady with a mother and father and her own children, who was doing nothing but helping sick and wounded people in Dili."

Joko raised his hands in a *What can you do?* gesture. "So much evil in the world."

Dox looked at him. "Yeah, well, we do what we can to make less of it, don't we?"

"We do what we do. Some people are more honest about it than others. The doctor. Did you sleep with her?"

Dox shook his head. "How did Roger Moore put it in *Live and Let Die?* 'That's not the sort of question a gentleman answers.'"

"Wasn't that right before Kananga fed him to the sharks?"

"Actually, that was later in the film. First Kananga tried to feed him to the crocodiles. But Bond escaped both times."

"I suppose if you're James Bond, you have nothing to worry about. Did you learn anything? About the doctor's involvement with Falintil and foreign journalists?"

"It's bad enough you expect a woman to sleep with me on the first date, but you expect her to fall in love with me, too? No, she didn't tell me about any of those things. I think we hit it off, and I think I acted in such a way that she trusts me. I'll try to build on that. But I doubt it'll happen overnight."

"It better happen quickly. There's a procession tomorrow. Timorese vermin honoring a fellow vermin named Sebastião Gomes. They'll be marching from the Motael Church to the Santa Cruz cemetery. The left hand in Jakarta allowed some foreign journalists in for a Portuguese delegation that never happened, and the right hand forgot to revoke their visas. So now they're here. The good news is, maybe the woman will try to make contact. I assume you'll be watching for that."

Dox didn't let on that A, he'd heard about the procession for Gomes, that B, he'd met the foreign journalists in question, or that C, he and Isobel had already arranged to meet outside the church.

"I will," he said.

Joko smiled and stood. He went to holster the pistol, and then quick as a cobra whipped it around and smashed Dox across the temple with the barrel. Dox saw a flash of bright white lights and felt a *boom!* behind his eyes. Time seemed to skip a second, and he realized he was on his side, luckily on the mattress, though, not the floor. He touched the side of his head and his fingers came away bloody.

"Second time you caught me like that," he said, feeling woozy. "Ain't gonna be a third."

"You should have someone look at your head," Joko said. "Maybe another excuse to go to the clinic. Maybe this time you can get her to fuck you."

Dox looked at his bloody fingers. "*Fuck you* is the operative phrase, Joker. Joko, I mean."

He knew a headache was coming and in fact it was already rolling in. Well, headaches were why God made aspirin. He'd been hit in the head before, and harder than what Joko just dished out. Anyone who doubted it needed only to ask Roy.

"I probably shouldn't say this, Joko, but there's something I want you to know."

"Yes? And what's that?"

Dox looked in his eyes. "Before this is done? I'm going to kill you. And I don't need Felix's permission to do it, either."

Chapter 28

Dox had been standing outside Motael Church for an hour, feeling more and more uneasy as the crowd grew. When he'd arrived, there had been no more than a hundred Timorese milling around in the area, but now he estimated at least a thousand—not just on the church grounds, but standing on the retaining walls and on a statue pedestal, filling the street, and stretching all the way to the esplanade running along the seawall.

No one was being disorderly, but he could feel the crowd's growing confidence, could hear it in the increased passion of the voices of the speakers shouting from the building's portico as they addressed the people assembled, and in the answering chants of *Liberdade!* And *Timor-Leste!* There were clusters of Indonesian soldiers in the area, watching tensely as more and more locals arrived. The soldiers looked like no more than teenagers, and probably they were wondering whether the higher-ups had fucked the dog again and sent too few of them to manage too many angry protesters. Of course, the soldiers had all the guns, but you didn't need a PhD in protests and riots to know that an increasingly emboldened crowd combined with immature, outnumbered, nervous occupying soldiers probably better trained in small-unit tactics than in urban policing was a bad combination. On top of which, tempers tended to flare in the heat, and a warm morning was now giving way to a sultry afternoon.

Yeah, if it hadn't been for Isobel, Dox would have been happy to wait this one out in the hotel room with an icepack on his head. But he didn't like the idea of her being here without him. Of course, she hadn't been wrong in asking what he could do if things got ugly. The truth was, probably not much. But certainly more than nothing, which would have been the only available option if he'd stayed away instead.

He cut back and forth for the dozenth time. He saw Goodman and Nairn interviewing people but didn't spot Stahl. Still no sign of Isobel. She had said that she would look for him in front of the church, and that she would be there early. Now he realized *in front of the church* was too imprecise a plan. When he agreed to it, he had envisioned a few dozen people, which in fairness was how things had started out. But now . . . even if he'd knocked a few onlookers off the statue pedestal and climbed it himself—which would have been an extremely bad idea for one of the few obvious foreigners in the area—it would have taken a lot of luck to spot her. There were just too many shifting people.

He kept moving back and forth and the crowd kept growing. He fought the temptation to go to the clinic, afraid that if he did, Isobel would show up while he was gone and they'd miss each other entirely.

After another hour, there were thousands of chanting protesters jamming the street as far as he could see, the din so loud he wouldn't have objected to earplugs. He was close to the water now, and too far back to hear what the latest speaker was saying from the church portico, but whatever it was, it must have been a stemwinder because it got the crowd roaring *Timor-Leste! Timor-Leste!* in unison. And then suddenly, as though some unspoken command had reached everyone all at once, the crowd began moving southeast. Dox had already reconnoitered and knew this was the route to the cemetery. But where the hell was Isobel?

He let the masses carry him along, the seawall to their left, doing what he could to drift back and forth, like a swimmer caught in a strong river current, looking for her. Some of the protesters eyed him with curiosity. A few, probably hoping he was a foreign reporter, even tried to explain in limited English what the procession was about. To these he held up his hands palms forward and said, "Sorry, not a reporter, just here to do what I can," all of which was true, and all of which could be read however anyone might want to read it. There was an ebullience in the air, a feeling dramatically different from what he'd sensed on that first walk through the city.

As the crowd proceeded along the water, its pace accelerated from a walk to a trot. A helicopter passed overhead, and the marchers chanted more loudly over the roar of its rotors. Banners began to appear: images of Xanana Gusmão, who Dox knew from the briefing papers he'd read was a resistance leader; slogans in Tetum; the yellows, blacks, and reds of the Timorese flag. People were holding up their fingers in peace signs, or maybe *V* for *victory*, but there were a lot of clenched fists pumping up and down as well. Some of the marchers pulled off sweatshirts, revealing Falintil tee-shirts beneath, and started running ahead, the crowd increasing its pace to follow. He began to see masks, and knew nothing good would come of it. It would be bad enough if it was just ordinary people covering their faces, because anonymous marchers could turn into a mob fast. But there was a worse possibility—false flags and agents provocateurs. The chanting grew to a roar, some in Tetum, but always returning to a refrain of *Viva Timor-Leste! Viva Timor-Leste!*

People jostled him left and right. He looked for escape routes and didn't see anything promising. To his right was a concrete wall. To his left stood a high steel fence, naval ships docked in the waters on the other side of it, Indonesian sailors watching sullenly from their decks as the protesters raced by. Dox and the marchers might as well have been running through a cattle chute for all the options they had. And none of the Indonesian soldiers he saw had anything resembling riot gear, just rifles. That was bad. For one thing, it meant the soldiers would feel vulnerable, which would make them scared. On top of which, to deal with any problems, they'd have only two options: retreat on the one hand, start shooting on the other. The bad feeling he had about where this was going was getting worse. And still no sign of Isobel.

Nor of Joko, for that matter. Another disquieting sign. Dox doubted the man would miss a shindig like this one, and if he was keeping himself unseen, it was likely because he was up to something nefarious. Maybe looking for new hearts to eat or whatever else he did to while away the hours.

They reached the walls of the cemetery and the crowd began to flow through the gates. Dox knew from his earlier reconnaissance that the grounds wouldn't easily hold so many, so he hung back. He saw Max Stahl standing along the entry path, holding a video camera and interviewing people as they passed him. Some of the protesters made sure to get handmade English signs in front of him: *Why the Indonesian Army Shoot Our Church? Independent Is What We Inspire! Check All the Prison and Liberate the Prisoners!* The spelling was off in a few, but whatever they lacked in English skills, they made up for in understanding who their audience was, and it sure wasn't Indonesia.

Within ten minutes, protesters of all ages were standing along every inch of the white concrete retaining walls, holding aloft banners in Tetum and English. There were schoolgirls in blue-and-white uniforms; bare-chested teen boys probably hoping to impress them; even some spry-looking gray-haired oldsters. People were climbing into the surrounding banyan trees for a better view, and the chanting was getting cacophonous. Someone started shouting in Tetum through a bullhorn. Dox wiped sweat from his eyes and looked around wildly, wondering if Isobel might have been inside the cemetery already, his head pounding and his bad feeling growing steadily worse.

And just like that, he saw her, pressed in the center of the approaching crowd that was still flowing into the cemetery. "Isobel!" he shouted, waving. "Hey!"

She broke into a smile at the sight of him and returned the wave. He fought his way against the current of people until he reached her.

"Where've you been?" he said. "I was worried." The crowd jostled them as it moved toward the cemetery gates, but he barely noticed.

"I had to wait for Rosa's family," she said. "I couldn't leave her."

"I'm sorry, I should have realized. Are they all right?"

"No. They're devastated. But . . . I don't want to talk about that now. I want to focus on this. Because it's wonderful. And I need that." She looked around. "See? There's even a Western cameraman. The whole world will see."

She must have been referring to Stahl. Dox started to answer, but someone bumped Isobel's shoulder on the way past, hard enough to knock her back a step. Dox gave the guy an angry look, but he was already gone, with twenty protesters flowing behind him. Immediately the crowd started pouring through the gap that had opened between Dox and Isobel. He struggled forward and stood close to make sure no one could come between them again.

"Don't look so worried," she said. "I was feeling resentful about coming. Because of Santiago. But now . . . look at all the people! Can't you feel it? This is a great day."

Dox was feeling something, all right, but a great day wasn't it. He looked around. "This is a bad place to stand," he said. "We're like a couple of leaves in a damn river."

She nodded to the cemetery gates. "Let's go in. There will be speakers at Gomes's grave. Maybe we can get close."

"I doubt it. See how the crowd is moving more slowly at the gates? They're congealing there because the entrance is a chokepoint. Not likely to be a lot of room to maneuver inside."

"Why would we need to maneuver?"

"I don't know, the soldiers I've seen feel twitchy to me. And that's just the ones in uniform. There could be others around, in street clothes, even masks."

"What can they do? There are thousands of people here! Come on. Let's go in."

He wanted to argue, but he could see she was caught up in the excitement and knew she wouldn't listen. "All right," he said. "You win. But listen, let everyone else get carried away by what a great day it is, all right? You keep your eyes and ears open."

"For what?"

"For anything that doesn't seem right. And stay close to me. If we get separated, let's try to meet back here again."

For a moment, she didn't respond. Then she surprised him by reaching out and taking his hands. "Are you asking me to trust you?" she said.

It made him happy, but somehow it hurt, too. "You shouldn't. You're not supposed to."

She gave him one of her beautiful smiles. "Then you shouldn't be trustworthy. Come on."

Going in was easy enough—all they had to do was stop resisting the crowd. Dox saw Stahl enter ahead of them and figured the man had decided it was time to go to the gravesite.

They walked along a wide dirt road toward the center. The air was thick with dust the procession was kicking up. As they passed a cluster of trees to their left, Isobel pointed ahead. "It's just up there," she said. "Let's try to get close."

Dox would have preferred far to close, but before he could respond, a tall man just ahead of them and to their left tripped or got pushed—it happened too fast to be clear on which, but the man stumbled toward Isobel, and just as they were about to collide, the man's head erupted and blood and brains sprayed onto Isobel and Dox. Isobel froze in shock. An instant later, Dox heard the crack of the shot. A single word blared Klaxon-loud in his head:

Sniper!

Behind them came the sudden report of dozens of rifle shots. The crowd started screaming and stampeding. Dox realized all at once what was happening:

—*Supposed to take her out just before the shooting started, maybe me, too. The guy who tripped saved her*—

Sirens started wailing. Dox threw an arm around Isobel and dove behind a raised concrete tomb. They crashed into the dirt. He looked back to see a dust cloud kicked up by a round that had hit just beyond where they'd been standing, heard the crack of the shot an instant later.

While reconnoitering that morning, he'd passed a small construction site—a store or a school or such. It was framed for two stories but only the first had been built, and there was an aluminum scaffold alongside it, the same type Dox had perched on while doing summer construction work as a teenager back home. He'd seen nothing else in the area that was both deserted enough for discretion and high enough to cover the necessary parts of the cemetery, and had noted the scaffolding as a good sniping position. Of course at the time, it was merely hypothetical, the kind of thing he noticed everywhere he went, an occupational hazard of being a Hunter of Gunmen. But now he knew someone else had seen that scaffolding, and decided to actually use it. He was furious with himself for not having treated the possibility seriously. Absent the dumbest of luck, right now Isobel would be dead, and it would have been his fault.

Isobel groaned, the wind knocked out of her. She tried to come to her knees, but Dox kept his arm around her back and pushed her down.

"There's a sniper!" he shouted. "On our left!"

He looked back and saw soldiers entering through the gates, shooting into the crowd. Panicked people stampeded past them. A young girl got hit in the neck, corkscrewed, and went down in a spray of blood. Isobel saw and struggled as though to go to her. Dox held her tight.

"We're pinned down!" he shouted. "They're shooting at us!"

"They're shooting at everyone!"

"No, you and me specifically! The shooting is random, the sniper is about us! Understand? You move from behind this crypt, he'll take you out!"

"But that girl—"

"You can't help her! That guy is good, he was going for your head and he would have had it, too, if someone hadn't stumbled!"

"Why? Why would they—"

"I don't know. We'll worry about why later."

He glanced around. They'd been lucky—the guy stumbling, of course, but also being right next to a tomb that offered reasonable cover. There were headstones in the area, and other tombs, too, but a lot of exposure involved in reaching them. A bizarre thought zigzagged through his brain: *If anyone ever asks me to define irony, I swear I'll tell them my life was saved by a damn tomb.*

Over the wail of sirens, he heard more rifle shots from the cemetery entrance. He looked over and saw additional soldiers racing through, firing as they moved. But not panic firing—it was deliberate. They were chasing marchers into the cemetery and mowing them down. All around, people were screaming, hiding, running, coughing from all the dust getting kicked up from the road. Here and there were bodies and pools of blood. One man tried to drag one of the fallen to safety, then he himself fell back from a shot through the chest.

Dox didn't like being downrange from the soldiers, but he'd take his chances with random fire over a sniper any day. And anyway, it wasn't like he had a choice.

He looked at Isobel. "You can't move from here. Not to save someone, not for anything. You can't even raise your head above the top edge of the tomb. You don't understand what a sniper sees through his scope. One inch of scalp and you'll lose your head, do you understand me?"

Her eyes were wide with fear. "What are we going to do?"

Dox glanced around. It looked like half the procession was running, and the other half was sheltering behind whatever cover they could find. The guy the sniper had hit was sprawled facedown just a few feet away. Dox checked the angle of the tomb and thought he could make it. But only if he was flat, and from that position he wouldn't be able to drag the dead guy back.

"I'm gonna stretch out," he said. "You stay close to the tomb and pull me back."

"Why?"

"No time to explain. Just pull me. I'll push with my free arm, and between the two of us, I think we can manage."

He got on his stomach, squirmed forward, extended an arm, and managed to snag one of the guy's pant legs without moving from behind the cover of the tomb. He pulled, but it didn't work—the guy's pants just started coming down. The guy was wearing a belt, too, obviously not cinched very tight. Worse, a second after Dox's hand had been exposed, a round tore into the guy's leg right where Dox had been gripping it.

Gonna get you for that, Mr. Sniper. You'll see.

He hooked his fingers inside one of the guy's sneakers, hoping the laces were snugger than the belt had been, and jerked hard just to get his hand out of danger. Then he glanced back, his eyes watering from all the dust. "Okay, pull me!"

Isobel grabbed his pant leg and did as he said. Luckily, Dox's belt was a little tighter than the unfortunate dead guy's, and between Isobel's efforts and his own pushing with his free hand, he was able to belly back to the edge of the tomb, dragging the dead guy along with him.

Isobel must have thought he'd been trying to help the guy, because she immediately turned him onto his back. But you didn't have to be a doctor to see there was nothing to be done. Half the guy's head was gone, and the remaining half was a mess of blood and brains and bone. Dox undid the guy's belt, then cinched it as tightly as he could.

More people ran past, screaming. "What are you doing?" Isobel said.

He didn't want to waste time explaining, but if she didn't understand, she might not listen.

"They didn't know where we'd be," he said. "Or when we'd get here. And maybe they didn't want anyone to witness anything done up close. Whatever it was, they decided to place a man in an elevated position with a clear view of the cemetery entrance, Gomes's grave, and everything in between. They knew we'd show up. All this shooting . . . it was planned. And the *Go* sign was the initial shot. No one would be able to distinguish that from all the random shooting right after."

"Why didn't he shoot us when we were outside the gates?"

"Where he's hiding, he's got a better view of the cemetery itself."

"How do you know where he's hiding?"

"I might be the world's worst spy, but I know a thing or two about sniping. I know where he is, and I'm going to take him out."

"How?"

"I haven't gotten that far yet. But you gotta promise me you'll stay here. Keep still and it'll be less likely those soldiers will key on you, there are hundreds of other people doing the same. The sniper's not in contact with the soldiers—if he were, they'd already be here shooting us at close range. Dumbasses didn't have a plan B."

It sounded encouraging. But the truth was, it wasn't clear that the "dumbasses" needed a plan B. The sniper had missed, but he still had them pinned down.

"I don't—"

"Promise me!"

"All right, I promise."

He took her hand. "You trust me, right?"

"Yes."

"Then trust me to come back. And don't move 'til I do."

Without thinking, he leaned forward and kissed her hard on the mouth. She kissed him back with equal ardor.

It couldn't have lasted for more than a couple of seconds, but it seemed like longer, maybe because it felt so good and he didn't want it to end. But somehow he managed to break away. "That was better than the first one," he said. Which was only a half truth, because in fact it was better than any he'd ever had.

She looked at him—her mouth half-open, her brow furrowed as though in consternation or shock. "That was the first one," she said.

He grinned. "Well, I can't wait for the second. Okay, I gotta go. Remember. Don't move."

What he had to do sucked, and the only reason he was going to do it was because everything else sucked even more. Going west back to the gate would have him running against the crowd and into the soldiers. Going north would have him running straight at the sniper. Any other direction would be equally exposed, and take too long besides. His only chance was northwest to the banyan trees lining the west side of the cemetery. But that was thirty yards of dirt with only headstones and low tombs for cover. His legs would be protected, but it wasn't his legs he was worried about.

He managed to push the dead guy into a sitting position with the guy's back against the tomb. Then he got on his knees in front of him, let the guy collapse onto his shoulder, and hoisted him by the belt and sleeve up into a fireman's carry. The good news was the guy was light enough to probably not slow him down too much. The bad news was a slightly thicker specimen might have been better suited to stopping rifle rounds. Well, any port in a storm.

He sucked in a big breath, came to a squat, and rocketed out from behind the tomb, crouching as much as he could consistent with the imperative of moving as fast as possible, the dead guy draped like a shawl at the right side of his head and along his torso, one of the dangling arms slapping Dox in the ass like a rider telling his horse to giddyup. He shuffled faster than he expected any human had ever shuffled before, certainly faster than anyone had ever managed while wearing a corpse like a shawl, trying not to imagine how clearly he must have been showing up between the reticles of the sniper's scope. He felt a round tear past, and then another slam into the guy's torso right alongside Dox's head. He shuffled faster, something that a mere second before he had been certain would be impossible. And suddenly he was in the trees, his chest heaving, his eyes streaming from the dust, but fuck all that, he was alive and unhit.

He dumped the guy and saw that the round he had absorbed had landed laterally. That was lucky—the guy was skinny enough that if he'd been hit in the stomach or back, the bullet likely would have gone right through, with Dox's skull as the backstop. And while he knew he had a hard head, he had no desire to test it against a rifle shot, not even one that had just been slowed courtesy of a corpse.

"I'm sorry for what happened," he said. "And that I can't do anything but leave you here. But I'm gonna get that sumbitch. I wish you could see it when I do."

He dashed forward to the next tree. From a distance it had looked thick, but given his knowledge that a sniper was on the other side of it, it felt up close as slender as a sapling. He thought he had solid concealment now, but he zigzagged anyway, moving from one tree to the next until he was crouching at the northwestern corner of the cemetery. It was quieter here, *quieter* of course being a relative term, because sirens were still wailing everywhere and sporadic gunfire kept erupting back by the main gates. There were people running in the area, albeit fewer than at the cemetery's center, some with defiant raised fists and continued cries of *Timor-Leste!*

He snuck a quick peek over the wall, which was about shoulder high here, and saw reinforcements marching down the street toward the gates, one jeep leading the way and another bringing up the rear. The men were sweeping the muzzles of their rifles left and right as they moved but seemed disciplined, and weren't firing. He pictured Isobel and tried to push away his terror that some random soldier had come upon her, or a stray round, or—

Enough. You got one way to help her. Do it.

He used a shirttail to wipe the sweat and grit from his eyes, then took a moment to consider. The problem was getting behind the man's position. A direct approach from the cemetery would be suicide. The sniper would have a clear field of fire the whole way, and unless he thought Dox had been running away with his custom-made corpse shield, it was exactly the approach he'd be expecting.

The street. There's no other way. With the trees, he won't be able to see that section. And with all those soldiers, he wouldn't expect it.

Of course, the reason he wouldn't expect it is because it would be so dumb. But like everything else, if you were motivated enough, *dumb* could become a relative term.

He stood and held his hands high, palms forward. "Pardon me," he called out loudly enough to be heard, but hopefully not so loudly that he would sound aggressive. "I'm an American tourist and this is not what my American travel agent told me to expect on this trip from America."

Most of the soldiers glanced at him and kept marching, but two stopped. They were just boys, younger than he was. And while they didn't lower their rifles, they weren't exactly aiming at him, either.

"American tourist," he said again, walking slowly forward, still with his hands raised, hoping the blood and skull matter he'd gotten hit with would make him look sympathetic, or at least unpleasant enough for no one to want to get near. "Without a doubt in the wrong place at the wrong time. And with your kind permission, this American would like nothing more than to hop over this wall, get back to his hotel room, and pour his exhausted American self a stiff American drink."

For all he knew, none of these people spoke English, in which case his blather was wasted and the word *American* would have to do all the heavy lifting. If so, he wanted to make sure they got plenty of it.

No one responded. The two soldiers glanced at each other. Dox knew the look well: *You want to fill out the paperwork for this, or pretend we didn't see it?*

More marching soldiers glanced at him, but when they saw that two of their number had been dumb enough to stop and handle it, whatever "it" was, they were happy to keep right on going.

"I'm just going to put my hands on the top of this wall," Dox said to the two soldiers, "and haul my American ass over it, and go back to my hotel room. Hopefully with a story to one day tell my American grandchildren. All right?"

Again, no response.

Oh, man. Moment-of-truth time.

He pressed his palms to the top of the wall, boosted himself up onto it, and vaulted over to the street. The soldiers watched, their rifles ready but still not exactly aimed at him.

Dox brushed the dust off his pants and straightened up. "What a day," he said. "Well, I'll just return to the aforementioned hotel room for the aforementioned American drink, most likely a Bombay Sapphire martini if you're curious. I apologize for interfering with whatever it is you're doing here and hope you have a pleasant rest of the day. American."

And then he turned and walked smartly away, forcing himself to put a little cavalier in his gait and to ignore the insane itching he could feel between his shoulder blades, which was the spot he expected the bullets to hit if the two soldiers changed their minds about the paperwork.

Ten feet. Twenty. He passed more soldiers. They eyed him, but the sight of a big, bloodied Westerner calmly walking in the opposite direction seemed sufficiently confusing to dissuade anyone from challenging him. Plus every soldier he passed could see that he'd already passed a dozen others, and if no one else had given him a hard time, his presence must have been authorized. Probably nuclear secrets had been stolen on less bluff than that.

About sixty yards along, he turned right onto a narrow street that paralleled the northern wall of the cemetery. Suddenly the soldiers were gone, the sounds of shooting and sirens muted. No one was around. He knew from instinct and experience that for the time being he absolutely could not consider how close he'd just come to dying—not just once but several times. That was for later, assuming he didn't die before later, and by God if he made it that far he planned to enjoy his legs wobbling and hands trembling and the feeling that he might puke from the undeserved freak luck of it all. But for now, he still had to focus.

Ten yards down, he cut right again, this time into an empty lot, scanning as he moved, seeing no problems. A girl was cowering behind a plant that offered neither cover nor concealment, despite the presence of various concrete structures nearby. Poor thing was too petrified to budge. He wanted to help her but there was nothing to be done. He wasn't even sure that a bad hiding place was a worse option than hoofing it.

He kept moving, intent on keeping structures between himself and the construction site. In a moment he reached a small house. Beyond it he could just make out the top of the scaffolding, sunlight glinting off the aluminum posts.

He eased to his right, mindful of his footing, avoiding some plastic wrappers and bottles strewn along the ground, probably detritus from workers breaking for lunch. He did a quick sneak-and-peek around the side of the building. Nothing.

He eased out and crept forward to a dumpster—the last cover or concealment between himself and the sniper. He could see the platform at the top of the scaffolding now, a pair of boots at the edge of it. The sniper was facing the cemetery, as expected. Of course, that could change, in which case Dox would be exposed and facing a proven-accurate sniper who held an elevated position and who, if he decided not to bother with a bullet, was close enough to kill him with just some rocks instead.

He hadn't expected a spotter and didn't see one, thank God. Not enough room on the platform, and no real need, either, given the distances involved. Still, it was good to get the confirmation that however outmatched he might otherwise be, at least the fight was one-on-one.

He eased out and crept closer and closer, hating how slowly he had to move and how long the last twenty feet was taking. But if he made a sound and the bastard turned around, it would be over for sure.

He's concentrating on the cemetery. He doesn't know you're here. Doesn't expect you at all. Stay slow. Slow. Almost there now. Nice and slow.

He made it to the side of the scaffolding and felt weirdly relieved and maximally exposed. Relieved because the last place in the world the guy would think to check would be the area directly beneath him. Exposed because if for some crazy reason the guy did look down, it would all be over in less than a second.

He looked up and didn't see anything—a rope, a chain, a hook—securing the side of the rig to the adjacent structure. Ten years earlier, when he'd been climbing up and down these things at construction sites, a failure to attach scaffolding to a stable structure would have landed you with a major safety infraction, and maybe a fine levied by an OSHA inspector. Well, thank God standards were a little more flexible in East Timor.

He got in a half crouch, wiped his palms on his pants, and took hold of two of the vertical metal struts. He knew rigs this size could weigh over four hundred pounds. That would be more than he could lift. But he didn't need to lift the whole thing. All he needed to do was tilt it.

One. Two. Three!

He exploded up and out like an offensive tackle surging off the line. There was a yelp of surprise and fear from eighteen feet above him, but the rig was heavier than he'd expected and he hadn't tilted it enough to send the sniper flying. Instead the guy slid back, grabbed hold of a post, and hung on, the baseball cap he must have been wearing sailing over the edge and toward Dox. The guy looked down. Dox recognized him from the hotel—one of Joko's men. But there was no time to process any of that, because somehow, the man had managed to bring his rifle around with one hand, the muzzle swinging toward Dox . . .

No, no, no, no, no—

With a wild yell Dox shoved harder. The rig tilted more. The guy shrieked in panic, went sliding farther, and grabbed on to one of the uprights just as he went over. A length of rope went slithering over the side like a snake trying to reach the ground—the rope the guy must have been suddenly wishing he'd used to secure the rig to the structure alongside it.

The good news was, the guy dropped the rifle. The bad news was, he himself managed to hang on. The worse news was, the rifle was now plummeting straight at Dox's upturned face like a bolt of lightning. Instinctively Dox released his hold and leaped back. The rig slammed back into the ground and shuddered. An instant later, the rifle landed alongside it with a heavy *thunk,* burying itself muzzle-down all the way to the forestock. Dox yanked it out of the ground like King Arthur pulling free Excalibur and recognized it immediately—a Vietnam-era M21, 20-round detachable box magazine, Redfield 3–9x adjustable ranging telescope. Not his preferred M40A1, but as the saying goes, the best gun to have is the one you can reach when you need it—

Bam bam bam!

A spray of bullets kicked up the dirt to his right. The guy was dangling eighteen feet up, boots churning uselessly against the air, with only an arm hooked around one of the uprights keeping him from falling. But despite his predicament, he'd still managed to draw a sidearm with his free hand and was now using said sidearm to shoot at Dox. The man's position was for shit, but still, given time, he was going to compensate and start walking those shots in to where he wanted them to go—

Dox leaped left and started running for the dumpster, instinctively recognizing that forcing the guy to track him counterclockwise would both weaken the guy's grip on the upright and make for a nearly impossible shooting angle. But more shots came as he ran, the guy apparently realizing that if shooting backward didn't succeed, he was going to be stuck at the top of an exposed eighteen-foot platform against someone aiming a rifle at him from cover close by. Shooting in the direction of your own ass was dumb at best. But again, if you were motivated enough, *dumb* could become a relative term.

Dox dove behind the dumpster just ahead of the guy's shots, eating a mouthful of dirt as he landed. The shots stopped. Had it been eight? He thought so, but he didn't know what the guy was shooting or what was in the magazine when he'd first opened fire.

He snuck a quick peek past the edge of the dumpster. The guy was struggling to pull himself up. Dox aimed the M21. The guy must have sensed the danger, because he glanced back, saw Dox had him dead to rights—

The guy let go of the strut he'd been holding and immediately plummeted to the dirt eighteen feet below, landing on his back with a resounding *whump* and a half groan, half scream as the wind got thoroughly knocked out of him.

But as hard as he hit, the guy must have understood that if he didn't get off the *X*, he was going to die there, and somehow he managed to pop up on his hands and feet and start scuttling away backward like that crab-legged head in John Carpenter's *The Thing*. Dox watched for a second, impressed by the guy's determination, then raised the rifle and put a round in his face, blowing his brains out the back of his skull.

"That's for the man you killed," he said. "And for trying to kill a good woman who does nothing here but help people who need it."

He walked over and found the sidearm the guy had been firing—a trusty Colt 1911. He ejected the magazine and saw it was empty. Yeah, eight shots. And hanging on for dear life, the guy couldn't manage a reload. Well, tough shit for him.

The guy was wearing plain olive cargo pants. Dox found two extra magazines in his pockets, each with a full load of eight rounds. And even better, on the ground a short distance from the rig, a box of match-grade 7.62 ammunition. Dox checked the magazine on the

M21. Twenty-round capacity, five shots fired. Okay. He inserted five cartridges, preferring whenever possible to drive with a full tank.

He looked around. Still all quiet. The soldiers must have heard the gunfight, but it had all happened fast and against the background of what was going on in the cemetery. Either they didn't make anything of it, or again the paperwork wasn't worth it.

His plan had been to head straight back to Isobel. But he hadn't counted on all those reinforcements clogging the road. And anyway, suddenly he had a better idea.

He slid his arm through the rifle sling, pushed the Colt into the back of his pants, pocketed all the ammo, and started climbing. A moment later he was at the top of the scaffolding, the center of the cemetery a hundred and fifty yards distant.

He proned out, looked through the scope, and found the tomb he and Isobel had taken cover behind. He saw the bodies of the two men who'd been hit, and the drag marks from the man he'd used as a shield. No sign of Isobel. He wished he could have known for sure, but in all likelihood she was still on the other side of the tomb, staying put like he'd told her. And hopefully unharmed.

He saw roaming soldiers, still firing at fleeing marchers. His plan had been to start dropping them. He could take out a bunch, no question. But watching now, he realized they'd know what was happening, and within a minute, all the reinforcements he'd passed on the road would be heading his way. There were just too many, and too spread out, for him to be able to make a difference.

He kept scanning and saw Max Stahl, standing with his back to a tomb, his hands held high, three soldiers detaining him at rifle point. Stahl seemed to be arguing, which was either one of the bravest or dumbest things possible under the circumstances. One of the soldiers raised his rifle so that he was looking right down the sites at Stahl's face. That seemed to call Stahl's bluff. He started nodding vigorously. He lowered the video camera, popped open the bay, removed the cassette, and held it out to one of the soldiers.

So that's what they wanted, and what Stahl was so reluctant to give. They were worried Stahl had videotaped their massacre. And they must have been right. What else would the man have been filming?

The soldier took the videotape and looked at it, nodding slowly and deliberately. Dox could tell Stahl was done. They were going to kill him now, Westerner, reporter, whatever.

No time to think it through. He put the reticles on the first soldier's head. Took a nice, deep breath. Let it start to flow out. And pressed the trigger.

Boom! The rifle kicked. The soldier's head exploded. Stahl's mouth dropped open in shock. The other two soldiers made the very sad mistake of looking frantically left and right instead of immediately taking cover.

"Dumbasses," Dox said quietly. He dropped them a second apart, both with head shots.

He watched as Stahl stared in shock at the bodies. Probably the man was struggling with the sight of all that gore—some of which had gotten on him—while also trying to process his sudden reversal of fortune. Then he seemed to get ahold of himself. He dropped his camera, picked up the video cassette, fell to his knees, and started frantically digging barehanded into the dirt at the edge of a fresh grave with a curly-haired statue above it. A moment later, he shoved the cassette into the hole he'd dug and smoothed it over. Then he grabbed the camera again, stood, and flung it away like an Olympian hurling the discus.

Dox instantly understood what the man was thinking. He would come back for the cassette when he felt it was safe. As for the camera, he didn't even want to be seen with it.

Good plan, amigo. You'll never know, but I'm glad I was able to help.

Within a minute, Stahl was surrounded by soldiers, too many for Dox to do anything about. Stahl raised his hands high and allowed the soldiers to lead him away. Dox had a feeling the man was in for a long interrogation, but that he'd survive. If the soldiers had thought he needed killing, they'd have done it right there, like the three who'd first confronted him. But if they didn't know about the videotape, they wouldn't have a reason. At least not that one.

He checked for Isobel again. Nothing had changed around the tomb. It was torture to not know whether she was still on the other side of it, or whether she was all right. But he couldn't help her now, at least not directly.

He tracked back and forth, looking through the scope, not knowing what else he could do but wanting to do something. People were still running but it seemed more had hunkered down. And there, near the entrance, Goodman and Nairn were trying to stop an entire column of advancing soldiers with nothing more than their upraised hands, which officially made them even braver or dumber than Stahl had been a minute earlier.

The soldiers didn't even slow. One of them butt-stroked Goodman in the head and she went down. Other soldiers started smashing her with their rifle butts. Nairn threw himself over Goodman to protect her and was promptly rewarded with a half-dozen butts raining down on him.

Dox gritted his teeth. He wanted to take out the soldiers so much he was actually caressing the M21's trigger. But unlike with Stahl, there were dozens of them surrounding Goodman and Nairn. Shooting a few, or even ten or twenty, might not have made things better, and could easily have made things worse. After all, in general if you want to kill someone with a rifle, you don't beat him with it, you shoot him. Which is what the soldiers were doing to the Timorese. By comparison, with the journalists they were holding back.

After a minute, the soldiers seemed to have vented enough of their fury. They grabbed Goodman and Nairn, pulled them to their feet, and started leading them away. Both were bleeding badly from their heads, Nairn in particular. But they were alive. Dox felt guilty for not having intervened. He had to keep reminding himself that he could have gotten both of them killed—and himself as well by giving away his position.

He didn't see what more he could do. And he couldn't stand being away from Isobel any longer. He had to find a way back to her.

He slung the M21 over his shoulder and climbed down the rig. He started to head off, then looked back at the scaffolding.

No chance someone's going to get another sniper up here while I'm back in the cemetery, right?

Of course there was no chance. He was being overcautious.

Still, the thought of running back to the very spot where A, Isobel and he had just nearly been killed, and where B, the three soldiers lay who he himself had just killed, somehow wasn't an appealing one.

The rope that had come off the rig was dangling down its side, secured at the top, moving ever so slightly a few feet above the ground.

Okay. It wouldn't quite be Archimedes, but close enough for government work.

He found a broken cinder block and kicked it into the dirt at the base of the scaffolding, making it a makeshift chock. Then he grabbed the rope, turned, and started walking away like a horse hitched to a wagon. There was a moment of resistance, and then the top was moving, and then suddenly it was falling, and Dox had to run to get out of the way. It landed with a heavy metallic clang behind him, though interestingly not as loud a thud as the sniper had made when he'd fallen from it.

Okay, good to go.

He didn't want to give up the rifle, but if he were seen with it, he doubted all those soldiers, hot and bothered from massacring God knew how many civilians, would wait for an explanation before shooting him dead.

He looked around for a place to hide it. The dumpster, maybe, but it felt a little close to the scene of the crime. At some point, whoever had given the sniper his orders would send someone to check on him. What they'd find would be the sniper sniped, which would likely make them worried, and peevish besides. Anyway, it would be too risky to come back here. He'd have to find somewhere else.

Something occurred to him. If Joko were in the mix, they might even conclude that the fly in their ointment was Dox himself. If that were the case, he doubted that invoking Felix's name again would be enough to shield him from retribution.

He headed east, crouching as he moved, zigzagging through alleys between houses of cinder block and rusted corrugated metal. Here and there in the distance he could still hear sirens, police or ambulances or both, as well as intermittent shooting.

Just before the street that formed the eastern side of the cemetery, he came upon a small playground, which looked like it doubled as a junkyard. There were giant disused truck tires piled up alongside a sad-looking swing set and a slide. Maybe the kids used the tires for hiding or climbing. Well, it didn't matter. He doubted anyone would be playing here today.

He hid the rifle and the 7.62 ammo inside one of the tires. Keeping the pistol was a risk, he knew, because if he got searched and was found with it, it would be both unexplainable and evidence that he'd killed the sniper. But in light of recent events, he found he couldn't part with it. So he left it in the back of his pants, concealed by his dirty, untucked, bloodstained shirt. The extra mags he kept in his pockets. He wiped the sweat from his eyes, took a deep breath, and walked out into the street and back toward the cemetery.

Chapter 29

By the time Dox reached the eastern side of the cemetery, the sirens and shooting had stopped. But the relative quiet was hardly comforting, punctuated as it was by the sounds of moans and sobbing. Everywhere were crumpled bodies, some probably playing dead, but others no doubt the genuine article.

Dox walked in through the gate. The air was heavy with dust and gun smoke. Here and there, small bands of soldiers patrolled, sweeping their rifles back and forth as though expecting some sudden resistance.

Dox shook his head in disgust and kept moving. *No one was resisting to begin with,* he thought. *And you bastards shot them all anyway.*

A cluster of three soldiers saw him and came marching over, rifles pointed at him. They were issuing what sounded from the tone like commands. But it was Bahasa, and Dox couldn't understand the specifics.

"Joko Sutrisno," he said. "Kopassus. I'm an American, working with Joko Sutrisno and Kopassus. You understand?"

The three looked at each other and started talking fast in Bahasa. Yeah, they understood, all right. Their expressions had gotten worried just at the mention of Joko's name. Plus every third word was *Sutrisno* and every fourth *Kopassus*.

"That's right," he added. "Don't fuck up. Old Joko will eat your hearts."

After a moment, they lowered their rifles and nodded in the direction he'd been walking.

"Terima kasih," Dox said, the words for *thank you* being about the only Bahasa he knew.

He kept walking. He passed what seemed like scores of fallen people, maybe hundreds, some wailing and weeping, but most lying still. It was a massacre. An absolute massacre.

But there was nothing he could do to help. And he had to get to Isobel.

He reached the tomb where he had left her and saw instantly that she was gone. His heart seemed to freeze, and he fought the certain feeling that something terrible had happened.

And then he saw her. Not fifty feet away, leaning over someone on the ground.

Dox ran to her, in the overwhelming rush of relief forgetting for a moment to be cognizant of his surroundings. Belatedly, he glanced left and right. He saw no problems, just drifting smoke and dust and the sad tableau of so many killed and dying.

It was a boy lying under Isobel, the ground around him soaked in blood. Isobel had tied a tourniquet around his thigh and was talking to him in Tetum, probably instructing him on how to hold it. The boy was grimacing and groaning and his face was streaked with sweat and grime. From all the blood, Dox didn't think he was going to make it. But he knew it wasn't in Isobel to accept something like that.

She saw Dox and nodded, then turned back to the boy and said a few more words. She stood and looked around, no doubt for the next person she might help.

"I didn't bring my bag," she said. She was crying, though she seemed unaware of it. "Stupid, stupid, stupid."

"You had no reason to expect this," Dox said. "Nobody did."

She shook her head as though his point was too idiotic even to bear arguing.

He wanted to chastise her for disobeying his instructions and exposing herself when the sniper might still have been active, but what would have been the point? Being criticized would be about the last thing she needed. Besides, she must have listened at least a little. It had taken Dox a good three minutes after leaving her to neutralize the sniper. If she'd come out before then, she would have been dead for sure.

"We have to go," he said.

She was still looking left and right for people to help. But none of the bodies around them was moving. She started walking. He stayed with her, his head swiveling, alert for danger.

"We have to go," he said again. "This is bad."

She didn't even look at him. "Oh, it's bad?"

"That's not what I mean. Someone made the decision to kill you. You, personally. And I think me, too. When they realize their plan A didn't come to fruition, you can count on them to try another way. We can't stay here."

"I have to help people."

"Help them how? Isobel, most of them are dead. The ones who aren't either soon will be, tourniquet or no, or they'll make it to a hospital or clinic. And if you stay here, the wrong person will see you and you'll die. How's your being dead going to help your people?"

That seemed to get through to her. She stopped walking, her body shaking for a moment with the effort of just standing still. She was thinking about something, thinking about it hard. He wished he knew what it was.

Then she turned to him. "Can I trust you?"

"I told you, it's not—"

"No! No more games. No more stupid spy stuff. Look me in the eye. Can I trust you?"

He looked her in the eye. "Yes."

"Can I rely on you?"

"Yes."

"If you're lying to me, manipulating me, using me—"

"I'm not. I'm all in for you, Isobel. I think I was from the first time I saw you."

She nodded. "Then take me to Maliana. I'll tell you everything on the way."

Chapter 30

Joko stood looking down at Bambang's body. The man was scarcely recognizable—half his face shot away, the other half grotesquely swollen, the back of his head blown out and sprayed all over the ground behind him.

But there was no doubt. Bambang had positioned himself here, at the top of the scaffolding, on Joko's orders. Orders that included taking out the doctor, Isobel Amaral, and the sniper, Dox.

It had been a good plan. And a necessary one. Joko had seen that Dox was useless. He was never going to learn anything from Amaral, who Joko judged to be smarter, braver, and more focused than this sniper-cum-spy could ever hope to be.

Unbeknownst to Felix, Jakarta had ordered a show of force against the protesters. An unusually happy instance of the left hand not knowing what the right was doing. And presenting a perfect opportunity to conceal a murder, or rather two, in a massacre. No one would be able to complain. Not Jakarta, not Felix . . . no one. It could all be chalked up to *Shit happens.*

It hadn't worked. Somehow, Dox had managed to turn the tables, killing Bambang, taking his rifle and position, and killing three soldiers in the cemetery, the only Indonesian casualties of the entire operation. All of them had been dispatched with head shots. There was no other explanation. It had to have been Dox.

Why those three, and no others?

AMOK

He didn't know. Had the three been threatening the doctor? Did Dox really care about her that much, enough to risk giving away his own position to hundreds of marauding soldiers?

Or maybe . . . maybe something else had been happening there, something Dox had wanted to stop. The army had arrested three foreign journalists and was interrogating them. Joko thought the interrogations would be pointless. The better alternative would be to release them and then observe from a distance. Where would they go? What would they do? Who would they meet with?

They wouldn't be thinking clearly. They'd be shaken, their instincts dulled, desperation dictating their decisions. They would assume they had been freed, when in fact they were merely being . . . supervised.

He'd have to consider intervening. The interrogations were the purview of the regular army, but in the end the regulars would do as Kopassus commanded. They always did.

He looked at the scaffolding for a moment. It lay toppled, and it wasn't hard to see what had toppled it. Dox had jammed a broken cinder block in at the base and pulled a rope attached to the top. Judging from Bambang's position, the rig had come down afterwards. Because . . .

Because Dox was planning to return to the cemetery, to Amaral. Snipers are paranoid about other snipers. He didn't want anyone else climbing up here while he was newly exposed.

He wished there had been a reason for Dox's fears. But in fact, Bambang was the only competent sniper in Joko's unit. It was a big loss, and for a moment he felt rage begin to take hold of him. He breathed deeply, willing it to pass.

He closed his eyes and tried to imagine where the two of them would go. Not to the hotel. Joko had men positioned there, just in case, but he didn't expect Dox, as stupid as he sometimes seemed, would be

259

that stupid. He would have considered things from Joko's position, as Joko was considering things from his. He would have known that Joko would understand who had killed Bambang. And that no one, not Felix or anyone else, would stop Joko from taking his revenge.

He wants to protect the woman. Where would he take her?

It was the wrong question. Dox didn't know the country.

Then where would she take him?

He didn't know enough about either of them, he realized. His fault. Things had developed quickly, it was true, but the more important factor was that Joko had underestimated both. After all, was Dox really as stupid as he seemed? Bambang was as competent a man as Joko had ever commanded, and yet the American had somehow managed not only to survive him, but to kill him in the process.

He sighed. Things had gotten unacceptably messy. He knew the phenomenon because he had encountered it before. Of course, some messiness was a part of war, as it was a part of life. Because war was life, or at least the most important part of it.

The problem was that past a certain point, messiness could become impossible to control. And even short of the point of impossibility, the cost of containing it could become prohibitive, the chances of success increasingly remote. Understanding all this, Joko had already taken certain prudent steps to . . . tidy things. Effective steps. Gratifying ones. He had discussed none of this with Felix. He had planned to seek forgiveness later, when everything was done.

But now it wasn't done. It was only partially done. No, it was worse than partially done; it was at risk of becoming *undone*. Because Dox and Amaral, who were supposed to be the end of the cleanup process, had instead caused a great deal more messiness, and indeed were now poised to multiply it.

He stared at Bambang, shaking his head. What a waste.

Still, only a setback. He knew he would find his quarry. The one was only a doctor. And the other, though former military, knew nothing of Timor. They were frightened, forced suddenly to flee, certainly improvising. It was only a matter of time.

"I won't kill them first," he said to Bambang. "I'll take their hearts from them living. They'll watch as I do it."

It wouldn't make up for losing Bambang. But . . . almost.

Chapter 31

Isobel had wanted to go to the clinic for its sole ambulance, a battered but reliable Toyota pickup. But Dox, walking them briskly out of the cemetery and into a warren of alleys on its western side, insisted that the clinic would be too dangerous, because it would be the first place they'd be looking for her.

"The Americans you talked about," Dox said. "What do they drive?"

"Jeeps. The same as the Indonesian soldiers."

"Then that's what we need. If we get challenged, I'll be one of those Americans. You'll be my prisoner. The rest will be a hell of a bluff."

She didn't know what else she could do but trust him, but still she didn't understand how they could bring any of this off. "How are we going to get a jeep?"

"I think I know where we can find one. I can't promise that whoever's driving will hand it over on nothing more than my charm, but I'll try."

They stopped at a playground, where Dox retrieved a rifle and a box of bullets from some abandoned truck tires. "This was what that sniper was using," he said. "He doesn't need it anymore, but we might."

They kept moving, staying in alleys and yards as much as they could. From the glimpses they stole of the main roads, they could see hundreds of dazed, bloody Timorese, scores of soldiers herding them along.

They cut through an alley with crumbling cinder-block walls and came to a clump of trees at the edge of the hotel parking lot. Dox crept forward, peeked through the foliage, and turned back to her.

"One open-top jeep, complete with driver," he said in a low voice. "At the edge of the parking lot."

"How did you know?"

"Joko's got people waiting for me here, just like he has people waiting for you at the clinic. They're probably in my room. Maybe even Joko himself. He likes that kind of thing. They're planning to bundle me into that jeep, take me to God knows where, and do God knows what."

He reached deep inside a hole in the wall, felt around for a moment, and came out with a small bag.

"What is that?" she said.

"A little just-in-case gear I left here during happier times. Emergency items, that kind of thing." He handed it to her. "Now listen. I'm going to sneak up on that sumbitch—"

"What? What if he sees you?"

Dox took a gun from the back of his pants. "Then I'll have to shoot him. But I'd rather not, because it'll make noise. Now don't worry, I'm good at sneaking. It's how I got behind that sniper who was trying to kill us both. I told you then I'd be fine, and I was right, wasn't I?"

She wanted to say something about past performance being no guarantee of future results, but she was far too frightened. So she only nodded instead.

He started to move out from the trees, then turned to her. "I almost forgot the most important thing," he said, his expression worried.

"What?"

"You better kiss me. It was good luck last time."

It made her angry enough to shake him, and under any other circumstances, she would have.

"You scared me!"

He smiled. "My bad. But come on now. We don't want to take any chances."

She didn't know whether to laugh or cry or scream. She kissed him, meaning for it to be short and businesslike, but somehow quickly forgetting all that, forgetting everything but the taste of him, and the feel of his tongue, his teeth, his mouth.

It was Dox who finally pulled back. "If that was the second time," he said a little breathlessly, "I can't imagine the third."

She shook her head, confused. How long had they been kissing? She touched his face and whispered, "I can't, either."

"Maybe we should get a room. We are at a hotel, you know."

She knew he was making jokes because he was scared. "We will," she said. "I want to."

"Really?"

"Yes."

He smiled again. "I want that, too. But I gotta go get that jeep. Thanks for the good luck."

He turned and walked out of the trees. It was strange—he was a big man, and he was moving upright and reasonably fast. But somehow, he seemed . . . unobtrusive. As though he was just a part of the parking area, like he belonged there, no more out of place or noteworthy than a car or lamppost or tree. She wondered if it was a sniper thing, and decided it probably was.

And the approach he was using—she noticed that, too. Not from the side, where the driver could have seen him in his peripheral vision. And not from directly behind, where the rearview would have been a problem. Instead, he came in at an angle, the blind spot of the driver's side mirror.

The driver never even glanced around, not even when Dox was right behind him. Dox raised the pistol high and smashed the butt directly into the top of the driver's head. The man shook from the impact and began to keel over to his right. Dox arrested the fall with one hand, shoved the pistol back in his pants with the other, then dragged the limp body over the front seat and dumped it in back.

Isobel realized from the force of the blow that Dox must have killed the man. Must have *intended* to kill him. She couldn't get her head around it. That one moment he could be so sweet, even boyish. And then . . . that he could do something like that.

You promised yourself. That you would do anything to combat these monsters. What did you think that meant?

This was her chance, maybe her only chance, to smuggle the videotapes out of Timor and get them into the hands of people who could make those girls' voices heard. That's what these soldiers were trying to prevent. They wanted to stop the world from knowing what they had done here. She wouldn't allow that. She couldn't. No matter what.

Dox jumped into the driver's seat, keyed the engine, and wheeled the jeep around to the trees. Isobel got in and shoved the bag under the seat. Dox immediately drove off—fast, but not obtrusively fast. The same way he had approached the driver.

She looked in back. The man had a deep gash in the top of his head. It was strange to have no desire to render aid. "Is he dead?" she said.

"I hope so. I didn't have time to check him. Would you mind? I can't dump him here, and I don't want him waking up irate and causing problems."

She glanced at the gas gauge—nearly full. But still not enough to make it to Maliana. "Do you know where you're going?"

"You bet. Like I said, I've spent my brief time here living my cover, doing site surveys on the ground and using topographical maps. Maliana's southwest."

"Yes. Just keep the ocean to your right."

"Way to the right. My understanding from briefing papers is that the Indonesians control the coasts, but the interior not so much. The main roads are going to have too many patrols. We need another way out of the city."

They cut across the main street, which was chaotic with soldiers and Timorese, and onto a quieter road. Isobel leaned into the back. Despite its severity, the gash was bleeding only a little, which suggested the man's heart had stopped. Still, she felt for a pulse. There was none.

"He's dead," she said, surprised at how little she felt about it. It had always been her policy to treat everyone at the clinic with the same level of concern. She wondered distantly whether she was now a bad doctor, maybe even a bad person.

I don't care. I'll be happy to burn in hell. Just let me get those videotapes to someone who can show them to the world. Please, just that.

They passed the back of a mercantile with a dumpster behind it. Dox pulled over, jumped out, and dragged the driver from the back. The body spilled to the ground. Isobel started to get out, too, thinking it would take both of them to get the dead weight up and into the dumpster, which she assumed was the plan. But Dox surprised her. He dropped and lay perpendicular across the body, his back on the chest, hooked an arm around the far leg, flung his other arm in the other direction, and rolled straight to his feet, the body secured across his shoulder. It happened so fast, Isobel wasn't even sure what he had done. Then he backed up against the dumpster, arched, and let the body fall inside. He pulled the lid closed, and they were back on the road in what couldn't have been half a minute.

"How did you . . . ," she said.

"It's a Marine trick for moving a casualty. Or maybe an army trick, I've heard Rangers taking credit for inventing it. Who can say? All I care about is it works. Are there ways across the Comoro River besides the bridges? The water is low right now, low enough to cross, but the banks are too steep here and I didn't explore all the way south."

"Checkpoints on the bridges?"

"Exactly. In fact, I went through one on my way in from the airport, and that was when things were relatively calm in these parts."

She realized she should have thought to avoid the bridges herself. She was a fugitive now. She had to start thinking like one.

"Yes," she told him. "The banks flatten out farther south. There are places we can drive across. Go left here, under the Nicolau Lobato, the main road."

"Roger that."

He drove well for an out-of-towner, smoothly and confidently. But just a few kilometers south, where the land flattened enough to drive across the river, there was a jeep parked in the road, two soldiers standing in front, pointing their rifles.

"Let me do the talking," Dox said, sounding tense.

"Should I hide the rifle?" It was propped up between them.

"No, I want it in plain sight. I'm with Joko and the CIA and you're my prisoner, remember? I've got nothing to hide."

They stopped a few meters from the checkpoint. Dox stood and said loudly, "Let us through." Isobel saw the gun, protruding from the back of his waistband.

"Who are you?" one of the soldiers said in accented but clear English.

"I'm American. Working with Joko Sutrisno of Kopassus and you know who else. You want more than that, you can explain to Joko why you didn't let me through."

The soldiers looked at each other worriedly and exchanged a few words in Bahasa. The first one glanced at Isobel, then back to Dox. "Who is the woman?"

"My prisoner. And my business."

The man said, "How did you get that blood on you?"

"How do you think I got it on me? Now either let me through or call Joko. I've identified myself, and I've got no more time to waste with your questions."

Isobel thought it was a good bluff—at least, she thought it would have worked on her. And the soldiers looked worried. They conferred again in Bahasa, then nodded, as though they'd agreed on a solution.

The man looked at Dox again. "Just one minute, sir." He lowered his rifle and walked to his jeep, probably to use the radio. The other soldier watched him, lowering his rifle, as well.

There was a sudden *Bam bam! Bam bam!* from right next to her. Isobel jerked away so hard she would have fallen out of the jeep if the door hadn't stopped her. She saw Dox holding the pistol in both hands, high and close to his chin. She looked at what he was looking at. The soldiers were down. He had shot them both.

Dox leaped from the jeep, raced closer, and shot them each a third time, both in the head. Then he jumped back in the jeep, cut right, and headed across the riverbed, the jeep's tires churning up muddy water as they drove.

They reached the other side, which was as much trail as road. "Going to be a bumpy ride for a bit," he said. "I want to stay off primary routes until we're past Tasitolu Lake. We'll be well clear of Dili then, and the roads should be safer."

"How did you learn all this so fast?"

"Oh, I wasn't much for school, but I can be a quick study when my life might depend on it. I wasn't joking when I said I was living my cover doing site surveys, at least up until all hell broke loose. Here, take the wheel for a minute. I need to reload."

She did as he asked, watching the road. In her peripheral vision, she saw him pull a fresh magazine from his pocket. The jeep bounced on the uneven terrain, and she was glad they hadn't tried to take the ambulance.

"I don't want you to think I'm cold-blooded," he said. "I know they were just boys doing their job. I doubt they were even at the cemetery, probably they pulled guard duty at some outpost no one was worried about. Their bad luck, running into us."

He ejected and pocketed the used magazine. "If they'd been a little dumber, they might have let us through. But they were just dumb enough to think I was fine, and just smart enough to think they should check with Joko or his people to be on the safe side. Well, if you're uncertain enough to check with command, you better not be lowering your rifle. Worst of both worlds."

AMOK

He slapped in the fresh magazine, got the gun back into his waist-band, and took the wheel again. "Wish we could have you drive. You know the terrain and I don't, and if you have experience in an ambulance, I'll bet you're hell on wheels when you need to be. But if we get stopped again, you driving would look all wrong."

They emerged from the forest and onto the sandy flats south of the lake. She watched him for a moment, wanting to touch him but afraid it would distract him. "I don't think you're cold-blooded," she said.

He glanced at her, then ahead again. "Thanks for that. In some ways I feel like we've gotten to know each other pretty well, but in other ways, we're just getting started. You know, not long ago, a man said something to me that stuck. He said, 'There's judges, and court orders, and announcements from on high. And then there's the way things are.' Well, right now, this is the way things are. And for us to get through it, I'm going to have to do what needs to be done. And a lot of it probably won't be pretty. You okay with that?"

This time she did touch him, on the thigh. "I'm okay with it."

He smiled. "I like you doing that."

"It won't distract you?"

"Not as long as you leave your hand where it is and don't move it any higher."

She laughed, feeling weirdly exhilarated. "I want to kiss you again."

His smile widened but he kept his eyes ahead. "How long is it to Maliana? Maybe five hours if we stay off the coastal road?"

"With luck."

"Can you wait that long?"

She laughed. "Can you?"

"Barely. I think."

She laughed again, and then was surprised to feel the laughter suddenly turn to tears. "I don't understand how I feel," she said, wiping her eyes. "All those people, and seeing you kill those soldiers . . . How can I be laughing?"

They cut through a ravine and suddenly were on a real road again, albeit rutted and washed out along the sides. The jeep was still bouncing, but not nearly as badly.

"'Cause you're alive," Dox said. "That's why. You feel guilty, too, because you survived while so many others didn't, and that's normal. But let me tell you, the first time you come close to dying, really dying, your head can spin for days. Not many people know it, or like to talk about it, but coming really close to dying and managing not to? That's one of the most intense experiences a person can have. It's hyperreal. Nothing makes you feel more alive than almost dying. It's why people get addicted to crazy sports like parasailing and whatnot."

She remembered a quote she'd heard, attributed to Winston Churchill: *Nothing in life is so exhilarating as to be shot at without result.*

"I can see that," she said.

"It has another effect, too."

"What?"

"Well, if you're wanting to kiss me so much, I think you already know."

She laughed again, embarrassed but also, she couldn't deny, excited. It was true, she hadn't felt this way in a long time. No, she hadn't felt this way ever. Her skin tingled as though from a mild electric current. Moving just a little, she could feel the fabric of her shirt sliding over her bra, irritating in a pleasant way, as though she was slightly sunburned. She crossed her ankles and was almost shocked at the delicious feeling it produced between her legs. Was she wet? She realized she was, and it excited her more. She wanted to feel his mouth pressed hard over hers, his hot skin, his weight on her . . .

She almost told him to find a place to pull over. But she was desperate to get to Maliana, to retrieve the videotapes.

Besides . . . she knew they would. And waiting, anticipating, was itself a pleasure.

He glanced in the rearview and pulled over onto the dirt. She looked, but no one was behind them. Was he . . . Were they going to do it right here?

"I forgot," he said. "There's one other effect." At that, he started shaking violently.

She watched for a moment, surprised. But of course. It was only natural.

He gripped the steering wheel hard. It steadied his hands, but his arms kept vibrating. "Damn," he said. "This is embarrassing."

She eased closer and put a hand on his back. "It's just adrenaline. It's okay."

"I know," he said. "Not my first rodeo. I've been staving it off. But I think we're in the clear now, and when I realized, I . . . I finally couldn't anymore. Damn."

She pulled him close and held him as he shook, one arm across his shoulders, her other hand on the back of his neck. "Shhh," she said. "Shhh."

She held him like that while the shakes passed through him, stroking his cheek and his hair, whispering to him that it was all right, it was okay.

When the trembling had abated, he disengaged. He blew out a long breath and looked at her. "That was nice."

She shook her head. "It was nothing."

He took her hand and kissed it. "Not to me, it wasn't."

Chapter 32

They drove on, zigzagging south and west along switchbacks, some with drop-offs so sheer Isobel was afraid to look down, sunlight slicing through the trees above them. She told him about Santiago's visit that morning, and how Dox had been right: Santiago seemed to believe her. And he told her Joko had been waiting in the hotel room and had hit him in the head with a gun, obviously not as hard as Dox had hit the man who'd been driving the jeep, but hard enough to stalemate the aspirin he'd taken afterward.

They passed a deep mountain stream alongside the road, and stopped to do what they could about the blood and dust they were coated with. The water was clear and delightfully cool, and Isobel wished they could have taken off their clothes. Dox had stood behind her and scooped water onto her neck, and then she felt his hands there, lightly stroking her skin, and she turned to him and they kissed so hard she felt she was melting into him. If they hadn't been right next to the road, she knew they would have made love right there. But they had to keep moving, and somehow they managed to get back on the road, the air blowing dry their hair and clothes, caressing the skin on her arms and chest into goose pimples.

They stopped and bought gas in the town of Gleno. They weren't low, but were still far from Maliana and unsure of when they would find another station. Isobel had never come this way—the coastal route was a lot longer, but those roads were much better maintained and with much more infrastructure. Still, the mountains were beautiful. They would be driving through forest so thick that the sky was barely visible through the tree canopy, and suddenly they would emerge along a ridge with a breathtaking view of the plains below and hills beyond, so high up they were looking down at the clouds.

Dox, as though reading her mind, said, "I wish I could look. But I need to keep my eyes on the asphalt, such as it is. Maybe you could describe it for me?"

She did. And in so doing, told him also about growing up in Dili, and losing her mother when she was small, and her dreams of becoming a doctor, and her fears that she wouldn't be able to make it at an American university. And how those fears had made her study ardently, obsessively, to the point where no, there hadn't been a boyfriend, at least none serious, not then and not since, her insecurities impeding her initially, her dedication to the clinic becoming the impediment afterward. Dox asked her if she'd ever been with anyone at all, and she knew what he meant by that, and told him the truth, that she had, but not since before medical school, and that it had been all right, but not so good that she couldn't live without it. She couldn't believe she was telling him these things, or how easy it was to do it. No, more than easy—she wanted to tell him, wanted him to know her, wanted him to hear. There were so many things she had wanted to talk about for so long. But having no one to talk about them with, she realized, she had denied the feeling, repressed it. And now it was bursting through, she supposed as part of that hyperrealness he had described. That and maybe the feeling of being on the run together, sharing danger together, having to and being able to rely only on each other. She felt she had never trusted anyone so much, and the sensation was half-exhilarating, half-terrifying.

And he told her things, too—about how his father was still in prison but soon to get out, how his family was afraid of his father and wanted Dox to try to keep him from being released, and how Dox had taken this spying job in Timor both to run from his dilemma and also in the hope that the job would help him solve it. And that he loved his small town, Tuscola, in Texas, but he also wanted to get away from it, which made him feel guilty because his family needed him. He couldn't stay and he couldn't leave, and he couldn't keep his father in prison, but he was afraid of what his father would do if he were released.

They kept going, the sun gradually moving west, its rays slanting through the trees into their eyes. She realized he had never once asked why she needed to go to Maliana, and for a moment her gratitude almost overwhelmed her. She told him then about the girls. What had been done to them. How they had agreed to let Isobel record their stories, and how terrified she had been to do it, but also how determined, now more than ever, after Beeler had been taken. She told him the duty she felt to those girls was sacred to her, and she was afraid he might belittle the notion, thinking it was self-important.

But she was wrong. "I think those girls were very unlucky," he said hoarsely when she was done. "But then, after that, I don't think they could have been luckier than to know you. To have you as their champion. We'll find a way to get their voices heard."

She almost said, *You always say the right thing,* because it was true and because it was such a beautiful gift. But maybe she'd told him too many times already. She didn't want to make him self-conscious about it.

"But how?" she said.

"One way or another. I don't know any journalists, but my step-dad . . . People respect him. He'll know who to ask."

"But how can we get the tapes out?"

"From what you told me, that journalist, Beeler, had the right idea. But . . . damn, this is why Joko—and the CIA—got interested in you, isn't it?"

"Joko's the one who took her."

"How do you know?"

She told him what had happened by the well. Her fear. Her guilt. How she had recognized the mohawk haircut from some of the girls' recountings, and how in her terror, she had tried to convince herself it was someone else.

"It's not your fault," he said when she was done. "You couldn't have helped her. They just would have taken you, too."

She knew it was true. But it didn't really make a difference. "I'm sorry I didn't tell you sooner."

"It's okay. I knew there was something you were holding back, I just couldn't tell what. My guess would be they got Beeler to give you up. But no, on second thought, if she'd given you up, and they knew about the recordings you made of those girls, they wouldn't have brought me in to try to cultivate you. They would have snatched you and made you cough up what they wanted. But that's not what happened. They knew you were up to something, they just didn't know what, and were trying to figure it out. Those soldiers who took Beeler . . . Could they have seen you? Tracked you?"

"I don't know. I suppose it's possible."

"Or maybe Beeler told them who you were, but didn't tell them what you were doing."

"Do you think . . . Is there any chance . . ."

He blew out a long breath. "I wouldn't bet on it, I'm sorry to say. We can hope, but we should also assume the worst. Meaning we need to smuggle those videos out ourselves. East Timor is too tightly controlled because of the occupation, the airport especially. But Indonesia is another matter. Hell, I've been to Bali, beautiful island, without a hint of what's happening here. Sneak across the border, and you can go anywhere."

"Can you do that? Get us across the border?"

"Oh, I've gone back and forth across borders tougher than this one. Just ask the Uzbeks."

She didn't understand. "Uzbeks?"

"It's a long story. But yeah, Maliana's not five miles from the border. Guessing it's tough terrain, but if Beeler managed to navigate it, we can, too. I got people I can call on once we're across. Not the guy who sent me here—he's a snake. Others I know from being a Marine."

"You can't tell them about the videotapes. I don't care how much you trust them—"

"I'm not going to tell a single soul about those tapes without your explicit say-so. All right?"

She was overwhelmed again by what she was feeling for him, something so intense she didn't have a name for it or even a point of reference. For a moment, she couldn't speak. She put her hand on his leg and squeezed.

He smiled but kept his eyes on the road. "Nothing about this mission was what it was supposed to be," he said. "I was going to be fighting for the wrong side, and I think my reasons for coming were for shit. But"—he stole a glance at her, then looked back to the road "I'm sure glad I did."

They stopped in a tiny town called Lauana, where they gassed up again and bought boxed lunches of hard-boiled eggs and rice. She knew it wouldn't be enough for a man of Dox's size, but there was little else in the town's mercantile and it would have to do. Luckily, the jeep was well equipped—with a tarp, wool blankets, ammunition, and some prepackaged military food Dox called MREs, or meals ready to eat, among other things. "We'll save the 'meals rejected by everyone' for later," he said. "Don't know what's ahead or whether we'll be able to buy more food."

Soon they were back on the twisting mountain road. They had been driving for hours and had seen no soldiers and almost no people. She couldn't help feeling optimistic. She was even looking forward to seeing Joana and Mateus and Alonsa again. She couldn't tell them the truth, of course, but she would explain that she had forgotten something. They would suspect it was more than that—Joana especially, who struck Isobel as having keen instincts—but she doubted they would even ask.

They passed a weathered sign announcing that they were leaving the district of Ermera and entering Bobonaro, thirty-five kilometers to Maliana. On these roads, that would be close to two hours. They wouldn't make it before dark.

"We're going to have to stop," Dox said, thinking the same thing she was. "Or at least I am. I didn't sleep last night and I'm starting to feel it. Besides, headlights show up for a long way at night. Better to bunk down and start again at first light."

As soon as he said it, she realized how exhausted she was. But exhausted or not, at the thought of "bunking down" with him, her throat went dry and her heart started pounding.

"Where?" she managed to say.

"Well, we could try to find a guesthouse. But there hasn't been much of anything since Lauana. And I'd rather not be seen. Joko's gonna figure out we stole this jeep, and that it was us that killed those two soldiers by the river. That's not much to go on, but if he gets a report we're here, he'll think Maliana again. Maybe figure we're making for the border, and try to anticipate us."

"There are those blankets in back."

"I'm thinking the same. The forest is deep around here. We'll find a flat patch and stretch the tarp from the side of the jeep to the ground. Even with the blankets, though, it'll be a little chilly once the sun goes down, but I think we'll manage."

"We'll keep each other warm," Isobel said, and then laughed, embarrassed at the words, which seemed to have come out on their own.

Dox blew out a breath. "Hey, I thought you said you were worried about distracting me."

"I'm sorry."

He smiled and snuck a glance at her. "Apologize to me later," he said. "While we're keeping each other warm."

Chapter 33

Joko was back at Felix's encampment. He'd thought about using the radio, but he knew Felix would be upset about events at the cemetery, and wanted the opportunity to gauge both Felix's reaction and his thinking on the tidying Joko knew needed to be done next.

Now he knew he'd been right to be concerned. Ordinarily, no matter what he was doing, Felix's demeanor was notably dispassionate, even professorial. But in the fading light of evening, the professor was largely gone, replaced by an angry headmaster.

"This is beyond a setback," he said. "Jakarta turned Surgical Hatchet into Self-inflicted Sledgehammer. How many Timorese dead?"

"Unknown. Two hundred. Maybe three."

"That's three hundred martyrs the Timorese will never forget. For sixteen years, indiscriminate brutality hasn't worked, and they go *back* to it? Just as we're making progress with something less primitive? Madness. I can't help people who don't want my help. It's useless. It's a waste."

Ostensibly, he was talking about Jakarta, but some of his ire was directed at Joko. "It wasn't my decision," Joko said.

"But you knew about it."

"I knew Jakarta wanted a show of force. A show—that is, columns of soldiers marching in formation. Not a shooting gallery in a cemetery."

That wasn't exactly true. The scuttlebutt was that the commander-in-chief of the Indonesian military himself had been very clear about what was expected, saying "Agitators must be shot, and they will be."

Felix shook his head. "After all we've been through, Joko. If I can't count on you to help me professionalize tactics, I just . . ."

He threw up his hands as though in despair.

Joko found himself getting irritated. Even though he had known what was coming at the cemetery, even though he had taken advantage of it to try to tie up the loose ends represented by Dox and Amaral . . . it wasn't as though he'd given the order himself.

Beyond which, there was Felix's holier-than-thou hypocrisy.

"Professionalization is like charity," Joko said. "It begins at home."

Felix looked at him. "Meaning what?"

"Meaning you know as well as I do that when it comes to slaking their appetites on Timorese girls, your men have never even paused. Waster in particular. Those girls are martyrs, too. You look the other way at what your men actually do, while blaming me for the decisions of others?"

Felix gave him the vivisection stare. "Are you trying to tell me your men haven't continued doing the same?"

"I'm telling you sauce for the goose is sauce for the gander."

Felix pulled off his glasses, wiped them on his shirttail, and refixed them behind his ears. Joko recognized the tell—Felix was trying to give himself time to think.

"You knew I would be upset," Felix said, after a moment.

"Yes."

"You didn't come just to confirm something you already knew."

"No."

"Then why?"

"That sniper you decided to repurpose as a spy? Dox? The doctor, Amaral, turned him. He's working with her now, meaning he's working with Falintil."

Whatever Felix had been expecting, it wasn't that. He looked aghast. "How do you know this?"

"I had a sniper positioned for overwatch at the cemetery. My best man, Bambang. Dox killed him, took his rifle, and disappeared with Amaral. I had men waiting for them at his hotel and at her clinic. The jeep outside the hotel was taken. Its driver is missing and presumed dead. Two soldiers manning a checkpoint at the Comoro River are also dead. I came here to brief you personally. But if we want to use this meeting to fix blame instead, let's talk about how you injected into my operation someone as dangerous and unreliable as this loose cannon of a sniper. Or, if you prefer, we can talk instead about how to fix the problem."

Fix the problem, not the blame was another Felixism, and Joko knew from experience that whatever else his shortcomings, Felix wasn't so much of a hypocrite that he would ignore his own aphorisms when they were deployed against him.

"I'd be happy to fix the problem," Felix said. "If it were fixable. But the shitstorm from this massacre is above my pay grade. There were Western journalists there, now being held at Lembaga. The US and British governments are demanding they be released."

"Jakarta should have revoked the visas," Joko said. "Politicians, they don't know whether to eat or wipe their asses."

Another Felixism, and in Joko's experience, true for all countries, not just for Indonesia.

"Unfortunately," Felix said, "that's now academic. It was a problem when you had one journalist witness a murder. Now we have three who witnessed a massacre."

A reference to Beeler—but no direct questions. Did Felix know? Was conjoining the first journalist with the other three a subtle green light? He needed a bit more to be sure.

"But your government knows the stakes," Joko said. "There's no way to neutralize their stories?"

Felix sighed. "We can survive their firsthand accounts. Maybe. We already have PR specialists shaping an appropriate narrative—Falintil provocateurs firing on peaceful soldiers, using civilians as human shields. That kind of thing. If we pump enough sewage into the pipes, they'll clog."

No, there was no green light. The plan was to neutralize the stories, not the journalists themselves. It was stupid. Ineffective. Pathetic.

Joko would have to do things on his own recognizance. And seek forgiveness later.

He smiled. "You see? We'll be all right. There have been countless massacres in this war. One more one way or the other won't make a difference."

The beauty of it was, it made sense. It was true. It was just . . . Joko had a better way.

Felix looked at him. "It could make a difference. If there's physical evidence."

"Physical evidence . . ."

"Photographs. Video footage. Anything that would back the journalists' accounts, and contradict the official ones."

Joko blinked. The journalists were in custody. They'd been searched. But . . .

His mind's eye flashed back to the three dead soldiers. The only ones Dox had shot.

Felix waited, and despite the fraught tenor of their conversation, Joko was gratified by the man's patience. Felix trusted Joko's instincts, and knew that when Joko was thinking, imagining, *feeling* for something . . . it was worth giving him space to do so.

Just three. All in a cluster. And not one other.

"If there is physical evidence," Joko said, "I think I know where to look for it."

He told Felix of his initial bafflement that Dox would kill only those three soldiers. That he had initially thought Dox had done so to protect the doctor. But that now he thought there might have been a different motive in play.

After all, Dox had clearly gone over to the other side. The man wanted Falintil to win. If one of the Western journalists had filmed the shootings, and those three soldiers had been on the verge of confiscating the video . . . then a sniper, watching, working for Falintil, certainly would have killed them, even at the risk of exposing his own position.

"But you can't be sure," Felix said, when he was done. "Assuming this video even exists. And there are three journalists. Do you have the manpower to follow that many?"

It was heartening that Felix was asking practical questions. This was pressure-checking, not opposition.

Though the truth was Joko was going to be stretched thin. Bambang was gone. Half the remainder he planned to deploy to potential border crossings because after what had happened at the Comoro River, he didn't trust the regular army to stop Dox. And the others he'd have to distribute among Goodman, Nairn, and Stahl.

But he didn't care about any of that. All he cared about was that he himself would remain static, lurking in the part of the cemetery where the three soldiers had been killed. His gut told him that's where the action would be. The rest was just bet-hedging.

"I have the manpower," he said.

"What about Dox?"

"Judging from the dead soldiers at the Comoro River checkpoint, I think he and the doctor are somewhere in the interior. But they can only stay submerged for so long. Eventually they'll resurface."

Felix nodded slightly as though considering. "The journalists. You have to give them a wide berth. If they sense they're being watched—"

"They won't."

"Then do it."

"I'll head back now. And have them released in the morning."

He turned to go. From behind him, Felix said, "Joko."

Joko turned.

AMOK

"All we want," Felix continued. "All we need. Is that video. Assuming it exists. What we definitely do not need is martyred journalists. Balibo was bad enough."

Still no questions about Beeler. On that, Felix really didn't want to know. But it was equally obvious he wanted nothing to happen to the other three. The man had good instincts. Though not quite as good as he thought. Not as good as Joko's.

And it wasn't just the journalists Felix's instincts were off about. It was Dox and Amaral, as well. Because as confident as Joko was about the video, he was even more confident that the sniper and the doctor would be back at the cemetery. Where Joko would be waiting for them.

"Of course," Joko said. He turned again and walked away.

Felix watched Joko's jeep disappearing into the forest, then walked over to Waster's position. The man was watching Joko, too, his ever-present Franchi SPAS-12 held almost high enough to be aiming at Joko's taillights.

Waster glanced at Felix. In the fading light, the vertical scar down his eye seemed deeper than it really was, as though the man's skull had been cleaved, but by some miracle cohered.

"That looked contentious," Waster said.

"It was."

"I don't know why you trust that guy. He's obviously a psycho. Eating people's hearts? Jesus."

Felix nodded. He might have said something about the pot calling the kettle black, but people could rarely see in themselves the defects they found so obvious in others.

Instead, he merely said, "We all have our proclivities. And, I suppose, our uses."

"What did he want? He didn't have a prisoner."

283

Unsurprisingly, Waster hadn't gleaned Felix's meaning. Which was fine. As Felix had just observed, everyone had their uses, and Waster was a hunter, not a philosopher.

"I think he was concerned about my reaction to the massacre. And to some other developments. He wanted my blessing for something."

"Did you give it to him?"

"He thinks I did. Or that, in the end, he didn't actually need it."

Waster waited.

"I want you to leave for Dili at first light," Felix said. "And, at nightfall, I want you to position yourself in the Santa Cruz cemetery."

"Where the shooting just happened?"

Felix nodded. "Yes."

"Who am I taking?"

"Don't take anyone. I want you there only to observe. Besides, too many and Joko will smell you."

Waster snorted. "You give that psycho too much credit. What will I be observing?"

"I'm not certain. But . . . something is going to happen there. And it isn't quite what Joko is telling me."

Chapter 34

Dox drove on for longer than Isobel had been expecting. She was about to ask what he was looking for when they came to another shallow roadside stream. He glanced at it and said, "That's what I'm talking about." But it sounded more to himself than to her, and he kept driving.

A minute later, he pulled into the stream, then drove along in it for a few hundred meters, and then, when it started to get wider, he stopped, turned the jeep around, and drove back in the direction they'd come from.

"Covering our tracks?" Isobel said.

"Exactly. No reason to think anyone has any idea where we are. But we don't know how Joko learned about you being involved with Beeler. The trick of driving in the middle of a stream won't fool a good tracker. But it'll slow him down."

A few minutes later, they pulled out of the stream and drove deeper into the forest, the jeep bouncing on rocks and tree roots. In no time, the road was invisible behind them. Dox found a grove of Australian pines and stopped alongside it. He cut the engine, and they were immediately engulfed by a vast silence, broken only by the sound of the wind rustling the tree leaves and the occasional call of a forest bird.

"This'll do," Dox said, nodding in satisfaction. "You need the bathroom?"

She laughed, a little embarrassed. "Badly."

"Go ahead and find a spot. I'll start getting us set up."

She walked off just enough to put a few trees between them. She was afraid to go too far. Not so much because of Joko or anything like that. More because the forest felt so infinite and impersonal. She thought of floating in the ocean, and imagined that doing it out at sea rather than near the beach would feel like this, with nothing around you but waves and the water below miles deep.

When she was done, she cleaned up in a stream and came back. She saw the jeep but not Dox, and for a moment, she felt a wave of fear that carried her back to the well in Maliana, to Beeler and the murdered girl.

"Over here," he called.

She looked, and there he was, about ten meters away, on his knees and doing something on the forest floor, the rifle alongside him. She walked over.

"Guess an air mattress would have been too much to hope for," he said, and she saw what he was up to—sweeping together a pile of underbrush.

"But not to worry," he went on. "Lots of pine needles we can use. And that tarp in the jeep is more than I thought—it's a shelter-half, like a pup tent. Nothing you'd want to vacation in, but it'll keep out the mosquitos at least."

She got down next to him and started sweeping, too. Soon they had assembled a soft, deep bed of needles.

"We can get that tent set up in a minute," he said. "But first things first. Have you ever fired a gun?"

"No."

"That's fine. It's one of those things that's hard to do well but easy to do okay. And for now, okay will be enough."

He stood and offered a hand, which made her smile because while she didn't need it, the gesture was also just so him. He had been right—they were getting to know a lot about each other. The danger, she supposed. The intensity. It compressed everything, including time.

He took the pistol from the back of his pants. "This is a .45 caliber Colt 1911. Classic handgun, easy to operate. In a better world, we'd give you some live-fire practice, but even though it feels like there's no one around for miles, I don't want to take a chance on that kind of noise. So you're going to handle the gun, but the rest will have to be conceptual. Okay?"

She was nervous, but excited, too. Everything with him felt new. *Was* new. "Okay," she said.

He nodded. "Now, the most important thing is this. And there's no wrong answer, as long as it's the truth. Are you capable of killing a man? Not everyone is, and there's no shame in it if you're not. This world needs doctors more than it needs soldiers, and you're a fine one. If saving lives is who you are, and you can't take one, then you go on doing just that."

She thought of the girl by the well, and of Beeler, and the girls at the clinic, and how they had entrusted her with their recountings of horror and shame.

"I'm capable," she said.

He nodded again. "I had a feeling. But best to be sure. Okay, safety first. Good safety is layered. That means every layer has to fail for an accident to happen. And if even just one layer holds, the accident won't happen. You understand?"

"I think so."

"Here, that means first that you always assume the gun is loaded. Which this one certainly is. And you never point the gun at something you're not willing to shoot. You never even let the muzzle cross anything you're not willing to shoot. Pretend the gun has a laser coming out of it that'll slice right through anything it crosses."

"Okay."

"And you don't put your finger on the trigger until you're ready to shoot. See how every one of these things would have to go wrong for you to shoot someone by accident?"

She nodded.

"Okay. If you've seen people shoot guns in movies, that's more or less the idea. Just don't hold the gun sideways like gangsters do. That's dumb in every way dumb can be dumb. We're only going to cover the things you might not know, or that you might think you know but might have wrong."

He held the gun in front of them.

"See how I'm pointing it only in a safe direction? And my finger's not on the trigger?"

"You told me."

"But I also told you safety is layered. That'll be true of my safety instructions, too."

She noticed that despite all the jokes he had made in the face of various dangers, this time he was being entirely serious.

"Okay," she said. "That makes sense."

He gave her a quick primer on how to use the gun, including grip safety and thumb safety, how to hold it with two hands, how they'd keep the gun "cocked and locked," and how she had to squeeze extra tightly to compensate for the gun being too big for her hands, and also for the fact that the ammunition it used would give it a big kick.

"It's heavier than I expected," she said, assuming an aggressive, two-handed stance as he had shown her, and sighting down the barrel at a tree. While keeping her finger off the trigger.

"That's actually a good thing: it'll help with the kick. Same as with a clothes iron. Heavier is easier. You don't have to press as hard to get the wrinkles out. Now look, I'm not expecting any trouble, but—"

"Good safety is layered."

He smiled. "Okay, the Colt stays close to you for the duration. I'll handle the rifle."

"I want you to show me how to use that, too. Not today. But . . . when this is done."

He looked at her for a long moment. Then he nodded. "When this is done."

He glanced up at the sky, and she realized why—they were losing light fast. "Okay," he said. "My turn for a bathroom break. You hold on to that gun, and remember—"

"Finger off the trigger. And no pointing in an unsafe direction."

He smiled. "You make your teacher proud."

When he was back, they strung up the tent between two saplings, using paracord from the bag he'd retrieved outside the hotel. As he asked her for the items he needed, she was surprised to see condoms. Was he . . . Had he been planning on this?

"Hand me the duct tape?" he said, holding one of the cords he had just tied off. "This tent has a hole in it big enough to march a battalion of mosquitos through."

She handed him a condom instead, and was surprised and gratified to see him instantly blush. "It's . . . not what you think it is," he stammered. "Well, I mean, it could be, but you'd be surprised at what you can do with a proper condom in a pinch."

"Just don't waste them," she said, surprising herself again with her boldness. "We might need them later."

"Oh, man," he said. "I think that's the most distracting thing you've said yet."

She smiled. "Well, you're not driving."

Soon they had the tent set up over the pine needles they had gathered. The tent was too small for two people to move around in, so she watched as Dox spread out the blankets inside it—one to sleep on, the other to sleep under. Watching him prepare it excited her.

They used the last of the fading light to eat two of the MREs from the jeep. She was surprised to find that they weren't bad at all.

"This is good," she said, greedily swallowing a mouthful of pasta and sauce. "Why did you call them 'meals rejected by everyone'?"

"Some are worse than others," he said, laughing. "And some of the reputation is just Marines having fun complaining. I've heard people say, *Three lies for the price of one . . . not a meal, not ready, and you can't eat it.* Also, eating too many can get you constipated right quick, so they're also known as meals requiring enemas, meals refusing to exit, and other such variations I won't regale you with, even though you're a medical professional and probably could handle it."

She laughed. "I don't care. I like them."

"Well, they beat going hungry, that's a fact."

The mosquitos were getting bad, and there was only a glimmer of light remaining in the sky above the tree canopy.

"All right," he said. "I wish we had claymores and tripwires. You don't want to wake up with the enemy inside your perimeter. But . . . I'd have to rate the chances of that as low."

She didn't answer. Her heart was beating too hard, and besides, she didn't know what to say.

He held open one of the tent flaps and she crawled inside. He came in after, snapping the flap closed behind them. Inside it was very dark. The pine needles under them were soft. For a moment, as they moved around she could hear the rustle of their clothes against the blankets and the tarp walls. Once they stopped, the only sound was their breathing.

She had thought it might be awkward after all the anticipation, but it wasn't. She felt his hand on her shoulder, and then on her face, and she found his face with her hands, and then they were kissing, and then everything else was gone, all the months of horror and danger and fear, the world itself reduced to this tiny dark enclosure and the two of them inside it, his mouth on hers, his hands on her body, her clothes coming off, and his mouth everywhere, doing things to her no one had done before, things she'd imagined but never believed she would actually try. And she was shocked at how natural it was, how uninhibited she felt, and she heard herself saying, "Please keep doing that, *meu Deus*, please keep doing that, just that, just that," and he reached under one of her legs and found her hand and squeezed, and his other hand was touching her in time with his mouth, and she pushed harder into his face and raised her hips and suddenly she was coming, and she couldn't believe the force of it, it made her feel the sea again, like being swept out by the surging tide, and it went on and on and she didn't care that she was crying out, she couldn't have stopped herself even if she had wanted to.

Finally the force of it ebbed, and she lay back on the cushion of pine needles, trying to catch her breath as Dox disentangled himself and crept up next to her. He said nothing. He just stroked her face and hair, the sound of his breathing in her ear.

"*Meu Deus,*" she said again, turning toward him unseeing in the dark. "Is that what I've been missing?"

She could sense him smiling. "Maybe among other things," he said.

She smiled back. "Like what?"

She heard the sound of a wrapper peeling. "Put this on me," he said breathlessly. "And let's find out."

But there was something else she wanted. "Not yet. I want . . . I want to taste you first. Like you tasted me. But . . ."

"Please, don't put *but* at the end of a sentence like that one. It'll destroy me for sure."

She laughed. "I don't . . . I don't really know how."

"I think it's probably not an easy thing to get wrong. Just . . . do whatever you feel like. Don't think about it. In the unlikely event there's a problem, I promise to speak up."

She laughed again, feeling awkward where a moment ago she had felt so natural. But she thought his advice was good. She didn't think, she just reached forward in the dark. He moaned when she touched him, and the feel of her fingers curling around his hardness, and the sound of his pleasure, gave her more confidence. She dipped down and kissed, then kissed again, and then licked. His breath caught, and she put her mouth around him, just a little, and he moaned again, and suddenly she felt worried, because he was big, much bigger than she'd known before, and then he moaned louder, and she didn't care, didn't care about anything but tasting more of him, doing for him what he had just done for her, and she took more of him into her mouth, and he moaned longer this time, almost as though he was in pain, and he said, "Put the condom on me, Isobel, please," and he pressed it into her hand. She rolled it onto him, and it was tight and she was afraid it was going to hurt him, but his moans seemed only of pleasure. And then he took her hand and said, "You can be on top if you'd like."

She almost said yes, but it wasn't what she wanted—wasn't what she had imagined. "No," she breathed. "You be on top. I want to feel . . . I want your weight on me. Is that okay?"

He was already coming up and easing her onto her back. "I think it's the most okay thing anyone's ever said to me."

She lay back and he moved between her legs, his hands on either side of her, taking most of his weight. She was very wet, wetter than she thought she'd ever been, but still he was big and the condom was dry. She spit on her hand and wiped it on the condom, raised her knees, then took hold of him, scared, excited, hearing the sound of his breathing, even louder than hers.

She tried to guide him in, but it wasn't working, he was being too gentle. "More," she whispered, once again amazed at how unselfconscious she was being, with the realization of the unselfconsciousness exciting her even more. "You won't hurt me. Go ahead."

He eased his hips forward and suddenly he was inside her. She knew she'd been lying about it not hurting, and it did, but maybe he sensed that because he paused, partway in, and she moved a little, grimacing, a few millimeters back and forth, giving herself a moment to get used to him. "Is it okay?" he said, breathing hard, and rather than answer she pushed against him, pushed hard, and he moved inside her more deeply, and instantly the pain was worse and she cried out without meaning to, and she was afraid he'd think it was too much and stop, but he must have been too excited because he kept moving, slowly in and out of her, and in a moment the pain had faded, replaced by a sensation so beautiful it shocked her, the feeling of him there and also at the same time everywhere, and suddenly she couldn't tell where she stopped and he began, and he moved faster and his breathing deepened, and she felt more of his weight on her and she realized he was forgetting himself, and knowing he was that excited made her more excited, and she said, "Don't hold back, put your weight on me, I want to feel that, I want to feel all of you, please don't hold back."

He said nothing in response. He slid his arms under hers and took her face in his hands and kissed her hard, his weight bearing down on her, his hips driving into her, and she realized she was tasting herself as well as him, and that feeling of not knowing where she ended and he began deepened, and he moaned and moved faster, deeper, and it hurt but the pleasure was so much more than the pain, and she moaned, too, louder than he had, and she felt herself coming again and couldn't believe it, and he cried out into her mouth and held her tighter and she felt him coming too, coming inside her, or maybe what she felt was herself coming, she no longer had any idea of which was which or who was who.

Gradually their movement slowed, their breathing along with it. She felt him take some of his weight onto his arms again and realized he'd nearly been crushing her. And that she had loved it.

"Isobel," he said. "Oh, my God."

She touched his face in the dark and repeated it. "Oh, my God."

"I like when you say it in Portuguese even better."

"I'll say it any way you like. But you have to make me."

He laughed. "I live to serve."

She laughed, too, and then he got on his side next to her and they held each other, laughing, kissing, talking. He said he was sorry, that he'd been trying to hold back, and she told him she hadn't wanted him to even though she'd been afraid because he was so big, and he asked how she would know, given her claimed scant experience, and she reminded him that she was a doctor, and they laughed again and it was beautiful, the most beautiful thing she thought had ever happened to her.

He told her it would be better if they took turns at sentry, but that on the other hand the chances anyone could find them just now were slim. "Besides which," he added, "I'm at thirty-six hours straight now. I know from experience that forty-eight is my legal limit, after which my shooting, driving, and pretty much everything else will suffer. I need just a couple hours to forestall that."

"I can stay up," she said. "I probably got less sleep in medical school than you did in the Marines."

He laughed. "I hate to ask, but if I can have the first hour, you can have the rest of the night. All you need to do is sit up, listening. Anyone trying to get anywhere near this tent is going to give himself away crunching on all the forest debris."

"Take the first two hours," she said. "Doctor's orders."

He leaned in and kissed her at that, then lay back and was breathing deeply and evenly only seconds later. She realized it was going to get cold, so she pulled the blanket up over them both, then lay there next to him, listening to him breathe, the feeling of what had just happened between them and of his lying asleep next to her too beautiful for her to do anything else. She wanted more time with him, and as wonderful as this intense, hyperreal experience had been, she wanted more slow time. Time to get to know him in different ways. And for him to get to know her.

And, she realized, for them to get to know themselves through each other. It sounded silly, and it would have embarrassed her to say it out loud. But she wanted it. She'd never realized how much her obsessive devotion to the clinic had been costing her, what she'd been giving up.

She needed to find a better balance. *Self-care is other-care,* they'd taught her at UCLA, and though she'd spent years resisting the notion, she realized belatedly that it was true.

But it was all right. They would have time. They would. They'd get the videotapes across the border. Find a reporter who would get them published. And then it would be just the two of them.

With all the time in the world.

Chapter 35

Dox slept far longer than the promised two hours. He awakened to find Isobel in his arms, sound asleep, something he realized he should have anticipated, but that he'd been too tired himself to do anything to prevent.

He listened for anything outside the tent, and heard nothing.

She groaned, probably at the feeling of his stirring. *"Merda,"* she said. "I fell asleep."

"It's okay. No harm, no foul."

"What time is it?"

He checked his watch, a Traser with a tritium dial. "Midnight. Over four hours. No wonder I feel so good. Well, the sleep, and earlier, too."

She went outside the tent to pee, and he did the same when she was done. It had gotten cold—not surprising, given the elevation—and when they were both back inside, they got under the blanket and snuggled to get warm. Within a minute, they were all over each other again. And it was beautiful. He knew it was wrong to compare, but as much as he'd enjoyed his time with Marla—and he had enjoyed it—the feeling he had with Isobel was different. He'd always loved girls, but he could tell this was another realm.

"You sleep again," she told him afterward. "You kept the vigil over Rosa. You need it more than I do."

"You sure?" he said, realizing a little more would do him good, but not wanting to deny her.

"Positive."

"Okay, give me just an hour. Or less if you start to get sleepy."

The next thing he knew, he heard birdsong. The interior of the tent was aglow with faint morning light. Isobel was in his arms, out cold. He couldn't help laughing, and it woke her.

"Merda," she said. "I did it again. I'm so sorry."

He kissed her. "Like I said, no harm, no foul."

"You say you're the worst spy in the world, but I'm the worst sentry."

"No. We got lucky, and now we're both rested. That's a good thing."

They shared an MRE, broke down the tent, and were back on the road before the sun had crested the mountains.

They traveled south, zigzagging down dirt switchbacks, then climbing again, this time west, the sun rising behind them. In less than two hours, they were on the outskirts of Maliana.

"Right here," Isobel told him. Dox turned onto a narrower dirt road lined with palm trees. In the distance, he could see squat green hills, white clouds clinging to their peaks, and before them rice fields and what he thought were orchards. It might have been paradise, if the folks who lived here could just be left alone.

There were a few people about. They stared at the jeep as it passed. They looked tired, hungry, and not very friendly. Not that he blamed them.

"Will Joana and Mateus be awake this early?" he said, scanning as he drove.

"They were when I was here. Don't worry."

The road came to a dead end. "Okay," Isobel said. "This is fine. We have to walk from here. Just a few hundred meters."

For whatever reason, Dox didn't have a good feeling about it. "Don't like to leave the jeep," he said. "And I especially don't want to leave the rifle in it. But on the other hand, I don't know that a white guy with a rifle showing up at their door in the early-morning hours is likely to put them at their ease."

"They know me. I helped their daughter. Come on. It's a short walk. We'll get what we came for and be on our way."

They trudged along a line of trees, Dox holding the M21 low and as nonthreateningly as he could, and came to cluster of thatched-roof huts. The one at the far end, which looked as though it had been larger than the others, had been destroyed—judging from the blackened remains, by fire.

Isobel gasped. "Oh no," she said, breaking into a run. "No, no, no."

She was completely focused on the ruin of the hut. Dox made sure to keep his head turning. He didn't see any problems. The remains weren't even smoldering, so whatever had happened, happened at least a day before. But still it put him on edge.

"Joana!" Isobel called out. "Mateus! Alonsa!"

Well, if anyone hadn't been awake before, they would be now. Dox hung back. Isobel kept calling out, her tone increasingly frantic.

People started emerging from the adjacent huts—an old woman. A younger couple. A woman with a baby in her arms.

Isobel began talking to them in Tetum, her tone extremely agitated. Occasionally the people would glance at Dox, but their suspicion seemed muted. They knew Isobel and seemed to trust her.

After a moment, Isobel came over to him, her face ashen. "A fire," she said. "Two nights ago. Everyone in the house killed." She wiped her forearm across her eyes furiously.

"They couldn't get out?" Dox said, already knowing the answer.

"No, they couldn't get out. There was the body of a white woman in the house, too. The people could tell from what was left of her."

"Oh no. Beeler?"

"Who else? Joko did this. He and his men."

Dox struggled to tamp down a cold rage. "She never gave you up," he said, beginning to put the pieces together. "He tracked you. He saw you staying with this family. He must have been here, interrogating them, learning what he needed about who you are and where he could find you. And then they came back to tie up loose ends. Including Beeler. He must have killed them all and burned the house with the bodies inside. I guess they wanted to make the whole thing look like an accident."

"It's my fault," she said. "My fault."

"It's not your fault," he said, more forcefully than he'd meant to.

"Do you understand?" she said, her voice breaking. "What those monsters do . . . what they did, to those good people . . ."

"None of this is your fault," he said, dropping his tone a notch. "The blame lies with exactly one person—the one who did this. Joko. And with his men."

"But if I hadn't come here—"

"You didn't do anything wrong. In fact, you did everything right. Isn't that what you told those girls you helped? They didn't do anything wrong. Well, you didn't, either."

She gave a half laugh, half cry, as though what he was telling her was the most absurd thing ever uttered.

"Isobel, listen to me. I know you knew them, and that they were good people. I know it hurts. But we came for the tapes. Let's focus on that. Where did you hide them? Is there any chance they survived the fire?"

For a moment, she seemed not even to understand. Then hope flared in her eyes. She glanced at what was left of the house, then back to him. "Come with me," she said.

They walked over. Closer to the structure, he could smell the woodsmoke and melted plastic, and an underlying quasi-meat smell that he knew was charred human flesh. *My lord,* he thought. *My lord.*

There wasn't much left beyond the foundation. A stove. A refrigerator. Some sort of metal cabinet—

"Here," Isobel said, her voice rising in hope. "This freezer. Please, please . . ."

The appliance had a glass door across the top, coated with brown soot. She tried to slide it open but couldn't.

"It's stuck," she said, tears of frustration springing to her eyes. "Help me, help me pull it open . . ."

Dox could see she was so overwrought she wasn't thinking clearly. "Step back," he said. "I'll get it."

She stepped back. He raised the M21. And smashed through the glass with the butt.

Immediately she stepped forward and started to reach out. "Hold on," he said. "You'll get cut. Hold on."

He swept the buttstock along the edges of the top, clearing the remaining glass. Then he set down the rifle and pushed the freezer onto its side. A dozen or so books came sliding out. No, not books. Photo albums, some of the photos slipping out onto the blackened floor. The fronts were browned and the edges were singed, but the images were still recognizable. A beaming young couple, three laughing children.

Amid the albums were two plastic VHS cassettes. "They're okay!" Isobel said, snatching them up. "They're okay, *meu Deus*, thank you, they're okay . . ."

She held up one of the cassettes and looked more closely. "No," she said. "No, no, no!"

She looked at the other cassette, then at Dox. He'd never seen an expression so stricken.

Wordlessly he took the cassettes and examined them.

The plastic was intact. But the film inside was a morass. They hadn't burned. But they had melted.

"Oh goddamn," he said, wishing he could think of something to comfort her. "Goddamn."

She looked at him, and then her despair seemed to overwhelm her. She sank to her knees on the blackened floor and sobbed.

He tried to think of a plan B. Couldn't she interview the girls again? It would be horribly unfair to them to have to relive their ordeals a second time, but the way Isobel had described it, they were determined to use their voices to get justice. He couldn't know, of course, but it was hard to imagine them backing down.

But no, he was being ridiculous. Joko and Kopassus wanted Isobel dead. She couldn't meet with those girls again; she couldn't even go back to the clinic. In fact, it wasn't just the videos they'd needed to smuggle out of East Timor; it was Isobel herself.

Wait. What about Stahl's video? It wasn't the same thing, but it might at least give Isobel some hope.

He squatted next to her and glanced around. "Listen to me," he said. "Isobel. You know, we're not the only ones trying to sneak video out of the country. That Western cameraman you saw outside the cemetery gates—Max Stahl is his name, remember? Well, he was inside during the whole massacre. He filmed it."

"It doesn't matter," she said, still crying. "Those girls . . . You don't understand what it cost them to . . . to have to recount, to have to relive, what they went through. And . . . I know it's not fair, but what it cost me to . . . to have to relive with them . . ."

She dropped her head and sobbed again.

"I know," Dox said. "I think I understand. I know nothing is going to make up for what they went through, what you went through, in making those videos. But what Stahl did . . . It's different, but it could have a similar effect, couldn't it? I mean, imagine the whole world seeing footage of what we saw. Those soldiers, firing at unarmed people, just mowing them down. People screaming and trying to hide, and the soldiers shooting them while they cowered. Stahl filmed it all. What if the world saw that?"

She looked at him, her eyes wet. "How do you know he filmed it?"

"I saw him."

"You saw him filming?"

"More than that," he said, glad he'd at least found a way to distract her from her grief. "When I was in the sniper hide, I saw him surrounded by three Indonesian soldiers who were trying to make him give them the cassette from his camera. He was arguing, but he saw they were going to kill him if he didn't comply, so he handed it over. But then I could see they were going to kill him anyway, so I shot all three dead. Then I saw Stahl hide the cassette in a grave and throw away the camera, and then some other soldiers came and arrested him. I'm guessing eventually they'll have to release him, at which point he must be planning on retrieving the cassette. I know it's not the same as those girls testifying, but—"

"No," she said, shaking her head violently. "You're right. This is very important. Very."

She stood. Dox did the same.

"You're sure?" she said. "That he filmed what happened inside the cemetery? You're sure?"

"Well, I didn't see him filming inside. But he was filming outside before the massacre. And those three soldiers sure thought he was filming inside. Plus why else would he have been so hot to hide that cassette, if there were nothing explosive on it?"

"Why didn't you tell me this sooner?"

From her tone, he could tell she was angry that he hadn't. "I didn't think . . . Well, not that it didn't matter, but I didn't see what it had to do with us. We were going the other way. You wanted to get to Maliana, and then we decided we'd cross the border, and, I mean, what could we have done to help Stahl?"

"But now his video is *everything*," she said fiercely. "Don't you see? And you're right, of course the Indonesians would be terrified of that video! They've spent sixteen years restricting foreign access precisely because they don't want the world to know what they've been doing here. I don't like Santiago—he's a narcissist and a bully—but he's right that the way this occupation ends is when the world learns its true nature. I thought the girls' testimony would do that. Now we'll never know. But the massacre . . . It could be just as damaging to them. Maybe more so!"

Dox didn't know where she was going with her thoughts, but he was getting uneasy. "Well, that's good. In a silver lining way, I mean."

She looked at him. "We have to go back."

"Back? We just came from there. Plus you got Joko and who knows who else gunning for you in Dili. And for me, too."

"But we have to help Stahl."

"Help him how?"

She was quiet for a moment, obviously thinking.

"How about this?" he said. "Can't you yourself bear witness?"

"What do you mean?"

"You interviewed all those girls. You're an American-trained doctor, people would have to—"

"No. Beeler was right. Without documentary proof, the stories won't get written. And even if they did, it's just words. Stahl filmed the thing itself!"

He could see he wasn't going to be able to persuade her. "Tell you what," he said. "Let's talk about this while we're driving. I don't know where we should go, but I do think we should keep moving."

They went back to the jeep. As soon as they were in, she said, "Go back the way we came."

It felt like a bad idea. "We should gas up first," he said.

"Fine. And then go back the way we came."

She certainly had a will. He'd known already, from what she'd told him about medical school and being a doctor, and of course by the risks she'd been taking in helping those girls. But now he was seeing it. And while it made him nervous to know how determined she was—determined enough to be heedless of contrary advice, even of obvious risks—he also couldn't help admiring her for it.

Still, he was worried that in the shock of losing her chance to help those girls, she was boomeranging too hard to Stahl's video. He wanted to talk some sense into her. Though unfortunately he had no idea how.

She was quiet while they looked for a gas station, and quiet while he filled the jeep. But as soon as they drove off, she started talking.

"First, Stahl might not even be released. You think he will be because he's British and a journalist. But they killed Beeler. You don't know they won't kill Stahl. And if they do, you're the only person in the world who knows where he hid that video! Don't you understand how important that makes you?"

"What about you?" he said, still hoping there might be some chance he could get her to see things differently. "You're the only witness to those girls' testimony. You're important, too. And we're risking you going back to Dili."

"I told you, my words alone won't matter."

"Okay, fine, but they'll probably release Stahl anyway."

"But you don't know. And even if they do . . . he hid the video near where you killed those three soldiers, right?"

"That's right."

"Did you kill any others?"

The question caused him a pang of guilt. "No. I wanted to, but there were too many. It could have made things worse, along with bringing the entire Indonesian army down on my position."

"I'm not blaming you, just trying to understand the facts. Now look at it from Joko's perspective. He'll know the one who killed the soldiers was you. Because he was trying to kill you, and you killed the sniper and took his rifle. He'll know all that. And he'll wonder why those particular soldiers? Why only those three and no others?"

"But he won't know."

"That's the point. He won't know, but he'll want to know. It's what he does, I can see that now. He and his men left with Beeler, at which point I should have been safe. But he knew something was off, and he came back to the well where I was supposed to meet her. He tracked me, just like you said. To Joana and Mateus's house, and then to Dili. And then he came here again, and he killed them all and burned them.

He'll know something was going on in that graveyard, something near where you killed the three soldiers, and he'll go there and try to figure out what it was."

He didn't want to admit it because he didn't want to go back, but she made a compelling case.

After a moment, he sighed. "I think you might already be better at this spy stuff than I ever was. You're worried they'll release Stahl, Stahl will go to the graveyard to retrieve the tape, and Joko will be waiting for him."

"Exactly."

He sighed again. "Goddamn. All right. We can't let that happen."

Chapter 36

Joko stood across the street from Lembaga Prison beside a banyan tree, concealed from the prison by its twisted trunk, shaded from the morning sun by the leaves high overhead. He didn't much like Timor, or maybe it was just the Timorese. But the banyan trees—roots growing down from their branches, their way of enveloping host trees, earning them the English sobriquet "strangler figs"—were different. They reminded him of Sumatra. Of home.

Joko had come to the prison an hour earlier and made it clear to the commandant that the three journalists were to be released that very morning. The commandant protested that he had received no such orders from Jakarta.

"Jakarta is busy right now," Joko had told him. "Smoothing out the aftereffects of yesterday's disturbances."

He thought *yesterday's disturbances* was a good euphemism, akin to *the Late Unpleasantness* as a reference to the American Civil War.

The commandant didn't seem to appreciate the wordplay. The man eyed him nervously, but still hesitated.

"So," Joko continued, "the journalists are a Kopassus operation now. Do you understand?"

The man continued to look at him. After a moment, he nodded meekly. Yes, the man understood. He understood extremely well. It made Joko happy.

He checked his surroundings, letting the muzzle of his CAR-15 track his gaze. Everything was quiet. His men were deployed where he needed them. Now it was just a question of waiting.

It wasn't long before he saw a guard swing wide the barred outer gate of the prison, then hold it open against the lichen-covered concrete wall behind it. Goodman, Nairn, and Stahl walked out. The clothes of the first two were covered in dried blood, and they looked unsteady on their feet. Stahl seemed to be okay.

Which was good. Because for whatever reason, Joko sensed that Stahl was the one he would see later. In the cemetery. When night came.

Chapter 37

They were back at the cemetery, and if Dox had been grappling with a bad feeling the last time they'd been here, now it was downright terrible.

There was a lot of moonlight, which had helped as they navigated through yards and alleys. But moonlight was like tracer rounds: it went both ways, making it easier for you to see, but also to be seen.

They had paused outside the southeast corner, the only part that wasn't abutted by roads, only by a thicket of corrugated houses. There were surprisingly few patrols, and Dox thought he knew why. Judging from the sounds of sporadic gunfire all around the city, Falintil was hitting back, meaning more Indonesian soldiers were needed for combat, with fewer available for police duty. Still, it made sense to stay clear of the roads whenever possible, hence the southeast corner.

They waited for several minutes, listening and looking. The cemetery was as quiet as the proverbial grave, but that didn't do much to ease Dox's discomfort.

"I wish you'd wait out here," he said. "I can sneak better alone."

"No," she said, as he knew she would. "I'm coming with you."

He had tried to get her to wait on the other side of the Comoro River. He hated the idea of leaving her, but he would have preferred for her to be in the rear rather than in the thick of fighting. Not that there was necessarily going to be a fight—it was possible they'd gotten all dressed up for the prom and wouldn't even wind up on the dance floor—but he didn't see a reason to take a chance.

She did, though. And he supposed in some ways, it was his fault. She'd quarreled with his initial tactical impulses back in Maliana, and, as he'd admitted at the time, she was making more sense than he was, at least if the objective was to ensure the safety of Stahl's recording. Now she wanted to be in on everything, and it was plain that all the hopes she'd invested in the videotapes she'd made of those poor girls, she'd now transferred to Stahl's video, and then some.

The good news was, they'd confirmed the scaffolding was still down. If it had been up again, there was no way in hell Dox was going back into that cemetery, especially knowing anyone on the scaffolding would likely have night vision. Maybe he could have found a way to take out a new sniper—he had the M21 now, after all—but it was better they didn't have to worry about snipers in the first place.

And the other thing that was better was that if no one was doing overwatch of the cemetery—and that scaffolding was the only place worth a damn—it might have meant no one was watching the cemetery at all. Meaning maybe they'd just get to see Max Stahl digging up the cassette he'd buried, wish him well, and get the hell out of Dodge.

All right, it had been quiet long enough. It was time to go in. "At least stay behind me," he whispered. "No closer than ten meters back. You stop when I stop, and move when I move. That way, at least if I draw fire or run into some other problem, you'll have options short of being in the middle of a gunfight."

He could tell she didn't like it. But there was no sensible reason to argue, either, and she didn't. She just nodded. He nodded back, then turned to the cemetery and started creeping forward. He was glad she had the Colt and wished they'd had an opportunity to practice with it live.

He went to the wall, looked into the cemetery, and saw nothing but the helter-skelter collection of crypts and headstones, alternately bathed in moonlight and shadows.

He pulled himself over, the M21 slung across his back and the fanny-pack bug-out kit tight around his waist. A moment later, Isobel joined him. He unslung the rifle, nodded at her, then went ahead, keeping low, moving from one monument to another, pausing to look and listen, then proceeding to the next place offering cover. With all the tombs in the silver moonlight, on any other night it might have been spooky, instead of being downright scary for the entirely pedestrian reason that from any one of the myriad shadows might emerge a certain angry psychopath with a penchant for eating human hearts.

As he moved, he heard the periodic crackle of small-arms fire, some of it in the distance, some not far from the cemetery itself. Well, at least if there were any shooting, the sound wouldn't draw undue attention. He just hoped the one doing the shooting would be him.

About halfway to the spot where Stahl had buried the video and just past a tall monument topped by a broken crucifix, he heard a low voice behind him say in American-accented English: "Don't turn around or you're dead right there."

Dox froze, his throat suddenly tight and his heart pounding. All he could think was, *Don't move, Isobel. Don't move.*

"Transfer the rifle to your left hand. Then kneel slowly and set it on the ground. Slowly, Dox. I'm not here to kill you, but I will if I have to."

Dox did as the voice commanded. *Stay back, Isobel. He doesn't know you're here. Just stay back.*

"All right," the voice said. "Keep your hands where I can see them. And slowly turn around."

Dox kept his hands up and turned around. There in the moonlight was a stocky white guy, hair in a buzz cut and a scar running up and down the left side of his face straight over his eye. From his hip, he was pointing a pistol-grip shotgun at Dox, something with the stock folded back over the top.

"You must be the one they call Waster," Dox said, glad his voice sounded reasonably steady despite the pounding in his chest.

The guy eyeballed him. "How did you know?"

Stay back, Isobel. Stay back. I got this.

"Let's just say your reputation precedes you."

"What are you doing here?"

"Oh, a little moonlight stroll, same as you I imagine. How's Felix?"

"Felix is fine. What are you doing here?"

"I feel conversationally we're going in circles. But it's all right—sometimes that's just part of two people getting to know each other on the way to being friends."

Beyond Waster, Dox could see movement. Isobel, creeping forward. *No,* he wanted to shout. *He doesn't know you're here. Stay back. Please, stay back.*

"Where's the girl?" Waster said.

"What girl?"

"The doctor. Isobel Amaral. The one working with Falintil. Joko says she turned you. Tell me where she is, and we'll know that's not true. And you and I can be friends, like you said."

Isobel was still moving forward. She was twenty feet away. Dox could see she was holding the Colt out in front of her with both hands, though untrained as she was, she was as likely to shoot Waster as to miss and hit Dox, instead.

She obviously had no intention of staying concealed. The only thing to do was try to give her a chance to get closer instead.

"This'll sound strange," Dox said, "but I'd be more moved by your protestations of incipient friendship if you'd lower that shotgun. What you got there anyway, a Franchi?"

"Loaded with buckshot. One more time, Dox, and then I'm afraid our friendship is going to be over just as it was getting started. Where's the girl?"

"Okay," Dox said. "You got me. She's closer than you'd expect."

Waster stared at him. "You think something like that is going to get me to, what, look around?"

Isobel crept forward another step. And another . . .

Dox shook his head. "Perish the thought. I mean, anyone who's earned the call sign Waster would be far too smart for a trick like—"

From behind Waster came a muzzle flash and a *boom!* Waster jerked forward, obviously hit. He staggered, started to turn—

Dox raced forward, grabbed the Franchi with both hands, and twisted. Waster tried to hang on, but he had no leverage and anyway had just been shot. As Dox tore the shotgun away, possibly taking Waster's trigger finger with it, the gun went off. It kicked, and Waster lost his grip entirely. The man had good instincts, though, lunging for Dox instead of trying to run, but Dox got a leg up and planted a foot solidly in his midsection, shoving him back. Then he stepped to the side to be sure anything that didn't stop inside Waster wouldn't hit Isobel, raised the gun, racked the pump, and pulled the trigger. The gun kicked and there was another *boom!*—louder this time—and a fist-sized hole blossomed in the center of Waster's chest, the wet inside it showing up silver in the moonlight. Waster did a half turn, and for a second his legs twitched as though they'd received one last *Run away!* command from his brain. Then he flopped forward onto his face and lay still.

Dox racked the pump again, then glanced up and saw Isobel running over, the Colt still pointing ahead of her. "You can lower it now," he said, his heart pounding even harder than it had been a moment earlier. "Nice shooting."

But she must have been so juiced on adrenaline she didn't hear, or she couldn't process it.

"Let me amend that," Dox said. "I guess what I'm saying is, could you please lower it?"

That time, she understood. She lowered the Colt and came up alongside him.

Dox kept the Franchi aimed at Waster. He would have liked to put one more load into him to be sure, but despite the presence of plenty of other gunfire in the city, he thought it better not to make any more noise.

He glanced at Isobel. "I forgot to tell you. They don't always die from just one shot. Better to keep shooting until you're sure. On the other hand, being that I was downrange, too, maybe one shot was the way to go."

He turned Waster over with a boot, and could instantly see from both his face and the wound that the man was dead.

"I killed him," Isobel said in a tone of disbelief. "I . . . killed him."

"I think it was more of a joint effort," Dox said. "Regardless, you're going to get the shakes from it later. And I will, too. That'll be fine. This time we can hold each other. For now, though, you can't think about it. You gotta just keep going. It's like being in the emergency room when you have too many patients. You can feel overwhelmed afterward, but not during. Right?"

She looked at him and nodded grimly. "Right."

"Okay, good. Let's keep moving. The grave where Stahl buried that video is only fifty meters from here."

He saw a shape hunched next to a tombstone and felt a flash of fear. He raised the Franchi, but even as he did so some part of his mind was telling him the shape wasn't a threat, the hiding spot was too clear in the moonlight, offering neither cover nor concealment. An operator would never have tried to lurk there.

"Identify yourself," Dox called out in a stage whisper. "If you don't want to get shot."

The shape stood, hands raised. Dox saw instantly who it was: Max Stahl.

"You," Stahl said.

Dox lowered the Franchi and looked around. "Are you alone?"

Stahl didn't answer. Dox realized the man must have been some combination of suspicious and terrified.

"Mr. Stahl," Isobel said. "We know what you did. We're here to help you. With the recording you made."

"I don't know what you mean," Stahl said.

"Please," Isobel said. "I'm Isobel Amaral. I'm a doctor at Clínica Médica Internacional. We're on your side. All we want is for the world to see what happened here. What the Indonesians have been doing to my country."

Stahl didn't respond.

"I can tell you exactly where you buried it," Dox said. "It was in that fresh grave by the curly-haired statue."

Stahl stared at him. "How . . ."

"I'm the guy who shot the soldiers who were trying to take it from you. That's *why* I shot them. You're welcome, by the way."

"Do you understand?" Isobel said. "If we wanted that video, we could just take it ourselves. We don't. We want you to get it out of Timor so the world will know. Do you have a way?"

There was a long pause. Stahl said, "Yes."

"Thank God," Isobel said. "Let's hurry."

"I'll lead the way," Dox said. He stopped, picked up the M21, and handed it to Stahl. "You know how to use this?"

"I've . . . shot before."

Dox handed him the rifle. "Well, let's hope you don't have to again. This one's ready to fire. Just don't point it at me, okay?"

Stahl took the rifle and nodded.

"You two stay behind," Dox said. "Let me get a little ahead before you start moving."

They both nodded. He nodded back and started to turn.

Isobel said, "Dox!"

He didn't think. By instinct he spun in the direction she'd been looking in, crouched, brought around the shotgun, and fired at the man he saw there. The Franchi kicked at exactly the same moment he saw a muzzle flash from ahead and heard a three-round burst of rifle fire, the rounds sizzling past him.

The man folded up, hit—

Dox raced forward, racking the pump, and fired again. The second round tore into the man and knocked him onto his back. The man dropped the short-barreled carbine he'd been holding, and the boonie hat he was wearing flew off. Dox saw the mohawk and felt a surge of grim joy. He racked the pump again, and within a second was standing over a badly bleeding Joko, the shotgun aimed at the man's face.

Dox glanced back and saw Isobel and Stahl watching. *Okay, good.* It had all happened so fast they hadn't even tried to take cover—or, fortunately, tried to return fire with Dox in the middle.

Joko was groaning. Dox scanned quickly but saw nothing. Was the man here by himself?

Maybe. Waster had been, and the two of them obviously hadn't been coordinating. Maybe their forces were stretched thin. Even better, maybe they'd had an argument and all killed each other. It didn't matter. All that mattered was killing Joko, getting that video, and getting clear of Dili.

Dox looked back to Joko. The man's hand was halfway to his belt. Dox stepped on his wrist, pinning it to the ground.

"Told you there wouldn't be a third time."

Joko grimaced and tried to jerk his hand free, but there was too much weight on it. "You can't kill me," he wheezed. "I won't die. I've taken the strength of all my enemies."

"Not all of them, asshole."

Joko coughed out a spray of blood, then spat. "I told you, stupid American. We believe things you could never understand."

"I understand one thing. It's an expression we've got in Texas. It goes *Some folks just need killing.* Well, Joker, I've never met anyone it applies to more than you."

Joko's breathing was getting more labored. "I'll come back."

"No, you won't. I told you I was going to kill you. And the last thing you're going to know is I keep my word."

Joko opened his mouth as though to respond, but never got to actually say anything, seeing as Dox fired the next round directly into it, pulping the man's entire head, mohawk and all.

Dox racked the pump and scanned again. No problems. He knelt and took the karambit, sheath and all, then stood and headed back to Isobel and Stahl.

He saw instantly that something was wrong. Isobel was holding her chest and looking down at her torso, and Stahl was gripping her elbow as though to support her.

He felt his heart freeze. *No, no, no, no, no—*

He raced over. She looked up and saw him coming. Her legs wobbled and she started to go down. Stahl tried to stop her, but he wasn't holding her right and lost his grip. Dox dropped the shotgun and got an arm around her just before her legs went out.

He lowered her to the ground, looking at her chest. Under her hand, her shirt was soaked with blood. And not just the front—he could feel it in back, too, and smell it in the humid night air.

The rounds Joko had fired. One of them had hit her. And gone right through.

"Isobel," he said. "I'm here. I've got you."

"What can I do?" Stahl said from behind.

Dox barely heard him. He was fumbling one-handed with the bug-out bag, trying to get to the medical kit, his fingers shaking—

Isobel looked past him at Stahl. Her breathing was fast and shallow. "Get the video," she said. "That's all that matters."

But Stahl didn't move. Isobel looked at Dox. "The video," she said. "Please."

Dox glanced back at Stahl. "Do as she says! And bring it back here. Hurry."

Stahl took off running.

Dox looked at Isobel. "I need to take my arm from behind you," he said. "There's gauze in the kit. I'm going to patch you up. Luckily we got a doctor here, the best in the world, so it's going to go fine." He blinked hard and realized he was crying.

She shook her head. "No. Don't let me go."

"But you're bleeding bad. I need to stop it."

"You can't." She reached out with her free hand and cupped a palm to his face.

He knew she was right. There was so much blood coming out of her back he could feel it flowing past his fingers.

"You're a doctor, Isobel, you tell me what to do. Please, tell me."

"Just hold me. That . . . and the ocean, that's the best feeling in the world."

"You're going to be okay. Come on now. Let's get you up and out of here. I'll keep holding you. I'll never stop. Come on now."

He could feel her trying to get her legs moving. But it wasn't working.

"I'll do that trick I showed you," he said. "I'll get you right up my back and carry you on out. It'll feel like you're riding the waves, the best of both worlds, okay?"

She shook her head. "No. Just stay with me. Keep talking to me."

He felt the tears flowing harder. "I don't know what to talk about."

She gave him a weak laugh. "That's never stopped you before."

He tried to smile, but he couldn't. "Let me pick you up. Come on now."

He heard footsteps approaching fast, loud and not the least bit stealthy. He glanced back and saw Stahl, holding the cassette.

"I got it," Stahl said. "I'll get help."

"There's no time," Isobel said, her voice weaker now. "You really . . . You really have a way to get the video out of Timor?"

"Yes," Stahl said. "I promise."

She nodded. "Make the world know what happened here."

Stahl didn't move. Dox turned to him and said through his tears, "Do as she says. Right now. I'll take care of her. You take care of that video."

"I'm sorry," Stahl said, and then he was walking away fast. A moment later, he had disappeared, lost among the shadows of the tombstones.

Dox turned back to Isobel. "Did you hear that, darlin'? He's . . . The whole world's gonna know. And if you hadn't made us come back here, Joko would have killed him and taken that video himself. You did this, Isobel. The whole world's gonna know what happened here, because of you."

She smiled at that, and he remembered the first time he'd made her smile, at the clinic, and how happy it made him to make her happy, and then her smile was fading, and he didn't know how to make it come back, and there was nothing he'd ever wanted more in the world than that, and he didn't know how to do it.

"Isobel," he said, a sob catching in his throat. "Please. Please don't die. I love you. I love you, Isobel."

For a second, she seemed to be looking through him at something far away. And then her eyes found his, and she smiled again, that beautiful smile.

"You always say the right thing," she whispered.

And then she was gone.

Chapter 38

Dox paused outside the arrival gate at Abilene Airport, other passengers from the flight from Dallas flowing past him. CNN was playing on a big television set bolted to the wall. It was footage Dox recognized too well, with the chyron reading in big block letters, *INDONESIAN TROOPS MASSACRE INDEPENDENCE PROTESTORS IN EAST TIMOR.*

He looked away, having no stomach to see it all again, but he listened as the announcer detailed what had happened. Over two hundred and fifty peaceful protestors dead. Medical clinics overrun with victims. The UN Special Rapporteur on Human Rights and Torture demanding access. Spontaneous international protests in solidarity with the Timorese. Party bigwigs in Congress claiming shock and dismay, and promising to revisit the issue of Washington's military assistance to Jakarta in light of this gross violation of human rights. *Indonesia's occupation is in its sixteenth year,* the announcer said. *This looks like the beginning of the end.*

It was all good, of course. Better than good. But it made Dox feel like crying.

He tamped down the feeling, which had dogged him for the entire forty-eight-hour trip home. Hell, he hadn't even been sure he'd make it home. He'd half expected to find CIA people waiting at customs in Los Angeles, ready to disappear him for fucking up their Timor operation. But Magnus, who he'd called before leaving, said he'd take care of it, and as always the man had been as good as his word. Not that this time there would have been so much for Magnus to do. Probably Christians in Action had bigger things to worry about post-massacre than the fly that had landed in their ointment and then buzzed off.

Henry was waiting at the curb. Dox had called from Dallas, explaining that he was coming home earlier than planned and asking that just Henry meet him at the airport. They shared a brief hug, then got in Henry's pickup.

A few minutes down the road, Henry broke the ice. "Didn't expect you back quite so soon."

Dox nodded. Despite feeling far longer, it had been only a week. "I know."

Henry, who always had good instincts about such things, didn't press further. And though he didn't much feel like talking, Dox said, "Everybody all right?"

"Everybody's fine. Looking forward to seeing you. A little bad news. That fellow you spoke to. George Whitaker. He's in the hospital."

Dox felt a pang of alarm. "What happened?"

"He got jumped and beat up pretty bad. But he's going to be okay."

"When did this happen?"

"Right after you left."

Dox shook his head, thinking, *Of course it did.*

"What hospital's he in?"

"Abilene Regional."

"That's on the way. Take me there?"

"Right now?"

"Please."

"You sure? I know it was a long trip."

Dox stared out the window at the dried scrub grass paralleling the road, and the pale blue sky beyond it, feeling nothing but a cold rage.

"I'm sure, all right."

Chapter 39

Dox stood in the doorway of Whitaker's room, horrified at all the bandages and swelling. Henry, who Dox had asked to wait in the pickup, had filled him in on the details. Whitaker had almost lost an eye. One arm was broken. Likewise his jaw.

Whitaker glanced over and looked at Dox through his unbandaged eye. "Didn't expect to see you again," he said, his teeth clenched by the wiring.

Dox walked over to the bed. "You mean you didn't want to. Which I more than understand."

Whitaker didn't say anything to disabuse him.

"This is my fault," Dox said.

Whitaker shook his head. "Nobody's fault but the men who did it."

"And the one who ordered it."

Whitaker said nothing.

"Who were they?" Dox said.

Whitaker shook his head. "That'll just make it worse."

"It'll make it right."

Again, Whitaker said nothing.

"The police aren't going to do anything," Dox went on. "You said it yourself. There's the way people think things are, and the way they really are."

Whitaker nodded. "That's true."

"Well, you know what I am?"

Whitaker looked at him. Something in his one-eyed gaze seemed to be sizing up Dox differently than at the Purple Sage. Which made sense, because the Purple Sage felt like a lifetime ago.

"What?" Whitaker said.

"I'm the way things really are."

Chapter 40

Before returning to Henry and the pickup, Dox used a hospital payphone to call Magnus.

"Hey," he said, once the base people had put the call through. "I'm home. Thanks for greasing the skids to get me out of there without a problem."

"It was the least I could do," Magnus said. "After getting you into such a clusterfuck in the first place."

"Not your fault. I know you thought you were helping me out, and I appreciate it."

"Well, I guess Felix's operation was spinning its wheels anyway."

"Yeah," Dox said. "And with the Timorese under the tires."

"He's being recalled. Word is, Congress is going to cut off military aid to Indonesia. If Jakarta wants the spigots to open again, they'll have to withdraw."

Distraught as Dox was, at least there was some satisfaction in that.

"I'm calling because I need another favor," Dox said. "Two more, actually."

"Go."

"I need a good rifle with a box magazine. Suppressor. Night scope. And match-grade ammunition. All disposable and untraceable."

There was a pause. Magnus said, "What are you . . . planning to do with this hardware?"

"Gonna go hunting."

"Is it hunting season there?"

"No, I'll be poaching. But the game I take, no one's gonna miss."

Another pause. "I'll make some calls. I'm sure we can find something at Dyess."

"I won't forget it, Magnus."

"I'd rather you did. And the other favor?"

Dox told him. When it was all arranged, he headed back out to Henry.

Chapter 41

Dinner was tense. Dox couldn't have been less talkative. Even Janey and Sue seemed to sense it would be better not to ask about where he'd been or what had happened. Or who was involved.

Afterward, he went out to the porch. Henry might join him later, he knew, but if so, Dox thought he'd have to excuse himself and go for a walk. He just had too much on his mind, and it was too surreal to be back, with everyone else the same and himself feeling so different.

But it wasn't Henry who came out. It was Ronnie. He realized he should have expected that.

"You all right?" she said.

"I'm fine."

"You don't seem fine. I've never seen you this quiet. You probably talk more in your sleep than you did at the dinner table."

"I wouldn't know."

"Have you come to any conclusions?"

He'd been thinking so much about George Whitaker that for a second, he didn't know what she meant.

"About what?"

"You know about what. About Roy."

Dox nodded. "Yes, I have."

"And?"

"Roy's not going to hurt anyone in this family. I'm going to take care of it."

"Take care of it how?"

"I really don't want to talk about it."

Ronnie eyed him with what looked like suspicion. Or maybe it was worry. "Carl," she said. "Don't go doing some crazy thing."

"Do I seem crazy?"

"Well, like I said, you're awfully quiet."

"Quiet doesn't mean crazy."

"For you it might."

He couldn't help laughing a little at that. Ronnie just didn't know when to stop. In fairness, he supposed it took one to know one.

"Ronnie, listen. No one's going to testify at that hearing. Not you, not Mom, not me, nobody."

Ronnie went slightly bug-eyed and her mouth dropped open. "I told you—"

"It'll just make him angrier. And he's going to be released regardless."

"You don't know that."

"Yes, I do."

He could tell by the worried way she was looking at him that she believed it. "How?" she said.

"I already said I don't want to talk about it. Look, you told me you and Mom protected me when I was small. And you were right, you did. And I'm grateful. But you also said that now I need to protect you, remember?"

"Yes, but I didn't mean by doing something crazy."

"I'm not doing anything crazy. Just what you asked. But I'm doing it my way."

She opened her mouth as though to argue, but she must have seen something in his eyes that made her decide not to. After a moment, she said, "I wish I knew what you're not telling me, Carl."

He nodded. "I know you do. But trust me, it's better you don't."

Chapter 42

Early the next morning, Dox was back at Huddle House. Evonne came by seconds after he'd sat down, filling his mug with steaming black coffee and giving him that bright Texas smile.

"Nice to see you again, honey. Let me guess. Big House Platter?"

He shook his head. "No, I'm not going to be here that long. Just a short meeting."

"Same fella as last time?"

Dox nodded.

She scowled. "Didn't care for the look of him. Hope you don't mind my saying."

"I don't mind."

She paused, eyeing him. "You all right? You seem different than last time I saw you."

"Different how?"

"You seem older."

"I am older."

She laughed. "Not that much older, honey. But okay. If you change your mind about breakfast, just holler. I'll be sure we've got a pot of decaf for that friend of yours."

"He's no friend of mine."

"Yeah, I suppose I could tell that."

Mossberg, for whom punctuality seemed a personal religion, walked in at eight o'clock sharp. This time, Dox didn't stand to greet him. He just waited until Mossberg was settled across from him.

"Well," Mossberg said by way of greeting. "That was a disaster if ever there was one."

"It sure was. But don't worry, I won't charge you extra for it. My first week's five thousand, plus the fifty thousand bonus we agreed on will be fine."

Mossberg started to answer, but there was Evonne, filling his mug with decaf. She didn't bother asking for his order.

"Extra?" Mossberg said after Evonne had moved on. "When you arrived, Felix was making progress and Falintil was on the run. Less than a week later, Felix is being recalled, and Falintil is poised to take over the country."

"I wish I could take the credit for that. But I don't deserve it."

"The word is, you didn't develop the woman, you helped her."

Just the mention of Isobel in the mouth of this human ass-crack made Dox want to grab him by the throat.

Mossberg held up his hands. "At least, that's what Felix said."

"Did Felix tell you where he heard that?"

"Yes, from a now-deceased Kopassus soldier who was part of his operation."

"Yeah, a guy named Joko. Who was doing nothing but running his own gang, raping Timorese girls, and eating people's hearts while Felix looked the other way. That how Felix was planning on pacifying Timor for Jakarta, democracy, and the American Way?"

"I already told you, the geopolitics—"

"Are complicated, I remember. I guess that was a roundabout way of saying you were going to send me over there on false pretenses, fighting for the wrong side, using the wrong methods, and with the wrong information, all to cover up for a bunch of rapists and torturers."

"Look—"

"Forget it. Here's the deal, and if you really do know things, like you're fond of saying you do, you'll know the consequences for reneging."

Mossberg looked at him, and Dox could tell he had the man's full attention. Good.

"The parole hearing is in less than a month," Dox said. "No one's going to testify one way or the other. And you're going to make sure my father is released."

"What? I thought—"

"I don't care what you thought."

"I can't promise—"

"You already did, remember? You telling me now you were lying?"

Mossberg watched him for a moment and slowly shook his head. "Why can't you just follow orders?"

"Because I'm unorthodox, like you pointed out and knew full well before you hired me. If you wanted a robot, you should have found someone with a different nom de guerre. Now, tell me if you were lying when you guaranteed that, absent Christians in Action intervention, Roy would be released. I'll find out anyway if he gets kept in prison."

Mossberg eyed him nervously. "I wasn't lying."

"Good. That's settled, then. Plus I'll expect the fifty thousand we agreed upon in my bank account by tomorrow. And five thousand for the week I was there. I'll be sure to put it to better use than you ever would."

He stood and placed a ten on the table for Evonne.

"Now goodbye, Mr. Mossberg. I promise, you don't want to see me again. And for that matter neither does your boy Felix."

Chapter 43

A week later, Dox went back to the Purple Sage. He would have come sooner, but there had been the matter of hunting with the rifle Magnus had procured for him. It had been a fine weapon, too—an Accuracy International Arctic Warfare model, its cold-weather features wasted in Texas, true, but as accurate as promised in the company name. It was a shame that it, an integral suppressor, a Zeiss scope, and some unused ammunition now all lay scattered at the bottom of Lake Fort Phantom Hill, but some trophies were better left unkept.

Wenzel was working the door, same as last time. "Didn't expect you back," he said when he saw Dox rolling up. "I heard you left town."

"You heard right. I'm just back for a bit."

This time Wenzel just nodded, skipping the chitchat. Dox gave him a nod in return and continued on his way.

He went through the red metal door and down the rickety wooden stairs. There was the same smell as always, tobacco smoke and beer and salted popcorn. But somehow, now it was different. There was no nostalgia to it. Maybe something elegiac, instead

He walked over to the bar. Geeber and Guppy were there, their faces bruised. He wasn't surprised to see them. He hoped for their sakes they weren't going to give him a hard time.

They didn't. They eyed him but said not one word. Maybe they had learned their lesson from the last time, from the rocks and the threat to turn them into baseball-bat Popsicles. But Dox had a feeling that wasn't really it. Something in his demeanor had changed, and people could sense it, even ones as dumb as the Skove boys.

He didn't see Marla. He'd called, so he knew she was here tonight. Well, maybe she was on her break. He watched the television set on the bar while he waited. This time, it wasn't tuned to a game. It was a local news channel, covering the story of Marvin Hatfield, Robert Miller, and James Callaway, the three former felons who'd been shot to death three nights before outside a Clyde pool hall. All were previous inmates at the infamous Walls Unit and were known to law enforcement for their gang affiliations, both within the prison and without. Police believed the killings were gang related, and the consensus seemed to be that the killer was unlikely to be found, in part because the police had better things to do.

"Hey, you," he heard from his left. He turned and saw Marla, smiling and coming his way.

For whatever reason, the sight of her gave him a terrible pang of sadness. They hugged, and then she stepped back and gave him one of her trademark head waggles, saying, "I didn't expect to see you back so soon."

"That seems to be the consensus. Can we talk for a minute?"

"You bet."

She asked the other girl working the bar to cover for her for a few minutes longer, and she and Dox went to the back room, where a long time before, George Whitaker had told him how the world really worked.

"I've been in town for a week," Dox said. "I meant to come sooner, but I've had a lot going on."

"I knew. Word gets around. Your father?"

Coming from Marla, it didn't feel intrusive. "That. And some other things, too. I'm going to be leaving, and . . . I don't know when I'll be back."

"You mean . . . if you'll be back."

He nodded. "I guess that's right."

She smiled, a little sadly. "I won't lie to you, Carl Williams. I liked having you here. But nothing lasts forever, does it?"

"I won't lie to you either, Marla. I don't think I much cared to be back. But . . . I liked being with you. And no, nothing does."

They were quiet for a moment. She said, "Where'd you go, anyway?"

He shook his head. "I can't talk about it."

He thought he meant it in an *It's top secret* kind of way, but apparently Marla heard it differently.

"I'm sorry," she said. "She must have been special."

Dox nodded. "I'm sorry, too. She was."

Chapter 44

Three weeks later, Dox was back in the parking lot at the Huntsville Unit, leaning against the door of the Ford F-250 pickup he'd driven over, squinting into the morning sun. He watched as the minute hand on the big clock face at the top of the brick facade clicked to twelve. Eight o'clock sharp.

The doors opened, and a line of men started filing out, each carrying a potato sack filled with personal items. No prison whites for the released men, Dox saw. Instead, they were dressed in street clothes, presumably the ones they'd been wearing on the day they went in, which for some might have meant just a few months earlier, but for others could have meant years. Maybe decades.

The column turned left at the bottom of the stairs. A few of the men, mostly younger ones, had family waiting—wives and mothers and some toddlers, too—and there were ecstatic greetings and laughter and tears. But most of the men kept trudging along, seeming dazed and even in shock, on their way to the Greyhound station a few blocks away.

A couple dozen men had already exited when Dox finally saw Roy, bringing up the rear. He was surprised Roy would be so far back. Maybe it was just happenstance, or maybe the administrators liked to line up prisoners alphabetically, or by the length of time served. But Dox wondered if maybe now that the day had finally come, Roy had found some reason to be at the end of the line, because on some level he was afraid to leave.

Dox didn't wave, he just waited. After a moment, Roy saw him, then glanced around. This time, the scan didn't have that air of confidence and dominion Dox had noted in the visitors' area. This time, Dox was seeing a man trying to get his bearings. A man who found himself suddenly lost.

Roy hefted his potato sack higher and walked over, his shadow long on the cracked pavement in front of him. He stopped and glanced around again, then eyed Dox.

"I might have known it was you that did it," he said, shaking his head slowly.

"Might have known it was me that did what?"

"Marv. And Bobby. And Jimmy Blue. Outside the pool hall. Guess that's what that bullet around your neck is about."

Dox stared at him. "They shouldn't have done what they did."

"You shouldn't have done it. Sticking your nose where it don't belong."

"You ever think you sicced those three on a man who was doing nothing more than trying to help your son?"

"Like I said. You were sticking your nose, just like he was sticking his."

"Well, Marv and Bobby and Jimmy Blue were sticking their noses in my business. What do you got to say to that?"

Apparently, Roy had not much to say to that. He just looked around again.

"Sorry they're not coming to get you," Dox said. "That's why I'm here. Or would you rather take the bus, like the men on their way to the Greyhound station? The ones without family?"

"I got no family."

"No? What am I?"

Again, Roy said nothing.

"Nobody testified against you," Dox said. "We could have. All of us. And I could have pulled some other strings, too. None of us did. We all stepped aside. And now you're out. The question is, what are you going to do about it?"

Roy gave him a stare that just a month before would have made Dox buckle. Not anymore. And it wasn't just because Dox felt different. He saw things differently, too. Because behind that fearsome gaze Roy trained on him, he could sense a man whose bluff had been called, and who didn't have another card to play. Who was confused and scared and trying not to show it.

"I'm going to make a deal with you," Dox said. "You want to hear it?"

Roy kept looking at him. "What if I don't like it?"

"Then don't take it. I'm sure they told you inside how to get to the bus station."

They were quiet for a moment. Dox said, "Last time I was here, you could have fed me a bunch of bullshit about how you were reformed and a different man and didn't want to hurt anyone anymore. Bygones be bygones and water under the bridge. I wanted to help you, and you could have taken advantage of that. Could have given me everything I needed to rationalize not only not testifying against you, but testifying in your favor. But you didn't. Why not?"

"I ain't a liar."

"Damn straight you're not. Which is why I'm trusting you now to make this deal. If you want it."

"What damn deal? You keep saying you have a deal. What is it?"

"The deal is, you look me in the eye and you tell me. Tell me you know the past is done. And you're not going to hurt any of our family, or even scare them or bother them. You do that long enough, by the way, they might even come to you. You ever think about that? Your first grandchild's on the way. Don't you want a shot at getting to know him? Or her, I don't know which it is."

Roy shook his head, but more in confusion than denial. "Veronica?"

"That's right."

"She's married?"

"Yes, Dad, she is."

Roy looked away for a moment, still shaking his head.

"If you can promise me all that," Dox went on, "then I can promise something to you."

Roy looked back at him. He didn't say anything, and Dox wondered whether it was because he didn't trust himself to speak.

Dox gestured to the Ford. "I promise you this truck is yours, for one thing. I bought it used in Abilene, but the tires are new, and I took care of the engine myself. It drives great. And all your tools are in back. I used them in high school on summer jobs, by the way, just like you taught me. Plus I added a few new ones."

"What am I supposed to do with all this?" Roy said.

Dox tried to tamp it down, but he couldn't help feeling encouraged. Roy could have told him to go fuck himself. Or said nothing at all, just turned and hoofed it to the Greyhound station. Instead, he was asking questions. The tone was aggressive, true, but the questions themselves were practical.

"You're supposed to get a job," Dox said. "Doing construction. What do you think you're supposed to do with it?"

"Maybe you're not keeping up with current events," Roy said, "but I'm now and always will be an ex-convict. I'm as good as unemployable, by anyone and for anything."

Dox shook his head. "That's not true. You got work waiting for you if you want it, at Marine Corps Air Station in Yuma. There's civilian construction work there, and I have a friend who can make sure you get it. It's about a thousand miles from Tuscola, but the Marines don't have any bases in Texas. And besides, it might not be the worst thing for everyone to have a little space to get used to the new circumstances."

Roy furrowed his brow. "Why are you doing this?" he said, and his voice was slightly thick.

"Because you're my daddy. And I ain't never giving up on you. Would you give up on me?"

Roy looked away. After a long moment, he said, "I thought I had."

"Well, that's up to you."

Roy kept looking away. But he nodded.

"There's one more thing," Dox said. "One more thing I need from you."

Roy didn't respond. He just kept looking away.

"I've got five thousand dollars from a job I just did. It's yours, to help you get set up. But you gotta send half to George Whitaker. Half of that, and half your wages, until Whitaker is back on his feet. Which could be a while, because your boys messed him up pretty bad."

Roy turned back and eyed him, suddenly confident again, on familiar ground.

"I told you, he was—"

"No, sir. I already told you. Anything he was doing in someone else's business, your boys were doing in my business. Which means *you* were doing it, too. Which means you received special dispensation, being that you and I are having a conversation in the sunshine and your boys are dead as dirt. And I hope you'll believe me when I tell you that if you'd been anyone other than my father, there'd be four of you dead now instead of only three."

Roy looked him slowly up and down. "What happened to you since you were here last? You're not the same."

Dox blew out a long breath. "I guess a lot."

Roy nodded as though considering. He said, "You want to tell me about it?"

Dox shook his head. "Let's start with other things. We got plenty to talk about and lots of time to do it. It's a long drive to Yuma."

"Oh, you're coming with me?"

"Well, it's your truck. But if you'll have me, then yeah."

337

Roy glanced at the truck, then at the prison, then out at the cracked pavement of the street that led into the town of Huntsville and to whatever lay beyond it. He started to speak, but his throat caught.

He cleared it. Then, still looking at the street, he said, "I could use a decent breakfast. You know any places between here and Yuma?"

Dox put a hand on his shoulder. "Let's go find one."

Epilogue

Two weeks later, Dox was back in Dili.

He would have liked to rent a motorcycle, or even a car, so he could get around by himself. But tourist infrastructure in East Timor seemed limited to guesthouses and a few hotels, so Fernando was waiting for him at the airport like last time, with his sunny smile and too-young-to-drive face.

On the ride to the Turismo, Fernando told him everything was different now—the Indonesians were cowed, Falintil had expanded its control of the countryside, people were emboldened. It seemed the whole country was united in its determination that the two hundred and fifty killed not have died in vain, and that their loss be a catalyst for the independence the Timorese craved.

Dox could see it was all true. The military presence was far less than it had been before. There weren't even any checkpoints. He'd seen something similar in Afghanistan, where toward the end the Russian troops he and his Muj engaged didn't even want to fight. They knew the fight was already done, and all they wanted was to make it home.

He realized it might have been Fernando who reported him to Falintil last time. Or maybe it was João. Or the woman who checked him in. He didn't care. He didn't blame them, and anyway it felt a long time ago. Another lifetime, in fact. He supposed it was possible someone might want to snatch him now. But if he was wrong, he didn't care about that, either. What he was doing here was more important.

Fernando asked if he would need a driver later that day, after he was settled in. Dox told him he would. In fact, he didn't need to get settled at all. They'd go to the hotel later. His first stop would be the clinic.

When they pulled up in front, he was gratified to see that ground had already been broken on the new wing, which when completed would double the clinic's patient capacity. And the new name had already been painted across the front. It was no longer Clínica Médica Internacional de Dili. Now it was Clínica Médica Internacional de Isobel Amaral.

Seeing the sign, Dox felt the tears start to come, but Fernando was watching and he didn't want the boy seeing him cry. So he cleared his throat, told Fernando he'd be back in a minute, and got out of the car.

Magnus had arranged everything after Dox called him from the hospital in Abilene—the rifle, the job for Roy, and the routing of Dox's $50,000 payday to the clinic, along with related matters. The man was a genius at getting things done—language, cultural, and other barriers be damned—and would have made a fine diplomat if he hadn't decided to become an even better Marine. Dox would look hard for a way to repay him, but it wouldn't be easy to find something commensurate.

The clinic people at the check-in area recognized him right away, and he had to wait only a moment before a slight man with wiry, receding hair came out and rushed over. "Hello, Mr. Dox," the man said in English, pumping Dox's hand effusively. "I'm Dr. Ramos. We're so grateful for what you've done for the clinic. I don't think I have the words to adequately thank you."

Dox shook his head. "I'm glad I was in a position to help."

"Can you stay for lunch? We don't have much, but . . ."

"I wish I could, but I'm afraid I'm in something of a hurry. If I could just trouble you for . . . the other thing."

"Of course. Of course." Ramos turned and nodded to a woman who was hanging back, who Dox assumed was an assistant. A moment later, the woman returned, holding a wooden cylinder, about nine inches high and six inches wide. The woman gently handed the cylinder to Ramos, and Ramos handed it gravely to Dox.

"Dr. Amaral had many admirers at the clinic," Ramos said. "Everyone loved her. But she had no family. We would have buried her ashes ourselves, of course. But . . ."

"I know," Dox said, wanting to go. "And I'm grateful for the trust you've put in me by allowing me to . . ." He had to pause for a moment, then went on. "To lay her to rest."

To that, Ramos dipped his head solemnly, almost as though he was going to bow.

Dox suddenly had a bad thought. "Pardon me," he said. "But . . . you're sure . . . This urn . . ."

Ramos nodded again. "There's a certificate inside. The crematorium we work with takes great care with the remains of everyone entrusted to it, not just to treat the remains with the utmost dignity and respect, but also to give the next of kin complete confidence in the rightfulness of the ashes. And I assure you that this time, I involved myself personally. The urn you're holding contains Dr. Amaral's earthly remains. All of them, and nothing else."

They shook hands. Dox went back to the car and had Fernando take him to Aidabalaten.

He was as exhausted from the trip as he was by being back, and spent most of the two-hour drive dozing, remembering, and dozing again. When they arrived, he asked Fernando to wait in the car. He wanted to walk along the beach. Fernando didn't ask why, only told him to take his time.

He stepped out of the car and was immediately grateful for the weather—warm and not too humid at all, with a breeze that smelled like the ocean and a pale blue sky over the water. It was a good spot, and he knew it would have made her happy to know he was doing this. And then the thought undid him, and he started to cry.

"Come on now," he said aloud. "Come on."

He found a cluster of mangrove trees, where he took a much-needed leak. It was such a pedestrian thing to have to attend to under the circumstances, but it made him happy to imagine how Isobel would have told him it was only natural, like the adrenaline shakes in the aftermath of combat. In response, he probably would have said something to make her laugh, like *But will you hold me the way you do after I get the shakes?*, and imagining it made him cry again.

And then he walked along the water, looking for nothing in particular, watching small waves break on the rocky beach and on larger rocks farther out in the surf. The urn was light. He carried it pressed to his chest.

Soon he came to a small cove with a sandy beach. To one side were mountains with clouds clinging to them; to the other, the undulating coastline. There were stands here and there, the kind of places that rented surfboards and floats and such, and the beach was dotted with pleasure seekers, mostly couples, but also two young parents with a child. Of course he couldn't be sure, but he felt strongly that this must be the very place Isobel's folks had taken her when she was small.

And suddenly he felt her presence surging against him like a wave, even though he was still on the beach and not yet in the water.

"This is the place, isn't it?" he said aloud in a cracked voice, as though he was talking to her, and he was surprised that he didn't feel foolish doing it. He'd never been the least bit superstitious. He'd always believed that when you were dead, you were just dead. He supposed he still believed it, but then what the hell was he doing here, anyway?

AMOK

"I don't know what's wrong with me," he said, and again he wasn't sure who he was talking to, himself or Isobel or the two of them.

He stripped down to his skivvies and waded into the water. He noticed a few of the beachgoers watching, but he didn't care.

Soon he was stomach deep. The water was warm and felt soft against his skin. The waves were small, and the way they were lapping against him reminded him of what she'd told him about how she felt being in the sea and letting the waves carry her along, how for those precious moments she felt as though she was with her parents again.

"Hello, ma'am," he said aloud, feeling he was talking to Isobel's mother. "She still talked about you, all these years later." He paused to collect himself. "Coming here with you, and you teaching her to bodysurf. She told me those were some of the best memories of her life."

He blew out a long breath. "And you, sir," he went on. "She told me what a good father you were. How you helped keep her studying. And how you cried at her graduation from medical school. That was another of her best memories, I could tell from the way she described it."

He breathed deeply for a minute, letting the wave of grief flow through him. Then he opened the top of the urn.

It was filled most of the way with powdery gray ash. At the top was a certificate, as Ramos had promised. It was in Portuguese, but there was some sort of official seal, and he could read the name easily enough: *Isobel Amaral*.

He took out the certificate, set it on the water, and watched as it gently bobbed away.

He blew out another long breath, reached into the urn, and started gently ladling its contents into the sea. "Isobel," he said, shaking his head and crying. "I'm so sorry."

When he had ladled all he could, he submerged the urn to make sure the sea would take everything inside it. He held it under the water like that, watching the remaining ash unfurl and spiral away to infinity.

"You told me I always say the right thing," he went on. "But now I don't know what to say. I love you. I'm glad I got to tell you that. I wish we could have lived it longer. And I think . . . I think I'm always going to miss you. Miss what we might have had. I think . . . I think it would have been so good."

Another wave of grief hit him, and for a moment, he couldn't tell the difference between the grief and the swells he was standing in. He waited for it to pass, then spoke again.

"I'm going to live a good life. At least, that's the plan. And I hope a long one. And I'm going to try to make it one you would have been proud of."

He started crying again, and then laughed because he'd never been such a wreck, at least not since he'd been a little boy. And then he remembered saying to Isobel, *I think we're all a little younger inside than we like to admit,* and it made him cry harder.

After a moment, he felt more in control of himself. He let go of the urn. It floated to the surface and began to drift away. He lay on his back then, letting the swells carry him gently along, looking up at the sky.

As unmarked as it was, this would have to be her place. Her monument would be the clinic. Of course, the fresh paint that now proclaimed her name would fade in time in the tropical sun. But he hoped his memories never would. They were all he had, after all. And what did she have? Not even a gravesite. Just the sea that she loved, and this country, and its people.

He felt he could have loved it, too. And maybe, in another life, a better life, the life that had been stolen just as he was understanding how much he longed for it, he would have lived here. With her.

But that was that life.

AMOK

He started back toward the beach. To the car, to the hotel, then to the airport. After that, he didn't know. Maybe Bali. He'd always liked Southeast Asia.

Yeah, that felt right. See some more of the region. And more of the world. There were a lot of places he still had to visit.

But he would never come back here.

Acknowledgments

The Legislative Drafting Institute for Child Protection (LDICP)—an organization that does work Isobel would be proud to support.

https://ldicp.org

And a particularly easy and effective way to support the LDICP is through AmazonSmile. It's simple to sign up and have Amazon donate 0.5 percent of your purchases to the LDICP (or other charity of your choice).

http://barryeisler.blogspot.com/2018/11/if-you-buy-from-amazon-do-it-at.html

I've never been a Marine, but I'm lucky to know a few people who have, and their explanations, stories, and reminiscences were invaluable as I went about writing this book. Dave Beckley, Travis Kelton, James Lucas, and Mike Killman—thank you. The Olongapo tales in particular were so good that they really deserve their own story, and Mike's contributions regarding Joko's tracking skills would make a great work of nonfiction.

And to another former Marine, this one Force Recon, and also a CIA Special Operations Group veteran—Dox's namesake, Carl. You might not remember, my friend, but the first thing you ever said to me was, "Don't fuck up." Good advice and I've tried to take it to heart.

Though I've been all over Texas and spent some time in Abilene and Tuscola researching this book, I've never lived in the state. So I'm lucky to count as friends both a transplant—Dave Beckley (one of the former Marines noted above)—and two natives, former Federal Air Marshal Montie Guthrie, who in addition to performing his Texas duties makes sure I'm getting firearms tools and tactics right, and CIA veteran Doug Patteson, who's also an encyclopedia of clandestine tactics. Thanks to you all for helping this New Jersey native develop a deeper feeling for the great state of Texas.

I should have gotten the names of the kind people in the Tuscola Allsup's who took the trouble to answer my questions about the town—I would have liked to thank you more personally. Well, if you happen to read this book, at least you'll know. If anyone wonders how I could have known that the Tuscola Café was formerly Vickie's, but in Dox's time, before becoming Vickie's, was called Lantrip's, my secret is revealed—it was those friendly Texans at Allsup's.

My medical training is limited to CPR, so huge thanks to Nurse Practitioner Lindsay Harris, former combat medic Mike Killman, and Dr. Peter Zimetbaum, for making sure I was doing justice to Isobel's training, instincts, and behavior. And Lindsay, thanks, too, for the winning "a brain feels like an overripe melon" description. ☺

Thanks to Lurdes Pires, a producer of the film *Beatriz's War,* for sharing her memories of and thoughts on the Hotel Turismo, the Santa Cruz cemetery massacre, and all things Timor.

If you want to be a writer, it helps to ask good questions, and once again, no one is better at answering mine than Mike Killman. Mike helps with more aspects of these books than I can reasonably fit in an acknowledgments section, including as noted above military and medical information, everything you ever wanted to know about airfield site surveys, the dos and don'ts of overland travel in a country like Timor, and much more.

It's not easy to conjure a place that's remote in both space and time, but there are resources that make it easier. One such is the Facebook page *Memories of the Old Hotel Turismo: Dili, Timor-Leste.* I'm grateful to Helen Mary Hill, one of the page's administrators, and to everyone who has taken the trouble to post photos, videos, links, and reminiscences there. Tony Maniaty's photos of and thoughts about the old Hotel Turismo were particularly helpful.

https://www.facebook.com/groups/10150127526410599/

I listened to a lot of country music while writing the Texas sequences of the book, two soundtracks in particular—George Strait's *Pure Country*, and the multiartist album *The Thing Called Love*. Plus of course a lot of Johnny Cash, Patsy Cline, Merle Haggard, and k. d. lang. Dan Levin, thanks for recommending "Copperhead Road." Good choice.

To the extent I get violence right in my fiction, I have many great instructors to thank, including Massad Ayoob, Tony Blauer, Alain Burrese, Loren Christensen, Wim Demeere, Dave Grossman, Tim Larkin, Marc MacYoung, Rory Miller, Clint Overland, Peyton Quinn, and Terry Trahan. I highly recommend their books and courses for anyone who wants to be safer in the world, or just to create more realistic violence on the page:

http://www.massadayoobgroup.com
https://blauerspear.com
http://yourwarriorsedge.com/about-alain-burrese
http://www.lorenchristensen.com
http://www.wimsblog.com
http://www.killology.com
http://www.targetfocustraining.com
https://www.nononsenseselfdefense.com
http://www.chirontraining.com

Thanks as always to the extraordinarily eclectic group of "foodies with a violence problem" who hang out at Marc "Animal" MacYoung and Dianna Gordon MacYoung's No Nonsense Self-Defense, for good humor, good fellowship, and a ton of insights, particularly regarding the real costs of violence.

Thanks to Naomi Andrews, Wim Demeere, Alan Eisler, Judith Eisler, Ben Grossblatt, Bart Gellman, Rachael Herbert, Mike Killman, Rebecca Matte, Liz Pearsons, Laura Rennert, Ken Rosenberg, Ted Schlein, Hannah Streetman, and Wanda Zimba for terrific feedback on the manuscript. And to Laura also for doing so much to help me write it. I love you, babe.

Notes

Chapter 1

For more on the freeze and how to break it, I recommend Rory Miller's *Facing Violence: Preparing for the Unexpected* (for which I was honored to write the foreword).

https://www.amazon.com/gp/product/B0182WEMGA/ref=dbs_a_def_rwt_hsch_vapi_tkin_p1_i1

Chapter 2

In addition to Jorge Antonio Renaud's eye-opening and moving book *Behind the Walls* and the other books noted in the bibliography below, in trying to understand Roy's experience in the Huntsville Unit, aka the Walls Unit, I drew on the following:

A PBS interview with Renaud in which he delivers some hard-earned conclusions on reimagining incarceration:

https://m.facebook.com/newshour/videos/jorge-antonio-renaud-gives-his-brief-but-spectacular-take-on-re-imagining-incarc/152705276980493/

A short video on the Texas Field Ministry. I respect the work of the ministry, but I think it's important to approach the video itself, technically a news broadcast, as a press release issued by the Texas Department of

Criminal Justice (no slight to the TDCJ; government officials launder press releases into "news" with the connivance of media partners all the time).

https://www.youtube.com/watch?v=RPMEYoCS9f4

A short video from a drive around the Huntsville Unit, making plain why the unit is called "the Walls":

https://www.youtube.com/watch?v=Kn7TPo1s3JI

A video of a scientist examining an unfixed (that is, fresh and not yet preserved in formaldehyde) human brain. If you're squeamish, you might want to skip this one.

https://www.youtube.com/watch?v=jHxyP-nUhUY

Chapter 4

I wish I could have visited Marobo Hot Springs for research, but the pandemic has made such things infeasible. Hopefully one day.

https://www.atlasobscura.com/places/marobo-hot-springs

Chapter 5

I first heard of chicken-fried steak in the same year this book is set—from the father of Doug Patteson, one of the gentlemen I thank above for helping me in my depictions of Texas. It was a long time ago, sir, but as you can see I was listening!

Chapter 6

Though Joko's sense of smell might seem supernatural, in fact he's just hyperosmic.

https://www.theguardian.com/society/2022/jan/23/ive-got-this-little-extra-strength-the-rare-intense-world-of-a-super-smeller

Chapter 7

Many sports franchises have been changing their names from Native American references. I don't know about the current status of the Jim Ned High School teams, but in 1991, when this story is set, Jim Ned's football team was the Indians.

https://www.economist.com/united-states/2022/03/26/the-debate-about-native-american-themed-team-names-goes-local

Chapter 9

An ad for Dox's 1977 Harley-Davidson Sportster:
https://www.ebay.com/itm/392832180840

I've never been to Olongapo, but these two articles made me feel like I have:
https://dennisclevenger.wordpress.com/2012/02/21/liberty-call-olongapo-city/
https://www.usswilhoite.org/index.php/sea-stories/olongapo

The Purple Sage was inspired in part by Arkey Blue's Silver Dollar. I badly wanted to visit for research, but Texas is a big place, and I had to concentrate on Abilene and Tuscola. Here's hoping I'll be back.
https://www.texasmonthly.com/being-texan/the-best-honky-tonks-in-texas/

And if you want to learn to line-dance to "Copperhead Road," here you go:
https://www.youtube.com/watch?v=0LWfnJyZgP0
https://www.youtube.com/watch?v=KRfIdWmKdfE

Chapter 10

I don't know what "proclivities" CIA personnel were instructed to over-look in Afghanistan during Operation Cyclone. But during America's subsequent war there, US military personnel were ordered to ignore child rape.

https://www.nytimes.com/2015/09/21/world/asia/us-soldiers-told-to-ignore-afghan-allies-abuse-of-boys.html

Similar orders for Canadian military personnel in Iraq:

https://ottawacitizen.com/news/national/defence-watch/canadian-soldiers-complained-iraqi-troops-they-were-training-were-war-criminals

Chapter 12

The notion that eating your enemy, and particularly the heart, is a way to acquire your enemy's strength is an old one among humans.

https://www.seeker.com/eating-the-enemy-a-savage-act-but-not-new-1767508224.html

North Sumatra, Joko's home, has some history of the practice.

https://en.wikipedia.org/wiki/Exocannibalism#List_of_cultures_known_for_exocannibalism

That said, I have no reason to believe cannibalism is any more practiced today in Sumatra than it is in Sacramento, and it's possible Joko was either fabricating the idea, or, more likely, that he believed it because he wanted to believe it, as humans are wont to do.

Chapter 14

America was no mere bystander to the 1965 Indonesian genocide.
https://www.theatlantic.com/international/archive/2017/10/the-indonesia-documents-and-the-us-agenda/543534/

How America trained the butchers of Timor:
https://www.theguardian.com/world/1999/sep/19/indonesia.easttimor2

Chapter 15

The Phoenix Program:
https://www.nytimes.com/2017/12/29/opinion/behind-the-phoenix-program.html

I first heard *False Evidence Appearing Real* from Tony Blauer.
https://www.knowfearnow.com

And *Fuck Everything and Run* is courtesy of Marc MacYoung.
http://www.nononsenseselfdefense.com

(Not saying these gentlemen invented the terms; I don't know the origins. But those were the origins for me.)

Chapter 18

Lots of nonsexual uses for condoms, including substituting for the companion you don't have!
https://willowhavenoutdoor.com/1-ways-a-condom-can-save-your-life-multi-functional-survival-uses-for-a-condom/

https://www.instructables.com/Ten-Unusual-Uses-for-a-Condom-That-Can-Save-Your-L/

Building and maintaining an airstrip is tricky business.
https://www.flyingdoctor.org.au/preparing-airstrip/
https://www.wsp.com/en-ZA/insights/rehabilitating-a-critical-airstrip

And Dox's interpretation of *Taxi Driver* is more fully laid out here:
https://screenrant.com/taxi-driver-ending-travis-bickle-explained/

Chapter 21

It wasn't just Indonesia and East Timor. Systematic rape is a widespread weapon of war. For example:
https://www.amnesty.org/en/latest/news/2021/08/ethiopia-troops-and-militia-rape-abduct-women-and-girls-in-tigray-conflict-new-report

Chapter 23

Isobel has good instincts about interrogation. But even if you know the tricks, they can be hard to resist when you're on the wrong end of them.

Here's former FBI agent and body language expert Joe Navarro, who I was proud to work alongside lobbying against torture with Human Rights First, breaking down some of the tricks of the trade.
https://www.youtube.com/watch?v=KfkOSYpMToo
https://www.humanrightsfirst.org/interrogation-and-intelligence-professionals/biographies

Oil was discovered in the Timor Sea in 1974, one year before Indonesia invaded. Coincidence? You be the judge.
    https://en.wikipedia.org/wiki/Woodside_Petroleum#Sunrise_LNG_development

Chapter 24

I couldn't find any photos or descriptions of the bar at the old Hotel Turismo, so my depiction is entirely the product of my imagination— the polite way of saying I made it up.

Fathers crying out of love for and pride in their daughters puts me in mind of Paul and Mira Sorvino at the 1996 Academy Awards:
    https://youtu.be/Y5QsDSeGv_k?t=120

Chapter 25

Of course the Soviet atrocities Dox recalls from Afghanistan were real.
    https://www.latimes.com/archives/la-xpm-1985-05-06-me-4493-story.html

But it would be misleading to suggest that atrocities are confined to wars carried out by our adversaries. The very word *atrocity* is used almost exclusively to describe what our enemies do; while the results of our own wars are merely regrettable "collateral damage."
    https://boingboing.net/2016/03/02/how-would-you-explain-the-diff.html

For more, I recommend Nick Turse's book *Kill Anything That Moves: The Real American War In Vietnam.*
    https://www.amazon.com/Kill-Anything-That-Moves-American-ebook/dp/B008FPSTOQ/ref=sr_1_1

The psychology of atrocity and counter-atrocity:
https://nonzero.substack.com/p/the-psychology-of-atrocity

It's a good idea to be skeptical about atrocity claims—especially when they're being used to justify going to war or to justify retaliatory atrocities.
https://en.wikipedia.org/wiki/Atrocity_propaganda

Chapter 28

Footage of the November 12, 1991, procession and the Santa Cruz cemetery massacre:
https://www.youtube.com/watch?v=7HkktBcIDzg

Amy Goodman, Allan Nairn, and Max Stahl's account of the massacre, with video:
https://www.democracynow.org/2006/11/13/amy_goodman_recounts_the_east_timor

More, including the aftermath:
https://www.youtube.com/watch?v=kDVNAe6TSK4

While taking notes in Shibuya, Tokyo, in 2001 for a scene in the manuscript that became my first book, *A Clean Kill in Tokyo* (originally *Rain Fall*), I fell seventeen feet and seven inches at an unmarked construction site, landing on bare concrete. I know the exact height because a month later, I went back with a tape measure. I had horrific bruising on my butt and heels and whiplash, too, but miraculously no permanent injuries (except maybe for some hip problems that started showing up about twelve years later, but who knows). That's all a long way of saying I know firsthand you can fall that far and if you hit just right still literally walk away from it (well, more like stagger away, gasping and wheezing and groaning).

Here are videos of two such incidents—the first with someone who was lucky; the second with someone less so. Wouldn't have guessed that a car can do so much to cushion a fall. Definitely preferable to concrete.
https://www.dailymotion.com/video/x3dnh1l
https://www.youtube.com/watch?v=H64o_x34Hko

Chapter 31

How did Dox lift the dead driver so quickly and easily? Here you go:
https://www.youtube.com/watch?v=KPrATJ-u5Rg

Chapter 33

"Agitators must be shot, and they will be."
https://en.wikipedia.org/wiki/Santa_Cruz_massacre#The_massacre

Chapter 38

The aftermath of the Santa Cruz cemetery massacre and how it led to Timorese independence:
https://en.wikipedia.org/wiki/Santa_Cruz_massacre#Aftermath
https://en.wikipedia.org/wiki/History_of_East_Timor#Towards_independence

Chapter 44

Video of prisoners being released from the Huntsville Unit:
https://www.texastribune.org/2011/03/13/out-on-their-own-re-entering-society-after-prison/

Bibliography

Bevins, Vincent. *The Jakarta Method: Washington's Anticommunist Crusade & the Mass Murder Program that Shaped Our World.* https://www.amazon.com/Jakarta-Method-Washingtons-Anticommunist-Crusade ebook/dp/B07XDMCSJM/ref=tmm_kin_swatch_0?_encoding=UTF8&qid=1624828331&sr=1-1

Bissinger, H. G. *Friday Night Lights: A Town, a Team, and a Dream.* https://www.amazon.com/Friday-Night-Lights-25th-Anniversary-ebook/dp/B00X2ZW684/ref=tmm_kin_swatch_0?_encoding=UTF8&qid=1624827536&sr=1-3

Burrough, Bryan, Jason Stanford, Chris Tomlinson. *Forget the Alamo: The Rise and Fall of an American Myth.* https://www.amazon.com/Forget-Alamo-Rise-Fall-American-ebook/dp/B08JKN9RCM/ref=tmm_kin_swatch_0?_encoding=UTF8&qid=1624827592&sr=1-1

Cardoso, Luis. *The Crossing: A Story of East Timor.* https://www.amazon.com/Crossing-Story-East-Timor/dp/1862074356/ref=tmm_pap_swatch_0

Dooley, James W. *Inside Huntsville Prison.* https://www.amazon.com/Inside-Huntsville-Prison-James-Dooley/dp/0960557601/ref=sr_1_1

Gwynne, S. C. *Empire of the Summer Moon: Quanah Parker and the Rise and Fall of the Comanches, the Most Powerful Indian Tribe in American History.* https://www.amazon.com/Empire-Summer-Moon-Comanches-Powerful-ebook/dp/B003KN3MDG/ref=tmm_kin_swatch_0?_encoding=UTF8&qid=1624827299&sr=1-1

Lyon, Danny. *Conversations with the Dead: Photographs of Prison Life with the Letters and Drawings of Billy McCune #122054.* https://www.amazon.com/Conversations-Dead-Danny-Lyon/dp/071487051X

Mo, Timothy. *The Redundancy of Courage.* https://www.amazon.com/Redundancy-Courage-Timothy-Mo/dp/0952419343/ref=sr_1_3

O'Neill, Bill. *The Great Book of Texas: The Crazy History of Texas with Amazing Random Facts & Trivia.* https://www.amazon.com/Great-Book-Texas-History-Amazing-ebook/dp/B07B11952R/ref=tmm_kin_swatch_0?_encoding=UTF8&qid=1624827498&sr=1-1-spons

Renaud, Jorge Antonio. *Behind the Walls: A Guide for Families and Friends of Texas Prison Inmates.* https://www.amazon.com/Behind-Walls-Families-Friends-Criminal-ebook/dp/B00AG4IKRK/

Wright, Lawrence. *God Save Texas: A Journey into the Soul of the Lone Star State.* https://www.amazon.com/God-Save-Texas-Journey-State-ebook/dp/B072KCBWPYN/ref=tmm_kin_swatch_0?_encoding=UTF8&qid=1624827373&sr=1-1

Filmography

The Act of Killing—an extremely strange film in which the aged killers who carried out the 1965–1966 Indonesian genocide reenact and discuss their crimes: http://theactofkilling.com

Balibo—a biopic about the Balibo Five, the Australian, New Zealand, and British journalists killed by Indonesian soldiers on the eve of Indonesia's 1975 invasion of East Timor (plus a sixth, Australian Roger East, murdered two months later investigating the previous murders): https://www.imdb.com/title/tt1111876/

Beatriz's War—a Timorese film about the Indonesian occupation: https://www.youtube.com/watch?v=7RMJtJH5-7w

Max Stahl and Human Rights (each segment about three minutes):

https://www.youtube.com/watch?v=FoLXQHbzfFU&t=1s

https://www.youtube.com/watch?v=1AZ2jsgWY8s

https://www.youtube.com/watch?v=unJqSaUYpxY&t=1s

https://www.youtube.com/watch?v=4eaO6WEjAjY

https://www.youtube.com/watch?v=Hu8Ea9gj0Ks

https://www.youtube.com/watch?v=PsclSOdAz20&t=1s

https://www.youtube.com/watch?v=2z0hTbn5J04&t=1s

Tribute to Journalist Max Stahl: https://www.youtube.com/watch?v=rRVu6517kZs&t=1s

The pandemic has impeded my usual practice of visiting the places I write about. In addition to the books and articles I read, the interviews I watched, and the people I talked to, the following videos were helpful in getting an overall feel for Timor. I even tried some civet-selected coffee. Delicious—and glad to report no residual taste from the, er, means of production.

https://www.youtube.com/watch?v=QFnnXsMnl-s

https://www.youtube.com/watch?v=ES8LbmRTVKg

https://www.youtube.com/watch?v=mZPMQ_Xrmg

https://www.youtube.com/watch?v=5_2SXlaPCCQ

About the Author

Photo © Douglas Sonders

New York Times bestselling author Barry Eisler spent three years in a covert position with the CIA's Directorate of Operations, then worked as a technology lawyer and start-up executive in Silicon Valley and Japan, earning his black belt at the Kodokan Judo Institute along the way. Eisler's award-winning thrillers have been included in numerous "best of" lists; have been translated into nearly twenty languages; and include the #1 bestsellers *The Detachment*, *Livia Lone*, *The Night Trade*, and *The Killer Collective*. Eisler lives in the San Francisco Bay Area and, when he's not writing novels, blogs about national security and the media. For more information, visit www.barryeisler.com.